THE
ASSASSIN'S
CURSE

Also by Kevin Sands

The Blackthorn Key
Mark of the Plague

A

BLACKTHORN KEY
ADVENTURE

THE

ASSASSIN'S CURSE

KEVIN SANDS

ALADDIN

NEW YORK   LONDON   TORONTO   SYDNEY   NEW DELHI

ALADDIN

An imprint of Simon & Schuster Children's Publishing Division
1230 Avenue of the Americas, New York, New York 10020
First Aladdin hardcover edition September 2017
Text copyright © 2017 by Kevin Sands
Interior Historia Anglorum (knights on horseback) image on page 174
copyright © British Library / Granger, NYC
Interior illustrations copyright © 2017 by Jim Madsen
Jacket illustration copyright © 2017 by James Fraser
All rights reserved, including the right of reproduction in whole or in part in any form.
ALADDIN and related logo are registered trademarks of Simon & Schuster, Inc.
For information about special discounts for bulk purchases, please contact Simon & Schuster
Special Sales at 1-866-506-1949 or business@simonandschuster.com.
The Simon & Schuster Speakers Bureau can bring authors to your live event. For more
information or to book an event, contact the Simon & Schuster Speakers Bureau at
1-866-248-3049 or visit our website at www.simonspeakers.com.
Interior designed by Karin Paprocki
The text of this book was set in Adobe Garamond Pro.
Manufactured in the United States of America 0817 FFG
2 4 6 8 10 9 7 5 3 1
Library of Congress Cataloging-in-Publication Data
Names: Sands, Kevin, author.
Title: The assassin's curse / Kevin Sands.
Description: First Aladdin hardcover edition. | New York : Aladdin, 2017. |
Series: Blackthorn key ; 3 | Summary: When Christopher Rowe's
code-breaking uncovers the true target of an assassination attempt, he and
his friends are odered to Paris to investigate a centuries-old curse on
the French throne.
Identifiers: LCCN 2017003373 (print) | LCCN 2017030996 (eBook) |
ISBN 9781534405257 (eBook) | ISBN 9781534405233 (hc)
Subjects: | CYAC: Adventure and adventurers—Fiction. |
Supernatural—Fiction. | Friendship—Fiction. | Secret societies—Fiction. |
Paris (France)—History—17th century—Fiction. | France—History—
Louis XIII, 1610-1643—Fiction. | Mystery and detective stories. |
BISAC: JUVENILE FICTION / Mysteries & Detective Stories. |
JUVENILE FICTION / Action & Adventure / General. |
JUVENILE FICTION / Historical / General.
Classification: LCC PZ7.1.S26 (eBook) | LCC PZ7.1.S26 As 2017 (print) | DDC [Fic]—dc23
LC record available at https://lccn.loc.gov/2017003373

THE
ASSASSIN'S
CURSE

MONDAY, NOVEMBER 2, 1665

Matins

DO YOU BELIEVE IN FATE?

Once, after I'd become Master Benedict's apprentice, I'd asked him about it. He'd stirred his soup, his spoon clunking against his bowl. "An interesting question. What brought this up?"

"Well," I said, "the astronomy book you gave me says the universe is like a clock. That everything proceeds according to a grand design."

"It does."

"Yet we have free will, don't we? I mean, we're responsible for the things we do."

"Absolutely," he said.

"But . . . how can both of these be true?" I said. "If we have free will, how can there be a grand design? Couldn't you do something to change the universe's plan? And if the universe *is* just a giant clock, and we're only gears playing our part, then how can we be blamed for what we do? Isn't that just who we were born to be?"

My master regarded me sternly. "Is this about you breaking the Baileys' window?"

"Er . . . no." Though Tom and I wouldn't be playing Castle Siege at his house again anytime soon.

"Then wait here."

He went upstairs, where I heard him rooting through the library in the spare room. When he returned, he was carrying a stack of books so tall he had to peek his head around it to see where he was going. He dropped them on the table. I scrambled to stop the tower from spilling into my soup.

"Start with these," my master said. "Return when you're done."

With my regular duties, it took me several days to read them all. When I finally finished, I found Master Benedict in the workshop, experimenting with a new recipe to cure gout.

"Well?" he said. "What do you think? Does fate rule, or free will?"

I scratched my head, embarrassed. "I have no idea."

He sighed. "Nor do I. I was rather hoping you'd find the answer."

Which is all to say that this is an incredibly difficult

question. So as Tom and I bumped along in the carriage on the muddy road to Oxford, I tried to explain to him how history's greatest thinkers had pondered this exact query. How complicated the notion of blame really was.

To Tom, however, the answer was simple: This was all *my* fault.

CHAPTER

1

"THIS IS ALL YOUR FAULT," TOM said.

He folded his arms and turned away, gazing unhappily through the carriage window. Beyond the curtain, the lights of distant farmhouses dotted the darkness of the countryside.

"But I haven't *done* anything," I said.

"You think we're here because of me?"

"No, I—"

"*I'm* not the one setting fire to pear trees," Tom said.

"That was an accident."

"*I'm* not the one saying, 'Hey, let's blow up these pumpkins in the street.'"

"That was an experiment," I protested. "And it was *one* pumpkin. The rest were squash. What does that have to do with anything?"

"Maybe you destroyed an important pumpkin."

"How can a pumpkin be important?"

"Maybe it was a prize-winning pumpkin," Tom said. "Maybe it was England's pumpkin, to be entered into the International Pumpkin Fair. In Scotland."

"Now you're just stringing random words together."

"Oh? Then explain this." He grabbed the . . . invitation, I suppose you'd call it, that had fallen to the floor of the carriage and thrust it at me. "Explain it!"

That was the problem. I *couldn't* explain it. This whole business had come as a surprise.

Yesterday morning, Tom and I had been eating lunch in my apothecary shop when a heavy fist had hammered on the door. I'd opened it to find myself face-to-face with one of the King's Men, the royal coat of arms emblazoned on his tabard. Behind him was a carriage, a second soldier waiting beside it in the street.

"You Christopher Rowe?" the King's Man said. When I nodded, he handed me a letter. I stared at it, uncomprehending. When I read it, I understood even less.

Christopher:
Get Thomas Bailey and get in the carriage.
Ashcombe

Baron Richard Ashcombe, the King's Warden, was the Lord Protector of His Majesty, Charles II. I looked warily at the soldier. "Are we in trouble?"

He shrugged. "I was just ordered to bring you to Oxford."

Oxford? That's where the king's Court was staying. "Are we under arrest?"

The man tapped his foot impatiently. "Not yet."

And that was how Tom and I ended up bumping our way through the countryside in the back of this carriage. After a night under guard in an inn, Tom was convinced we were headed for doom.

"We're going to end up in the dungeon," he moaned.

"We're not going to end up in the dungeon," I said, not entirely certain of that.

"Do you know what happens in a dungeon? There's no food. They *starve* you."

"We're not even in irons."

Tom's lower lip trembled. "All you get is a single piece

of bread, once a night. And not the good bread, either, with poppy seeds and maybe a bit of cinnamon. No. It's hard bread. Hard bread for a hard life."

Trust the baker's son to critique the dungeon's bread. Still, I wished he'd stop. The more he spoke, the more the prospect of wasting away behind bars loomed large in my mind. I tried to push his worry aside and think of why Lord Ashcombe would call for us.

I'd only had contact with the King's Warden twice since we'd stopped the plot against the city at the height of the plague. The first was after Magistrate Aldebourne had told Lord Ashcombe what had happened. He'd written to me separately, asking for my account. The second was when he'd found a job for Sally, as promised.

His note, characteristically brief, said he'd found her a position as chambermaid to the Lady Pemberton, and a horse would come to collect her. As the baroness was with Court, which had fled London when the plague came, Sally had said a bittersweet goodbye to us back in September. Since she'd gone, I'd written her letters every week, but I hadn't heard back. That wasn't unexpected—her job wouldn't give her enough money to pay for post—but Lord Ashcombe's summons made me wonder if she was in some kind of trouble.

The carriage slowed. Tom and I watched from the window as we turned north, off the road to Oxford. It appeared the city wouldn't be our destination after all. We skirted the town, lumbering through deep ruts in the mud, until our driver pulled us onto the grounds of a private estate.

Oaks lined the pathway, autumn-copper leaves stained rusty orange by the torches staked between them. Our horses, their breath puffing wispy clouds in the November chill, dragged us up the road to the mansion atop the slope. Lamps glowed through the windows, adding their light to the haze in the frosty air.

This place was no prison. And, whatever reason we were here, we wouldn't be alone. Dozens of other carriages lined the lawn, flattening the grass under mud-caked wheels, while their drivers lounged about, waiting.

Our own transport pulled to a stop in front of the mansion, where a man in livery ushered us from the coach. The King's Men nudged us up the stairs, through a set of grand double doors. A coat of arms was carved into the stone above the entrance: crossed halberds over a shield emblazoned with antlers.

Wherever we were, this place was astounding. The entrance hall alone was as big as my entire house. A marble staircase curved upward from the center of the foyer to the upper floors. A pair of servants waited there, their livery matching the staff standing by the half dozen exits to the different wings of the estate. From somewhere beyond, I heard the sounds of a gathering and the faint strains of music.

"You're late."

Lord Ashcombe strode into the entryway, dressed in fine black silks. He wore a patch over his left eye and a glove on his three-fingered right hand, wounds from a battle with the men who'd murdered my master earlier this year. There was no sword at his side, but his pearl-handled pistol was jammed into his belt.

"Sorry, General," the King's Man accompanying us said. "The rain's turned the roads to slop."

Lord Ashcombe grunted and looked us over. "We'll need to get you ready." He motioned to the servants on the stairs.

"My lord?" I glanced at Tom, who, by this point, was close to fainting. "Are we in trouble?"

Lord Ashcombe raised an eyebrow. "Should you be?"

"Uh . . . no?"

"Then I suppose it'll depend on how this evening goes."

"This evening?"

"Yes," Lord Ashcombe said. "The king wants to speak with you."

CHAPTER

I NEARLY CHOKED. "THE KING?"

"The king," Lord Ashcombe said.

"What king?" Tom blurted.

"*Your* king."

"Our king? You mean the man on the coins?"

Lord Ashcombe closed his eyes and sighed. "Get them upstairs," he said to the servants.

Before the men could take us away, our driver entered the foyer, carrying a small metal cage. A rather plump bird marched around inside it, rustling her salt-and-pepper feathers against the wire.

Lord Ashcombe looked puzzled. "What is that?"

The soldier studied the cage. "A pigeon, innit?"

Lord Ashcombe pressed his lips together. "I know it's a pigeon. I'm asking you why you've brought it to me."

"She's . . . she's mine, my lord," I said, still dazed. *The king?* "That's Bridget."

Bridget poked her head through the cage and cooed at him.

"Why would you bring—never mind. I don't want to know. Go on, get them ready," he said to the servants, then walked back toward the sound of the music.

One of the servants collected Bridget's cage. "This way, please, sirs."

I followed him up the stairs, stomach churning. *We're going to meet the king.*

Tom grabbed my sleeve, more terrified than ever. "You have to get me out of this," he said.

"How am I supposed to do that?"

"You *have* to. I can't meet the king, Christopher. I can't." Tom's voice cracked. "I'm a baker. What am I supposed to say to him? 'Good evening, Your Majesty. Do you like buns?'"

I suddenly realized I had no idea what to say to him, either. Why did Lord Ashcombe always have to be so cryptic? What were we *doing* here?

They separated us on the second floor. As one of the men led him down the hall, Tom looked back at me accusingly. "This is all your fault."

Bodwin, the servant escorting me, took me down the opposite wing to a fancifully decorated bedroom. He held up Bridget's cage. "Was the bird intended for some purpose, sir?"

His question dragged me from my worries. "What? Oh. No. She's just . . . mine. Lord Ashcombe didn't say how long I was going to be away, and there wasn't anyone to care for her at home."

"Of course, sir. I'll see she's tended to. In the meantime, I'll help you wash."

I didn't think I needed help—I'd been washing myself successfully for years now—but, still in a daze, I didn't object. I followed him to an adjoining room, where a girl poured a bucket of hot water into an already steaming tub. Bodwin remained while I undressed, then worked to scrub the dust of the road from my skin.

When we returned to my room, my clothes were gone, a new kit laid out on the bed. The breeches, hose, and shirt I was left were of finer quality than any I'd ever worn before, with a half-baize, half-silk sapphire waistcoat and a soft woolen doublet overtop. The leather shoes had been polished so finely I could see my face on their tips. Clothes for a king—literally.

Once I was dressed, Bodwin hurried me back into the hall. Still distracted, I turned the corner and bumped into a man with bleary eyes inspecting a bronze bust of some bewigged gentleman next to one of the doors. The man teetered slightly as he peered at the statue, a bottle of wine dangling from his hand.

"Pardon me," he said, his speech a little slurred.

Bodwin cleared his throat. "Mr. Glover."

"A moment, please," Glover said. "I am trying to determine who this is."

Bodwin cleared his throat again, more forcefully. "Mr. *Glover*. You are needed downstairs."

"The next round of wine is already dec . . . decanting," he hiccupped. "Who's this? New boy?"

Now Bodwin was mortified. "This is one of the king's guests."

"Oh. My apologies, young master. John Glover, my lady's cellarman, at your service." He bowed, spilling wine on his shoes.

"Mr. *Glover*. Mr. Skipwith has warned you."

"It's my job to taste the wine, sir. What if it's poisoned?" He belched. "Pardon me."

"*Mr.—*"

Glover held up a hand. "Say no more. I am going."

He weaved his way around the corner and out of sight. Bodwin seemed sad. "Please accept my apologies, sir. Mr. Glover really is a decent man. Very kind to all. He just . . . slips, sometimes, with the drink."

That seemed a less-than-preferable quality for a cellar-man. "It's all right," I said.

"I'll report him, of course."

He sounded like he didn't want to do that. I wasn't particularly keen on it, either. If Glover was reported, he'd lose his job, and I didn't want to be the cause of anyone's troubles.

"I'd prefer it if you didn't," I said.

Bodwin looked at me, surprised, then bowed his head in gratitude. "As you wish."

He led me back down the stairs. Tom was already waiting for me, tugging at his breeches. "These do not sit right," he said.

Lord Ashcombe returned for us. Music came from behind him, louder than before. "Finally," he said. "Come, then. It's time to meet His Majesty."

CHAPTER

3

HE'D BROUGHT US TO A PARTY.

The ballroom was filled with satin and silk, grand nobles sipping wine from crystal glasses. Four balconies overlooked the chamber from the third floor, high above. In one of them, six musicians played, a consort of recorders. A host of couples danced below; several more ringed around them, clapping with the beat.

From the otherwise empty balconies hung yellow and purple streamers, dangling inches from the wigs of the men underneath. A massive chandelier, blazing with a hundred candles, glittered in the center, filling the room with its warmth.

"Close your mouth," Lord Ashcombe said.

I snapped my jaw shut. It left me no less dazzled by the throng as he led us through the crowd. I called to Master Benedict in my heart. *Look where I am, Master.*

I stopped for a moment as we passed a woman who, most strangely, was wearing a mask. Adorned with feathers, it covered the top half of her face. She'd drawn a crowd of men who appeared to be making a play for her hand. She laughed, a musical sound, and smiled brightly as she said in a heavily accented voice, "I am not available."

I looked at Lord Ashcombe. "She's French," he said, as if that was an explanation in itself. "Now listen. When you're introduced to the king, all you need to do is be polite. Call him 'Your Majesty' the first time you speak, then 'sire' after that. And, for the love of our Lord, be brief. Everyone always stammers on. They sound like idiots."

Tom's face had gone whiter than snow. My own stomach was tumbling. "What does he want from us?" I said.

"To meet you. He'd expressed interest after the business with the Cult of the Archangel, of course, but when I told him about the incident during the plague, he insisted I bring you to Court. I'd planned to wait until we returned to London, but from the way the sickness is hanging on, we won't be back anytime soon. So I thought you might like this instead." He regarded me critically. "If you don't pass out beforehand."

That was a very real possibility. I was on the verge of suggesting we wait for London after all, when Lord Ashcombe edged his way into a circle of people, their gaze all fixed on one man.

He was remarkably tall, and thin, with a large nose and a long, curly black wig. He plucked grapes from the plate of the lady next to him and popped them into his mouth as he spoke.

Tom gripped my arm so tightly I thought he might snap my bones. For we stood before the man himself: His Majesty, Charles II, by the grace of God, King of England, Scotland, France, and Ireland, Defender of the Faith.

He had a merry twinkle in his eye. Distracted by my fluttering nerves, it took me a moment to realize he was telling a joke. "And the shepherd says to her, 'Beggin' your pardon, my lady, but that's not my hat.'"

The men burst into laughter. The ladies standing on either side of him tittered with scandalous delight. One of them rapped him playfully on the arm with an ivory fan. "You're wicked," she said.

He grinned. "To my eternal shame. Hello, who's this?"

He'd spotted me trembling at the edge of the circle. Lord Ashcombe prodded me forward. "Your Majesty, may I present two of your subjects. This is Christopher Rowe, of London, former apprentice to the late Benedict Blackthorn."

The king brightened. "Oh! Yes! Welcome!"

I bowed, awestruck. In the back of my mind, I heard Lord Ashcombe. *For the love of our Lord, be brief.* "The—the honor is mine, Your Majesty," I stammered.

He turned to one of the ladies. "This boy solves murders, can you believe it? Christopher, you must join me for breakfast tomorrow. I want to hear all of your secrets."

A warm glow spread through my chest. "Of . . . of course, sire."

"Richard, make certain— Odd's fish, who's the giant? He's taller than me."

Charles stared curiously at Tom, who stood frozen in terror. Lord Ashcombe had to drag him in. "Thomas Bailey, sire," the King's Warden said. "Baker's son, and friend to Christopher."

"Aha! The master of the rolling pin!" Tom flushed as the king clapped his hands, grinning. "You must join my guard, Thomas. Our enemies will flee when they see you on the walls. Then afterward you can bake us all biscuits."

Everyone laughed. Tom turned so red his face looked like a cherry.

"Oh no, look," Charles said. "My poor jest has embarrassed the boy. Come here, Thomas, come."

Tom gaped as the king clasped his hand. "Richard told me what you did at Mortimer House. You not only saved the life of your own friend that day, you saved the life of mine as well. I am forever grateful. You are a true son of England."

Tom didn't say a word. But I'd never seen him beam so brightly.

"Thank you, sire," Lord Ashcombe said, and he pulled us away from the circle. As the ladies returned to vying for the king's attention, the King's Warden led us toward another chamber next to the main ballroom.

"So, that's done," he said. "If His Majesty wants you again, I'll find you. Otherwise, enjoy the party. There's food in there, and drinks everywhere. Plus dancing, if you like that sort of thing."

He left us then, among the crowd. I stood there, flush, still glowing. "This is the best day *ever*," I said.

If Tom got any happier, I thought he might float. He stopped a man as he passed us. "I'm a true son of England," Tom said to him.

The man looked at me, bemused. "He is," I said, and we laughed as we moved on.

Tom grabbed the hand of another gentleman and shook it. "Good evening. I'm Thomas Bailey of London. I'm a true son of England."

This man looked just as puzzled. "Are you, now?"

I couldn't get the grin off my face. "We met the king," I said.

"Oh, I see." He nodded understandingly. "Then congratulations. Enjoy your—urk!"

Tom wrapped the man in his arms and held him close. A guard, standing against the wall, lifted his halberd and began shoving his way through the crowd.

"Tom," I said hastily, "I don't think you should hug the guests."

"All right." He let go and drifted away. "I'm a true son of England."

I helped the man right his wig. "I'm very sorry, my lord. Tom just loves the king."

"Loyalty needs no defense," the man said, waving the

guard back to his post. "Tell your friend the Duke of York wishes him well."

I froze. "The Duke of . . . "

He winked and moved on.

This was getting out of hand. Tom had just hugged the Lord High Admiral—who also happened to be the king's brother. I needed to rein him in before he bumped into the queen.

Tom came back for me first. *"Christopher!"* He grabbed my arm and dragged me halfway across the room. "Look."

I did. And I blinked.

"Am I really seeing this?" Tom said.

I couldn't be sure myself. Laid out on either side of us were two tables, each one fifty feet long. Piled on one were meat and fowl of various kinds: roast beef, glazed venison, steaming pheasant. The other table held breads and sweets: pastries, pies, cakes, and fruits.

I didn't know where to put my eyes. They drifted from the sweets to the meats and back again. Tom squeezed my arm.

"Are those *chops*?" he said. "In *sauce*? Christopher, *they're in sauce!*"

He shook me so hard my brain rattled. When he let me

go, I had to steady myself to keep from falling. "Are you *crying*?" I said.

He sniffed. "It's just so beautiful."

He wasn't wrong. Because of the plague, neither one of us had seen meat in months. Tom ran straight toward that table, while I remained to think again of my master. *How I wish you were here, too.*

I suddenly got an image of him, raising an eyebrow at me. It made me laugh. Master Benedict would have hated this. He was never one for parties.

But *I* sure was. I turned my attention back to the tables, debating which one to attack first. And then someone poked me in the side.

CHAPTER

4

I TURNED TO SEE A GIRL, A HEAD shorter than I was, with a light dusting of freckles across her nose. She was dressed in a gown of forest green, which looked lovely against her auburn curls. She grinned up at me.

"Hello," she said.

"Sally!" Without thinking, I threw my arms around her and picked her up. She squealed in delight as I spun her about. Her arms wrapped around my neck, holding me close, and her hair fell softly against my cheek. I smelled lavender.

Suddenly confused, I put her down. Her hands slid over

my doublet and away. She looked up at me through her eye-lashes, face flushed. "Well," she said.

My own face had got pretty warm, too. We stood there awkwardly for a moment, until an older servant woman passing by leaned in with a conspiratorial smile. "You dropped something, dear."

She handed Sally a shoe with a green satin bow tied over the buckle. Sally turned away and slipped it over her stocking. When she turned back, she'd gone even redder.

"Did you . . . uh . . . get my letters?" I said.

"I did," she said. "I wrote you back for each one; they're with my things. I can give them to you after the party. If you want."

"Of course I do."

"Where's Tom?"

"You have one guess," I said.

Her eyes went immediately to the table with the meat. Sure enough, Tom had parked himself right in front of the chops in sauce. He had one in his mouth, and two more in each hand. When he spotted Sally, he raised them like he'd discovered fistfuls of gold. "Mmm uhh trr sunn uv Nnnglnd," he shouted.

She laughed. "What?"

"I'll tell you later," I said. I looked her over. The last time I'd seen her, she'd still been bandaged from the terrible fight two months ago. Now all that remained from that battle was a small pink scar on her cheek, and another on the bridge of her nose. "Are you here for Lord Ashcombe?"

She shook her head. "I'm working. Lady Pemberton's one of the king's guests."

"How's that going, by the way?" When she hesitated, I winced. "That bad?"

"No, no," she said. "The baroness is actually quite nice. She's just a little—"

"Sally!" a woman shrieked.

"—highly strung." Sally sighed.

A young woman rushed over, dressed in a canary silk gown decorated with brocade. Tears ran down her cheeks. "My dress," she moaned. "Paul spilled wine all over it. It's ruined!"

I saw the tiniest fleck of burgundy on one of her sleeves. I wouldn't even have noticed it if she hadn't been pointing at it like her arm had come off.

"My lady—" Sally began.

"Everyone's staring at me," the baroness said in a

trembling voice—and they were, because now she was making a scene. "I have to change *immediately*."

She grabbed Sally's arm and dragged her away. Sally threw a look of apology at me over her shoulder and mouthed, *I'll see you later.*

I'd barely had the chance to wave goodbye before someone called me. "Boy!"

I turned to see an elderly fellow with a badly crooked cravat beckoning to me. When I went over, he handed me his glass. "This is not very good. Surely your cellarman has better?"

It took me a moment to realize what he was asking. In seeing me talking to Sally, he must have thought I was one of the staff. "I'm sorry, my lord," I said. "I'm not a waiter."

"Wonderful. I'll have that."

It appeared the man was a little hard of hearing. "I'm not a waiter," I repeated, more loudly.

"Excellent news," he said. "I'm delighted."

I had to bite my lip so I wouldn't laugh. I was in such a good mood; why not help? Besides, it would give me the chance to see more of this incredible house. "I'll bring it right away."

"And more pickles."

"Of course. How can we have run out of pickles?" I grabbed an almond pastry from the dessert table and waved to Tom. *I'm just going to find more wine,* I mouthed.

"Whnngh?" he said, a massive bone clamped between his teeth.

I pointed toward the doors through which the servers kept coming. "I'll be back."

Tom held his arms out, as if to ask *How can you leave when there's all this food?* Normally, I'd have dragged him with me, but I couldn't possibly tear him away while chops were still in sauce. I stuffed the pastry in my mouth, snatched another, then stopped a man carrying a tray of empty glasses. "Have you seen Mr. Glover? I have a request from one of the guests."

"Downstairs, sir," the man said. "Preparing the next round of wine. It's through the kitchen." I followed his instruction and slipped into the realm of the servants.

It was almost startling to see the chaos behind the gilt. In the kitchen, which stretched nearly the entire east wing of the house, cooks screamed at their apprentices, pots clanged off the floors, staff buzzed in and out like bees, and, though its raucous aggression was nothing like Master Benedict's apothecary workshop, this place nonetheless felt much closer to my heart than the world I'd just left. The party had been wondrous, an extraordinary glimpse into a life I'd dreamed of, growing up in the Cripplegate orphanage. Yet, even as the glow from meeting the king filled me with warmth, it struck me how out of place I'd been in that ballroom. I'd been treated with nothing but kindness, yet I knew that I didn't really belong.

The other reason I found the kitchen so fascinating was simpler: I'd never seen so much food. The tables in the ballroom were already groaning; who was going to eat all this?

Tom is, I laughed to myself, and snatched a chop in sauce from a waiting plate. He'd just have to make do without this one. Several of the staff cast curious glances my way, but no one challenged me. I was about to ask for more directions to the cellar when I spotted the stairs down. I stood aside as a half dozen girls passed by, staggering under more silver trays laden with glasses filled with a deep burgundy liquid—hopefully good enough for my hard-of-hearing friend. I thought about returning to the party, but since I was here, and curious about the cellar, I continued downward.

It was cold, the autumn chill having seeped through the earth and stone. Flickering lamps hanging from the rafters illuminated the space, casting shadows that danced with the flames. Giant casks lay alongside one wall, one dripping ale from a leaking spigot. All the way down the middle of the room were racks upon racks of wine bottles, hundreds of them, a fortune in drink. A large table held several empties.

"Mr. Glover?"

He wasn't here, but he hadn't gone up with the trays. I half wondered if he'd succumbed to his tasting and passed out between the casks. Then I spotted faint light spilling in from the far side of the cellar.

I went a little closer and found myself at a door made of stone that blended into the wall. It was open just a crack; the source of the light. I pulled on it and saw a narrow ring of spiral steps, leading upward, an oil lamp hanging from the central column.

A secret passage, I thought. So that's where Glover had gone. I'd heard about these: narrow tunnels, built for servants to move behind the scenes without disturbing the masters. Interesting that they had one in the cellar. Whoever had built this house had, like their cellarman, apparently enjoyed their drink.

I took a step inside. As I did, a voice in my head told me I shouldn't be snooping. It sounded a lot like Tom. I ignored it. How could anyone see a secret passage and not want to know where it goes?

Just one little peek, I told my phantom friend, and I crept up the steps. I found another entrance, closed, on the second floor—and, strangely, a solitary boot, lying on its side. I picked it up and noticed the stain on the tip: wine. It was Glover's, the one on which he'd previously spilled his bottle.

What was this doing here?

More light shined from above. I continued up to find that the spiral steps ended at another doorway, this one open. I peeked my head around the corner to see what was beyond it.

It was a bedroom, much grander than mine. The master of the house's own chamber, I guessed, not only from the luxury, but from the crest on the tapestry hanging over the cushions: crossed halberds over antlers, the same as above the entryway outside.

And there was a man, fallen, hanging half off the bed.

I froze. It was Glover, wearing only one of his boots, a match for the mate I'd found on the stairs. My own boot clinked on glass, and a pair of bottles rolled away, one corked, one opened, spilling its contents in a sloppy line across the floorboards.

I wasn't sure what to do. I couldn't just leave Glover as he was; clearly, he needed help. But if I went to get someone, I'd have to explain why I was here—where *neither* of us were supposed to be.

I'd need to take care of this myself, then. I went to the bed and turned the cellarman over. The stink of wine and bile assaulted my nostrils, with a heavy scent of garlic. He'd thrown up, though not here; there was no vomit anywhere on the bed. I gagged as I turned him over, because now a much worse smell came: He'd soiled his breeches.

"Mr. Glover." I shook him, but he didn't wake. "Mr. Glover!"

His head lolled, and his eyes came open a little. For a moment, I thought I'd succeeded in rousing him. Except he didn't really seem to be looking at anything. And then I realized he wasn't breathing, either.

He was *dead*.

I stumbled backward, landing with a thud on the rug beside the bed. *Plague.* I began to crawl away, panicked, before I managed to calm myself.

It wasn't plague. The man had shown none of the symptoms, and the sickness hadn't followed us to Oxford.

Then . . . what had killed him?

Had he fallen, struck his head on the bedpost? I checked him over. There wasn't a wound anywhere to be seen.

His heart, then? No, that didn't match the symptoms, either: vomiting, uncontrolled bowels, a quick death.

It is *plague,* my mind screamed at me, but I shook my head. None of the marks were there. Based on what I could see, it was more likely he'd died by—

A chill sank deep into my bones as I remembered what the cellarman had said.

It's my job to taste the wine, sir. What if it's poisoned?

He'd meant it as a joke. But I realized, with horror: It fit. Not just the symptoms, but the speed of it.

Glover had been *poisoned.* He'd been drinking the wine, and one of the bottles had poisoned him. And a new round of wine was now on its way to—

The party.

The *king.*

My chest tightened. I scrambled to my feet, ready to run back downstairs.

And then I felt a cord slip around my throat.

CHAPTER

THE ROPE DREW TIGHT. PAIN GRIPPED
my neck as the cord hauled me upward.

I kicked out, trying to find the floor. I felt the press of a
man against me, his breath hot in my ear.

I grabbed for the cord, fingers scrabbling against it.
It tightened, cutting into my flesh. I couldn't breathe. I
couldn't think. I reached back at the man holding me. I felt
his big hands, his skin taut as his fingers twisted the loop
around my throat. My arms flailed, trying to beat him off,
but they were weak blows, landing against the hood that
covered his head.

He shook me, like a dog shaking a rat, and tightened

the cord once more. My face swelled as I gave up my useless beating and tried to pry my fingers under the loop. But it was too tight. The world began to flash with shooting stars; then my vision went black. My arms dragged, so heavy, and even as my brain screamed at them to *move*, they fell to my side.

Tom, my mind called out.

Tom.

no

no

tom

master

help

falling

I am falling

the floor

The floor. Sound. Heat. Someone shouting.
A fight.
A . . . shade? A spirit? A bear?
My neck. My neck hurt so much.

I heard glass shatter. I felt the coolness of a breeze, saw the sparkle of candlelight.

Hands lifted me—big, strong. They placed me on the bed.

The cord. The cord was pulled away from my neck. My skin was on fire.

Air. I gasped, and air returned, in great heaving breaths.

Tom loomed over me, afraid. He squinted, one eye red and tearing, a swelling pink mark on the cheek below. He pushed on my chest, as if he could will breath back into me. I coughed and hacked and struggled in his arms.

"It's all right," Tom said. "The man . . . the man's gone. He fell."

Dazed, I looked over. I saw the broken window, the cloak crumpled on the floor. Tom must have fought the assassin off, pushed him through the glass. Bad news for him; we were two floors up.

The autumn air blew in, turning the room cold. I breathed, fast and ragged. I was alive. I lay back, trying to rest, but a voice chimed in my head.

You're forgetting something.

I sat up with a jolt. Mr. Glover's body still lay beside me on the bed.

Poison, I said. Or I tried to say.

No words came out.

I tried again. *Stop them.* But my throat had seized, rebelled. The cord around it had silenced my voice. I couldn't speak.

I couldn't *speak.*

I grabbed Tom's arms. "Lie down," he said. "You'll be all right. Lie down."

I shook my head. No time. *You have to stop them from drinking the wine.* But my voice still wouldn't cooperate.

My soundless words were scaring him. "What's the matter? What do you need?"

I pointed to the bottles on the floor. *Wine,* I mouthed.

"Oh—yes. Of course." Tom picked up the opened bottle. He raised it to my lips. "It'll be all right. Drink."

Panicked, I swatted his hand away. The bottle spun from his fingers and cracked on the floorboards, bleeding the rest of the poisoned wine in rivulets under the dresser.

I wanted to scream in frustration, to scream for real. Any sound, anything. But I had no voice—and no time.

I dragged myself from the bed. Tom watched in confusion as, wobbling, I grabbed the unopened bottle and staggered toward the secret passage.

No. Treacherous steps. Down, belowground, then up again. My legs were like jelly; it would take too long. Instead, I stumbled out the bedroom door and lurched down the hall.

Tom followed, still scared. "What's wrong? Christopher!"

I'd have given anything to be able to answer. I just kept moving, weaving my way toward the sounds of the party. My legs shook; Tom had to right me twice as I fell.

I need to go down, I thought. *But I'll break my head on the stairs.*

Then I remembered the ballroom. The balconies.

The balconies. That was it. I moved faster now, more steadily, with a purpose. I found the hall to the nearest balcony, stumbled forward to the rail, and looked down.

The musicians sat across from me, still playing. Everyone else was below. The servants had already begun working their way through the guests, distributing the wine.

I scanned the crowd for the king. Taller than everyone, he was easy to spot. He already had his glass. The ladies and gentlemen around him had theirs, too, as did Lord Ashcombe, standing half a room away. The rest of the guests were plucking the wine from the servants' trays. One was handed to the French lady, still wearing her feathered mask.

"Stop."

My voice came, finally. But it was only a croak. Far too faint to be heard over their talk, their laughter, the music.

Charles raised his glass and spoke to those around him. I tried again.

"Stop."

But they didn't hear me, couldn't hear me.

The king finished speaking. He raised his glass to his lips.

I still held the unopened bottle that Glover had had with him. I could think of only one thing to do with it.

I threw it at the king.

The bottle twisted as it fell, tumbling in a slow, lazy arc. Then it landed, right in the middle of the circle.

It didn't just shatter. It *exploded*. Shards of glass splintered, peppering their boots. The wine burst outward in a great ruby star, staining all that fine silk hose and those gowns.

There were a few short shrieks. Then a stunned, horrified silence. The voices stopped, the music stopped, and everyone looked upward.

"What on God's good earth . . . ?" I heard Charles say.

And then the guards that ringed the ballroom sprang into action. Two pushed through the crowd, polearms in hand, elbowing the ladies out of the way to stand shoulder to shoulder with the king. A few clanged their halberds across the exits. The rest ran out of the room—coming for me, no doubt.

Lord Ashcombe's hand had gone automatically to his side and come up empty, his sword left behind because of the party. He grabbed instead the pearl handle of his pistol, scanning the balconies for the threat.

When he spotted me, he stopped, his flintlock half-drawn. He frowned.

Tom, equally confused, stepped away, mortified at what I'd done. I didn't have time to explain it to him. "Don't drink the wine," I called down. But my voice was still too faint, and the crowd had started up again, buzzing about the insanity they'd just witnessed. A lady near His Majesty, who'd been splashed the worst, cursed up at me in outrage. Everyone else looked over at the king.

Charles tried to defuse the tension with a joke. "That's some boy you brought us, Richard." He shook ruby drips from his fingers. "Someone should tell the lad: Wine is for drinking, not throwing."

The crowd chuckled, but all I could hear was the thunder of the guards' boots on the stairs. And all I could see was the glass. The king still had his glass.

I locked eyes with Lord Ashcombe. He cocked his head at me, puzzled. *Why?*

The guards were almost upon me. I thrust a hand out as if I were holding a goblet. I pointed frantically at the imaginary cup.

Lord Ashcombe watched.

Slowly, deliberately, I drew a finger across my neck.

Lord Ashcombe frowned.

Then I pointed directly at the king. I barely had time for the gesture before rough hands grabbed me and slammed me to the floor. The King's Men jumped on Tom, too. Backing away in fear, he made no attempt to defend himself; he hit the floor next to me.

But Lord Ashcombe had seen. And he turned.

Charles raised his glass once again. "To childhood," he laughed, and those who hadn't dropped their drinks raised theirs in return.

"To childhood!"

Lord Ashcombe's eye went wide.

Charles brought the glass to his lips.

There was no time to reach him. Instead, Lord Ashcombe finished drawing his pistol. With one smooth motion, he pointed it at the king and pulled the trigger.

The burst of gunpowder echoed deafeningly in the hall. The lead shot flew out with a puff of smoke, and hit the glass just as the liquid touched the king's lips. The crystal shattered, spattering his finery with scarlet. The shot continued on, knocking off a man's curled wig before punching splinters from the paneling of the ballroom wall behind.

The crowd gasped. The King's Men beside Charles froze for a moment, as if unable to believe what they'd just seen. Then they shoved the crowd aside to seize the arms of their own general. Even then, they looked at each other in confusion.

Charles was just as stunned. He stared at his old friend, and when he spoke, he didn't sound angry. He sounded hurt. "Richard," he said. "What wretched treason is this?"

Lord Ashcombe bowed his head. "Forgive me, sire," he said. "But I believe the wine may be poisoned."

CHAPTER

THEY LOCKED DOWN THE HOUSE
immediately. Charles was hustled from the ballroom by
a dozen guards as Lord Ashcombe ordered men to every
corner of the grounds to try to prevent anyone's escape. He
sent a rider on a sprint southward to Oxford for more men,
and, within the hour, so many soldiers had surrounded the
estate it looked like the house was under siege.

Despite my messy intervention, some of the guests
had already been poisoned. There was nothing I could do
for three of them: two lords who'd downed their wine as
soon as they'd received it, and a servant girl who'd snuck
a glass for herself before bringing out the trays. A score

of others had also drunk at least some of the wine, and since I didn't know what poison had been used, and so what remedy to apply, I thought it safest to just make them all throw up.

With Lord Ashcombe's permission, I collected my apothecary sash from my bedroom. An invention of my master's, the sash was stitched with pockets that contained dozens of vials of remedies and ingredients, plus a host of other useful tools as well. Master Benedict had always worn it when he left the shop to see his customers; after his murder, I usually wore it hidden under my shirt.

The best emetic in the sash was syrup of ipecac, made from a plant that grew only in the New World. The vial I carried, however, only held enough for two doses. I gave that to the guests who had drunk the most wine and used mustard powder on the others. While I only had two doses of that as well, the kitchen had plenty of mustard seeds for me to grind. The vomiting made for a nasty sight—and a worse smell—but, thankfully, though several fell ill, only one lady remained truly in danger.

Once the poisoned were taken care of, I limped into the library to treat myself. The bumps and bruises the King's Men had given me when they'd thrown me to the floor weren't anything serious, but my throat still ached from being strangled, and the skin of my neck burned like fire.

Tom pulled away the cloth I'd wrapped around it and had a look. "You're really hurt," he said.

I used the looking glass in my sash to see. There was an angry red ring all the way around my neck. Blood from the wound had already ruined the collar of my borrowed shirt. Sighing, I slumped in my chair and let Tom use the vial of spiderweb to pack the cut.

The door to the library opened. The guards Lord Ashcombe had ordered to stay with me for protection advanced with their halberds until I called them back.

"It's all right," I said. "She's a friend."

Sally eyed the guards warily as she slipped inside. She hurried over, looking as worried as Tom, and maybe a little exasperated, too.

"Does trouble follow you *everywhere*?" she said.

Tom grunted. "Don't get me started."

"Be nice to me," I said. "I'm wounded." I pointed to my neck. "See? Ow."

Tom shook his head as Sally pulled the vial of honey from my sash and dabbed it over the spiderweb in the cut. It stung, but the coolness of it helped to soothe the burn.

"What's going on out there?" I asked Sally.

"Lord Ashcombe's questioning the guests. He's trying to find out who the assassin was." She lowered her voice as she glanced at the King's Men. "He's scary."

I already knew that quite well. "What's scary is that an assassin can just walk around the house without anyone stopping him."

"That was the easy part." Sally dabbed the last of the cut with honey, then began gently rolling a cotton strip around the wound. "There are a hundred guests, any one of whom might have a grudge against the king. Plus all of them brought servants—that French lady alone has ten of them—and no one ever pays attention to servants. Whoever it was, servant or guest, he could have walked right past you, and nobody would have thought twice about it."

A fact I'd already recognized. I told them about being in the kitchen and going down to the cellar. "No one stopped me. They didn't even ask what I was doing."

Sally tied the cotton strip so it would stay in place. "Speaking of which, I'm not supposed to be here, either. Lady Pemberton's in hysterics, so I told her I'd go find a restorative. I really just wanted to see if you were all right."

I pulled a vial with a deep amber liquid from my sash. "That's brandy. It's as good a restorative as any. And it's guaranteed not to be poisoned."

"It might explode, though," Tom said.

Sally looked like she didn't know whether to laugh or scold us. "You fools."

The door opened again, and Lord Ashcombe appeared. Sally bowed her head, curtsied, then slipped past him into the hall.

He shut the door behind her. "Are you all right?" he asked me.

"I'll be fine," I said.

"You did well. Both of you." Lord Ashcombe folded his arms. "Now we have a traitor to catch. Say what you know."

I told him what had happened, every detail I could remember. He listened, then turned to Tom when I finished.

"I saw Christopher leave the party," Tom said, shrinking under Ashcombe's gaze. "So I followed him. When I got to the kitchen, one of the serving girls said he'd gone to the cellar, so I went there, and found the passageway up. I know Christopher can't resist a secret, so I went up, too. When I got there, I saw him being strangled."

"What did the man attacking him look like?"

"He was stocky. Built like a bull. I've never met anybody so strong."

"And his face?"

"I . . . I couldn't see it," Tom said apologetically. "He had a cloak on. The hood was covering his head." When Lord Ashcombe grunted and indicated for Tom to go on, he drew a breath before continuing. "Anyway, I grabbed the man to pull him off. He let Christopher go, and we wrestled. Then he poked me in the eye. I half let go of him, and when I saw his hand move toward his belt, I panicked and kicked him away. His cloak tore off, and he fell through the window. I think . . . I think I killed him."

Lord Ashcombe shook his head. "You didn't. The window was above the garden. The assassin fell into the bushes."

My throat throbbed at his words. "He's still alive?"

Lord Ashcombe nodded. "What did you do with the assassin's cloak?"

"Nothing," Tom said. "I just left it there."

Ashcombe ordered one of the King's Men to retrieve it. Then he studied us as we waited. The silence made me nervous. "Is the king all right?" I asked him, just to break it.

"Yes," he said curtly.

Another pause. "Sally was just mentioning the French woman at the party, and—"

"It's not her."

I didn't try for any more conversation. The King's Man returned with the cloak, and a scrap of shirt that had torn away with it. Lord Ashcombe laid them out on the table and stared.

Tom was dejected. He was the only person who'd seen the assassin, yet he hadn't been able to provide any real clues as to who it was. I ventured another few words, as much for Tom's sake as my own curiosity. "Excuse me, my lord. . . . Are you looking for something in particular?"

He regarded me a moment, his gaze inscrutable. Then he said, "Come here."

We went to stand beside him. He pointed to the clothes. "What do you see?"

I wasn't sure what I was supposed to be looking at. Tom wasn't either.

"It's not a trick," the King's Warden said. "Just tell me what you see. Everything, no matter how unimportant you think it is."

Tom certainly wasn't going to speak first, so I did, stomach fluttering, like I was back at Apothecaries' Hall, being grilled for an exam. "The cloak is wool. It's brown. It looks warm. The shirt is linen. It's white. The weave seems of fair quality."

"What does that tell you?"

I felt the sweat beading on my upper lip. "Uh . . ."

"Think. Who would wear this?"

I looked between him and Tom. Ashcombe's shirt was silk. Tom's was linen, like mine, like the scrap he'd torn from the assassin, though our shirts were of much better quality than—

And I understood.

CHAPTER

"A SERVANT," I SAID. "THESE ARE
the clothes of a servant."

Lord Ashcombe nodded and turned the scrap of shirt
over in his fingers. "None of the guests would wear linen of
this quality before the king."

"So we should question the servants?" Tom said.

"We already are. But we won't find him among them. The
assassin's run off, yet everyone's staff is accounted for. Which
means this was merely a disguise. So: What else does it tell you?"

I went back to the cloak. It had no distinguishing marks
I could see, so I decided to follow what Master Benedict
had taught me and investigate it like an unknown plant. I

smelled it but couldn't detect any scent. Except for the slight tang of sweat, I couldn't smell anything on the shirt, either. I wasn't about to taste it.

"Is that it, then?"

The way Lord Ashcombe spoke made me think I was still missing something. I racked my brain, but the only other thing I could think of was, "They're in good condition."

"How good?"

"They look new," Tom said.

"Yes," Lord Ashcombe said. "No staining, no wear. These were bought recently, and worn for the first time tonight."

"How does knowing that help us?" I asked.

"We find the tailor who made them and prompt him to remember whom he sold them to."

The growl in his voice made me glad I wasn't going to watch the prompting. Yet I did wonder: "How do we find the right tailor?"

"By the stitching." He flipped the cloak over and pointed at the seams. "Every tailor has their own pattern, learned from their master. So it's a matter of checking this stitch against . . ." He trailed off.

"My lord?"

He held out his hand. "Knife."

Neither Tom nor I had worn ours to the party, but I had a small one among the tools in my sash. I dug it out for him.

Lord Ashcombe spread the cloak over the table. He ran his fingers over the seam, near the bottom corner, where the stitching looked different from the rest.

"The *other* reason you study an assassin's clothes," he said, "is because there's occasionally something else you can find."

He sliced the seam open and pulled out what was hidden inside. It was a piece of paper, folded into a narrow strip. On one side of the fold, someone had inked a single letter.

Lord Ashcombe stared at it. Then he unfolded the paper to reveal the message inside.

Ro mv hfuurg kzh jfv ovh uroh wv 77 nvfivmg.
Ovh xlfhrmvh wlrevmg nlfiri, zfhhr, zevx ovfih
kzizhrgvh. Xlmgzxgva J klfi oz tfvirhlm. Uzrgvh
ivhhvnyovi jfv ov kvmwziw vhg oz xryov.

Qfhjf'zf nlnvmg.

I glanced over at Tom. He looked back at me, surprised. The assassin had been carrying a message in secret code. *Instructions?* I wondered.

Lord Ashcombe turned to the King's Man guarding the room. "His Majesty's spymaster is in Ipswich. Get him here *now*."

Despite the command, it would be some time before we saw the spymaster. Ipswich was a two-day ride away. The wound on my neck throbbed as I realized we'd have a royal assassin running around Oxford for half a week before the spymaster arrived. And that assassin now had a reason for a serious grudge against *me*.

"My lord?" I said. "My master taught me some things about secret codes. I . . . I might be able to help."

I half expected Lord Ashcombe to scoff at me, but he didn't. He just studied me for a moment. Then he held the message out. "What will you need?"

"Just a quill, some ink, and some paper," I said. "Lots of paper."

A soldier brought me what I'd asked for. On Lord Ashcombe's order, the first thing I did was make a copy of the message to send along with the courier sent to summon the king's spy-master. Then I got to work.

Ro mv hfuurg kzh jfv ovh uroh wv 77 nvfivmg.

Ovh xlfhrmvh wlrevmg nlfiri, zfhhr, zevx ovfih

kzizhrgvh. Xlmgzxgva J klfi oz tfvirhlm. Uzrgvh

ivhhvnyovi jfv ov kvmwziw vhg oz xryov.

Qfhjf'zf nlnvmg.

Tom looked it over. "Do you recognize this code?"

"Not offhand," I said. "But it looks like a simple letter sub-stitution. So I'll try a few of those and see if anything leaps out."

I started with the simplest type: the Caesar shift. This involved taking a standard alphabet and shifting each letter a certain number of spaces. Normally, I'd shift the whole message, in case the encoder was clever and put gibberish at the beginning to confuse a would-be code breaker. But for speed, I started by shifting only the first few words. One space to the right:

Sp nw igvvsh lai kgw pwi

And two:

Tq ox jhwwti mbj lhx qxj

And three:

Ur py kixxuj nck miy ryk

And so on. I continued, with all twenty-five shifts, but none of those gave me anything but gibberish.

On to the second attempt, then. If it wasn't a Caesar shift, maybe I could figure it out by examining the words in the cipher itself and seeing what substitutions might make sense. The most interesting one was near the bottom: *Qfhjf'zf.*

I frowned. I could only think of four contractions that fit that pattern: *could've, would've, where've, and there've.* But in the cipher, the second, fifth, and seventh letters were the same. So none of those contractions would work.

"I think we're in trouble," I said.

"Why?" Tom said.

"Because whoever wrote this code either used spaces and punctuation to confuse us into thinking these are what the words look like, or this is a cipher where the shift in the letters keeps changing."

"You can do that?"

"Absolutely. It's called the Vigenère cipher. And if that's what the assassin used, we're lost. Vigenère's unbreakable without a key."

"How would a key help with a cipher?" Tom said.

"Not a real key. I mean a word you use to translate the message," I said. "Like a password you say to a guard, to get past the castle gates. If you don't know it, they won't let you in."

"Maybe there's a hint as to how to solve it on the paper," Tom suggested. "Like that *A*."

That was an interesting idea. I turned the paper over and studied the symbol.

As I looked it over, I noticed something else. Near the bottom on the back, three more letters had been scratched on the paper with charcoal: *ILN*.

"Does that mean something?" Tom asked. "Could that be the key?"

"It might be," I said. "Though it looks like it's in a different hand than the code itself."

"Maybe it's part of the message, then."

"How do you mean?"

"Well, suppose the assassin started to decode the message on the back. Then maybe he thought he should do it somewhere else. That could be the start of a word, like 'illness.'" He sat up. "Like we've seen before! A poison made to look like an illness!"

"'Illness' has two *l*s," I said. But his idea was definitely worth pursuing. As Master Benedict had once pointed out, most people found deciphering codes incredibly difficult. If the assassin had written "ILN" to remind himself that he was decoding the message correctly, then that might give us a hint as to how to crack it.

I tried it. First, I wrote out the alphabet. Then, underneath it, I placed the first three letters from the cipher to see how they corresponded to *I*, *L*, and *N*.

A B C D E F G H I J K L M N O P Q R S T U V W X Y Z

R   O   M

"There! Look!" Tom pointed. "There's a shift, right there. *M* is one letter over."

"But look at the others," I said. "*O* is three letters back, and *R* is nine . . ."

I stopped.

"What's wrong?" Tom said.

"Nothing's wrong," I said. "Except that you're brilliant."

Tom scratched his head. "I have no idea what's going on."

"But you found it. You *found* it. It *is* a shift. It's *Atbash*."

"It's . . . what?"

"Atbash," I said. "It's one of the earliest ciphers we know of—and really easy to use." I took a blank piece of paper and began to scribble on it. "All you do is swap the first letter of the alphabet with the last letter of the alphabet, then the second letter with the second-to-last letter, and so on. So *A* with *Z*, *B* with *Y*, *C* with *X* . . . like this."

A B C D E F G H I J K L M
Z Y X W V U T S R Q P O N

"See?" I said. "It matches!"

I began to decipher the rest of the message. As before, I started with the first few words.

Il ne suffit pas que les

Tom shook his head. "It doesn't work," he said, deflated.

But my heart was thumping. Because it *did* work. And I suddenly understood why the contractions I'd looked at were wrong.

I kept going, faster and faster. When I finished, I sat for a moment and stared. Then I spoke.

"We need to find Lord Ashcombe," I said. "We need to get him here *now*."

CHAPTER

"IT *WAS* HER," I SAID.

Though the hour was late, Lord Ashcombe showed no signs of fatigue. "Who are you talking about?"

"That woman in the mask. She's behind the plot. Or someone else is, on her staff."

"I told you, that's impossible."

"But—look. I deciphered the message."

Lord Ashcombe seemed surprised as I handed him the solution. He studied it, his one eye widening as he read.

Il ne suffit pas que les fils de _ _ meurent. Les cousines doivent mourir, aussi, avec leurs parasites.

Contactez Q pour la guérison. Faites ressembler que
le pendard est la cible.

Jusqu'au moment.

"It's in *French*," I said. "So unless there were other French guests here—"

"It wasn't her," Lord Ashcombe said.

"How can you be so sure?"

"Because I know who the woman is. And there's absolutely no chance she'd kill the king."

I gave up trying to convince him. "I've translated the message—"

"I know the language," he said as he read it again.

Of course—I'd forgotten. Sixteen years ago, the Puritans of the Commonwealth had overthrown the monarchy and executed Charles's father—then went on the hunt for Charles himself. To keep the young king safe, Lord Ashcombe had snuck him away to France. They'd lived in exile on the Continent for years before Charles returned to the throne in 1660. His Majesty's ties to France remained strong: His mother and younger sister lived there still.

As for me, I knew French because of my master. I'd

learned some at the Cripplegate school, but when I joined Master Benedict, he'd had me study it intensely, along with several other tongues. *I will give you many things to read,* he'd said. *And the original is always better than the translation.*

Tom, on the other hand, didn't know a word of French. So I gave him the translation I'd worked out while Lord Ashcombe studied the original.

> *It is not sufficient that the sons of _ _ die. The cousins must go, too, with their parasites. Contact Q for the cure. Make it look like the good-for-nothing rascal is the target.*

> *Until the time.*

Lord Ashcombe frowned. "Are you sure you deciphered this correctly?"

I showed him the Atbash cipher and how I'd worked it out. "I'm guessing there's a second layer of code in here," I said, "where some of the words have a special meaning. I think 'cure,' for example, actually means 'poison.'"

"Yes, I've seen that before." He pointed to the blank spaces before the word "die." "What are these?"

"I'm not sure," I said. "In the original message, they're not letters—they're numbers."

"Numbers?"

I nodded. "Atbash is normally for letters, but you can encipher numbers with it as well. Just swap *0* with *9*, *1* with *8*, and so on. I left them blank because I wasn't sure if I should apply Atbash to them or not."

"What were the original numbers?"

"77," I said.

"And with Atbash?"

"22."

He stiffened.

Tom and I exchanged a glance. "Does that—"

The King's Warden held up a hand. He stared intently at the page. After a minute, he began to pace. Eventually, he stopped at the window, his face like stone.

Then he stalked over to us. He took the quill and inked *22* in the blank spaces on the paper. "Follow me," he said. "And bring your notes. We're going to see the king."

CHAPTER

FOUR GUARDS STOOD WATCH BEFORE
the door, halberds at the ready. By silent command, they
moved aside for the King's Warden.

The door led into a study. It was warm inside, heated
by a fire blazing in the hearth that filled the room with
a soft orange glow. The king lounged by the flames, legs
crossed, on a velvet-draped settee, staring off into the distance. Two more of the King's Men stood nearby, on either
side of the window.

Lord Ashcombe motioned to them. "Leave us."

Charles glanced over as they shuffled out. He looked me
up and down thoughtfully. "That's twice you've saved my

life," he said softly. Then he spoke to Tom. "And twice that *you've* saved *his*. Keep this up, I may have to knight you."

Tom flushed, proud. I flushed a bit myself.

"I don't suppose there's any unpoisoned food out there," the king said to Lord Ashcombe.

"The chops in sauce were wonderful," Tom said. Then he clapped his hand over his mouth, shocked beyond belief that he'd actually spoken.

"They would be fine," I said to Lord Ashcombe, as much to spare Tom the embarrassment as to confirm them as safe. Tom had eaten an entire sheep's worth, and he was still alive.

The King's Warden shook his head. "I'll not risk it. I'll have food sent up from Oxford."

The king sighed. "Tell me you've at least brought wine."

"Afraid not, sire." Lord Ashcombe handed him the paper. "Christopher deciphered the assassin's code. It explains the entire plot."

"Odd's fish." Charles stared at me. "Are you aiming for duke, instead of knight?" He read the deciphered message, then held it up. "I don't know what any of this means."

Lord Ashcombe turned to me. "What do you know of the French royal family?"

The question surprised me. "Not much, my lord. I

know Louis the Fourteenth is the king—they call him the Sun King. And I know His Majesty"—I motioned to Charles—"and Louis are related."

Lord Ashcombe nodded. "Louis used to have an advisor, a cardinal by the name of Mazarin. Cardinal Mazarin often wrote letters using coded phrases instead of names. 'The Confident,' for example, meant 'Louis'; 'the sea' meant Mazarin himself. Sometimes, he used numbers instead of letters. '16', again referred to Mazarin."

Charles tapped his chair's armrest as he read the page again.

It is not sufficient that the sons of **22** *die. The cousins must go, too, with their parasites. Contact Q for the cure. Make it look like the good-for-nothing rascal is the target.*

Until the time.

"There's a number here," he said, frowning. "22."

"Yes, sire. It appears whoever wrote these instructions used at least some of the same code Mazarin did."

"Then you know who 22 is?"

Lord Ashcombe nodded. "It's Louis's mother, Anne."

"And who's the good-for-nothing rascal?"

"I believe that's you."

Charles looked amused. "Not entirely inaccurate, I suppose. Nonetheless, I still don't understand. Why does it say it should *look* like the rascal is the target?"

"Because I don't believe you *were* the target," Lord Ashcombe said. "I'm almost certain the assassin was trying to kill your sister."

The king went pale. "What did you say?" He stood. His hand clenched around the paper, voice rising. *"What did you say?"*

The door to the study opened. One of the guards stepped in, alarmed by the shouting. "Your Majesty? Is everything—?"

"Out!"

The soldier slammed the door shut. Tom looked like he wished he were on the other side of it. So did I.

The king stalked across the rug, waving the message in Lord Ashcombe's face. "My *sister*? *Minette*? What madness are you speaking?"

Lord Ashcombe took his master's anger with calm. "If you would sit, sire, I'll explain."

Charles lowered himself to the settee, crumpling and uncrumpling the paper in his fingers.

"The message is clear," Lord Ashcombe said. "'It is not enough that the sons of 22 die.' '22' is Anne, so her sons are Louis the Fourteenth, and his brother, Philippe, duc d'Orléans—the Duke of Orléans."

"What does that have to do with Minette?"

"The next line explains that. 'The cousins must go, too, with their parasites.'"

Slowly it dawned on Charles what that meant. He looked up in horror. And, as little as I knew about royal families, I still knew why.

The English, French, and Spanish had all intermarried very closely. Louis XIV had married Maria Theresa of Spain, the daughter of Elizabeth of France—Louis's aunt. And Philippe had married Charles's sister, Henrietta—whom Charles called Minette—and their mother was Henrietta Maria of France, Philippe's aunt.

Louis and Philippe had both married cousins, one of whom was Charles's sister. I thought about the message. "If the 'cousins' are the wives," I said, "then the 'parasites' must be . . ."

"Their children," Lord Ashcombe said. "Kill the king; kill his brother; kill their wives; kill their children. Someone is trying to eliminate the entire royal line of France."

The thought was shocking. But I still didn't understand what that had to do with tonight's party. Lord Ashcombe explained.

"I told you," he said to me, "that the woman in the mask couldn't possibly be involved in a plot to kill the king. That's because she is Henrietta, duchesse d'Orléans—Minette. The king's sister."

Charles frowned. "No. No, you can't be right, Richard. No one knows she's here. Her trip to England is a secret."

"As I've told you many times, sire, anything known by more than two people is not a secret. The message is clear: Tonight's poisoning was only meant to *look* like it targeted you. It was aimed at the duchess."

Charles looked over at us. "Then I owe you even more than I thought," he said, "for Minette's life is dearer to me than my own. What is being done to find this assassin?"

"We're investigating," Ashcombe said. "The message mentions 'Q.' We've run across him before. It's the identity of an unknown poisoner in London."

· "Unknown? How helpful."

"We have other leads. For the moment, we should talk about your sister's return to France."

"Return?" the king said. "She can't return now. She'll remain here, with me."

"Impossible, sire. Her husband has recalled her to Paris."

"I don't give a fig about that weasel."

"Nor do I. But if Minette were to refuse Philippe's command, the scandal would ruin our relations with the French. With the war with the Dutch, we *need* Louis on our side."

"Then how do you propose to protect her?"

"You might encourage her to increase her guard."

The king regarded him sternly. "I don't want her frightened. I'll not tell her someone's trying to murder her."

"You don't need to, sire," Lord Ashcombe said. "Just say you're worried about tonight—if they could attack you, they could attack the people you love just as easily. In the meantime, I'll engage more spies, and place them in her household."

"*More* spies?" Charles scoffed. "The spies we have *now* are useless. If it wasn't for these boys—"

The king stopped. He turned to stare at Tom and me. "That's it. Yes, that's *it*."

"Sire?" Lord Ashcombe said.

"We *will* send someone as part of her household," Charles said. "We'll send *them*."

CHAPTER
10

TOM AND I GAPED AT HIM, JAWS hanging open.

"*Us?*" I said.

Even Lord Ashcombe seemed startled by the idea. "That's . . . an unusual suggestion, sire."

"Is it?" the king said. "Think. This one"—he pointed at me—"has now stopped not one, but two plots against my family—plus that business with the plague. He treats poisons, finds criminals—he even deciphers codes. Who better to go than him? And we'd *all* be dead without his giant friend, rolling pin or otherwise."

To my horror, I saw Lord Ashcombe looking at us

speculatively. Surely he wasn't taking this seriously! "They're a little young," he said finally.

"How old was I at the Battle of Edgehill?" Charles said. "And how old was I when my father made me commander of the West Country?"

"Twelve," the King's Warden said thoughtfully. "And fourteen."

"And did I not do my duty?"

Lord Ashcombe's growl softened. "You were very brave."

This was absurd. Lord Ashcombe was supposed to be sensible. Now he was *nodding*.

"My lord—Your Majesty—I think there's been some kind of mistake," I said. "I'm an apothecary's apprentice. Tom's a baker's son. We're not spies. We wouldn't even know where to begin."

"Was His Majesty wrong?" Lord Ashcombe said. "Have you not stopped two—no, *three* plots so far?"

"I . . . we . . . yes, but that was all—"

"Did you not decipher that code?"

"Well . . . yes, but that's just because my master taught me how—"

"And did you not spot the poison, and treat it?"

"Again, my master—"

"Appears to have prepared you quite *well* for being a spy."

I had a disconcerting image of Master Benedict laughing uproariously. Tom stared at me in horror. *Do something,* his eyes said.

Except I didn't know what else to say. A spy? For the Crown? In *France*? It was madness. But how do you tell your king he's lost his mind?

Charles stood. "Come here, boys."

We approached him warily. Tom stood next to me, his arm pressed against mine.

"This has been a hard year for England," Charles said. "And not only with the coming of the plague. Plots that have simmered for years all seem to be boiling over. I've learned there are very few people a king may trust. And most of them are here, in this room."

He clasped my shoulder. "I don't know why you've been so successful. Your master's training? Your master's blessing? Or maybe God Himself smiles upon you. Whatever the answer, I need you. In all the world, there's no one I love more than Minette. I'd be heartbroken if anything happened to her."

Now he took Tom's shoulder, too. "Christopher has served me well. And, Thomas, your strength has served both of us along the way. All your king is asking is that you serve him, one more time, as true sons of England."

Oh, that was *cheating*. Tom swelled with pride. "I will, sire," he boomed.

He'd regret that soon. So would I. But what else could I say? "All right."

The king smiled. Lord Ashcombe, however, noted a problem. "This is all fine, sire, but a point remains. If investigating the people around Minette is the mission, then, in one important respect, these boys are entirely unqualified."

Now he says so. "How?" Charles said.

"Because they're *boys*," Lord Ashcombe said. "If we're serious about shadowing Minette, we'll need someone close to the duchess. Someone who can move freely within her circle, even her chambers, when necessary. We need to find a girl. Someone we can trust. And it'll have to be someone who knows French."

Tom glanced over at me in surprise. I already knew what he was thinking. Might as well spread the misery.

"My lord?" I said. "I believe I know someone who fits that description."

• • •

Sally's eyes went wide when she saw who was in the room. The King's Man who'd escorted her shut the door behind her. She looked at me, questioning, and slightly scared.

Lord Ashcombe spoke first. "Christopher says you were essential in stopping that scheme during the plague. That they'd both have died without you."

"I . . . didn't do much, my lord," she said.

"That's not how he tells it. How old are you?"

"I just turned thirteen."

"Christopher says your parents died when you were eight. That your father was French."

"Yes, my lord."

"Bien: a-t-il t'apprit à parler sa langue?" Well then, did he teach you to speak it?

She seemed surprised at the switch. *"Oui, monsieur."* He did, my lord.

"Mais il est mort depuis longtemps. Tu t'en souviens encore?" But he died a long time ago. Do you still remember it?

Sally drew herself up. *"Monsieur . . . je ne pourrais pas plus oublier la langue de mon père que vous pourriez oublier celle de vôtre."* My lord, I could no more forget the language of my father than you could forget the language of yours.

The king clapped the arm of his chair. "Well said, girl."

Sally flushed under his praise, though she still seemed confused. She listened as Lord Ashcombe told her what we'd learned, and of our mission to investigate the assassin. "They'll be traveling to Paris with the duchess, but they'll be unable to get close enough to her circle. I need a girl—"

"I'll do it," she said.

Lord Ashcombe blinked. "You understand it's dangerous—"

"I'll do it."

The king laughed. "You make me wish I was thirteen again."

Sally blushed.

"Then it's settled," Lord Ashcombe said. "The duchess leaves for Paris at first light. All of you, get some sleep. You'll receive your instructions in the morning. Dismissed."

He ordered the King's Men to take us to our quarters. Sally looked puzzled by what had just happened. As for Tom, his proud glow was fading, and I knew he'd regret what he'd agreed to soon.

As it turned out, soon was very, *very* soon. "Wait," he gasped as the soldier led him away. "What did I just do?"

NOVEMBER 3–16, 1665

Lauds

CHAPTER
11

IT WAS THE SECOND SWORD TO the crotch that made Tom cry.

I saw it coming. I was sitting outside the inn, by the fire in the stones, keeping one eye on my master's notes and one on Tom's training session. As new companions to Minette—or, as the rest of the world knew her, Henriette d'Angleterre, duchesse d'Orléans—Lord Ashcombe had assigned us counterfeit identities, so we'd be welcome in her circle.

"You'll be posing as a nobleman," Lord Ashcombe had told me as Minette's servants carted her luggage to the carriages that would take us to Dover. "It's clear this mission will be dangerous, so I want you to carry a sword."

That made my eyes go wide. "I'm an apprentice. I'm not allowed to carry a sword."

"I don't care about Apothecaries' Guild rules. From this point on, you are what I say you are. And I say you wear a sword. Now, in Paris, no one's allowed to carry a weapon unless they're a soldier or a noble—and you're clearly no soldier. So, congratulations: You are now the Baron of Chillingham."

I blinked. "But . . . aren't *you* the Baron of Chillingham?"

"Not anymore. My father died this summer, so now I'm the marquess. The title of baron passed to my grandson. He's just a couple years younger than you, and also named Christopher. So it'll make an excellent disguise. You are Christopher Ashcombe, grandson of the King's Warden."

I didn't even know what to think of that. "What if someone recognizes me as a fake?"

"It's France. Most of them won't even have heard of Chillingham. The ones who have will know me, not my grandson. Your identity is safe. You'll have to start *acting* like a noble, however."

"How do I do that?"

"Just pretend the world owes you a living." He nodded toward Tom, who was helping load the carriages. "He's going as your personal guard, so he's wearing your livery, but the main point of it is that he'll *also* be allowed to wear a sword. I'm sending an old master of mine with you to train him along the way, so he won't look a complete fool with the blade."

All of this set my head spinning. As for Tom, despite his proud declaration placing him in the king's service, he did *not* want to be going on this trip. He came to me that very night, wringing his hands as I took Bridget from her cage to feed her. "What did I do? What did I do?"

"We'll be fine," I assured him, though my stomach was fluttering like Bridget's wings.

"I can't go to France," he said. "I don't even speak the language. How will I get by?"

"You'll be with me. I won't leave you."

"But I don't want to go to Paris. It's full of foreigners."

"Actually, in Paris, we'll be the foreigners."

"Englishmen can't be foreigners, Christopher."

"But that's what—never mind." I could only think of one thing that might take his mind off it. "At least you'll get to learn how to use a sword."

He brightened. "That's true."

As it turned out, however, that was not to be quite as fun as he thought.

The sword master's name was Sir William Leech. He had closely cropped snowy hair and penetrating eyes, and, though long retired, he still walked with a military bearing. When they first met, Tom stood nervously at attention as the old man looked him up and down. Finally, Sir William spoke.

"Every child," he said, "thinks a sword is a toy. It is not. It is a weapon of distinction, and, for a soldier, it must become his very arm. I will teach you to respect it. I will not teach you to master it—that takes a lifetime, not a fortnight—but I will show you one or two things so that, hopefully, you will not embarrass me when you draw your blade."

Tom glanced over at me, looking even more nervous than before.

"Here is how our lessons will go," Sir William said. "I will work with you as we travel. I will teach you something new every day. Then, once the day is finished, I will test you on what you have learned. I will do this by taking *my* sword and beating you senseless."

Tom's eyes widened.

"You will cry," Sir William said. "You will plead. You will beg me to stop. I will not. If you wish *not* to be beaten senseless, you will have to learn to defend yourself. Understood? Good. Then we begin."

And so they did. Lord Ashcombe had commissioned an uncovered wagon to follow the carriages so Tom could practice even while we were moving. The lessons themselves looked excellent. Tom, as was only natural, was rather clumsy at first; he'd never wielded anything but a rolling pin. As a master, however, Sir William was brilliant: clear and, despite his rigid manner, surprisingly patient. He never once yelled or cursed as Tom struggled to pick up the various strikes, guards, and parries the sword master sought to teach him.

It was grueling. Tom huffed and puffed through hours of training every day, his arm weary, his muscles aching for release. Yet, as the time passed, he began to follow Sir William's instructions with some skill, and I couldn't help but feel a pang of envy that I wasn't going to get to learn swordplay too.

That first evening, as the sun went down, our carriages stopped at the inn where we'd spend the night. After supper,

Tom's training resumed. Then came the final hour of the day.

"All right, Bailey," Sir William said. "Now we fight for true."

Tom motioned nervously to their swords. "With these?"

"What else would we use? A bunch of daisies?"

"But . . . won't I get cut?"

"A scratch or two, perhaps. They're only practice swords, quite dull. And I'll hit you with the flat of my blade."

"But what if I hit you?"

Sir William threw his head back and laughed with delight. "You're funny, Bailey. I like you."

Then it began. Sir William was true to his word: Using nothing but the flat of the blade, he beat Tom senseless. I began by watching with interest; within minutes, I could only watch by peeking through my fingers. Sally, curious to see a real fight, had wandered over from the circle of ladies surrounding Minette. It wasn't long before she fled back to it.

I didn't blame her. Poor Tom. He got hit *everywhere*. I actually saw what the old sword master was doing: The blows he struck, and the openings he left, were carefully chosen to correspond to the parries and strikes he'd taught earlier that day. But Tom, unused to all this swordplay, couldn't always get there quick enough. After the second smack between the legs, he collapsed.

"AAAAAAUUUUGGGGGHHHHGGGGHHHH," he said.

Sir William put up his sword. "I agree. That's enough for tonight. Don't forget to wipe down your blade before you retire." He nodded to me as he left. "Ashcombe."

Tom lay on the grass, curled into a ball, tears running down his cheeks. I pulled the vial of willow bark from my sash and set water to boil on the fire.

Tom wasn't the only one who felt the flat of a blade that trip. I'd been excited when Lord Ashcombe had handed me the sword I'd take with me to Paris. I'd buckled it onto my waist and strutted around with it proudly all day long. What I hadn't realized was how much of a pain wearing a sword would be.

It got in the way *all the time*. Every turn I made, it bumped into something. Sitting was a chore; I had to try to slide the sword down the side of my leg. And it tugged constantly at my waist. After a few days, Tom said he was used to it, but I took to unbelting it in the evenings, while I was reading.

One night, after sitting by the fire outside, I forgot to take it with me when I returned to the inn to sleep. When I woke the next morning, I went to put it on, and a burst of panic seized my chest. I bolted past a sore and moaning Tom and ran out to the charred remains of the fire.

It wasn't there. I'd left the sword next to the log, but it wasn't there. I searched beside the log, beneath it, in the grass. Nothing. All I found were faint tracks in the frost.

My guts sank. Someone had stolen it. I'd lost the weapon Lord Ashcombe had given me. What was I going to do?

"Looking for something?"

I turned to see Sir William leaning against a tree. He had a rag out, oiling a sword—*my* sword.

I let out a breath. "Thank goodness," I said. "I thought I'd lost—"

"Do you know what happens when a sword gets wet, my lord?" Sir William said.

"It . . . uh . . . it rusts?"

"It does. And what good is a rusty sword?"

I swallowed. "None?"

"Well done, Ashcombe. Well done." He gave the blade one last polish, then held it up. "A sword is the tool with which a man may defend himself, his king, and the people he loves. It should never be left unattended. And it should certainly *never* be left on the grass, where the dew will collect and summon forth that plague of soldiers: rust."

He pushed himself from the tree. "I have not yet had the honor to train you, and, to my regret, we will have no time for lessons on this journey. But—with my lord's permission, of course—I will pause a moment in my day to instruct you nonetheless."

His instruction involved bending me over the log and whapping me with the sword on the backside until tears welled in my eyes. When he was done, Sir William handed the weapon back. "Good blade," he said approvingly.

I waddled my way back upstairs and lowered my bottom into a basin of water to cool it. Fortunately, it was early, so only Tom saw my humiliation, though Sally did ask me later why I wouldn't sit down. I kept the lesson to myself, but I did learn it: I never forgot a sword in the grass again.

CHAPTER

12

THOUGH IT MIGHT HAVE SEEMED otherwise, blades and their associated beatings were not the sum total of our journey. Lord Ashcombe had warned us that no one, not even Minette, must know who any of us really were.

This wasn't only to maintain secrecy for our mission. The nobles of Paris would never allow a commoner to live with them, regardless of circumstances. Impersonating a noble, in fact, was a crime, the punishment for which was death. And, as the King's Warden pointed out, it was good practice to keep as many secrets as possible: With a poisoner on the loose, one would never know whom to trust.

To that end, Tom, Sally, and I didn't get to spend nearly as much time together as I would have liked. Besides the wagons that carried our supplies, Minette had three carriages just for herself and the ladies-in-waiting accompanying her, which now included Sally: like me, her true identity a secret, posing as a noblewoman, a distant cousin of Lord Ashcombe's from the old country. Lord Ashcombe had arranged a separate carriage for the newly minted Baron of Chillingham so I could study along the way, plus the open wagon for Tom to train with Sir William while we moved. His lessons meant that even when I watched him, we were apart most of the time.

At least I still had Bridget for company. I let her out of her cage, and she swooped joyously between the bumpy carriages, free to stretch her wings for the first time in months. Whenever we passed a pond, she splashed about in it while we moved on, bathing her feathers, then chased after us to flutter through my window, cooing contentedly. I asked Sally to sit with me, too, but she refused.

"I can't. Besides, it's better if I stay with the girls. They gossip constantly. It might be useful for figuring out who's trying to kill Minette."

I was disappointed, but her reason made sense. "Have you learned anything?"

"Too much," she said. "Did you know there are nearly a thousand people living in the Palais-Royal?" The Palais-Royal was Minette's home in Paris, where she lived with her husband, the king's brother, Philippe. "They're not just servants, either; they always have visitors and house-guests, too."

Houseguests at the Palais were what we were going to be. That would allow us to investigate Minette's circle and mix with those closest to her. Though to investigate a thousand people . . . my guts, already on edge, fluttered again. I called to my master. *What am I supposed to do?*

He didn't have an answer. And now I *really* didn't want to be alone. "Why not spend a couple hours in my carriage?" I said to Sally. "We can go over what the ladies are talking about, work out if you've found any suspects."

"I told you, I can't."

"Just an hour, then. You won't miss *that* much."

"It's not appropriate."

"What does that mean?"

"You keep forgetting: You're a baron now. And I'm the Lady Grace. I can't spend time alone with a boy in his cur-tained carriage. Unless you want all of Paris to think I'm your mistress."

I was shocked. I hadn't even considered that. I realized I needed to spend a lot more time thinking of what Christopher Ashcombe would do, instead of Christopher Rowe. Having those girls titter about me keeping Sally as my mistress? "Absolutely *not*," I said.

Sally's jaw hardened. She pressed her lips together, then spun on her heel and stomped away.

I looked over at Tom, who was taking a break from his training. "What did *I* do?" I said.

Tom shrugged, just as puzzled. Sir William raised an eyebrow. "And I heard you were good at secret codes."

With Tom training every day, and Sally turned somewhat frosty, I had plenty of time to pursue my own studies. The king's hope that I'd ferret out the assassin meant I needed to learn as much as I could about poisons. So, when Minette's carriage train skirted the still-plague-touched London, I rode with one of the King's Men into the city. He escorted me to Blackthorn, where I packed everything that might prove useful on the journey.

Master Benedict had several notes and books on poisons, venoms, their administration, and their remedies. I collected those and bundled them in a strap with his journals from 1652. He'd spent several months in Paris that year while studying the plague, staying with an old friend of his: Marin Chastellain, the comte de Gravigny. His journals mostly recorded his attempts at creating a plague cure, but he'd jotted a few notes about the city itself. While Lord Ashcombe had provided me with a map of Paris, I figured any thoughts of my master's might be of help.

While home, I also picked up some seed for Bridget, plus something else most curious. After that business with the plague cure in September, I'd made more of an effort to learn what my master knew about poisons. One night, while going through his things, I'd found a box tucked away deep under his papers.

It was a sturdy but simple cherrywood case, unadorned except for a pair of heavy locks. When I'd first found it, I'd searched everywhere for the keys. I eventually discovered where Master Benedict had hidden them: One was in his room, and one was in the workshop. When I finally opened the box, I understood why he'd gone to all that trouble to keep them separate.

Poisons.

The box was *full* of poisons in tiny jars, ampoules, and

vials. Each one was labeled clearly: arsenic, nightshade, hemlock, plus dozens more, and a sheaf of notes tucked into a pouch in the lid. From what he'd written, I could see he'd kept the poisons to study them, to better identify their properties and manufacture antidotes against them.

It was alarming—and, to my slight worry, strangely compelling—to hold a box full of death. When I'd first found it, my duties in making Venice treacle for the city's plague doctors had kept me too busy to study my master's notes in detail. Fortunately, the journey to Paris gave me plenty of time to go through them, since all there was for me to do was read. And, though I didn't like being alone so much, I enjoyed having that time with my master's words. I would read what he'd written on this poison or that, then close my eyes, and imagine his voice, and sometimes, for a few sweet moments, I could feel him sitting next to me once again.

I kept to his notes in the carriage, and left the study of the box and vials themselves to evenings in my rooms at the inns where we stayed: Bumpy wheels and poison ampoules didn't mix.

"Those things give me a chill," Tom said one night, with a shudder.

They did to me, too, but I also found them fascinating. Especially because some of them were so exotic. "Look at this one." I pulled out a jar sealed with wax. Inside was a dark, sticky paste. "This comes all the way from the southern Americas. It's called urare."

"What happens if you drink it?"

"Nothing, actually. It only works if you put it on a weapon. When it gets into your victim's blood, it paralyzes them. They can't move a muscle. But apparently they still feel everything while they die."

Tom was horrified. "Who would invent such a thing?"

"It wasn't meant for people, originally. The Macusi Indians in Guyana dip their arrows in it for hunting."

"So why did Master Benedict want it?"

"To experiment. Just a little of it relaxes the muscles, makes you weak. He thought small doses might help those afflicted with the falling sickness. And look at this."

I put the jar back and picked up a new one. Curled inside were three thin, graying strips. "This is from Japan. It's a fish."

"That's a fish?"

"Well, part of one. It's called fugu. Apparently, it can blow itself up like a bladder and stick out spikes."

"Ridiculous."

"That's what Master Benedict says in his notes," I insisted. "Apparently this is incredibly poisonous, but the Japanese eat it anyway."

"See, now I know you're making this up," he said, and after that, I couldn't convince him I wasn't just playing a trick on him.

I spent most of the trip, then, studying poisons, venoms, and the deceptive methods of murder, trying to commit as many details to memory as I could. Remembering the smell of garlic on John Glover's breath, I worked out the poison the assassin had used was most likely arsenic. It could come in many forms, the deadliest of which was a simple white powder. It was colorless and odorless, which meant unless the assassin was clumsy, it was nearly impossible to detect.

Master Benedict had a vial of it, and I studied it intently. Though I didn't focus solely on it. One time, when I closed my eyes to hear the echo of my master's voice, he spoke instead with a warning. *Be prepared for anything, Christopher. A poisoner is an insidious soul—and one never, ever to be underestimated. Remember, the assassins have already tried to disguise their true target by pretending to attack the king.*

What he said reminded me of Lord Ashcombe's own

warning, before we left. He'd waited until Charles was out of earshot to say it.

"This attack is troubling," he'd said. "Not just because it was poison. Striking against the wives of the French crown? It doesn't make sense."

"Why not?" I'd said. "If the assassins are trying to eliminate the royal family, wouldn't they need to get rid of the queens, too?"

"No. That's my point. France is not like England, where an Elizabeth could rule. Their country is under Salic law: Women are forbidden from inheriting the throne. Killing the children—the boys, anyway—that has purpose. But to murder the wives? That's a sign of wicked spite." He shook his head. "Stay wary, Christopher. Whoever our enemies are, they're cruel."

His warning put a chill inside me, made me study even harder. I regretted I didn't have much time to enjoy the scenery as we moved. It was beautiful. We traveled over rolling hills, through trees and fields, narrow woods and open spaces. We passed through many villages, saw their stone houses and thatched roofs, smoke rising from their chimneys. I watched the villagers we passed, as they milked their cows and tended their sheep, and I wondered what life would have been like if I'd grown up there. Simple, I thought, and maybe a little boring—as lovely as it was, part of me already missed the bustle of the city—but I also felt a kind of serenity here, and I finally understood why the farmers I'd spoken to at market insisted they didn't know how we could live in such dirty, smelly places. And so I daydreamed, imagining a different life.

One thing I decided: Following royalty was definitely the way to travel. Though it slowed the journey some-what—the trip to Paris would last a fortnight—we always took the time to find an inn of decent quality to rest our heads. Then, in the evening, there would be entertainment: The ladies would sing or play games, especially cards. I also discovered that at some point after Sally left London, Lady Pembroke had found her a lute. I remembered she'd told me she'd learned to play at Cripplegate, and that music was her favorite thing, but I hadn't known how skilled she was. Her fingers danced over the strings, bringing the tunes to life as she sang. Minette was beyond delighted—she was mad about music—and, though I sat apart from the ladies, I found myself looking forward to hearing Sally play, too.

"You never told me you were so good," I said to her one night.

"Hmph," she said, and drifted away. But she stopped being so cool to me after that.

It took five days to get from Oxford to Dover. A boat ferried us across the channel, and here I *did* put aside my master's notes, standing with Tom on the prow, smelling the salt of the ocean, braving the ice-cold mist of the waves on my face. Seven hours later, we disembarked in Calais, and for the first time ever, I was standing on foreign soil.

The French countryside looked much the same as the English. From the time we landed, Tom remained wary, like a soldier in enemy territory. I did my best to reassure him, because his caution wasn't solely a mistrust of foreigners: Now he genuinely was an outsider. Except for Sir William, who couldn't have cared less about the French, Tom was the only one of us who didn't speak the language.

To my surprise, I discovered the opposite was true of Minette: Her English was terrible. This struck me as very odd for the sister of our king before I remembered that she'd lived in France exclusively since she was three. I could speak to her in French, of course, but I did my best to avoid interacting with her as much as I could.

It wasn't because I didn't like her. If anything, it was the opposite. Twenty-one years old, she radiated warmth, a sort of pure, distilled charm. She was incredibly thin, almost fragile, and though she rarely ate, she bustled with a kind of nervous energy, like a hummingbird, flitting here and there, hovering for only a moment.

To my confusion, I found myself flushing when she turned her attention to me. "Your grandfather has been our family's greatest friend," she said. "I'm so glad you're coming to stay in our home. I hope you enjoy your time in France."

"You're very kind to have me," I said, my face warm.

"Anything you need. And I hope you'll dine with us as well"—she gazed up at the sky with a sunlit smile—"and come with your darling little bird."

"Of course, Madame," I said, bowing my head to cover my fluster. Now I was torn. The more I thought about it, the more I found I didn't mind the idea of spending time with her. But that was, I knew, a *bad* idea. Sally had spent the last couple of months in the halls of nobility, so she was better able to imitate the behavior of an aristocrat. I hadn't, and it left me constantly afraid of tripping up and revealing myself as an impostor. Lord Ashcombe assured me that I could play off any errors as a difference between the English and French, but if I was discovered, it would be my neck on the block—literally.

So, as much as I would have liked to spend my days in Minette's company, I left that job to Sally. Instead, I concentrated harder on my books, even more certain I had to prevent Minette from being hurt. To that end, I read the deciphered code that gave the assassin his instructions until I could recite it backward. Lord Ashcombe had worked out everything, except for that one last line.

Until the time.

Until what time? No one seemed to know what that meant. But the more I reread it, the more it scared me. The tone of it felt ritualistic, like the words of a fanatic. And I'd dealt with fanatics before. The first one had scarred my chest and murdered my master. The second had broken my arm—broken us all—and killed a good, decent man in the process.

I'd have been happy to never encounter such things again. But here the message remained, mocking me.

Until the time.

Soon, I thought. And I shuddered.

TUESDAY, NOVEMBER 17, 1665

Prime

CHAPTER

WE SMELLED THE CITY BEFORE WE
saw it.

Tom scrunched up his nose. It was like someone had
stirred a rotten egg in a chamber pot. "What *is* that?"

"Your new home." Sir William, riding next to our carriage window, nodded forward. "Welcome to Paris."

We leaned out and watched as we drew closer to the
city walls. They loomed above us, thirty feet high, seven
feet thick, with a moat in front that wrapped around the
town. Unlike London, whose neighborhoods had grown
sprawling beyond its defenses, outside these walls was little
but open farmland, with the occasional cottage dotting the

landscape. Bridget swooped down to the moat to splash around, irritating some ducks who were trying to sleep. I was surprised to see the birds there so late in the autumn, until I remembered I was now a couple hundred miles farther south than I'd ever been.

We entered through the Porte Saint-Denis, one of the two stony medieval gates on the north side of the city. Traffic thickened as we approached until we got inside, and our carriage train crawled to a halt in the raucous noise of the streets. The roads were jammed: carts laden with bales of wheat and baskets of vegetables; farmers driving livestock toward the markets; workmen on their way to their jobs, tools hanging from their belts; soldiers on horseback, booting angry travelers out of their way; tonsured monks in sackcloth robes on pilgrimage; and I could have gone on forever with the sights. And carriages, carriages were everywhere; there might have been as many of them as people.

"Look at that," Tom said, astonished.

A man stood on a street corner, waiting under one of the hanging shop signs that jutted into the road. There weren't any words on it, just a symbol: a pig and a bloody knife. The man had pulled his hat down to his forehead and brought his cloak high to cover most of his face. He stared over the cloth at the passing crowd with narrowed eyes.

"Is that a *criminal*?" Tom said.

Sir William laughed. "In a manner of speaking. It's a nobleman."

"Why is he dressed like that?"

"That's the fashion for nobles on the streets. When they go out, the commoners gawk at them, so they hide their faces. The men cover theirs with their cloaks, and the women . . ." He scanned the crowd, then pointed to a sedan chair: a large, curtain-shrouded throne carted by four servants hoisting it on sturdy poles.

A lady peeked out between the curtains. Her face was covered by a mask: soft, shapeless black velvet. "They claim it's for anonymity," Sir William said. "But you'll notice the woman is hanging out of her chair. Look, everyone's staring, trying to figure out who she is."

Our lead horseman finally beat enough of a path to get us moving again, though barely. Tom and I covered our noses. London may never have smelled pretty, but Paris was something else. We were practically swimming in stink. A quick glance at the ground showed why: a gutter ran in the center of our paved street, with all kinds of slop running inside it. Off the main roads, smaller, unpaved streets were covered with a thick black muck that stuck to everyone's shoes.

And yet the stench *still* got worse. Tom was practically gagging. "It's like something died," he said.

"Something did," Sir William said. He pointed to a walled compound on our right, the spires of a church visible behind the stone. "That's the Cimetière des Innocents— Holy Innocents' Cemetery. It's kept the bones of Parisians for five hundred years."

Tom was appalled. "Who builds a city around a *cemetery*?"

"Frenchmen, apparently. They say the place is haunted."

We turned right as we passed the Cimetière, leaving Rue Saint-Denis and continuing along Rue Saint-Honoré. Since we were strangers to the city, Lord Ashcombe had given us a map of Paris to guide our way. I studied it, trying to orient myself.

Sir William helped. "The River Seine is to the south. We're now going west. The Louvre, where Louis the Fourteenth lives, is to your left. And now . . . you are here."

Our carriages stopped in front of an enormous palace on the right. The main building, two stories high, faced Rue Saint-Honoré, with pillars flanking a grand arch over the entrance.

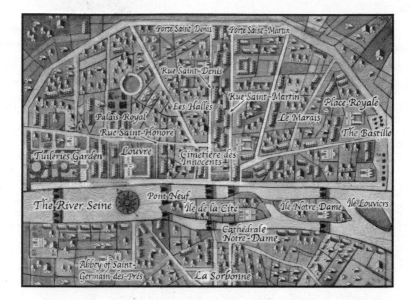

"The Palais-Royal," Sir William said. "This is where I leave you."

We'd known that Sir William was only going to accompany us while we were traveling. Yet Tom was still disappointed. Though he was covered in yellowing bruises, as he'd improved, he'd really started to enjoy learning the sword. "Thank you for training me, Master."

"You're welcome, Bailey. But I'm not done yet. We have time for one final lesson."

He nudged his horse closer to the carriage and spoke quietly. "You're strong, boy, and you've worked very hard, and that's helped you start down a new path. Yet the important word to remember here is 'start.' What I've taught you will save you in a pinch, but don't be fooled: If you square yourself against a master swordsman, he'll carve you to pieces."

Sir William looked up at the Palais. "The marquess never told me what you'll face here. I suspect it won't be good. Keep your sense about you. I've seen too many boys get a sword in their hands and think they're now God's own crusaders. If you stick with your training, perhaps one day that might be true. But that glorious day is not *this* one. So be smart. Avoiding fights is always better than seeking them."

And with that, he wheeled his horse and rode away.

The Palais's servants unloaded our belongings and carried them to our rooms. We followed them, chilled by Sir William's warning. He'd reminded me that the lives, not only of Minette and the royal family, but of my friends, as well, were now my responsibility. It was, after all, *my* actions that had got them into this. And somewhere out there—or perhaps somewhere in *here*, I thought with a shudder—was an assassin, waiting for his opportunity.

Still, arriving at the Palais was at least something of a relief. After two weeks on the road, it was good to finally come to rest. And a palace—an *actual* palace—was now, at least temporarily, my home.

The beauty, the majesty, the sheer wealth on display was astounding. Friezes and tapestries lined the walls, with paintings by Europe's grand masters between them: van Dycks, Caravaggios, and Titians hung everywhere. The ceilings were sculpted and painted with colorful designs. Even the floors were stunning: parquet wood worked with copper and pewter, gleaming with polish. Besides all this opulence, there was a theater on the east side—the home base of the famous French playwright Molière and his *compagnie*—and behind the palace, an immense, beautiful walled garden, surrounded by narrow homes on quiet streets.

And yet, as we moved along, we saw behind the pretty face. The Palais was, in places, falling apart. As Sally drifted away with the ladies, the *maître d'hôtel* escorting us explained that since the king had moved into the Louvre, the Palais had fallen into disrepair. Now, by the duke's command, it was under constant renovation. Workmen stomped along the parquet floors, muddying the polish with that greasy black tar that covered the city streets. On the west side, a section of roof had caved in, and many rooms showed the corrosion of weather, with water damage running down the walls and seeping into the wood below.

It was into such a small, water-stained room on the second floor that Tom and I were shown. As master and servant, we'd live together. I was pleased to see we had our own fireplace—the Palais was cold—plus there were various chests and drawers in which I could keep my things. Though when it came time to retire, we might have a problem. There was only a single, narrow bed with a straw mattress for me, and for Tom, a nice hard floor.

"That's it?" he said, dejected, after the steward had left.

"We'll find something," I said. "Or we can just swap nights on the bed."

"No, we can't. What if someone came in and saw the Baron of Chillingam on the floor?"

I'd forgotten about that *again*. I really needed to keep my new status at the front of my mind. "Well, then, I'll buy a bed. The Baron of Chillingham is the sort of fellow who buys what he wants."

I certainly had the money to do it. Lord Ashcombe had given me an entire purse of French coins for the mission. Inside were several gold *louis*, worth about a pound; dozens of silver *écus*, roughly two-and-a-half shillings each; plus many more silver *sous*, half a penny in value.

"Lord Ashcombe said only spend that when necessary," Tom said.

"Not having a grumpy servant *is* necessary."

His eyes narrowed as I suppressed a grin. "That's going to get old pretty fast," he said.

The chamber smelled heavily of mildew, so I opened the window to air it out a bit—though, given the smell in the streets, I wasn't sure if that made it better or worse. A pair of servants brought in our trunks. A chambermaid joined them, carrying Bridget's cage, then started a fire. I took Bridget out and stroked her feathers. She looked around curiously and cooed.

"Can you bring me some water for my pigeon?" I asked the chambermaid. I realized, too late, that Baron Ashcombe would have made it a command, not a request. At least I'd stopped myself before I said please.

"Right away, monsieur." When she returned, Tom and I stared at the bowl.

"Is that *gold*?" I said.

The girl hesitated, not sure if she'd given offense. "Would the bird prefer silver, monsieur?"

"Uh . . . no. Gold is fine." Though my pigeon was now drinking better than I ever had.

"Where *are* we?" Tom said after the servants left.

I didn't get the chance to answer. The moment he shut the door, I heard the sound of people running. I poked my head out to see what was going on.

And then, in the distance, I heard screaming.

CHAPTER
14

WE CHASED THE SCREAMS THROUGH
the Palais. Our path took us from the run-down wing of
the palace back into beauty—and that made us run even
faster. *Minette.*

Near the end of the hall, nobles and servants clustered
around a door, afraid to go inside. My stomach lurched as
we shoved them out of the way; from what the nobles were
saying, these were the duchess's chambers.

But it wasn't her that was screaming.

In the center of the room was a bed with four carved
walnut posts and a pavilion, covering a mattress so wide it
could have slept six in comfort. The sheets, sapphire silk,

were crumpled and hanging off the end. A servant girl lay on the floor beside them, holding her leg and howling. Another pair of girls huddled in the far corner, shrieking just as loudly. Only one girl seemed to have her head together: Sally, wielding one of the bedsheets like a gladiator's net.

She spotted me. *"Look out!"* she shouted, and from the corner of my eye I saw the thing dart toward me.

It was a snake. A little more than two feet long, it was brown, with thick black stripes along its length. *An asp,* I thought incredulously as I leaped back, more from instinct than anything else. It snapped at me. I stumbled into Tom, and as we toppled, I felt something snag my breeches at the knee. I began to crawl away in panic, and then a blue shroud seemed to cover the room.

It was the sheet Sally had been holding. It fanned out as she threw it over the snake, catching my boots underneath as well. I yanked my feet out and scrambled away. The silk coiled and hissed as the snake beneath hunted for escape.

"Did it get you?" Tom said, breathless.

I was too scared to look. "Everyone out!" I yelled at the maids, but they just kept screaming. Tom ran forward to pick up the girl on the ground, whose stocking was stained with blood. Sally yanked a second sheet from the bed and tried to throw it over the first one, but it crumpled in the air and fell in a lump on the rug.

"Come on!" I shouted, but the girls wouldn't move. I had to go grab them, and though they fought me at first, pulling them away from the wall seemed to crack their terror. They shoved me as they bolted past, and, off balance, I fell.

"Christopher!" Sally screamed.

The snake had gotten loose. It reared, jaws opening, its body coiled to strike.

I tried to climb to my feet, but my heel slipped on the bedsheet. I fell again, cracking my knee against the parquet.

Writhing in pain, I twisted, hoping to somehow get away from the snake. Then, suddenly, Tom was there, sword in hand. He stepped between us, and the snake hissed, turning on him instead.

"No! Don't!" I said.

The snake lashed out for him, aiming right between his legs. I saw the snake's fangs, distended from its jaw, drops of venom glistening in the sunlight.

Then, in one smooth motion, Tom whirled his sword, swinging it in a wide, downward swoop.

He caught the snake just in time. Its severed head sailed

forward, bouncing on the wood next to me, its jaws opening and closing, as if trying to bite me even in death. The decapitated body writhed, blood pumping from the end.

I scrambled away, still half in panic, climbing up Tom like a cat clawing its way up a curtain.

He stood there, shocked. "I *got* it!" he shouted. "Christopher! *I got it!*"

You sure did, I thought, and I slumped back to the floor, leaning against his legs.

"Are you all right?" he said.

My breeches were punctured at the knee. Though I was scared, I needed to look underneath. I pulled them up and searched, but I couldn't see any marks on my skin. I took a deep breath, trying to calm my thumping heart.

Tom helped me back to my feet. I steadied myself, turning away from the severed snake's head, still snapping at the air. "That was very nicely done," I said.

"Did you see where that thing was aiming?" he said. "I took a sword there twice already. I'm not taking a viper in the soft bits, too."

"It was an asp."

"That's even worse."

The wailing from the hallway reminded me there was

someone in much bigger trouble than us. We hurried outside to see Sally tending to the girl the snake had bitten. She'd removed the girl's stocking to see the damage.

There were three pairs of punctures on her calf. They oozed blood in thin trickles down her skin. The flesh beneath them swelled, dark red.

Sally looked worried. "Can you do something?"

"Grab the bedsheet," I said. As she ran back into Minette's chambers, I reached under my shirt, searching my apothecary sash for the vial of Venice treacle.

"Swallow this," I told the girl, but she couldn't hear me; she was too hysterical. Eventually I just grabbed her nose and held the vial to her mouth, making her down the sticky liquid inside.

Sally returned with the sheet. *I'm making bandages out of silk,* I thought wildly as I ripped a strip down the side. I wrapped it tightly around her leg, four inches above the rapidly swelling bites.

"Hold her down," I said to Tom.

I pulled my knife. Tom held the girl against the floor as I slit open her wounds. She screamed, then fainted.

"Will that save her?" Sally asked.

"I don't know." We had only one venomous snake in

England—the adder—and its venom wasn't particularly deadly. The bites on this girl's leg were darkening worse than any I'd seen. "We need a surgeon," I said to one of the servants nearby.

He ran, leather heels echoing off the floorboards. The girl began to rouse, though, mercifully, she didn't return to her wailing. She just cried silently, leaning against Tom.

Sally spoke to the maids who'd been in the chamber with her. "What happened?"

"We were making the duchess's bed, mademoiselle," one of them said, terrified. "Lisette was being silly, hopping on it every time we straightened the sheets. I'd pulled her off the bed and was scolding her when she just screamed. That's when we saw the snake."

The crowd grew as we waited for the surgeon, more guests of the duke and duchess coming to see. They stared at Lisette in Tom's arms, and at the mess in the room, chittering with gossipy delight at the wound on the girl's leg and the segmented snake in the bedchamber. The only one who didn't seem pleased was a red-faced man shaped like a barrel.

The asp must have been this man's pet, for he gasped when he saw all the blood. "No!" he said, almost desperately. He looked around, and his eyes fell on Tom's sword, lying on the ground beside him as he held Lisette. "What have you done? You killed Marguerite!"

Tom, confused, looked to me. The man had shouted in French, of course, and Tom didn't understand.

"Don't yell at him," I said to the man. "Your snake attacked us. My friend saved our lives."

"She was pregnant!" he said. "She was only defending herself."

This was getting crazier by the moment. What kind of idiot keeps a venomous snake? "It bit this girl."

"A servant? Who cares? Do you have any idea how much Marguerite will cost to replace? You'll pay for a new one."

Now I was annoyed. "I'll pay for nothing. What was your snake doing in the duchess's bedchamber, anyway?"

"She escaped her cage, obviously. Snakes are clever, fool. Sometimes they do that."

"Well, sometimes they get their heads chopped off, too."

A large purple vein on the man's temple throbbed so heavily I thought it might burst through his skin. He was about to bellow at me again when the surgeon arrived; Palissy, his name was, I'd learn.

"Out of the way," Palissy said gruffly, bumping the

assembled nobles aside without regard. He examined the girl's leg. "Who bound this?"

"I did." I explained what had happened. "I also gave her some . . ." I didn't know the French word for Venice treacle, so I switched to Latin. "Theriac."

The surgeon examined the wounds, which had now darkened alarmingly. He shook his head. "The theriac hasn't stopped the venom. I think it'll be the leg."

Sally went pale.

"We can't do anything here," Palissy said. "Carry her down to the kitchen. I'll need the table."

I told Tom what the surgeon had ordered. He picked the girl up and carried her down as Palissy told his apprentices to prepare his tools. The servants hurried in front of them to ready the space. Sally went with them, still pale, along with most of the assembled houseguests; to watch the show, I imagined. I went to go down, too—the surgeon might need some remedies for Lisette—but then I remembered Christopher Ashcombe wouldn't have any knowledge of that sort of thing. I probably shouldn't have even given her the Venice treacle. I reassured myself that Palissy, who seemed to know what he was doing, would certainly have his own supply of remedies as needed.

Besides, the half-barrel, half-man snake owner—or former snake owner, anyway—wasn't through with me. He placed a finger on my chest. "What's your name?"

Not all of the houseguests had gone with the surgeon; the ones who remained watched us curiously. Silently, I cursed. I hadn't wanted to attract attention to myself on this mission. Now this man was challenging me in front of everyone. I wanted to end things quietly—actually, I wanted to end things by putting a firework in his breeches—but Baron Ashcombe surely wouldn't back down.

I tried to channel the King's Warden. "I'm Christopher, Baron Ashcombe of Chillingham," I said coldly.

He sneered. "You're English."

"You mean like our host, the duchess? Why, yes."

That stung him. "You'll pay for Marguerite, or I'll take this matter to His Grace, the duke."

"Do as you please. But—who are you again?"

He drew himself up. "Pierre Amyot, comte de Colmar."

"Well, Comte," I said in my best Lord Ashcombe growl, "touch me again, and we'll resolve this with steel instead of silver." I placed my hand on the hilt of my sword.

Amyot sputtered. "Dueling is outlawed in France."

"Who said anything about a duel?"

Very Ashcombey, I thought proudly, as Amyot turned bright red. He seemed suddenly aware of the amused faces surrounding him. Without a word, he spun on his heel and stomped off.

I'd have liked to run from their gazes myself. But now I had a job to do. Regardless of what Amyot had said, I didn't believe a venomous snake in Minette's bedchamber was an accident. I needed to get back inside and investigate.

I picked up the torn silk sheet and carried it into the bedroom, under the pretense of using it to wipe my sword blade clean. That was probably a ridiculous idea; I'd never even drawn the thing. But with only a moment to think, it was more or less the best I could come up with.

No one seemed to notice the oddity of it. The show finished, the assembled houseguests walked away, chattering about what they'd just seen. The moment I thought no one was watching, I shut the door.

Minette would be horrified. Blood decorated her floor, seeping into the rug, crawling a slow stain up the bedsheets hanging from the mattress—to say nothing of the decapitated snake. I needed to work quickly; once the servants had prepared the surgeon's table, they'd return to clean the room.

I knelt next to the snake's head, which had finally stopped its grisly snapping. Its mouth gaped open, drops of amber venom swelling at the tips of its fangs. Not willing to touch it, I turned it back and forth with the tip of my blade.

The head was triangular, blunted at the nose. The markings, as on the body, were a murky sort of brown with hashed black bands. Definitely an asp—a European asp, if I remembered my master's notes. I thought of what he'd written. *As deadly as any snake native to the Continent.*

A good choice for an assassin. But how did it get here?

I looked about the room. There were plenty of places a snake could hide: under the dresser, the drawers, the chairs, the bed—

The bed. I remembered what the servant girl had told Sally. *Lisette was jumping on the bed.*

I bent down and looked underneath it. Silhouetted against the light from the window on the other side was a boxy shape. I stretched a hand to pull it out. My fingers touched metal, and then I felt a sharp prick against the heel of my palm.

My chest tightened. I fell back, gasping, and peered at my palm, expecting to see a snakebite. Instead, I saw a tiny piece of glass embedded in my skin.

Where had that come from? I plucked it out and returned to the bed, this time reaching underneath it with my sword. The blade swept everything toward me, bouncing little shards of glass along the floor in front of a gold mesh cage.

I stared at the mess for a moment. Then I scooped everything up and snuck down the hall to a nearby study, where I spread it all out on the desk.

The cage was the sort of thing one might use to carry a small pet, like a bird or a mouse—or a snake. The latch was missing. I examined the shards of glass and noticed they were small and cylindrical. I laid them out in a line and found that some of the pieces fit neatly together.

So the pieces of glass had once been a long, thin rod. I sat there, puzzled, trying to figure out what I was looking at, until I spotted a shard of glass stuck in the mesh of the cage door. Then I understood.

A trap.

That's what this was: a trap. Someone had taken Amyot's asp, stuck it in the cage, then slipped it under Minette's bed. Then, instead of locking the cage with the latch, they'd pinned the glass rod between the floor and the bed in front of the cage door to hold it shut. When Lisette had jumped on the bed, the mattress had sagged, cracking the rod and freeing the snake.

The girl should never have been on the bed. Which meant this trap had been left for Minette. The cage would have remained locked by the glass rod until the night, when the duchess retired. She'd have been alone with a venomous snake—or maybe Philippe might have been there, too—and the asp would have bitten them while they slept.

My stomach churned. This trap had only been sprung by accident, by a playful young girl. If not for her, I'd have failed in my mission the very day I arrived at the Palais.

My face grew hot, sweat beading on my cheeks, as my guts sank in despair. They'd made a mistake. Lord Ashcombe. The *king*. They'd made a terrible mistake sending me here. I was meant to find the assassins. I wasn't prepared to find *anything*. What was I supposed to do? Look under every bed? Every chair? In every drawer? Should I take the thousand people at the Palais and question them one by one?

I buried my head in my hands. *What am I supposed to do? Oh, Master, what do I do?*

"What are you doing?"

The question echoed my own thoughts so perfectly that, for a moment, I thought it had come from inside my head. But the voice was unfamiliar, melodic, and when I turned, I saw a man, dressed in finery, with a jewel-pommelled blade at his side. He watched me from the doorway to the study. I got the feeling he'd been standing there for a while.

I wasn't sure how to respond. "Just . . . examining this cage," I said.

The man studied me. He looked young—in his early twenties, maybe—and he gazed at me with intense blue eyes. That gaze flicked to the cage on the desk. "You took that from the duchess's bedchamber."

I flushed. I could have sworn no one was in the hall when I'd left. "It's . . . fine workmanship," I said. "I wanted to examine it in better light."

Suddenly he switched to perfect, unaccented English. "Who are you?"

The change threw me off guard. "I'm . . . Christopher Ashcombe. The Baron of Chillingham. I'm a friend of the duchess."

"Yes, I heard you say that to Amyot. Except *Richard* Ashcombe is the Baron of Chillingham."

"That's my grandfather. He's the marquess now. I inherited my title this summer."

"Oh?" He cocked his head. "You have a curious knowledge, Baron. I wouldn't have thought you an expert at treating snakebites."

"We . . . get them all the time out hunting."

"Is that why you were carrying Venice treacle? In case you found yourself on a hunt in the halls of the Palais?"

So he'd been watching from the very beginning. Inwardly, I cursed. I'd treated Lisette without thought—and of course I did; was I supposed to let her die? Except it occurred to me that, to keep to my cover, I *should* have let her die. What had I got myself into?

I thought quickly. Venice treacle was used for much more than snake venom. "I . . . passed by London on the way here," I said. "There's still plague in the city, and the treacle works against the sickness. So I thought I'd better have some with me, just in case."

"That's a good answer." The young man smiled slightly. "Unfortunately for you, I don't believe a word of it." Slowly, he shut the door to the study behind him. Then he drew his sword. "Who are you, really?"

CHAPTER

15

I TOOK A STEP BACK. MY LEG BUMPED against the desk. "I told you who I am."

The man stepped closer, the point of his blade toward me. "And I said I don't believe you."

I thought of Sir William's final words to us. *Avoiding fights is always better than seeking them.* Fine enough, but I didn't seek this. It found *me*. Even so, I knew: I had no training. All I'd ever done was watch Tom. I had to hope that, as with Amyot, channeling Lord Ashcombe would be enough.

I drew my sword and pointed it at him. "Shall we fight right here in the study, then?" I said.

He looked at me incredulously. Then, with the quickness of a cat, he leaped forward, his blade flashing in the light. He wrapped his sword around mine in a circular motion, wrenching the weapon from my hand. It flew through the air, smacked against the shelf beside us, and clattered to the floor.

I stared at him. He grinned.

"Now I *know* you're not Ashcombe's grandson," he said. "No one with the King's Warden's blood could wield a sword that badly. Have you even picked one up before?"

"The duchess will confirm—"

"The duchess isn't here. And she won't return in time to stop me running you through." He looked me up and down. "You know what I think? You're more than just an impostor. That cage was for the snake, wasn't it? You planted it in her room. And now you're trying to get rid of the evidence. You're an *assassin*."

My stomach tumbled as I realized that's *exactly* what this looked like. What had I done? "I swear to you—"

He pressed his sword against my lips. "Swear nothing. You're clearly no baron. You have all the wrong skills. You called your servant your 'friend.' So I'm warning you. Tell me who you are, and what you're doing with that cage. Or I'll cut your tongue out."

Panic rose in my chest. I had no doubt the man would do as he threatened. But I didn't know what to say. Admitting I wasn't a noble would be as much a death sentence as lying to him.

On the other hand, telling the truth would get me killed *later*. Lying to him would end my life right *now*. That left me with only one choice.

"My name is Christopher Rowe," I said. "I was sent here by King Charles and Lord Ashcombe to protect the duchess. There was an attempt on their lives in England, and His Majesty was worried about his sister. I didn't know there was a cage underneath the bed. I just found it when I went looking to see where the snake had come from."

"If you didn't know about the cage, why were you carrying Venice treacle? How did you know there'd be a snake?"

"I didn't. I just had the medicine with me because I'm an apothecary's apprentice."

He snorted. "Why would the king send an apothecary's apprentice to protect his sister?"

"Whoever tried to kill them used poison," I said. "They sent me because I know about poisons."

"That still doesn't explain: Why you? Why an apprentice? Why not send your master instead?"

"I . . . that's a long story."

His blade bit into my lip. "Make it a short one."

"I've served His Majesty before," I said, trying to move my mouth as little as possible. "So Lord Ashcombe trusts me. And he couldn't send my master because he was murdered."

"Oh? Who was this murdered master? And careful, now: I know London."

"Benedict Blackthorn."

The man's jaw dropped. His blade left my lips, drifted downward. "Benedict . . . ," he whispered.

And then, suddenly, I was falling.

CHAPTER
16

THE MAN SPRANG ON ME SO QUICKLY,
I didn't even see him move. He shoved me backward, landing on top of me on the floor. All the air rushed from my lungs. I tried to push him off, but he grabbed my hair, yanked my head back, and laid the edge of his blade against my neck.

"Who sent you?" he shouted. *"Who sent you?"*

"The king! Lord Ashcombe!" I said. "I swear!"

He pinned my arms to the floor with his knees. Then he lifted his sword from my neck and placed the point of the blade against my abdomen.

"Listen to me very carefully," he hissed. "If you don't

tell me the truth—*everything*—I'm going to gut you. I'm going to slice you open, and pull out your entrails, until they string a ribbon around this room."

I didn't know what to do. I couldn't move. Calling for help wouldn't bring anyone in time to stop him gutting me—which I was more than certain he would do. My master's name had alarmed him, and I didn't have any idea why. But I didn't have anything better than the truth.

"Please," I said. "Lord Ashcombe sent me, on orders from the king. Ask the duchess what happened—"

His eyes hardened. "I warned you."

He pressed the blade down.

"No! Wait!" I began.

Clink.

We heard the sound of breaking glass as the man's sword pressed into me. It threw him for a moment. Puzzled, he pulled up my shirt.

The apothecary sash was around my waist. Broken glass spilled out of it, spilling fine purple powder from one of the pockets.

The man stared at the mess beneath his blade, mouth hanging open once again. Slowly, he climbed off me. He couldn't stop staring at the sash.

"Take that off," he said.

Numbly, I complied. I held it out, and he took it, gently, almost reverently.

"This *is* his," the man said, flabbergasted. "This is Master Benedict's. How . . . how did you get it?"

Did he just call him Master Benedict? "I told you. I was his apprentice. He left everything to me when he died."

"He's dead?" The man's face fell. "Truly? I didn't . . . I didn't realize he was gone."

I blinked. "You *knew* him?"

"A little," the man said. "It . . . it was a long time ago."

The man sheathed his sword. He didn't seem to care about me anymore, so, keeping my eyes on him, I stood. Purple powder and broken glass fell from my stomach, scattering across the floor.

I didn't understand what was happening. "Who are you?" I said.

"What?" He looked up from the sash, still dazed. "Oh. I'm Simon. Simon Chastellain. I'm the vicomte d'Aviron. Your master . . . was a great friend to my uncle."

My jaw dropped. "Your uncle . . . *Chastellain*? You're not talking about . . . *Marin* Chastellain, are you?"

"You know him?"

"Master Benedict wrote about him in his journals." I couldn't believe my luck. Once again, my master's past had weaved its way into my life—and once again, it had saved me from a terrible fate. "Why did you attack me?"

Simon looked embarrassed. "I'm . . . I'm sorry about that. I didn't hurt you, did I?"

Yes, you did, I thought, wiping blood from my lip. "I'm all right."

"I didn't know . . . it's just . . . you were behaving so *strangely.* The Venice treacle . . . the way you bandaged that girl's leg . . . what you said about your 'friend.' Something just wasn't right. And it was your master who'd once taught me to notice when things are strange." He smiled sadly, as if recalling a distant memory. "Anyway, I was suspicious. So when everyone left, I stayed hidden to see what you would do. When you went into the duchess's bedchamber, and came out with that cage . . . well, what would you have thought? Especially if you already knew someone had tried to poison your king."

I understood that completely. Though . . . "How did you already know someone tried to poison him?"

"The whole city knows. It was in this week's *Gazette de France.* Don't expect to keep secrets here, Christopher. In

Paris, gold is only a secondary currency. The primary coin is gossip."

A fair enough answer, though it still left me with a question. "Why were you so angry when I mentioned Master Benedict?"

He pursed his lips. "As you said earlier, that's a long story. I'll tell you, but first . . . could I ask a favor of you?"

"A . . . what?"

Simon looked rueful. "I know," he said. "It's shameful of me to ask after what I did to you. But the favor's not really for me. It's for my uncle. Would you come and see him? He's . . . not well, and I think . . . I think you might be able to help."

Still rattled by Simon's assault, my first thought was: Not a chance. Let him find another apothecary. But my refusal froze on my lips as I thought of my master.

He'd cared for Marin Chastellain. They'd been friends since Master Benedict was a boy. If Marin really was sick, I couldn't just abandon him. What would my master think?

If I could help him, I had to. That didn't mean I was willing to go alone. "I have to wait for Tom," I said.

"Of course." Almost regretfully, Simon returned my

master's sash. He also unbuckled his sword and held it out. "So you know I mean you no harm."

Graciousness would have allowed him to keep his weapon. Then again, graciousness didn't have a sliced lip and a sore backside. I took the blade.

We waited in silence. I was burning with curiosity about Simon and my master, but I decided to hold any questions until Tom came back. It didn't take long. The surgeon, with his own journeymen and apprentices to help with the operation, sent everyone out of the room. When Sally returned with Tom, I called them into the study. She hesitated when she saw Simon. I explained who he was, and she, in turn, confirmed what Palissy had predicted: Lisette would have to lose the leg.

Sally was upset. Of all of us, she knew best what would happen to the girl. "She'll lose her job now. Even if the surgeon saves her, she'll end up begging in the streets."

I showed them the cage trap and explained how the attack had been staged. "Surely Minette will keep her on," Tom said. "Accident or not, Lisette saved her life."

"I wouldn't count on it," Simon said. "There's not much charity for servants here."

"We have to find these assassins, Christopher," Sally said fiercely. "We *have* to."

My heart began to sink again. I still didn't know how.

"I don't know about assassins," Simon said, "but I might be able to help you nonetheless. Here's what I propose: Christopher, you come and try to help Uncle Marin. In return, I'll speak to Rémi, our *maître d'hôtel*, about Lisette. I'm sure he can find something she'll be able to do in my uncle's house."

Sally looked hopeful. "You'd do that?"

"Why not? A simple trade—everyone benefits. That's fair, isn't it?"

Very fair, I thought, considering I'd planned to help Marin anyway. Though I still needed to add something to the deal. "You won't tell anyone at the Palais we're not who we claim to be, will you?"

He seemed surprised, like the thought hadn't even occurred to him. "Oh. No. Of course. That would not be good." He looked at me, amused. "But if you'd really like to keep it secret that you're not an Ashcombe, Christopher, take my advice: Don't draw that sword of yours again."

• • •

Maison Chastellain was on the Île Notre-Dame—which, despite its name, was not the same island that held that famous cathedral. "That's the Île de la Cité," Simon said, pointing to Lord Ashcombe's map. "This island is called Île Notre-Dame because it's *next* to the cathedral."

Tom gave me a look. Simon saw it. "If you think *that's* confusing, try walking the streets for a day. I'll not spoil the surprise; you'll see what I mean soon enough."

We weren't going to be walking any streets on this outing. Simon had his own carriage. "Everyone of quality does in Paris," he said. "The streets are clogged with them. There's even a public carriage system, which makes timed stops around the city, if you don't mind mingling with someone below your class."

I'd noticed the excess of carriages on the way in, and this particular journey did nothing to change that observation. Though Marin's home was a little more than a mile from the Palais, it took longer to ride there then it would have to walk. Simon used the time to explain why he'd been so angry at my mention of Master Benedict.

"My parents moved me around a lot when I was young," he said. "When I was eight, they sent me to live with Uncle Marin for a year. That year, unfortunately, was 1652—the same year the plague came to Paris. My parents wouldn't move me away—they forbade me to step out of the house until the plague disappeared—so I was terribly bored by the time Blackthorn came to stay, to hunt for his cure.

"I liked him immediately. I was a bit wild back then"—*not much different from now,* I thought, my lip still stinging—"but he was very kind to me. He would talk to me as I sat in his workshop, teaching me, like what I told you about watching for things out of place. And the potions he made, his concoctions . . . well, I suppose I don't have to tell *you* how fascinating they were.

"I was especially enthralled by that sash of his. He wouldn't let me have it, of course—God knows how many ways I might have poisoned myself—but he did let me play with some of the tools inside. My favorite was the magnet."

I reached into the sash and pulled out a small, rectangular prism of iron.

Simon gasped. "That's it!"

I handed it to him. Like a child, he proceeded to try to stick it to everything in the carriage, laughing with delight. Eventually, he handed it back.

"That's the memory I have of your master," he said wistfully. "A kind and patient man. Anyway, once the sickness ran its course, my parents came for me, and we moved to an estate we owned in England, in Nottinghamshire, on the edge of Sherwood Forest. After the plague scare, they wouldn't send me to Paris anymore, so that's where I spent the rest of my youth."

"I was wondering why your English is so good," I said. "I can't even hear an accent."

He made a face. "You try being a French boy in an English school. I worked very hard to lose it. Though not before I learned how to fight." He nodded toward his blade, which I carried beside my own.

"Did you see Master Benedict again?"

"Sadly, no. I was lying when I told you I knew London; our estate was too far north to make many trips. But my time in Paris was a good one, so my uncle and I wrote each other letters. Then, a couple years ago, what he wrote made me begin to worry about his health. Eventually, it got so bad that, back in April, I journeyed to Paris to check on him. What I found enraged me.

"As my uncle's health deteriorated, his servants began to prey on him. You see, he's rather gullible, and, despite his enormous wealth, he'd been obsessed with hunting treasure since he was a boy. He'd get ideas in his head about secrets and conspiracies, and the type of people he surrounded himself with often took advantage of that. It made your master so exasperated, but there wasn't much any of us could do. It was just my uncle's way.

"Anyway, as Uncle Marin weakened, his own servants started to rob him blind. When I arrived in Paris and discovered what they were doing, I taught them a lesson." He said it with steel in his voice. "That's why I was so harsh with you. When you mentioned Blackthorn, I thought you were another thief, here to prey on my family once again. I tell you, Christopher, I'm so grateful you were wearing your master's sash. Otherwise, I'd have run you through."

I told Tom and Sally what had happened. Tom stared, and Sally, sitting on the carriage bench beside me, stuck her finger through the hole his blade had made in my shirt.

"I hadn't even seen that," I said.

Simon flushed. "I can't apologize enough. I'll pay for a new shirt, of course."

"It's fine; Lord Ashcombe gave me others."

"Absolutely not. You'll have that replaced; that's a promise."

Suddenly, there was a fluttering of wings. Bridget flew through the window of the carriage and landed on my lap.

"What on earth . . . ?" Simon said, and he reached forward to toss her back out.

"No!" I scooped her up. "She's mine. This is Bridget."

"Where did she come from?" Simon said, still amazed.

"You'd be surprised," Tom said. "That pigeon follows him *everywhere*."

I'd left the window open in our quarters. She must have gone out to explore. Simon held out his hands, gently, this time. "May I?"

I handed her over, and he brought her up to his face. Cooing, she stretched out her beak to rest against his nose.

"This is the sweetest bird I've ever seen. How long have you—oh!" She flapped her wings, startling him; then she flew out the window, swooping from rooftop to rooftop as she followed the carriage. "What an extraordinary thing." He watched her for a while, then pointed into the distance. "Oh, we're almost there. Look."

Tom, Sally, and I leaned out the window to see. We'd already turned onto the Pont Marie, the bridge that led to the Île Notre-Dame.

I'd never seen anything like it. The island, Simon told us, was man-made: built up forty years ago from two smaller islands in the middle of the Seine. Unlike the twisting, alley-marked streets of London, Île Notre-Dame was laid out in a grid, with broader, more easily traveled avenues. The homes were all huge, gleaming mansions, built of white ashlar stone, making the island shine like a pearl at the center of its Parisian shell.

Maison Chastellain was one of the grandest palaces on the island. Tom, Sally, and I were reduced to gawking again as we walked up marble steps between a pair of stone lions and entered the house. The entryway was fascinating: The walls curved in an oval, decorated with so many banners and paintings of Europe's masters I half believed we were back in the Palais. There were several doors to the other wings of the house and, on the left, a staircase sweeping up along the wall to the second floor.

The *maître d'hôtel*, brought by the sound of our entrance, joined us in the oval from the stairs. Simon handed him his cloak. "How is he this afternoon?" he asked in French.

The servant hesitated.

"It's all right, Rémi," Simon said. "They're friends."

"Monsieur le Comte is not well," Rémi said. "He's been shouting all day about—"

"Assassins!"

CHAPTER 17

WE LOOKED UP. AT THE TOP OF THE curving stairs stood an elderly man in disarray. He was half-undressed, wearing only a long, stained nightshirt over hose and boots. His eyes were wild under his wig, which was tilted as if someone had cuffed him across the head. He waved a silver cane at us from atop the balcony.

"Murderers!" he shouted. "Blackguards! I want to go home!"

Simon's face fell. "This *is* home, Uncle. Remember?"

"I'm not your uncle!" Behind him, a tall, pretty servant girl came toward him, hands out, speaking softly. Marin backed away, coming dangerously close to the stairs. "Get away from me. I'll shoot you."

He trained the cane on the girl like it was a musket. She froze, mostly so he wouldn't topple down the steps.

Simon waved her back. "It's all right, Colette," he said. "Uncle. You have guests."

"I want to go home!"

"But look who I've brought you. It's Benedict Blackthorn's apprentice."

"Liar."

Tom and Sally shifted uncomfortably. "Maybe we should leave," I said.

"No, please," Simon said desperately. "I thought if Blackthorn . . ." He stopped. "Wait. The sash."

"What?"

"The sash. Show him Master Benedict's sash."

I lifted my shirt.

"Uncle, look," Simon said.

Marin's eyes narrowed, but he took his gaze off the servant girl to look down at us. When he saw me, he blinked.

"Benedict?" He lowered his cane. "Benedict? Is that really you?"

"No, I'm—" I began, but Simon grabbed my sleeve.

"Wait," he whispered.

"Benedict!" Marin began a slow descent toward us. Colette and Rémi both rushed to ensure he didn't fall. I thought he'd try to push them away, but he accepted their help without complaint.

They released Marin once he'd made it down the steps. He came toward me, arms outstretched, and wrapped me in a hug. "Where have you been?" he said, switching to English. "I've been looking all over for you."

"I . . ." I wasn't sure what to say. I didn't like the idea of pretending to be my master. But thinking Master Benedict was here seemed to have calmed Marin considerably. "I've . . . I've been in London," I said finally.

"London?" Marin looked puzzled. "Was there a plague?"

"Yes. It's mostly over now."

"That was yesterday," he said more forcefully. Then he turned to Tom and Sally. "Are these friends?"

"Yes," I said. "This is Sally."

He took her hand and kissed it, while she curtsied. "Enchanted."

"And this is Tom."

"Welcome. Welcome to my . . ." He frowned. "This is my home."

"Yes," I said. "And this is your nephew."

"Yes, Simon. I know. I'm not *that* old, Benedict."

Simon seemed to relax. "Uncle, why don't you escort Benedict's friends to the study?" he said. "We'll join you in a minute."

"Of course, of course." Marin spoke to Rémi. "We'll need more brandy."

"I'll make you something, Uncle," Simon said.

"I can drink if I want to," Marin said peevishly. He took Sally's arm, and she helped him up the stairs. "Sit with me, *chérie*," he said. "Tell me how London fares."

Tom and Rémi followed them upstairs. Simon ordered Colette to ready the water in the kitchen. Once she'd gone, he slumped against the wall and wiped his brow.

"Thank you," he said. "I know that was unpleasant, but . . . I didn't know what else to do. You see what's happened—" He choked, then cleared his throat. "I have a calmative that's good for him. Will you help me make it?"

"Of course," I said. "I have ingredients in the sash, if you want them."

"I have plenty. There's been a desperate need of them of late."

I followed him to the kitchen. Colette plunked down

a heavy pail next to me with a shy smile. Simon gathered ingredients from the cupboards while Colette set the fire, and I found a small pot to boil the water. Curious, I glanced over to see what Simon had collected: valerian, cowslip, basil, and honey.

I looked up at him, surprised.

He grinned. "You recognize it."

"That's Master Benedict's recipe," I said.

He nodded. "When I arrived in April, my uncle was as you saw. I didn't know what to do, and French apothecaries are worthless. So I wrote to Blackthorn to see if he could help."

Simon pulled a folded piece of paper from the cupboard and handed it to me. I opened it as he and Colette chopped the ingredients and cast them into the pot.

It was a letter. I recognized the smooth, angular hand immediately: It was Master Benedict's.

April 29, 1665

Dear Simon,

Of course I remember you—though I doubt you much resemble anymore that young boy who built forts out of firewood under my workbench.

I am most grateful to you for writing me, though I am deeply saddened to hear of Marin's decline. From his letters, I had begun to fear that something had taken hold of him, but you know your uncle: He'd rather die than consult an apothecary, even me.

I am incredibly sorry to say there is very little that can be done to help him now. Once the mind begins to falter in this way, no power on earth can stop it. You will find Marin increasingly confused by the world around him. The strangest puzzle of this disease is how it affects the memory: He will remember incidents from years ago with perfect clarity, yet be completely unaware of whether he ate his noontime meal. He will see dead friends come to life, while forgetting those still around him whom he loves.

I know this will be a terrible strain on you. Try not to be wounded by Marin's behavior. He is confused, and frightened, and this is why he lashes out. Please remember also that he always loved you. You must steel yourself to the fact that, as time progresses, he will recognize you less and less. Do not try to correct him; it will not help, and will only agitate him further. If his errors are of no danger to anyone, it is a kindness to simply let them be.

I am enclosing a recipe for a calmative you may find of use; the more rested Marin is, the more his faculties will return. I wish I could come there myself, but I am at a critical juncture in my

research and unable to leave London. Perhaps, if things go well, I
will visit with my apprentice in the summer.
With affection,
Benedict

I traced my fingers over the letters, then wiped my eyes. Simon and Colette remained silent until I'd collected myself. "I wrote to your master again a few months ago," Simon said, "but I never heard back. I'd assumed the plague had prevented couriers from traveling to London. I hadn't realized he'd died."

I didn't want to talk about this anymore. I watched him prepare my master's recipe. The way he wielded his knife actually reminded me of Master Benedict. "You're quite skilled at that," I said.

He smiled. "I learned from your master for months. To my parents' dismay, I've been sneaking into kitchens ever since. Sometimes I wish I wasn't a vicomte. I think I'd have very much liked being an apothecary." He sighed. "I suppose it's ungrateful to complain."

Perhaps, but he wasn't going to get any argument from me. There was nothing else I'd ever want to be. "Does the calmative work, then?"

"Incredibly well. Uncle Marin remembers me most of the time afterward, though his favorite subject remains the old days. I try to get him to take it regularly. Otherwise . . . well, you saw."

Over the years, I'd helped Master Benedict treat many patients who'd declined in the same way: Demency, he called it. So I knew Simon's uncle wasn't seeing things clearly. Nonetheless, his cry about assassins made me curious. "He seems particularly worried about murderers. Is that normal?"

"Yes," Simon said, looking dejected. "The old servants had been with him for years. Decades, some of them." He motioned to Colette, who was stirring my master's recipe in the pot over the fire. "Everyone here now, Colette and Rémi and the rest, are strangers to him. When he gets confused, he thinks we murdered the others."

"What *did* happen to them?" I said.

He shrugged. "Nothing. I filed a writ of arrest with the courts, but they'd disappeared by then. Fled the city, probably. Though I promise you, Christopher, if they return, I *will* see them hanged in the square. They'll answer to Uncle Marin, and then they'll answer to God."

Simon took a deep breath to calm himself. "Come, let's bring him his medicine."

We took the mug up to Marin's study. The curtains drawn over the French doors to the balcony made it a dark but warm sort of room, with deep red cherrywood paneling and its own impressive collection of artwork. A fire blazed in the hearth, illuminating the space.

Marin sat in front of it, drinking brandy from crystal in a plush, comfortable chair, with Tom and Sally in matching chairs around him. Rémi waited unobtrusively against the far wall, stepping forward only when it was time to refill Marin's glass. It appeared the brandy had already done some of the medicine's work, for Marin had put on breeches, and, still speaking English, he was in the middle of telling a story that had Tom doubled over in the cushions, crying with laughter. Sally covered her mouth.

"You're making this up," she gasped.

"I swear to you," Marin said. "The farmer insisted it was the only way to clear the blockage. So there's a duck on my head, these geese are attacking me, and I've got my arm all the way up this cow's—" He spotted the mug in Simon's hand. "I'm not drinking that."

"Come now, Uncle," Simon said. "Benedict says you must."

"Hmph." He looked me up and down. "Who are you?"

"It's Benedict."

"Are you daft? Benedict's taller. And he's gone back to London."

I felt relieved that I'd no longer have to keep up the charade. "I'm Master Benedict's apprentice, monsieur," I said. "I'm Christopher Rowe."

His eyes lit up. "Christopher? Benedict writes to me of you all the time! Sit, sit. Have a drink."

Rémi came forward to fill a new glass with brandy. I sipped at it lightly; the alcohol stung my nose and burned like fire down my throat. Marin returned to his story of the farmer's field, and when he was finished, launched immediately into a new one involving a blacksmith, a country lady, and a moose from Scandinavia named Karl.

He was transformed. We sat for ages, riveted to our seats, as Marin spun us a series of tales. He told of magical journeys, and of high adventures, and of dark and wicked plots; in Paris, in France, and all over the world. I saw easily why my master had liked him: He was the kind of friend you could have while never needing to say a single word in return. And his knowledge of history—and its conspiracies—seemed unparalleled, something else Master Benedict would have loved. Marin's stories were so vivid, it was as if we were there—and when I remembered my master's letter, I recognized, in Marin's mind, he probably was. *The strangest puzzle of this disease is how it affects the memory: He will remember incidents from years ago with perfect clarity, yet be completely unaware of whether he ate his noontime meal.*

His stories kept us much longer than I'd planned, long enough for me to begin to feel guilty. *You have a mission,* I chastised myself. *And listening to stories isn't it.* Still, I remained, held not only by Marin's tales, but by the connection to my master. I couldn't bring myself to pull away from it.

Yet it was as Marin told us the story of the Fronde—the failed rebellion against Louis XIV, fifteen years ago—that it struck me: Maybe I *hadn't* been wasting time. We were, after all, sitting with a living encyclopedia of French conspiracies.

"Monsieur Chastellain?" I said, when he paused to call Rémi forward to refill his glass.

"Call me Marin, son."

"Marin . . . have you ever heard the phrase 'until the time'?"

He looked at me with interest. "Why?" he asked. "Are you planning to kill the king?"

CHAPTER
18

I SAT UP, STARTLED. "YOU KNOW what it means?"

"Of course," he said. "*Jusqu'au moment*—until the time. It's from Molay's curse."

Neither Tom nor Sally had any idea what he was talking about. I looked over at Simon, who shook his head and shrugged.

"Hm," Marin said. "I'd have thought Benedict would have told you this one." He mulled it over. "What do you know about the Knights Templar?"

Tom's eyes lit up. He liked stories of knights. "They

were crusaders," he said. "And then the pope got rid of them, didn't he?"

"A much simplified version of the story—and somewhat inaccurate, I'm afraid. Perhaps we should start at the beginning."

Marin settled into his chair. "Our tale begins in Jerusalem, in 1119, twenty years after the First Crusade drove back the Saracens and returned the city to Christian hands. Though the town itself is secure, King Baldwin of Jerusalem is troubled: The roads are plagued with highwaymen, and there is no safe passage in the Holy Land.

"In the midst of this chaos, nine French knights appear before the king. 'Let us form a new knighthood,' they say, 'so we may protect the pilgrims on their way.' Baldwin agrees, and for their headquarters, he gives them the old royal palace, which rests over the ruins of the ancient Temple of Solomon. From this they get their name: the Poor Fellow-Soldiers of Christ and the Temple of Solomon—or, as they will come to be known, the Knights Templar.

"The earliest records of the Templars are lost. But, as far as we can tell, instead of guarding pilgrims, they spent their first eight years digging under the royal palace, excavating the old Temple ruins."

"What were they looking for?" Tom said.

"Nobody knows. What we *do* know is that, in 1127, their grand master, Hugh de Payns, leaves Jerusalem and returns to France. He holds a few secret meetings, and, within months, every noble in Europe has offered land, gold, and supplies to the Templars—suddenly making this unknown, undistinguished band of knights the wealthiest order in Christendom.

"With their newfound power, their ranks swell, reaching twenty thousand brothers at their peak. Entire armies scatter in their wake. But then they meet their greatest enemy, a foe much more dangerous than any Saracen."

Marin swirled his brandy in his glass, the firelight giving it an amber glow. "His name is Philippe the Fourth, the Iron King of France. They call him Philippe le Bel—Philip the Fair—for his handsome appearance and golden locks. And le Bel has ambitions greater than any king before him.

"He wishes to transform France into the greatest power the world has ever known: a new empire to rival the ancient Romans, with le Bel himself as Caesar. He makes war with his neighbors—England in particular—and the expense of his lavish lifestyle and never-ending conflict put him deeply into debt: most of all, to the Templars, who have lent him money. And so the Iron King begins to scheme.

"*I will arrest the Templars,* he thinks. *I will accuse them of terrible crimes. And as their punishment, I will confiscate everything they own.* It's a fine plan: Not only will he no longer be in debt, he'll be rich beyond his wildest dreams.

"So, in 1307, le Bel sends a summons to their commander, Jacques de Molay, the twenty-third grand master of the Templars. 'Come to Paris,' le Bel says, 'and we can talk about a new Crusade.' Though Molay is suspicious—he knows what kind of man le Bel is—he agrees. He travels to France with great wealth, knowing he will need it to gain support from the nobility.

"The sum he carries is vast: one hundred fifty thousand gold florins, heaps of jeweled relics, and enough silver to burden a dozen packhorses. When Molay arrives in Paris, he takes the treasure to the Templar headquarters and secures it deep within their stronghold. Le Bel, watching the caravan arrive, is driven mad with greed. And he pounces.

"It happens on Friday, October thirteenth. The Iron King arrests every Templar in the whole of France. The charges against them are evil: spitting on the Cross, heresy, even Devil worship. The pope, Clement the Fifth, objects: By law, the Templars answer to no one but him. But he is a weak pope, and a weak man, and when le Bel threatens to depose him, Clement, too, backs down, and officially disbands their order.

"The charges, of course, are lies: a fiction to allow le Bel to steal their treasure. Philippe rides triumphantly from the royal palace to the Templar stronghold, intending to seize the gold with his own hands. But when his men force their way into the compound, the king receives a shock that nearly stops his blackened heart.

"The treasure is gone. Nothing is left—well, *almost* nothing. All that remains is a single gold florin, glinting in the firelight, lying in the very center of the chamber, the Templar cross hammered into its face.

"Furious, Le Bel summons the city guards. They tell him that the night before, under cover of darkness, twelve Templars left the city, traveling in different directions, each one leading a wagon train. When le Bel checks with the harbor, he discovers the Templar ships are also gone, left that night for the coast.

"Panicked, he sends his men in pursuit. Three of the twelve knights are captured; the first two on the roads within a day, the third a week later in Nancy. Their wagons, however, carry nothing but straw. Livid, le Bel drags the arrested Templars to the dungeons, where he tries to torture confessions from their lips. Which of the knights took the treasure? And where was that man bound?

"The Templar high command—Jacques de Molay and his lieutenants—are held in the dungeon in the seized Templar stronghold itself. 'So you can reflect on your crimes,' le Bel says. When no one will tell him what he wants to know, he hauls fifty-four of the captured knights to the pyre, burning them alive. Still Molay refuses to talk—until March of 1314. After seven terrible years in prison, Molay finally confesses. And he agrees to tell Philippe where he sent the treasure.

"The Iron King gleefully sets an audience for the following day, so all the world can see how the Templars have broken before his will. And when Molay kneels before the king, he certainly seems but a shell of his former self: ragged and filthy, like a beggar in the street. Le Bel demands that Molay confess once again. Then it happens.

"In a strong, clear voice, Molay *recants* his confession. 'These charges you bring against us,' he says, 'are lies. And, though you may torture me for all eternity, I shall never give you what you want. For I serve something greater than you could ever hope to be.'

"The king goes mad with rage. Discarding all pretexts of justice, he orders Molay and his closest lieutenants to be burned as heretics. Molay is taken from the hall to the pyre. He walks silently, head unbowed. As they bind him to the stake, he asks only one request: tie him facing east, so he might look upon the Cathédrale Notre-Dame, the holiest place in France, before he dies.

"Then the fire is lit. The straw begins to blaze. And as the flames lick at his feet, with his final words, he calls down a terrifying curse.

"'The Knights Templar have been done a terrible injustice,' he says. 'And those responsible shall face the ultimate punishment. Philippe le Bel, for his treachery, and Pope Clement, for his cowardice, will stand in judgment before God before the year is through. *And the treasure for which the king sold his soul shall remain hidden until the time no prince of the blood sits upon the throne of Charlemagne.*'"

CHAPTER
19

UNTIL THE TIME.

The words of Molay's bitter curse hung in the air.

"Did it happen?" Tom asked breathlessly. "Did they really stand before God?"

"Indeed they did," Marin said. "Pope Clement, who was already in ill health before the curse, died within the month, bleeding into his belly. Le Bel died eight months later, while hunting. He chased a stag ahead of his men into the thickest part of the woods. When he didn't return, his guards went looking for him. They found him lying in the moss, dead after falling from his horse."

Sally listened, wide-eyed; Tom shuddered. I swallowed,

feeling the same chill. "So," I said, "'Until the time' . . . the phrase is used by people who are trying to find where Molay sent the Templar treasure."

"Yes," Marin said.

I sat back, mind racing. Now it all made sense. *The treasure for which the king sold his soul shall remain hidden until the time no prince of the blood sits upon the throne of Charlemagne.* Kill Louis and his brother, kill their wives, kill their children. Leave the French throne empty . . . and, by Molay's words, the treasure will be discovered.

"I don't understand," Sally said. "How would killing the king's family reveal where Molay sent the treasure?"

"Those who seek to fulfill the curse," Marin said, "believe what Molay was promising was actually a sort of oath. That he'd given orders to the knight who carried away the treasure, telling him that whoever eliminated the king and his descendants should be rewarded with its location. In other words, it's a payment for an assassination. It wouldn't be unheard of; the Templars did have close dealings with the original order of Assassins, a sect that operated in the Holy Land at the time."

"But that knight would have died ages ago."

"Certainly. But, like the king, he'd have descendants

of his own. And they would have instructions to honor the terms of the curse."

Something troubling occurred to me. "Marin," I said.

"Yes?"

"You said you once searched for the Templar treasure."

"I still do."

He fixed his gaze upon me, as the question hung between us. Then he laughed. "Ha! You should see your face. Don't look so sour, Benedict. You know very well I'd never kill anyone; least of all my own king."

I glanced over at Simon, whose slight shifting in his chair was the only indication he'd noticed that Marin's mind had started to slip again.

"Then what about the curse?" Tom said. "Didn't you say to find the treasure, the king's family would have to die?"

"I said *some* people believe that. There are other ways to interpret Molay's curse. Usually, the term 'prince of the blood' is taken to mean *any* descendant of Charlemagne, which Louis the Fourteenth is. But what if Molay meant something much simpler?

"Philippe le Bel had four sons. Three of them lived to become king after his death—and they themselves all died under suspicious circumstances. But none of them had sons of their own. So le Bel's line died in 1328, when the House of Valois took the throne. The answer, then, depends on whose blood Molay meant: Charlemagne's, or le Bel's?"

"I still don't understand," Sally said. "Why wouldn't Molay have meant 'prince of the blood' the same way everyone else does?"

Marin's eyes twinkled. "An excellent question." He drained his glass and, creaking, pushed himself to his feet. "The Templars were quite possibly the most important order of the Middle Ages. Yet we know so little about them. There's a reason for this: Everything they did was shrouded in secrecy. The Templars, you see, were masters of misdirection. Look."

Marin walked around the desk and pulled a weathered old tome from the shelf behind him. We huddled around it as he flipped through the yellowing parchment. The text, written in a clear and steady hand, was marked in different colors, with illumination and sketches inked in the margins. Marin stopped around forty pages in and pointed to a drawing at the bottom.

"This was the symbol of the Templars," he said.

It showed two knights in medieval armor, sitting astride a marching steed.

Tom frowned. "Are they both riding the same horse?"

"Hardly what you'd expect from the wealthiest knights in history, is it?" Marin said. "The usual interpretation is that this symbol is supposed to mean either poverty or brotherhood. But my own research suggests that by choosing this symbol, the Templars were hiding the true nature of their order in plain sight."

He pointed to the knights. "Two brothers on one horse. Two purposes in one order. Two meanings for one face. 'We appear to be one thing,' the symbol says, 'but we are in fact something else. Masters of misdirection.' Their order was born of it: Their stated purpose was to protect pilgrims, but they excavated ruins instead. Even their *name* is misdirection: the *Poor* Fellow-Soldiers of Christ. 'Poor' had a different meaning back then; it meant 'humble,' not 'without money.' Yet they were the mightiest force in the world, in almost every way possible. And then, of course, there's their greatest deceit of all."

He smiled. "The order of the Templars *still exists*."

CHAPTER

20

NOW I WAS CONFUSED. "YOU SAID the pope disbanded them."

"Officially, he did," Marin said. "But remember, nine knights escaped le Bel's clutches—just as nine founded the order, two hundred years before. An interesting symmetry, don't you think? What's more, their descendants continue to plague the royal line of France. Do you remember the gold florin le Bel found in the empty treasure room?"

We nodded.

"That's become the Templar's signature. It's said that upon the coronation of every French king, he goes to sleep in his bedchamber at night. And when he wakes up, lying beside him on his pillow is a single golden coin, stamped with the Templar cross. A threat, in the same style of their old associates, the Assassins."

Tom's eyes went wide. "Is that true?"

"Absolutely. The kings deny it, of course, but when we've been able to get their servants to talk, they all tell of their liege's fear the morning after."

"Surely the king's chambers are guarded," I said. "How would they get in?"

Marin shrugged. "You'd have to ask the Templars."

Masters of misdirection, I thought. They reminded me of my own master: secrets under secrets, codes inside codes. "Twelve knights, each going a different way," I said. "More misdirection."

"Always."

"So how would one search for the treasure?" Sally said. "The nine knights escaped three hundred and fifty years ago. If the Iron King never learned which one of them had it, how would anyone know where to look now?"

"Ah," Marin said. "That's *another* way we know the Templars still exist. Because apart from the coin on the pillow, since the end of le Bel's line, whenever a new king is crowned, a puzzle is revealed. If you can solve it, it will tell you where the Templars sent their treasure."

Now this I wanted to hear. "What kind of puzzle?"

Marin winked at Sally. "You see how clever I am? Benedict can't resist a mystery. It's how I get him to do things for me."

Sally laughed, even as she glanced over at Simon. Quietly, Simon nodded to Rémi to keep watch and left the room.

Marin continued. "The nature of the puzzle changes with every king. It might be a map, or a riddle, or a code; a symbol, a foreign language . . . sometimes, it's all of these at once. In Louis's father's time, it started with a map. I discovered it slipped between the pages of an old text in the Louvre's library. I even managed to find two of the clues hidden within before Louis's father died and Louis became king. After that, further clues vanished, and a new puzzle was set. Of course, *finding* the puzzle is often a puzzle in itself."

"Do you know where the puzzle begins for Louis?"

He grinned. "Lift that rug."

Marin pointed to the Persian carpet that rested in front of the fireplace. Tom flipped it aside, as asked. Then Marin, straining, tried to push his desk forward. "It's stuck," he said.

Sally and I moved to help him as Simon returned with a fresh mug of Marin's calmative. He stopped, puzzled, as we pushed on his uncle's desk. Then the bureau shifted. Tom, still in front of the fireplace, hopped back as the floorboards popped upward at his feet.

Simon looked astonished; he'd clearly never seen this before. Marin flipped the trapdoor open with his cane. Beneath it was a hidden space containing several sheets of paper and a small pinewood box. Marin scooped them all out and dropped them on the nearby daybed, where he shuffled through the papers. "Here it is."

He handed a piece of parchment to me. On it, someone had written a poem.

> *King triumphant, man is burned*
> *Fate brings forth a lesson learned.*
>
> *King triumphant, man is soot*
> *Path is followed underfoot.*
>
> *King is broken, man remains*
> *Answer hidden in the stains.*
>
> *King is rotting, man upstart*
> *Find the city's very heart.*

Simon came to read it over my shoulder. "Uncle, what is this?"

"That belonged to a poet named Vincent Voiture," Marin said. "He wrote it last month, just before he died." Simon looked up sharply but let his uncle continue. "It is the key to beginning the new hunt for the Templar treasure."

"How do you know?" Sally said.

"In three ways. First, the subject matter is clearly related to the story of le Bel, Molay, and the Templars. A victorious king defeats his enemy and burns him at the stake, then himself falls while the order rises from the ashes. That could be coincidence, of course, but the second reason is most curious. Tom should be able to guess what it is."

Tom looked up in surprise. "Me?" He scanned the paper again, nervous under everyone's gaze. "Why would *I* be able to guess?"

"Well, you can read it, can't you?"

He looked over at me, but I wasn't any more certain what Marin was getting at. Sally understood first. "It's in *English*."

Marin nodded. "Vincent Voiture was a French poet; he wrote in French. We have no record of him ever writing anything in English. Except this."

"You think he was a Templar, then?" I said.

"No. I think he was given the text, and then paid to claim it as his own. Which brings me to the third and most compelling reason it's a Templar riddle: what Voiture was paid with."

He picked up the pinewood box and handed it to Sally. She opened it. Then she gasped.

CHAPTER
21

IT WAS A COIN. A SINGLE GOLD

coin, stamped with a familiar symbol.

I took it out, amazed. "Is that . . . ?"

Marin nodded gleefully. "A Templar florin."

I turned it over in my hand. The coin was worn around the edges, the markings nearly flat with wear. *Baldvinus Rex,* it said on one side; *de Ierusalem* on the other. King Baldwin of Jerusalem, blessed patron of the Knights Templar. This florin was more than five hundred years old.

"You can hold on to that, Benedict, if it helps you," Marin said. "The boy next door has one, too."

Simon shifted uncomfortably. "Uncle," he said.

Marin ignored him. "The painter gave it to him."

"The painter?" I said. "You mean the poet? Voiture?"

"Yes." Marin paused, as if uncertain. "No. I . . . we discussed this, remember? I showed it to you."

I held up the poem. "This?"

Marin frowned. "No, no. You wrote it down." He bent over the papers on the daybed and shuffled through them again.

"Uncle." Simon tried to get Marin to take the mug. "It's time for your medicine again."

"I told you I don't want it." Marin pressed a piece of paper into my hands, then returned to sifting through the other pages. "That's yours. Just a moment—the rest is in here somewhere."

I read the paper, startled. It was the same poem as on

the parchment, but this copy was in Master Benedict's handwriting. "Where did this come from?" I said.

"What do you mean, where? You wrote it." When he saw me looking confused, he said, "In between working on the cure. This was last week; how can you not remember?" Marin stopped sifting through the pile. "It's not here. Did you take it?"

Simon glanced over at Rémi. The servant stepped forward. "Dinner is served, monsieur."

"Already?" Marin said. "Very well, let's get dressed for table. We can continue our discussion there."

Rémi escorted Marin out. Simon followed, pausing at the door to whisper, "Wait here."

My confusion faded as I realized what had happened. As Marin's mind had slipped, he'd begun to live in the past again. Clearly, his claim Voiture had written this poem last month was a mistake: Master Benedict would have copied it when he'd stayed with Marin, and that was over thirteen years ago. And Louis had become king a decade before that.

Regardless, the poem itself was what interested me. I looked between the original and my master's. They were identical, except for a single line Master Benedict had written on his own copy, right beside the first verse.

Start at the beginning.

"What does that mean?" Tom said.

It meant Master Benedict was being his usual cryptic self. Still, I read and reread the poem. And as I did, an idea began to form in my mind.

"Oh *no*," Tom said.

I frowned. "I haven't even said anything yet."

I didn't get the chance to, either, because Simon returned to the study. "We've managed to convince my uncle it's time for bed," he said.

"Will he be all right?" Sally asked.

Simon sighed. "As well as he can be. He'll improve once he's had a nap."

"We shouldn't have stayed so long," I apologized. "We taxed him."

"Are you mad? You three are the best thing that's happened to this house since I've been here. That was *him* again," Simon said, his voice thick. "That was my Uncle Marin."

He cleared his throat before continuing. "Please, I have another favor to ask." He lowered his voice, glancing toward the door as he spoke. "I told you before my uncle is wealthy—which I'm sure you'd have figured anyway, from this house. But his finances are in trouble. It's because of those bloody thieving servants."

Simon explained. "Most of my uncle's money comes from his appanage: the land granted to him to manage by the king. Before I came, those servants had looted it. For months, it's been floundering." He sounded almost desperate. "If Louis finds out, he'll take it away, and my uncle will be left with no source of income. I need to go there to put things right. I should have done it weeks ago, but I've kept delaying because of my uncle's health. Now that you're here . . . would you be willing to stop by and check on him?

"I know Charles sent you to the Palais-Royal for a reason," Simon said quickly, "but you've put Uncle Marin in better spirits than I ever have. With you here, I'd be free to hurry to Normandy and reorganize his business. I'd leave tomorrow, and only be gone a few days. I have no right to ask this of you, but . . . would you please come see him while I'm away?"

Tom looked at me as if expecting I'd refuse. So he was surprised when I said, "Absolutely. We'll stop in every day."

Simon clasped my hand in gratitude. "I'll have my carriage take you back to the Palais. In the meantime, if you need anything, tell Rémi. He'll have instructions that this home is yours."

We said our goodbyes and clambered into the carriage. "I'm glad we can help Marin," Tom said, as it began plodding through the streets, "but shouldn't we be hunting for the assassin? We can't stop him from Maison Chastellain."

"We can't stop him from the Palais, either," I said.

"We've done it twice already," Sally said.

"No, we haven't. *Lisette* stopped him the second time— and that was only by accident. Which, frankly, is how we foiled him the first time, too. If that man at the party hadn't asked me for better wine, if I hadn't followed his order when I didn't have to . . ." I shook my head. "That's what I realized, after I found that cage under Minette's bed. We've been lucky, that's all. Eventually, we won't be. We can stop the assassin a hundred times. He only needs to succeed once."

"But our mission was to find out who he is," Sally said. "And whom he works for."

"How? Whom do we ask? Where do we look? There are a thousand people in the Palais. Investigating them all would be like trying to drain the Thames with a cup."

"The man who owned that snake might be a good start," Tom said.

"Agreed," I said. "Sally, see if the ladies know anything about the comte de Colmar. I'll see what I can find out, too. But I'm not so sure Amyot's part of the plot. Even if he'd planned to recover the snake before anyone found it, the physicians would have seen the bites on the bodies. So would he really use his own snake?"

"He didn't seem all that clever," Sally pointed out.

"Which is why we'll investigate him. But keep in mind, the real assassins might have known he kept snakes, and stole one of them to use. So if Amyot's not our man, then what? Work our way on to number two of a thousand?"

"We have to do *something.*"

"And we will. Because I figured out how we're going to stop the assassins for good."

"How?" Tom said.

"It all comes down to this: Whoever's behind this plot wants Minette dead, along with the rest of the royal family, to fulfill Molay's curse. It's only to reveal the Templars' treasure. And that's how we can stop them. Because *that's* the one thing Master Benedict taught me to do."

I held up the florin Marin had given me. Then I held up the poem. "We're going to take away the assassins' purpose. We're going to find the treasure *first.*"

WEDNESDAY, NOVEMBER 18, 1665

Terce

CHAPTER

WE WOKE BEFORE THE SUN DID,
though not to go searching for treasure. Lying on his newly
purchased palliasse, Tom rubbed his eyes as I nudged him
awake.

"You're going to do what?" he said.

"I'm going to watch the king rise," I said. "Philippe and
Minette are taking some of their guests to the Louvre, and
I was invited. We'll go into Louis's bedroom; then the king
will be awakened and have his breakfast while we watch.
Apparently, it's a great honor."

Tom blinked. "You're going to do *what*?"

"Just get dressed," I said. "I can't be late."

Tom grumbled some rude words about the French. I didn't try to disagree.

The nobles gathered in the entrance hall of the Palais. A dozen couples waited in their best French finery, chatting among themselves, next to a handful of unaccompanied ladies. Sally was with them. For the trip to the Louvre, she'd dressed herself in the richest gown Lord Ashcombe had provided her: a stunning emerald brocade, cut low, that seemed to sparkle in the candlelight. Her auburn curls had been tied with a ribbon to cascade enticingly over one pale shoulder. I watched her from across the room, my gaze lingering—she looked *good*—until I was pulled away by something I didn't want to see.

Amyot had joined the crowd. He was escorting a plain, willowy sort of woman who I guessed must be his wife, the comtesse. He seemed to be haranguing her about something. She'd turned away from him slightly, head down, looking deflated, and somewhat embarrassed. It appeared his wife didn't like him much more than I did.

I sighed. I knew I needed to investigate him, but I was far too tired to deal with him right now. I tried to hide behind a man with a wig twice as large as his head, so Amyot wouldn't spot me. It didn't work.

He left his long-suffering wife and stalked over to me. "Twenty *louis*," he said. "That's what you owe me for replacing Marguerite."

My jaw dropped. I'd never have taken Amyot for an honest man, but the figure he'd quoted was so ludicrous it made me angry. Twenty *louis* was more than twenty pounds. A replacement snake—even a venomous one—couldn't possibly cost that much.

I stamped my anger down. *Be unobtrusive,* I said to myself. I couldn't afford another shouting match, especially with everyone watching. And everyone *was* watching, waiting for the entertainment to begin. It appeared they all knew the man quite well.

I gritted my teeth and answered as pleasantly as I could. "I'll be happy to discuss your snake later, Comte."

He intended to discuss it now. "You'll pay me in gold, or you'll pay me in kind."

That made me pause. "What are you talking about?"

"A head for a head. I understand you own a pigeon. Pay me twenty *louis*, or give me the bird."

So much for keeping my temper. "Touch one of Bridget's feathers and I'll run you through."

A voice came from above, sounding peevish. "What is all this *bother*?"

The crowd turned. Coming down the steps was a remarkably short, narrow-faced man with big eyes in a curly black wig, a wide-brimmed feathered hat, and three-inch heels. He was dressed in the absolute height of aristocratic French fashion. He wore a brocaded waistcoat and rhinegraves: loose breeches folded over to resemble a skirt. Under his waistcoat was a linen shirt with long, puffy sleeves, lace cuffs, and a lace cravat. Below his breeches were silk stockings, with fancy bows decorating his high-heeled shoes.

The crowd seemed impressed. I found his outfit slightly horrifying, and not just because it was so gaudy: From the richness of the material, I guessed it had probably cost around a hundred *louis*.

Minette trailed behind him, dressed just as regally. She wore a lavender gown and skirts with a matching lace-trimmed bodice. The top skirt was full and set off with rows of tiny green ribbons. Her corset was tapered at the waist and laced up with silk, cut low at the neck and finished with short puffed sleeves. A chambermaid behind her carried her long fur robe.

Minette had her hand on the man's arm, so this could only be Philippe, duc d'Orléans, brother to the king. Philippe reached the landing and glared at us. "Must there be all this *noise* in the morning?"

Amyot bowed, flushing. "My apologies, monsieur. A matter of business."

"Is this about that silly snake of yours that escaped?"

"Yes, monsieur."

"Well, my dear Comte, I must tell you: If I find one of those things in *my* bedroom, I'll have *your* head cut off."

Amyot went pale. "Y-yes, monsieur."

Philippe sniffed. "You have my permission to remain here today," he said, and then he strode out without a second glance. Minette went with him, sending a small smile my way.

Now Amyot had gone completely white. Behind him, his wife seemed to shrink, trying desperately not to cry. The girls with Sally, I noticed, looked viciously delighted with the comtesse's predicament as they followed the duke and duchess outside.

Not wishing to provoke Amyot further, I didn't look at him as I left. I'd barely exited the door before I heard the comtesse burst into tears and run away.

. . .

Despite Philippe's putting the matter of the snake to rest, I found I didn't much like him. Beyond the wastefulness of his outfit—I could have lived for years on what it cost—there was something about him that raised my hackles. He seemed to be constantly scanning the throng that surrounded him, as if trying to determine how best to manipulate it. Also, despite Minette's sweetness—it was clear every man present was smitten with her—he treated her with a coldness that veered frequently into disrespect, while at the same time looking jealous whenever another man was pleased with her company. If I hadn't known the assassins were trying to murder him as well, he'd have joined Amyot on my (admittedly short) list of suspects.

Though the carriages were already waiting, Philippe dallied, delaying our trip to the Louvre to no apparent purpose, until the sun peeked over the horizon. Though Louis's home was only a few hundred feet from the Palais, walking appeared to be out of the question—though not for the servants, of course. They arrived before we did; it took longer to wait for everyone to climb in and depart than it would have if we'd just gone on foot. Tom hurried to my side as I stepped out of the carriage, trying to get away from one of the bolder chambermaids who'd eyed my giant friend up and down and decided to "practizze herr Eeenglish."

To his dismay, I sent him back to the eyelash-fluttering girl. I had to, as the nobles separated from the servants again as we entered the Louvre. The place was stunning, a three-story palace in beige stone, encircled by grand pillars and exquisitely carved statues. Remembering who I was supposed to be, I tried not to gawk like the commoner I was, which was unfortunate, since I didn't get a chance to admire the view.

The *maître d'hôtel* hurried us along, chiding the duke for being late. Though I hadn't seen this attitude at Maison Chastellain, I'd noticed at the Palais that French servants were frequently rude to their masters. It was a bit shocking; in England, a tone like that would get one flogged.

The *maître* took us straight to the king's bedroom. The ladies waited in an antechamber while the gentlemen shuffled in. We huddled on one side of the room, which was dominated, as all noble French bedrooms seemed to be, by a massive four-poster bed, this one wide enough to sleep eight. A light, almost translucent blue curtain covered the canopy. Once we were inside, a servant drew it back so we could see Louis at rest. Then the attendant rang a chime, and the king sat up.

I admit I was curious to see what he looked like. The resemblance to Philippe was obvious—he had the same oval face, Roman nose, and full lips as the duke—but, though Louis didn't speak, he nonetheless seemed to possess a more pleasant, friendly manner than his brother. His servants brought him some bowls; he washed his face in one, nibbled fruits, meats, and pastries from the others, then dismissed them.

My master had always said politics bored him. I didn't think I'd ever fully grasped what that meant until now. I glanced around, and was surprised to see that everyone else was transfixed. I supposed on some level I could appreciate that—this *was* their king—but he wasn't *my* king, and, though he was unquestionably the most powerful man in France, in bedclothes he looked like any other man popping melon in his mouth. When we finally shuffled out of the room and rejoined our servants, I must have had a bemused sort of expression, because Tom smirked at me.

"Was it exciting, watching the king wake, monsieur?" he said.

"Like you wouldn't believe," I said.

"I want to hear everything, monsieur. Tell me what he did first."

"I'd really rather not."

"Did he open his eyes? Did he stretch? Did he yawn? Tell me he yawned."

"Will you stop, already?"

Tom looked wistful. "I wish I could watch a king sit up."

"Are you going to be like this all day?"

"This is France, monsieur," he said haughtily. "I can be as rude to you as I like."

Tom continued referring to me as "monsieur." I reminded him I had a whole box of poisons under my bed at the Palais. I also told him if he didn't stop calling me that, I'd take monsieur's privilege over *les serviteurs* and arrange a marriage between him and that overly eager chambermaid. He stopped.

After a few minutes to attend to any business, I had to leave Tom with the servants again. Now that the king had had his breakfast, the rest of us could have ours. We were ushered into a large chamber, where several plates of food waited on a long table. Everyone plucked what they liked from the spread while they talked, the women and men mostly separate.

Now that I had to actually interact with the crowd, I

started to get nervous. Besides Philippe—who I didn't *want* to talk to—I wasn't sure who anyone was. What's more, my need to investigate Amyot, or anyone else who might be in charge of the assassins, was tempered by the fact that I had no real idea how to speak to these people. It was all very well to sit in a carriage and pretend to be a baron. It was something else entirely to convince the jewels of French nobility I belonged among them. I'd practiced such conversations on the trip here, and, behind the curtains, I'd thought I'd sounded great. Now my brain stumbled over my words like a fool.

I was impressed to see Sally, once again, blending in perfectly well. She was surrounded by ladies who leaned in as she spoke, listening, eyes twinkling. Disconcertingly, every so often, they seemed to look speculatively over at me.

Inwardly, I groaned. I wished Simon were here. I should have asked him what to say to these people before I'd left Maison Chastellain. Now he was preparing to leave the city, once again leaving me all alone.

And then one of them decided to talk to *me*. A man in a gold-buttoned waistcoat drifted over and introduced himself as the marquis de Nogent-sur-Seine. "I heard the comte de Colmar made a scene this morning," he said.

Simon had told me the coin of the realm was gossip. Perhaps that was my way in. "Yes, monsieur," I said. "My fr—uh, my man cut his snake in two."

He laughed. "Oh, that was you. Well, good for you."

"Amyot said he'd make trouble for me."

The marquis waved his hand dismissively. "Pah. He's of the gown, not the sword." He looked at me curiously. "Which are you?"

". . . Marquis?"

"Your family."

My pulse quickened. I had no idea what he meant— and I got the feeling I should have. I tried to think of what to say.

Well, I *was* supposed to be an Ashcombe. So I guessed I'd have to be of the sword. "My grandfather is the warden to the King of England. He's been Charles's loyal general for decades."

That was apparently the right answer. The marquis nodded, satisfied. "You have the bearing of it," he said, and it took all I had to not stare at him like he was blind.

Another gentleman joined us, a friendly looking sort with a thin mustache. "Jean-Baptiste Colbert," he said with a nod.

Now I was even more nervous, because I recognized the name. Lord Ashcombe had mentioned the man to me before he left. *Jean-Baptiste Colbert is Louis's most trusted minister. If you need something done, you go to him.*

"I couldn't help but overhear," Colbert said. "You're from England? Are your estates near London?"

"Not far," I said warily. "Though I haven't been to the city for some time."

"Naturally, with the sickness. I wondered if you had news of it."

I suddenly felt an enormous sense of relief. This I *did* know, and better than anyone. Careful to leave myself out of it—Christopher Ashcombe wouldn't have been any-where near plague-infested London—I began to tell them of what had happened: of the comet and its ill portents, of the plague's coming and rise, of the terrible devastation it had wreaked upon our city. And as I spoke, the men around me began to gather.

I'd only intended to give them the barest news. But as the words spilled out of me, I felt a voice, almost a presence, inside, pushing me to tell them everything. I wanted them to know. I wanted them to hear our sorrow, and our pain; to hear of children hanging dead in their mothers' arms;

to recount the friends and family we'd lost. I wanted them to know who we were, the people: the courage I'd seen, the generosity, the sacrifice in the wake of the horror that was the plague. I talked, and I talked, and they listened in silence, and when I finished, they stayed that way, until one man finally broke the quiet.

CHAPTER

"SUCH A TERRIBLE THING."

I looked over . . . and saw the king. Louis himself had joined the crowd, risen and dressed in finery that outdid even his brother—though, on him, his frilled and ribboned clothes looked masculine and grand.

The king regarded me, his gaze inscrutable. "Welcome, Baron," he said. "The prayers of all of France have been with you and your people."

I felt the weight of everyone's eyes upon me. I had to respond, but what could I say? Wouldn't Louis, of all people, see through my fraud?

I remembered Lord Ashcombe's advice about kings—

be brief—but I also remembered something else he'd told me before we'd left England. *Louis's court flatters him shamelessly.*

And I heard another voice inside, my master's. *The Sun King. They call him the Sun King.*

I bowed with a flourish and held it. "Your Majesty. Your words touch my soul, and bring peace to a troubled city. Please know that the light of your radiance warms the hearts and hearths of all, even to the darkest corner of England."

Where on earth did that *come from?* I wondered. But it seemed to do the trick.

The tiniest smile appeared on Louis's lips. He nodded, slightly, in acknowledgement. Then he drifted away.

It was as if the very air in the room had changed. Over the next hour, nearly every man came to me and insisted I absolutely *must* dine with him and his family, it would be *such* an honor, and when was I available—perhaps tonight? Flustered, I desperately memorized everyone's names and told them all they were *so* kind, and of course I would be *delighted* to join them—though I was, sadly, already engaged this evening, I would return their invitations with haste.

Colbert watched from the side, looking amused and, when everyone had had their say, simply said, "If you need anything,

Baron, my door is open." And then, finally, I was alone. I wiped the sweat from my forehead and tried to quiet the fluttering in my guts. Now I *definitely* needed Simon's help.

But I'd done it. I'd convinced them I was one of their own. I wondered what my master was thinking. He'd never cared for politics, but I wasn't playing politics; I was here to find a killer. Would he be proud of me? I closed my eyes, and I thought I could see him smile.

As the gathering broke, Sally sidled up to me. "Everyone's talking about you," she said.

"They are?"

"The Sun King shined his light on you. You'd better prepare yourself; everyone's going to try to take advantage of that by manipulating you."

I kicked myself for being so naive. Of course they would. No wonder Master Benedict hated politics. No one ever said anything they meant.

"I guess I overdid it," I said glumly. "The ladies seem to like you a lot, too."

Sally regarded the departing girls with surprise. "Them? They despise me."

"What do you mean? They were hanging on your every word."

"Only because I was feeding them gossip."

"About what?"

"You, actually."

"Me?" That explained all the glances. "Wait . . . what did you say?"

"I told them about the snake, and Amyot. Plus I took some stories Lady Pemberton told me about her younger sister and put you in them. You're quite a cad."

"*What?*" I couldn't believe this. "Why would you do that?"

"Because now they want to know everything about you—and that keeps them talking to me, which they won't do otherwise. They loathe me, Christopher. To them, I'm just some backward country girl from a backward country. They rank me barely higher than a peasant. And they haven't been shy about letting me know it."

"How?"

"With oh-so-subtle remarks. My accent. My hair. My gown."

I was hardly an expert on fashion, but I thought she looked beautiful—distractingly so. "What's wrong with them?"

"Whatever they want to be wrong." She sighed. "You wouldn't understand."

"But . . . Lord Ashcombe said your title would give you status."

She laughed sadly. "You boys with your swords. You think they're so sharp. Nothing cuts deeper than a girl who wants to put you in your place. And highborn girls are the *worst*. They were kinder to me at the orphanage."

I wasn't entirely certain the men of Paris were all that different. I told her about the question I'd got—gown or sword?—and how I'd only answered it correctly by accident. "I still have no idea why."

"I do," Sally said. "And I think it's actually going to help us."

She leaned in to explain. "The aristocracy in France has two major classes. The *noblesse d'épée*—the nobles of the sword—were awarded their titles for serving the king in battle. The *noblesse de robe*—the nobles of the gown— got theirs through administrative service. The sword has contempt for the gown, and doesn't want them to have any power."

"I was told Amyot was of the gown."

"He is. But his wife *isn't*. And that's going to be our way in." Sally dropped her voice even further. "The comtesse's family is of the sword, so they have a lot of prestige, but they're penniless. Amyot's family is of the gown, but—"

"Wealthy," I guessed.

"*Incredibly* wealthy. So the comtesse's father arranged the marriage, trading his prestige for Amyot's money. Except Amyot turned out to be a fool, and he's squandered his inheritance already."

I stared at her. "Amyot needs money?"

"Desperately. The ladies say it's because of bad investments, shady business ventures with equally shady partners. That's what the snake was for, and why he's so angry Tom killed it. He's been trying to convince Louis to take it as a pet. If the king got one, then the whole court would have to get one, too, and Amyot would make a fortune."

"Why would the king want a bunch of venomous snakes in the Louvre?"

Sally shrugged. "I suppose that's why Amyot's poor now. Anyway, he's so deep in debt he's in danger of losing his estate."

My mind was racing. Was Amyot really behind this, after all? It seemed like madness for him to think he could put a snake under Minette's bed and not have suspicion fall on him. But if he was that desperate for money . . . and if he'd planned to remove the snake after it had done its job . . .

The Templars' treasure would solve every one of his problems. *Just like Philippe le Bel,* I thought, *all those centuries ago.*

"So how do we learn more?" I said. "Amyot clearly won't talk to us."

"No," Sally said. "But his wife might. You saw her this morning; she's humiliated by all this. And the other girls know how sad she is. So they pretend to be nice to her, even as they mock her behind her back. The comtesse knows she doesn't have any real friends, except for Minette, so she just wants to leave Paris and go home. But her husband won't leave, and Minette likes her; she doesn't want her to go, either. So the comtesse is stuck. And that gives me an opening. If I can talk to her, become friends, maybe I can find out more about her husband. See who these shady business partners are. Because maybe his business partners—"

"Are the assassins!" I said.

"Or hired them."

This was a *fantastic* plan. I'd been so worried about how I was going to navigate the aristocracy. It turned out Sally could do it instead—and with much more ease than me. "You really have a head for this sort of thing," I said.

She flushed, pleased. "I'll speak to the comtesse when we return to the Palais. In the meantime, the ladies are going to walk with the royal children in the Tuileries Garden. I'll see if they know anything else."

"All right," I said. "But . . . you're not going to make up any more stories about me, are you?"

"Of course I am," she said. "I haven't even got to the really good ones."

"That's not fair!"

She hid her laughter behind her hand. "We must all make sacrifices, my baron."

Sally hurried to join the ladies on their way to the garden. I rushed to Tom and told him what she'd discovered. With Sally on Amyot's trail, I could turn my mind away from court politics and back to what my master had taught me to do: solve riddles.

I pulled the paper with Voiture's poem from under my sash. Though I'd already memorized it, there was something about reading the actual words I found helpful.

King triumphant, man is burned
Fate brings forth a lesson learned.

King triumphant, man is soot
Path is followed underfoot.

King is broken, man remains
Answer hidden in the stains.

King is rotting, man upstart
Find the city's very heart.

And there, too, was Master Benedict's note: *Start at the beginning.*

The beginning of what? The poem? Where else would one start?

"Any ideas?" Tom said.

I sighed. "No." I was already trying to solve one riddle; did my master have to add to it by being so cryptic?

With no answers forthcoming, I suggested we have a look around the Louvre. After all, the threat wasn't just to Minette. The king and his family were in danger, too, so it stood to reason the assassins might make an attempt to kill someone here like they had in the Palais. Knowing the layout of the palace might be valuable.

There were plenty of guards, and plenty of guests,

and none of them seemed to mind that we wandered the halls. Like at the Palais, the Louvre was under renovation. I asked one of the workmen we encountered about it, and he explained that the old medieval palace where the king lived was being joined via a new wing to the more modern Palais des Tuileries. Beyond that was the magnificent private royal garden, where Sally had gone.

Also like the Palais-Royal, the Louvre was filled with art, though the collection put the Palais's offerings to shame. Every inch of wall seemed to be covered by grand masters. There were religious scenes, pastoral scenes, portraits: an angel visiting the Virgin; shepherds reading an inscription on a tomb; men and women long dead and gone, watching from on high like enthroned guards eternal. Even the ceilings abounded with masterpieces of illustration, details, and golden patterns. We walked the corridors, dazzled. I wondered what Master Benedict would have thought. He'd never been that interested in art, but if he'd seen this, I had to imagine he'd have changed his mind.

We left the Louvre proper and entered the Palais des Tuileries, heading toward the garden. As we did, my mind kept drifting back to Voiture's riddle, hoping to catch it unawares and reveal an answer. But, as we approached the Tuileries, no solution presented itself.

What do I do now, Master? I said in my head.

He didn't answer me. But maybe that was because he'd *already* answered me. *Start at the beginning,* he'd written.

All right. The beginning of what?

I thought about it. The only thing I knew so far was the poem. So . . . why not start at the beginning of that?

King triumphant. That had to be Philippe le Bel. He captures the last Templar grand master, Jacques de Molay: *man is burned.* And from this, *Fate brings forth a lesson learned.*

And that lesson is . . .

I frowned. "Did you hear that?" I could have sworn I'd heard shouting.

Tom was already looking around. We stopped, listened. The sound came again, faint, but growing louder.

Tom cocked his head. "I think it's coming from outside."

I went to the window, opened it. Now we heard it much more clearly. It was coming from the west, toward the Tuileries.

Someone was screaming in the garden.

CHAPTER
24

THEY WERE RUNNING.

We leaned out the window and watched the ladies of the court coming toward us. They ran as fast as they could, waving their arms. From a distance, it looked like they'd simply gone mad. Then as they came closer, I saw them.

Wasps.

The women were swatting at wasps. Their screams stretched from across the garden as they sprinted for safety, leaving bow-tied shoes behind in their wake.

Then came the swarm.

It was so thick, it looked like a cloud. It wavered, undulating, then swooped forward, a living thing, hunting for prey.

Sally. Sally was out there. And Minette. And the queen. And their children.

We ran. Tom and I sprinted through the palace, looking for a staircase down. I shouted at the startled nobles, servants, everyone we could see. "Cloaks! Tablecloths! Blankets! Hurry!"

The screams led us to the nearest exit. Ladies had already begun to pile through the door, sprawling on the floor, gowns ripping as they fell. Several were crying, covered in angry red welts swelling as large as grapes.

The wasps came with them. The men that had followed us swiped and swatted at the buzzing insects with whatever came to hand: lace-trimmed cushions, gilded plates, silver trays.

Tom had a better idea. He yanked a giant painting of a woman with a mirror from the wall—it might have been a Titian—and swung it like a board. Wasps bounced off the canvas as I ran to the door and scanned the fleeing crowd.

I racked my brain for something in my apothecary sash that might get rid of wasps, but I had nothing better than my cloak. The sugar and saltpeter could make smoke, but, as I'd learned one painful afternoon with Master Benedict, smoke only calms bees.

I squeezed through a gap of fleeing girls to stand outside, sweeping my cloak like a flag. A vicious buzzing snarled in my ear, and I felt the sharp jab of a needle in my shoulder. I slapped it, and heard the crunch of shell. Wasp guts smeared on my palm.

"Christopher!"

It was Sally. She was holding up an older woman who staggered toward us with a bundle in her arms. The woman's face had swollen grotesquely, her face and neck marked with stings.

Shoulder burning, I ran toward them, whirling my cloak. I got a pair of burning needles between my shoulder blades in return. The woman collapsed, her face hitting the stones, one hand clutching at her neck. Sally toppled with her. The woman's head turned to the side on the grass, eyes staring sightlessly into the distance.

"The child!" Sally shouted. She tugged at the woman's arm, trying to turn her over. "The *child*!"

Then I remembered. The bundle. The woman had been carrying a bundle. We rolled her onto her side, and beneath her, swaddled in thick cloth, was a boy, no more than one year old, howling in terror.

Sally scooped him up, covering him once more with the cloth. I gave her my own cover, throwing my cloak over her head as we ran for the door. Tom, who'd followed me outside, swung the Titian back and forth in wide arcs as we passed, batting down the buzzing horde that chased us. As soon as we were through, he leaped in behind and slammed the door.

Sally ran to the nearest table and removed the cloth from the squalling child. The boy screamed uncontrollably. Sally stripped him, looking for welts, but it looked like the woman who'd carried him had saved him from any stings—at the cost of her own life.

"Minette," I said to Sally. "And the queen. Where are they?"

"They went the other way around," she said, and I heard raised voices coming through the adjoining rooms. I followed them and saw with relief that both women had made it inside safely. Each of them had a few welts, but apart from a little hysteria, neither seemed in any further danger.

The queen found her son, the young *dauphin*, bawling but safe in that room, and fussed over him, along with the other ladies of the court who'd recovered from their fright. Minette ran to Sally and grasped her own crying child. She held him to her breast, chest heaving, then ran farther inside. The rest of the women, and most of the men, followed them. Sally moved to join them before I stopped her.

"What happened?" I said.

"I'm not sure," she said. "We were just walking in the garden when a chambermaid ran from the bushes, screaming. Then it was just . . . wasps. Everywhere. Everyone panicked. I lost sight of the duchess, so I went for her son. Marie-Hélène—the nursemaid—she bundled up the boy. She was terrified; she said the stings would be poison to him: He'd been stung once before and nearly died. Is she . . . ?"

I shook my head. "She's gone."

Sally looked deflated. "I have to go tell the duchess."

"Tell the servants to find some vinegar first," I said. "You can use it on the stings; it'll help with the pain and swelling."

She nodded her thanks and went, leaving Tom and me standing among the remaining shaken survivors. Tom was squinting—his left eyebrow had begun to swell—and he was rubbing the stings on his arms.

My own shoulder and back were absolutely burning. "Are you all right?" I said.

Tom nodded, pressing gingerly on his eyebrow. "Have you ever heard of a wasp attack in November?"

"No," I said. "I think we'd better have a look in the garden."

CHAPTER

25

WE STOPPED ONLY FOR ME TO SEND
Tom down to the kitchen for some vinegar of our own. I
poured it on a cloth and covered Tom's stings. He slumped
in relief as it soothed his skin, then returned the favor,
pressing the cloth against my back, under my shirt. The
pain began to cool as we walked into the Tuileries.

I shook my head. If I'd been here an hour ago, I'd have
called the garden paradise. Terraces led away in all directions,
surrounding gardens bordered by low boxwood hedges, with
flower beds shaped brilliantly into sweeping curled designs.
Where the paths crossed, fountains trickled water from
mineral-crusted spouts, splashing misty rainbows in the sun.

But the beauty of the garden was marred. The nurse-maid who'd saved the young prince by swaddling him lay twisted on the ground. A pair of men, standing there helplessly, had turned her on her back, revealing again her grotesquely swollen face. Her mouth hung open, and her tongue puffed out between her lips. We looked away.

"What did that?" Tom said, horrified.

"The wasps," I said.

"How many stung her?"

I shrugged. "Might have been a hundred, might have just been one. It wouldn't have made a difference. There are people for whom harmless things are poison. A wasp sting that merely hurts you or me will kill them. That's why she was worried about the prince; Sally said he'd nearly died from being stung before. It's not just insects, either. Even something like strawberries can be poison to the wrong person."

That struck a nerve; Tom loved strawberries. *"What?"*

I told him a story of Richard III, king of England nearly two hundred years ago. "Strawberries were his poison. He used them, once, to get rid of an enemy, Lord Hastings. Richard secretly ate some before an audience with the man. When he broke out in a rash, he accused Hastings of putting a curse on him. They dragged the poor baron away and cut off his head."

Tom seemed shaken that food could be deadly. "Don't tell me such things."

As we walked on, both of us kept an eye on the skies, but it appeared the attackers had all been driven off. We followed a trail of crushed wasps to the far side of the Tuileries, where a bearded gardener wearing heavy gloves was lighting an oil-soaked torch.

"Have a care, monsieur," he said. "There's a wasp's nest."

Standing a healthy distance back, I peered through the trees. I could just see the gray honeycomb paper of the nest on the ground behind one of them.

"I know France is warmer than England," I said to the gardener, "but is it normal for wasps to be alive this close to winter?"

"No, monsieur, very strange." He looked troubled—and more than a little scared. "I don't know where this nest came from."

"Did you knock it from the tree?"

"No, monsieur. It must have fallen on its own, when Her Majesty and her guests walked by."

I looked up. I was no expert on wasps, but I couldn't see

any scraps of nest paper, or anything to suggest it had ever been attached to that tree. I remembered what Sally had been told: stings were poison to the prince.

The gardener was right to be scared. He'd be punished for this; allowing a wasp's nest to grow in the middle of the king's garden was the height of incompetence. Except I'd bet every *louis* in my coin purse that that nest *hadn't* grown here. The assassin had to have placed it here, knowing the queen, the duchess, and their guests would walk with their sons through the Tuileries this morning.

This was another attempt on their family. This time, Minette's baby was the target. Once again, it had been designed to look like an accident.

And, once again, I'd failed to stop it.

I stood there, overwhelmed with despair. Adding more guards to the kitchen staff hadn't slowed down the assassins in the slightest. They'd just found other methods to try.

I thought of all those poisons tucked away in the cherry box hidden in my room. Perhaps the killers couldn't slip arsenic into the royal drink anymore, or add Japanese fugu to the stew. But what if they discovered something like urare? They wouldn't even need to go near the kitchen. They could just coat a pin with the poison and pierce it through the bottom of a chair. All Minette would have to do is *sit*, and everything would be over.

The gardener put the nest to the torch. The paper crackled. Ash floated in charred fragments, buffeted by rising smoke.

"Come on," I said to Tom.

"Where are we going?" he said.

"Into the city."

"The city? Where?"

I shook my head. "I really wish I knew."

We stopped at the Palais-Royal first. Minette and her retinue had returned home immediately, and I wanted to see that everyone—especially Sally—was all right before I went into the city. I found her already on her way out, having changed her gown into a less formal dress. She looked tired.

"One of the ladies died," she said. "Minette has locked herself in her bedchamber with her son and only her closest ladies-in-waiting. I think they're going to stay there all day."

I was glad for it. Staying locked up would keep them safe for the moment—unless, of course, someone poisoned their food. "Did you find the comtesse?"

Sally shook her head. "She's gone into the city. After

this morning's humiliation, she didn't want to be here when the girls came back."

"We're going into the city, too," I said. "I want to look around. I need . . ." I threw my arms up. "I don't know what I need."

"You're stuck on Voiture's riddle?"

"I feel like it has something to do with Paris," I said. "But I don't *know* Paris. Master Benedict always said that when you couldn't find an answer, you should step aside and let your mind find the answer for you. So that's what I'll do: wander around and hope something comes to me."

Sally traced a finger along the lace on her sleeve. "Can I walk with you for a while?"

"Always," I said. "You don't have to ask."

"There's somewhere I want to go."

"All right." I looked at her, curious. "What is it you want to see?"

She bit her lip. "My family."

CHAPTER

WE TOOK THE STREETS HEADING

east. The roads were packed as usual, carriages jamming the lanes. As nobles, Sally and I had the right to walk on the higher part of the slope in the road, Tom leading the way as our guard, avoiding the sewage in the central gutter where the commoners had to tread. Though there was no getting away from the smell.

Sally's declaration had been a surprise, to say the least. She'd arrived at the Cripplegate orphanage when she was eight, after her parents had died on a merchant voyage back to France. "I didn't realize you had any family left," I said.

"I don't, in England," she said. "My only relatives are here."

"Who are they?"

"My father had an older brother, Gaston. My grandfather died, so Gaston runs his business, but I was told my grandmother really rules the family." She chewed nervously on a fingernail. "I'm named after her."

"Have you met them before?" Tom asked.

"No. They . . . weren't very happy with my father when he left. He said once that they were angry he'd married my mother." She shook her head. "I'm not even sure they're still living in the old house. The masters at Cripplegate sent a letter there when I came, but they said they never heard back from either my grandmother or my uncle. I'm just hoping I'll find someone who lives nearby to tell me what happened to them."

Sally knew her father's old house was in the northeastern part of town called le Marais—the Swamp—because that part of the city had once been swampland, drained, in a curious coincidence, by the Templars, over four hundred years ago. The street her father's family had once lived on was Rue des Deux Portes. There had been a sign over the door, her father had told her, of a jewel and a mountain.

As we trekked there, I began to wonder if the reason the Cripplegate masters' letter had never reached Sally's family wasn't because they'd moved, but because the courier had never found the house at all. We asked a passing ink-seller where to find Rue des Deux Portes.

"Which one?" he said. "There's five of them."

The layout of the streets was beyond confusing. Most were unmarked, and several had exactly the same name. Like London, most of Paris's roads twisted and turned in medieval alleys darkened by the houses overhead, the upper stories stretching so far forward that they almost touched at the gable. We wandered for nearly an hour, trying to spot some mark that might guide us, or someone who could tell us where to go, without any luck.

Like yesterday, Bridget followed us, flying overhead, then disappearing for minutes at a time. I saw her fly toward a tall, square tower in the distance, with four round turrets at each corner, before she returned, swooping down to land at my feet. I picked her up and stroked her feathers. "I don't suppose you know where we're going?" I said.

She gave me an inquisitive coo.

Sally said nothing, but I could tell she was growing ever

more disappointed. "Let's just forget it," she said finally.

"No, come on," I said. "We're already here. Look, you ask that old woman, and I'll ask that man there. Someone who's lived here for years is bound to know who we're talking about."

Sally walked away without enthusiasm. I made to go to the man. But it was Tom who grabbed my arm. "Christopher."

"What is it?"

"I think I found them."

"Really?" I scanned the signs that hung above the shops, looking for the jewel and mountain.

"No," Tom said. "There."

He pointed down the street to a small patch of dirt between the roads. A pair of children sprawled on it, rolling a ball of knotted string back and forth. For a moment, I had no idea what he'd spotted. Then I got a closer look at the girl.

She was around eight years old. She was dressed in a simple smock of green, auburn curls tumbling over her shoulders. Her skin was pale, her slightly upturned nose dusted with freckles.

The resemblance was eerie. My mind flashed back to one Christmas in Cripplegate, where I'd cared for a similar young girl, nearly dying of the flux. "Sally!" I shouted.

She turned back. I pointed. Like me, at first she seemed puzzled. Then she froze.

Slowly, she approached the girl. The child looked up to see who was coming, shielding her eyes from the sun. Then she jumped to her feet, astonished.

They stood there, as if gazing into some strange mirror of time. "Who are you?" the girl said, her mouth hanging open.

"I'm . . . Sara-Claire," Sally said. I looked at her, just as astonished. "Sara-Claire Deschamps. My father was Nicolas Deschamps."

The girl stared at Sally in wonder. "You're my cousin!" She reached up and poked Sally in the cheek, as if to prove to herself that the girl before her was real.

"Do you live around here?" Sally said.

Without a word, the girl bolted into the street, weaving nimbly through the traffic. We hurried after her, bumping our way between carriages.

I translated what she'd said for Tom as we ran. He was as surprised as I'd been. "Did you know her real name was Sara-Claire?" he whispered.

I shook my head. I'd only ever known her as Sally. Still,

I understood why she'd kept it a secret. Sally was English—or at least half-English; her mother was from London—but, as Simon had said, growing up French in an English school wouldn't be fun. Cripplegate was bad enough; I couldn't imagine the nightmare it would have been with a foreign name.

The girl led us to a house, four stories high. A sign hung over the doorway, the one we'd been searching for: a jewel and a mountain. The girl flung the door open and ran inside, shouting. "*Mamie! Mamie!* It's your granddaughter! I mean, it's *another* granddaughter!"

Sally hesitated at the threshold. Her cousin ran back and grabbed Sally's hand. "Come see *Mamie!*"

She dragged us into a well-appointed parlor before bolting for the street again, slamming the front door behind her. The parlor's ceiling had been painted to look like the sky: aquamarine, with puffy white clouds. They led all the way to the window, merging with the real Paris sky outside.

A velvet-cushioned chair sat by the blue-and-white-tiled fireplace. Behind it stood three girls, two of them a year or two older than me, the third considerably younger. They all looked strangely familiar, like altered copies of Sally. But it was the woman in the chair who drew my gaze.

After three years visiting patients with Master Benedict,

I saw the signs immediately. On the right side of her face, the woman's mouth drooped, as did her eyelid, with a sag visible in the cheek. The fingers of her right hand, resting in her lap, were curled inward; her left held an ornately carved silver cane. At some point in the past, this woman had suffered a stroke.

Yet it was just as clear that the apoplexy hadn't touched her mind. She scanned us with intent, and when her eyes met mine, I saw a clarity, a sharpness, that told of an even sharper brain behind. Sally's father had said this woman had ruled over the family; I had no doubt that was true.

Madame Deschamps, aging queen of her home, looked Sally up and down as her granddaughters stared at their newfound cousin. After a moment, the old woman raised her silver cane, pointed its head at Sally, then pointed at the couch in front of her. *Sit.*

Sally obeyed the silent command. Madame regarded her for a moment more before rapping the table between them. The older girls behind her ran from the parlor, returning with fruit and pastries. The woman waved her cane over the plates. *Eat.*

Sally took a pastry, flaky dough filled with fresh cream, and nibbled on it. "Thank you," she said.

The woman nodded, then raised her cane. *Talk.*

And Sally did. She told of life in England—not of the orphanage, but of the time before. Of her father. She told of his arms, strong and loving, and his voice, just the same, and of days in his shop and nights by the fire and all those things she no longer had, all those things I'd never had, until Master Benedict had rescued me from a life of nothing. Standing with Tom in the hall, I remained silent, listening as intently as her grandmother did.

A poke on my arm interrupted me. When I turned, I found a boy of about eleven with a somewhat sour expression.

"Are you English?" he asked.

Though darker in complexion, he also had a faint resemblance to Sally; another cousin. A smaller boy, probably two years younger, stood behind him.

"Yes, I'm English," I said.

"Do you eat cows alive?"

I must have translated that wrong. "What did you say?"

"Cows. Do you eat them while they're still alive?"

I wasn't even sure how to answer that. "Of course not. Why would you ask such a thing?"

"Our father says Englishmen"—he used the French slur for Englishmen, *les goddons*—"eat cows and pigs while they're still alive. And that you eat chickens whole, without even plucking their feathers; you just grease them and stuff them down your gullets."

"I think your father's having a little fun with you," I said. "No one in England does anything like that."

"Uh-huh." He didn't sound like he believed me. "Are you married to Sara-Claire?"

It took me a second to remember he was referring to Sally. "No."

"What do you do?"

"I'm an—" I caught myself. "I'm the Baron of Chillingham."

"Uh-huh." He didn't seem impressed by that, either.

The younger boy piped up. "Our father's a silversmith."

"Is he? That's interesting."

"Do you want to see his work?"

"Sure," I said, more to be agreeable than out of any real curiosity. I turned to Tom. "I'll be back. You'll stay with Sally?"

He nodded, and the boys took me through the house to a second parlor. There they opened a chest of drawers and began pulling pieces from inside. They laid them on top of the chest as I examined them.

They were very well made. There was jewelry: rings,

bracelets, necklaces, some with stones inlaid. But there were also larger ornamental and functional pieces: a box, a cup, a knife. Several had been engraved with a particular, ornate pattern of swirls and loops, the same design I'd seen on Sally's grandmother's cane.

"These are excellent," I said.

"Of course they are," the older boy said.

I did my best not to roll my eyes and returned to examining the pieces. The younger boy wanted to show me the detail inside the box. But something much more interesting suddenly caught my attention.

CHAPTER
27

I PICKED UP ONE OF THE NECK-
laces the boys had laid out. Hanging from the chain was a
silver cross, flared at the ends, all four arms of equal length.

"That's a Templar cross," the younger boy said.

I turned it over in my fingers. "Your father makes these?"

"He sells them to travelers who come searching for treasure," the older boy said, a slight note of contempt in his voice.

I looked at him. "People come here searching for treasure?"

"Not here. At the old Templar headquarters."

"Where's that?"

"Did you see the tower to the north?" When I nodded,
the boy said, "That's where they used to be. People go there

searching for treasure all the time. Father says they're fools." He eyed me shrewdly as I stared at the cross. "Do you want that? I can sell it to you."

"How much?" I said.

"Three *louis*."

Even if I'd been naive enough not to know that was outrageously high, the shocked look on his younger brother's face would have given the game away. Regardless, I didn't need the cross; I'd already learned something more interesting.

"Maybe another time," I said. "I should return to my friends."

When I got back to the parlor, Sally was still talking to her grandmother, who sat without saying a word. Tom, not able to understand the language, was studying the room instead. He spied something over in the corner.

A little girl, no more than four years old, had poked her head from around the couch. She stared up in awe and fear at Tom, who was nearly three times her height. Tom curled his finger, beckoning her closer.

She looked toward her older sisters, trying to decide if it was safe or not. Slowly, hesitantly, she stepped forward. Just as slowly, Tom leaned down and reached toward her.

Her eyes widened. She lifted her arms, as if about to ward him off. But she let him slip his hands around her chest, and he picked her up.

She drew in a breath as she rose. Eye to eye, she stared at him. Suddenly, Tom winked—and flipped her upside down.

She gasped. Her dress slipped up, exposing her petticoat, but she didn't care. She looked down at the ground in wonder, then up. Slowly, she placed one bare foot against the painted sky, then another, until she was standing on the ceiling. Tom moved, and she began to walk, and suddenly she was screaming in delight.

"*Je marche sur le ciel! Je marche sur le ciel!*" She thrust her arms above her head—below her head, rather—and shouted to her sisters. "*Je suis la reine du ciel!*" I'm the queen of the sky!

Her sisters giggled, and the youngest, about six years old, ran forward. She tugged on Tom's shirt. "*Moi aussi! Moi aussi!*"

"Put her down."

The voice came from the doorway. We turned to see a man with strong arms and a ruddy face glaring at Tom. The girl who'd led us here stood behind him, somewhat breathless.

Tom didn't understand the words, but the tone was

unmistakable. He put the girl down. She ran behind the chair where her grandmother sat silently.

Sally stood. The man—who could only be Sally's uncle, Gaston—turned his glare to her. "What are you doing here?" he said.

The girl who'd run to get him began to answer. "I told you, this is our cousin—"

"I know who she is. What do you want?"

"Nothing," Sally said, taken aback. "I just came to—"

"Are you looking for money?"

"No, I—"

"Or maybe you want a place to stay?" Gaston said. "I wrote to your orphanage very clearly: No one wants you here. There's no room in this house for your father's shame."

Sally went pale.

"Do you have any idea how much pain Nicolas caused our mother when he left?" He waved at the old woman, who sat still without a word. "How she begged him not to go? How she cried for him every night? But he cared nothing for her, for us, for his family. Only for that *goddon* tramp."

Sally flinched, as if he'd hit her.

"Well, he made his choice," Gaston said. "So go back to England, go stay where you belong. Never come here again."

He stood aside. Pale as a ghost, Sally walked past him, her eyes on the ground.

We followed her out. The girls seemed crestfallen, the younger boy looked sad. Only the older boy looked smug.

Sally stood in the road, staring into the distance. Neither Tom nor I knew what to say. She took a breath. It rattled in her chest.

"It's all right," she said, her voice light. "I knew . . . *Papa* told me . . . I shouldn't have come."

She turned away. Then, behind us, the door opened.

It was her grandmother. The old woman came toward her, leaning heavily on her cane, struggling with every step. Her right foot slid across the ground. Sally watched, face inscrutable, as the woman approached.

Gaston appeared in the door. "*Maman! Maman!* Come inside immediately."

The old woman stopped. She didn't quite turn. Just a shift of the head, the faintest hint of a look backward. But Gaston went red and slammed the door.

Madame returned to her granddaughter. Then the old woman waved her gnarled hand at her home. The gesture was simple, but within it seemed a great many words. *It's no longer my house. He's the master there now.*

Sally nodded. "I understand. I'm sorry. I never meant to cause you pain."

The old woman tapped her chest with her fist. *No more pain. Only love.*

Sally trembled now. Still leaning on her cane, her grandmother reached up and, with great difficulty, pulled a silver chain hanging around her neck from beneath her dress. She looked over at Tom and tugged at it. He didn't move, and she pulled again, more insistently.

"I think she wants you to help her take it off," I said quietly.

Obediently, Tom reached behind her neck and undid the clasp. The ends of the chain slipped down and dangled over the woman's fingers. Again she looked at Tom and thrust her hand toward Sally.

Tom understood this time. Sally lifted her hair as Tom fastened the chain around her neck.

Sally looked down. There was a small silver medallion on the end of the chain. On its face was a man, a thick wooden staff in one hand. I recognized it easily, for the figure inside was my namesake. Saint Christopher, patron saint of travelers.

The old woman brought her gnarled hand to her mouth

and kissed her fingertips. Hand shaking, she reached forward. With her thumb, she drew a cross on Sally's forehead.

Then she spoke. She struggled, and her words came out slurred, but we heard every one.

"*Le sang . . . de mon sang,*" she whispered. "*Je . . . te . . . bénis.*" Blood of my blood. I bless you.

That was when Sally broke. She collapsed on the flagstones, weeping at her grandmother's feet. The old woman placed her hand on Sally's head and gently stroked her curls.

Tom and I moved a discreet distance away, to give them their privacy. When Sally finally came to us, we were waiting in the warmth of a blacksmith's forge.

Sally's eyes were red and puffy, but her color had returned. She wore her new necklace, rubbing the Saint Christopher medallion absently between her thumb and forefinger. When she spoke, she sounded like the weight of the world had been taken from her shoulders. "Where to now?"

I pointed north, to the square tower with the four turrets. "See that? Your cousins told me it belonged to the Templars. It was their dungeon, here in Paris."

"Do you think we could see inside it?"

"I don't know," I said. "But they said the old church is still standing. Apparently, treasure hunters go there a lot. I figured we'd have a look—unless either of you have a better idea?"

Neither did, so we made our way through the twisting streets, using the distant tower as a guide. Saint Mary's—the old Templar church—lay north of the giant tower, with a second, smaller tower north of that.

The church, built in the classic medieval Gothic style, was beautiful. Constructed of heavy stone, the entrance on the west was capped by a pointed arch. Inside, the nave was filled with colors that splashed through the stained-glass windows high above. From there, the church opened into a grand, two-floor round, with a circular gallery above supported by six giant pillars. Beyond that stretched the chancel and the altar, with a staircase to the south that led to the bell tower.

We stood in the round, gawking up at the gallery. "I wonder if we're allowed up there," I said.

"That depends," a voice said in accented English. "Are you a servant, or an enemy?"

CHAPTER

WE TURNED. AN OLD PRIEST STOOD in front of the stairs to the bell tower, watching us.

"What do you mean, enemy?" I said.

He held up a hand in apology. "I meant no offense, monsieur. But you are treasure hunters, yes?"

I glanced at my friends, surprised. "How did you know that?"

"My son, I've been a priest at Saint Mary's for forty-seven years. I've seen countless young lords and ladies like yourselves come searching. Every one of them stands there, in the round, and wonders what's hidden up above."

"What *is* hidden up above?" Sally said.

He smiled. "Nothing but pretty windows, I'm afraid."

"If you knew we were treasure hunters," I said, "why would you think we'd be your enemy?"

"Not *my* enemy. The Templars'. Because of the prophecy."

I'd had more than enough of prophecy this year. "Do you mean the thing about the princes of the blood? 'Until the time'?"

"No," he said. "That's Molay's curse. The knight's prophecy tells of *who* will find the treasure—or at least discover where the Templars sent it. You don't know of it?" He seemed surprised.

"We're new at this," I said.

"Then you have much to learn." He bowed. "I wish you good luck in your search."

"Wait." I stopped him. "I don't suppose you could tell us more about it."

"Sometimes I show guests around, when I have the time," he said. "But things are very busy at the moment. There are many poor in this parish, and collections have been low of late."

He wasn't being very subtle. Still, Lord Ashcombe had given me a coin purse for a reason, and this was as good a reason as any.

I wasn't sure how much to give him, so I decided to err on the high side. If this priest had been here long enough to recognize treasure hunters by sight, I wagered he had lots of good stories. I dropped a handful of coins into his palm: three gold *louis*, three silver *écus*, and a dozen *sou*.

He blinked. "Well, then." He called over the boy who'd been scrubbing the floor of the chancel and gave him the coins. "Put these in the strongbox immediately."

The boy's eyes widened, too, and I realized that I'd *far* overestimated how much of a donation he'd been expecting. Still, it appeared it paid off, because the priest straightened his cassock and said, "I think this deserves the grand tour."

His name was Father Bernard. He took us up to the gallery first, where we discovered he'd told the truth: We got a lovely view of the stained glass above and the marble floor below, but I couldn't see anything that might point to where the Templars had taken their treasure.

"You wouldn't," Father Bernard said. "The round was the original temple, built when the order first drained the swamp. That was in the 1100s, well before the treasure was even a question. The rest of the church was added some hundred years later, long before Molay came to Paris."

"What was that prophecy you mentioned?" I said.

"Do you know the story of the twelve, who crept from the city before the Templars were arrested?" When we nodded, he said, "Philippe le Bel tortured one of the knights who was captured. The only thing the man ever said was this: that the treasure could only be found by someone who was either the Templars' servant, or their enemy."

I could hear the skepticism in his voice. "You don't believe it."

"I don't put much stock in prophecy."

"That's an unusual view for a priest."

He laughed. "I believe there are prophets. I just don't think we've seen a real one since John's Revelation. Besides, it doesn't make sense. Wherever the Templars sent their treasure, that's where it is. What possible difference could the intent of the discoverer make? You either find it, or you don't. Come, I'll show you the grounds."

Father Bernard grabbed a set of keys from behind the doorway to the bell tower and took us outside. "So you don't believe there's a prophecy," I said, "but you do still think there's a treasure?"

"Oh, unquestionably. We know for a fact that Molay brought one with him, and that it had already disappeared by the time le Bel tried to confiscate it. The question is: Which one of the five escaped knights had it when he fled?"

"Five?" Tom said. "I thought nine escaped."

The old priest shook his head. "You see? That's what I'm talking about. All this mysticism wrapped around something so ordinary. Nine knights founded the Templars, so *of course* nine knights must have escaped. Except that's not true.

"Yes, twelve knights left under cover of darkness, traveling in all directions of the compass. And yes, three were caught almost immediately, leaving nine. But what people always omit from the story is that, over the next several months, *four more* knights were caught in various places around Europe. Subtract those, and you see that only five actually escaped."

"Do we know where they went?" I said.

Father Bernard nodded. "If you think of the knights traveling away from Paris as a circle moving outward, then noting the directions the captured knights were going allows you to identify the gaps in that circle. Of the five who escaped, one went south, to Spain. Two went eastward: one up to the Netherlands, the other down to the Swiss cantons. One went north, reportedly to England, though whether he stopped there or traveled on to Scotland isn't known. As for the fifth knight, the legends say he traveled westward by ship and made it all the way to the New World."

Tom frowned. "Wasn't that before the New World existed?"

"Well, it *existed*. We just hadn't discovered it yet."

"Could a ship from that time have made it that far?" Sally said.

The priest shrugged. "Stranger things have happened." He turned to face the grounds. "All this belonged to the Templars, though most of what they built has been torn down. The only things that remain are Saint Mary's, the storeroom over there, the hospital, and the two towers." He pointed to the shorter, squatter tower to the north. "That's called Caesar's Tower; it was the original Templar dungeon. Then, in the mid 1200s, they built the new Great Tower." He nodded to the square tower with the turrets and jingled his keys. "Come, I'll take you."

"We're going in the *dungeon*?" Tom said.

Father Bernard smiled. "It hasn't been a dungeon for years. Louis prefers to house his 'guests' in the Bastille."

"Then what's inside it?" I asked.

"Nothing, really. We use it for storage sometimes, but otherwise it's empty."

The Great Tower was even more intimidating up close. It stood over 150 feet high, with heavily barred windows dug into the stone at each of the tower's four floors. The central tower was square, fifty feet a side, with a crenellated rampart and a lookout post. At each corner was another circular tower, capped with a cone-shaped roof. Banners of royal blue fluttered from the spires, emblazoned with the fleur-de-lis, the royal emblem of France.

Father Bernard unlocked the door and ushered us in. The space inside was dark and musty, with very little light coming through the windows, which were barely more than arrow slits. The priest lit a torch, and the orange flame brightened the space.

We were in the tower's great hall. A massive pillar stretched upward in the center, stone ribs branching out to support the upper floors. I craned to see into the darkness for a moment, before my gaze was drawn to the carvings on the walls.

Between the windows, carved directly into the stone, were panels depicting the history of the Templars, each one engraved with Latin. The panel in front of me showed nine knights kneeling before a king. The king's hand was raised in blessing. The sun shined its light down on them. In the middle of the sun was a Templar cross, faint flecks of gold still painted on its surface.

I read the words above.

COMMILITONES CHRISTI TEMPLIQUE

DEO ET HOMINIBUS BENEDICTI

"The Order of the Templars," Father Bernard said. "Blessed by God and man."

The next panel showed two knights in front of a domed temple. "The Dome of the Rock," the priest said. "The Templars' first headquarters, above the ruins of the Temple of Solomon."

There were many more panels beyond. Father Bernard waved at them and said, "The story of the Templars continues all around—most of it, at least. But if you'd like to gaze upon something special, I'll show you what few treasure hunters have ever seen."

CHAPTER

HE TOOK US TO A SPIRAL STAIR-
case in one of the turrets. Yet instead of taking us up, he
led us down, into the earth.

The torch illuminated the space. The same kind of panels were carved into these walls, with items stacked here
and there: boxes, crates, some rolled-up tapestries. Under
normal circumstances, I'd have thought this a simple storeroom. Except all around us were dungeon cells, enclosed
with thick iron bars.

"Molay's prison," Father Bernard said.

I stared in awe. "This is where they kept him?"

"And several other knights as well. Though there were very few left by the time of Molay's death."

He led us into one of the larger cells. The door creaked on rusty iron hinges, and for one terrifying moment I thought it would lock us in. I could almost feel the presence of spirits, of the knights held here all those years, victims of the Iron King's greed.

"Before the Templars were imprisoned," Father Bernard said, "this tower was where they secured their treasure."

"Where did they keep it?" Sally said.

"Right here. If the treasure were here now, you'd be knee deep in it."

"They kept their treasure in their dungeon?" Tom said.

"What safer place for it? No one could get in. And—as the seven-year imprisonment of all those knights proved—if someone did manage to get in, they'd never be able to break out."

I stared around me, as if I wished hard enough, the treasure would suddenly appear. "Did they really leave a single florin to taunt Philippe?" I said.

"They did. As they leave florins for every French king upon coronation."

"So . . . the coin was in this room?"

He looked amused. "Move your foot."

I did and looked down. I saw I'd been standing on a small circle with a mark inside. I knelt to find the mark was a Templar cross.

"Behold where it all started," Father Bernard said. "The fall of the Templars, and later, the house of le Bel. That spot marks the actual location of the Iron King's florin. The legend says that God, angered by the treatment of His chosen knights, burned the imprint of the coin into the stone itself, so no man would doubt His wrath."

Tom's eyes went wide. "Really?"

Father Bernard chuckled. "That's the story. It's far more likely that one of the imprisoned knights carved it into the floor while he was held here. To keep their spirits up, and remind them what they must never let le Bel know. And they told him nothing, despite the terrible torture to which the Iron King subjected them."

"So Molay only pretended to confess to stop the torture?" Sally said.

"Masters of misdirection to the last."

I looked up at Father Bernard. "Someone else described the Templars in the exact same way."

"They were the best at it," he agreed. "Though their

penchant for misdirection didn't serve Molay this time. Unless, of course, he *wanted* to die."

"What do you mean?"

"It was well known le Bel had a terrible temper. When he realized Molay's false confession made him look the fool, he was livid. Despite his own advisors begging him not to act hastily, the Iron King ordered Molay to the stake at once. Molay had to know his trick would provoke the king. Especially since he'd seen his temper before. Look at this."

He held the torch near one of the panels, which had been damaged. It looked like the scene had once depicted the unearthing of some kind of treasure from deep below the city of Jerusalem. I could see the Dome of the Rock above, and the sun with the Templar cross inside shining over it. The rest of the panel showed three knights below-ground, lifting a large container. Most of what they were carrying had been hacked away from the stone. What remained looked like part of an angel statue.

"What happened to this?" I said.

"The Iron King got angry," the priest said. "The Templars had left him that florin, but it wasn't the only thing they'd left him. When Philippe arrived, underneath this panel, one of the knights had carved the words *non erit tibi hoc.*"

I translated. "This shall never be yours."

"When he saw it, le Bel flew into a rage. He hacked the words from the stone with his own sword. Broke the weapon in two, or he'd have kept at it until the whole tower fell down."

Sally asked Father Bernard a question, but I didn't hear it. Something the priest had said had finally begun to register in my brain.

He'd shown us the spot on which le Bel had found the florin. *Behold where it all started. The fall of the Templars, and later, the house of le Bel.*

I stared at the broken panel and thought of what my master had said.

Start at the beginning.

I pulled the poem from beneath my sash. I read it, just the first verse.

King triumphant, man is burned
Fate brings forth a lesson learned.

"Father Bernard?" I said.

"Yes?"

"Do you know where Jacques de Molay was burned?"

The priest looked surprised at the question, but he nodded. "On the Île des Juifs—the Island of the Jews. Many burnings took place there."

I scanned Lord Ashcombe's map, but the King's Warden hadn't marked it. "Where is that?"

"It doesn't exist anymore. It used to be to the west of the Île de la Cité, but it was joined to that island when the Pont Neuf was built. If you go to the Pont Neuf, and stand in front of the equestrian statue of Henri the Fourth, you'll be standing more or less where Molay was executed."

"Thank you," I said. "You've been incredibly helpful."

"You discovered something, then?"

I stopped, not sure what to say. He laughed.

"I don't really expect you to tell me," he said. "Regardless, I wish you well. You seem like decent people. Better you have the treasure than the Iron King."

He ushered us outside and locked the Great Tower before returning to his church. When he was gone, I showed Tom and Sally the poem again and told them what I was thinking.

Tom mulled it over. "Start at the beginning . . . where Molay was burned. I suppose that makes sense."

"But even if that's what Master Benedict meant," Sally

said, "how will that help us? Molay died three hundred and fifty years ago. The island isn't even there anymore. What do you expect to see?"

"I'm not sure," I said. "But if the poem's right, then there must be some sort of clue. We just have to go there and find it."

CHAPTER
30

OF ALL THE THINGS I MIGHT BE impressed by, I never imagined it would be a bridge.

But the Pont Neuf was extraordinary. Much wider than any street in London, it stretched all the way from the north bank to the south of the River Seine, just touching the western tip of the Île de la Cité. Unlike every other big bridge, there were no houses built along its sides; instead, we could stand right at the edge and have an unobstructed view of the river.

The three of us did just that for a while, watching the water flow beneath our feet. Hundreds of boats bobbed on the surface, from tiny one-man rowboats to the massive, flat-bottomed grain barges dragged against the current by dozens of horses, hooves churning in the mud of the riverbank.

Even being able to stand there was remarkable. Anywhere else, we'd have had to dodge a never-ending stampede of carriages. But the Pont Neuf had these raised platforms on each side—*allées*, they called them—reserved only for people on foot. I think even Tom was impressed.

Which is not to say we didn't get bumped around. The *allées* were still thick with travelers; the crowd itself remarkable in its own way. On the Pont Neuf, peasants and workmen lounged side-by-side with the nobility, some of whom covered their faces with those cloaks and masks, some who strolled without. There seemed to be little regard for status here; it felt more like a fairground than a bridge.

But we were here for a purpose. We wormed our way through the crowd toward the middle of the bridge. It was here we found the Bronze King: the equestrian statue of Henri IV, Louis's grandfather, the king who built the Pont Neuf.

The statue stood on an arched stone platform, surrounded by a wrought iron fence. The Bronze King sat majestically astride his muscled warhorse. Everyone seemed to treat his statue with respect—except for Bridget, who fluttered from the sky and sat on his head, preening a wing.

"So this is where Jacques de Molay was burned," I said.

"What do we do now?" Tom said.

I wasn't sure. I took a look around. To the west, we had an excellent view of the Seine, with the Louvre to the north against the riverbank. To the east was the Place Dauphine, a triangular plaza of high-quality shops: goldsmiths, jewelers, silk merchants, and the like. Beyond it, in the distance, we could see the twin towers and spire of the Cathédrale Notre-Dame. I thought for a moment, then pulled out the poem and read the first stanza.

> *King triumphant, man is burned*
> *Fate brings forth a lesson learned.*

"Here," I said. "Let's recreate Molay's execution. Tom, you be Molay. Stand in front of the statue."

He puffed himself up. "I'm a Knight Templar," he said proudly. Then he stopped. "Wait . . . you're not actually going to burn me, are you?"

"Of course I'm not going to burn you. Why would you even ask me that?"

"Don't sound so insulted. It's not like it's never happened before."

"That was *once*," I protested.

"It was *twice*," he said.

"It was *not* tw—" Then I remembered. "Oh . . . right."

"You see?" he said to Sally.

"Be fair," I said. "I didn't really set *you* on fire. It was just your breeches."

He looked at me incredulously. "Do you know what's under my breeches?"

"Unfortunately."

"Then you know I don't want it burned," he said. "I'm tired of this stupid country. It's always aiming at my crotch. First it's a sword. Then it's a viper. Then it's a wasp."

"It wasn't a viper—it was an asp."

"Who cares! It had fangs!" He jabbed a finger at me. "I'm warning you, if you even *think* about starting a fire, I'll throw you in the— What's this river called again?"

"The Seine," Sally said helpfully.

"I'll throw you in the Seine."

Now I was losing *my* patience. "I just said I wouldn't. You know what? Forget it. You don't get to be a Templar anymore. We'll burn Sally instead."

She raised her eyebrows, but moved in front of the statue.

"All right." I took a deep breath. "You're Jacques de Molay, twenty-third, and final, grand master of the Templars. You've just been tied to the stake."

"Wait—I'm facing the wrong way." Sally shifted. "Marin said I turned toward the east."

"Right, good. All right, we're lighting the fire."

"Ow," she said. "That fire certainly is hot. I fear it shall ruin my dress. Ow. Ow."

Tom applauded. "An excellent performance. I can really feel the flames."

Sally gave him a curtsy. I'd had enough.

"Are you two going to take this seriously or not?" I said. They snickered. "I'm trying to stop an assassin!"

"By staging a play on the Pont Neuf?" Tom said.

"By *trying* things. That's what Master Benedict said to do when you don't know how to solve a problem. You try different things and hope something shakes loose."

"All right," Sally said, mollifying me. "But what exactly are we trying to figure out?"

"What this line from the poem means. *Fate brings forth a lesson learned.*"

"We already know Molay's fate," Tom said. "He was burned to death. So I'd say the lesson is: Don't irritate the king."

"I don't think the lesson is what *Molay* learned. I think it's supposed to be what *we* learn. Look, the next verse talks about following a path. So the first verse must be meant to put us *on* that path. And somehow, that ties into his fate."

"But his fate was that he died."

"So what happened afterward?"

"To his bones?" Sally said. "Or his soul?"

I stopped. I hadn't really considered his soul—though, of course, *that* was a man's ultimate fate. Did he go to heaven, or hell?

"How could we possibly know that?" Tom said.

"I guess it depends on whether he'd done good or evil," I said. "If the charges against him were false, then I think he'd have gone to heaven."

Sally agreed. "Molay called God's wrath down on both king and pope, and they died. Plus, when they tied him to the stake, he asked to be allowed to look upon Notre-Dame one last time. That doesn't sound like a man who'd spent his life in service to the Devil."

"It doesn't, does it? So—"

I stopped.

Molay's last request, I thought. *His fate; his soul, in heaven.*

The man had died 350 years ago. The city had changed immeasurably since then; shifting, expanding. Modern Paris would have been unrecognizable to the last grand master; this very bridge we stood on was proof of that.

But some things remained. The Seine still flowed. The Louvre was still here. And the holiest place in France still stood above them all.

I blinked. "I think Molay's giving us the path himself. I think he just pointed us to Notre-Dame."

CHAPTER

MAGNIFICENT.

Nothing had prepared me for the Cathédrale Notre-Dame. We stood in front of the western entrance, the twin bell towers stretching up hundreds of feet, piercing the sky above the sloped lead roof. A rose-shaped stained glass window sat in the center of the facade, behind statues of angels that surrounded our Savior and the Virgin Mother. Below them were dozens of saints, carved above three massive oaken doors riveted with iron. The doors, sunken into arches, were themselves surrounded by intricate figures: Mary on the left, Saint Anne on the right, and the Day of the Last Judgment at the main entrance in the center.

Impossibly, the interior of the cathedral was even more majestic. Giant pillars rose three stories high to the ceiling, buttressed by heavy beams. Tapestries hung from each pillar, all the way down the aisle. Stained glass shined rainbow light through the clerestory, but most of the church's illumination was provided by hundreds and hundreds of candles, flickering in the chapels along the walls.

We were flanked by statues on either side. The first, and grandest, was a familiar, colossal figure, dozens of feet high: Saint Christopher, once again. I wasn't sure who the others were; more saints, I presumed, though there were far too many to identify them all. They looked so realistic, I half expected them to come to life.

Tom spoke quietly, not wishing to disturb the peace inside the church. "What do we do now?"

I opened the poem and read the second verse.

King triumphant, man is soot
Path is followed underfoot.

Underfoot, I thought.

Among the faithful praying were a pair of boys at work. One of them scrubbed the floor by the choir; the other lit candles at the side of the nave. I went to the one lighting candles. "Excuse me."

"Yes, monsieur?" he said.

"Is there a crypt, or are there any tombs, in this cathedral?" I said.

"Yes, monsieur."

"Would you be able to show us?"

"I'm not supposed to leave my duties."

I didn't think this would require nearly as large a donation as I'd given Father Bernard. I pulled a pair of *sou* from my purse.

It was enough. The boy pocketed the coins and led us along the side of the church, past the transept and main altar to the chapels at the back. He pointed to the tombs beside them. "Here you are, monsieur. There are a few men buried here."

The tombs were simple affairs. Each held an effigy of a man in robes lying at rest over a slab of marble. "Who are these people?" I said.

"I'm not sure, monsieur."

This wasn't really what I'd expected. "Isn't there a crypt *under* the cathedral?"

"No, monsieur. The city buries its dead in the cemeteries.

There are many tombs at the Cimetière des Innocents, if that's what you search for."

It wasn't. I frowned and thought about Voiture's poem. *Path is followed underfoot.*

I looked the tombs over again. They *might* match the second verse: The bodies were definitely "underfoot." Except none of these men could be Jacques de Molay. He'd been burned as a heretic; they'd never have buried him in consecrated ground. They'd probably just dumped his bones in the river. As for the Cimetière des Innocents, I didn't see any link between that and Jacques de Molay's fate. Besides, his gaze had led us to this cathedral.

I began to wonder if I'd got the riddle wrong. "What can you tell me about this church and the Knights Templar?"

The boy looked lost. "Nothing, monsieur."

"Is there anyone who might know?"

"One of the priests?" he suggested. "Father Lavalin knows some history."

He went to get the man. We wandered back toward the transept, studying the church, until a young priest with an easy smile approached us. "Odart said you had questions about the cathedral?"

"Yes," I said. "Do you have anything related to the Templars here?"

"No, monsieur. The Templars had their own church in their headquarters. It's still there, near the north wall of the city, if you'd like to see it."

We'd just come from there. "What about Jacques de Molay himself?"

"The last of the Templars?" Father Lavalin thought about it. "I don't know of any particular connection to this church. Though we know he was a pallbearer here once."

"He was?"

He nodded. "It was the day before le Bel had them arrested."

A pallbearer. "I don't suppose anything's left over from that time?"

"Well, the building is. The walls, the floors, the stained glass windows are all the original works. If you mean artifacts, however, I don't think so."

Apparently, he could see my disappointment, because he said, "You have to understand: This has been the most important church in France for five hundred years. There would be no circumstance under which the Iron King would have let his enemies remain as part of it. He wished to stand unopposed—triumphant, as always."

I started. "What do you mean, triumphant?"

"Philippe le Bel is still here."

"Where?"

"Right behind you."

I turned. Our path through the cathedral had led us back to the statues in the nave. The closest one—the one behind me—was an equestrian statue of a knight. Carved from polished wood, it stood on a platform eight feet high, supported by pillars.

The figure in the statue was imposing. The man was dressed in plate armor, his visor down. His warhorse was mailed and muscled, bred for combat. And as I looked, I saw: This was no ordinary knight. The coat that covered the horse's armor had the fleur-de-lis, the royal symbol of France, carved into it. And on this knight's helmet was a crown.

"That's the Iron King," Father Lavalin said. "The statue was installed in 1304, after he defeated the comte de Flandre at the battle of Mons-en-Pévèle. It was a mark of his victories as a warrior king. He'd never let a Templar stand nearby."

King triumphant, I thought.

"Thank you, Father," I said, and I gave him an *écu* for the poor. He thanked me graciously and left.

"This is it," I whispered to the others. "From the statue where Molay was burned to the statue of his tormentor. This has to be the next clue."

We huddled around the poem and reread the second verse.

King triumphant, man is soot
Path is followed underfoot.

I examined the floor underneath the statue. It looked the same as everywhere else, just simple interlocking stones.

"You think there's a path underneath?" Tom said. "But there's no crypt."

"Maybe there is," I said, excited. "A secret passage, forgotten over the years. One that the Templars knew about."

I handed Tom the poem. Then, after glancing to see that no one was watching, I crawled under the platform that held the statue and pried at the stones. They wouldn't budge. I looked around for some clue but couldn't see anything.

Sally had taken the poem from Tom. She stared at it, reading the second verse over and over. Then she looked up at the Iron King.

"Masters of misdirection," she said softly.

I saw her leave out of the corner of my eye as I continued to pry at the stones. When she came back, she held a candle, borrowed from one of the nearby chapels.

She gave the poem back to Tom. Then she clambered up the pillar and onto the platform with le Bel and his horse.

"What are you doing?" Tom whispered, horrified. "Get down from there!"

She brought the candle close and inspected the statue.

"Christopher," she said. "I think you should come up here."

"Keep watch," I said to Tom, and, ignoring his sputtering, pulled myself onto the platform beside her.

She held the candle near the king's mailed boot. "Underfoot," she said. "Under . . . foot."

I peered closer, and in the light—under the king's foot—I saw the same thing she had.

Someone had written on the statue. On the inside of the stirrup, letters had been marked in ink. It was faint against the darkened wood, but with the candle I could just make out what it said.

ARCADIA

CHAPTER
32

I STARED, THE WORD TUMBLING over in my mind.

Arcadia.

"I've seen this before," I said.

But where? I racked my brain, trying to recall the memory. I swear I'd seen that very word—

"Christopher."

Sally had moved to the right of the statue, looking beneath le Bel's other boot. I went to her and saw another message in the second stirrup.

la soluzione è dove pensa

I blinked.

"That's not Latin," Sally said.

I shook my head. "It's Italian."

"What does it mean?"

La soluzione è dove pensa. "The answer is where you think."

Now that was confusing. Where was I supposed to think the answer was?

Sally lifted the candle to examine the rest of the statue. Neither of us found anything, and soon Tom was tugging at my shoe.

"Someone's coming!" he hissed.

We hopped back down and landed right in front of Odart, the boy who'd helped us before. He stopped in his tracks, looking at the candle in Sally's hands.

"We wanted to say a prayer for my master," I said.

I dropped a *sou* into his hand as Sally returned the candle to its holder. As we left the cathedral, I glanced back. Odart had returned to his work, shaking his head at the strangeness of foreigners.

I paced in front of the church. *The answer is where you think.*

"I've seen it," I said. "I *know* I've seen it."

"What are you talking about?" Tom said. "Seen what?"

"Arcadia." I told him what Sally and I had found.

"What's that supposed to mean?" he asked.

"I don't know. But the message said Arcadia, and I know I've seen that word somewhere before."

"What *is* Arcadia?" Sally said.

"Paradise," I said, recalling my lessons with Master Benedict. "There's a real Arcadia, in Greece, but over time the word's come to mean 'paradise,' or 'utopia.' Not in the heavenly sense; Arcadia is an *earthly* perfection. People and animals in harmony with God's creation, that sort of thing." I threw my hands up in frustration. "And I've *seen* it recently. I just can't remember where."

"Was it in the cathedral?"

"No, it was before that."

"The Great Tower?"

I thought about it. Had it been carved into the panels of Templar history? "No."

So where was it?

Tom looked eastward, to the white stone mansions on the Île Notre-Dame. "Maybe we should ask Marin. He knows Paris better than us. If he's feeling well, maybe he'll know where you've seen it."

That was a great idea. I'd promised Simon I'd visit his uncle, anyway.

We began to make our way there. Tom and Sally chatted as we went, enjoying the sights. I walked ahead, searching my memory. The others let me think, and it wasn't until we were approaching Marin's house that I realized I'd left them behind.

I turned. They'd stopped about thirty feet back. Tom was gazing down the street toward the south, frowning. Sally just looked puzzled.

I joined them. "What's the matter?"

Sally shrugged and pointed at Tom. He seemed unsure of himself. "That man," he said.

I followed his gaze. There was considerably less traffic on the Île Notre-Dame, only a few people strolling among the carriages that rumbled on the paving. Tom pointed to a man, his face covered by a cloak, leaning against the wall of a private garden.

"What about him?" I said.

"He just jumped over that wall," Tom said.

"From the garden?" The cloak over the face was a nobleman's disguise. "That's probably his home. Or do you think he's a thief—wait a minute."

I tried to get an image of the layout of the streets. Marin's house was . . . nearby? Two estates eastward, if I remembered.

The man glanced over at us, sidelong. When he saw we were looking at him, he pushed himself from the wall and walked away.

"Christopher," Tom said.

"What?"

Tom took a step closer, alarmed. *"Christopher."*

"What's the matter?"

"That's . . . I think that's *him.*"

"Who?" I said.

"The man." He was tall, with a stocky build. He lumbered as he walked, like a bull. "The way he's moving. I . . . I think that's the man I saw back in England. I think that might be the assassin."

I stared. I'd never seen the assassin; he'd jumped me from behind. But I recalled Tom's description to Lord Ashcombe. *He was stocky. Built like a bull. I've never met anybody so strong.*

We began to follow. The man glanced behind him. His eyes met mine. And in them, I saw it.

He recognized me.

It *was* him.

Suddenly, he darted to the right. Clumsily, he swung himself over a garden wall.

"Hey!" I shouted.

I didn't think. I just broke into a sprint after him.

"Christopher!" Tom said.

"Go around!" I called back. "Cut him off!"

I didn't wait to see if they obeyed. I ran straight for the wall and clambered over it. I found myself in a narrow garden, a small green space with some grass and a flower bed. A gardener, on his knees, watched with bemusement as the man in the cloak hopped the wall on the other side.

I ran past the startled gardener and threw myself over the wall, tumbling to the street. The assassin, still holding his cloak over his face, looked back, and when he saw me hit the ground, I heard him curse.

I pointed. "Stop him! Someone stop him!" Everyone on the street looked at me curiously but did nothing. It took a moment to realize I'd shouted in English. *"Arrêtez-le!"*

They still did nothing, just watched as the assassin ran past them. Didn't want to get their finery dirty, I supposed. Nonetheless, as I ran after him, I saw I was closing the distance. He might have been big, but he was slow, and his need to keep his face covered slowed him even further. I felt a surge of elation as I realized he couldn't escape me without dropping his cloak.

Do it, I urged him in my mind. *Let someone see your face.*

He seemed to recognize his predicament. His twists and turns became increasingly frantic, as I gained on him with every step. With one final pivot, he bolted toward the coast of the island, and I was close enough to see the alarm in his eyes.

He reached beneath his cloak. For a moment, I thought he was going to stand and fight. I was half-right.

He threw a dagger at me.

I saw the glint of steel in the sunlight as he drew it from his cloak. Instinctively, I skidded into a slide—which probably saved my life. The dagger spun toward my face. I turned my head and felt the sting in my cheek as the blade scraped across my skin.

The knife clattered behind me on the pavement. My boot caught on a flagstone, and I tumbled before rolling to a stop. I sat there for a moment, bumped and bruised, shaken by how close I'd been to taking a dagger in the eye.

The man took advantage of my delay. Face still covered, he whirled and ran to the island's edge. Shaken or not, I couldn't let him get away. I leaped to my feet and ran after him faster than ever.

I gained, again. There were no more twists and turns now; we were in a straight-out sprint, boots thundering against the pavement as we hurtled down a slope toward the water. Several boats waited at the edge of the quay. The assassin sprinted for the closest, a rowboat. The boatman stood on the gunwale, holding his craft steady with one hand on the quay's wooden post, reaching with the other to help a velvet-masked young lady in a yellow dress step inside.

"Look out!" I shouted.

Startled, they turned to see the assassin barreling toward them. He was so close, just a few feet away. I stretched my fingers out to grab him.

Then the man surprised us all. He seized the lady by the arm and spun her around, flinging her in a circle toward me.

I was moving too quickly to stop. I slammed into her with a *whump*. She cried out as she tumbled head over heels into the Seine. I fell, landing heavily, bouncing to the edge of the dock.

I skidded, my shirt tearing against the wood. I felt a splinter drive into my forearm, and suddenly the quay dropped away.

Then I hit the water, too.

CHAPTER

THE SHOCK OF THE COLD KNOCKED

me senseless. I sank, disoriented, not knowing which way
was up. I had a moment of panic before I realized the rip-
pling bands of light below my feet must be from the sun.
I flipped myself over in the water, then kicked frantically
upward until I broke the surface, gasping.

I banged my head against the rowboat. The assassin was
inside it, scrambling to get to his feet; when he'd flung the
lady at me, his momentum had carried him crashing into the
bottom boards. And his cloak . . . his cloak had fallen away.

It lay crumpled in a heap beside him. But he was facing
away from me. I couldn't see him. I couldn't *see*.

The boatman, confused, tried to help him up. As he reached out, the assassin hooked his arms under the boatman's legs and sent him plunging into the drink on the opposite side. The assassin scrambled to grab his cloak.

Then I heard a cry.

"Help!"

It was the lady I'd knocked into the river. She flailed her arms, splashing water, gasping. "Help!" she cried once more, and then her head went under.

Her dress, I realized. All that finery, waterlogged, was weighing her down. She couldn't swim.

My heart sank. I was so close, so *close.* The assassin, fumbling to reattach his cloak, still had his back to me. If I left the woman behind, pulled myself up, drew my sword . . . I could end this, here, right now.

But I couldn't. I couldn't let her drown. My mind screamed in frustration as I let the boat go and dove back down into the Seine.

The water was murky, muddy, with a greasy feel to it. And cold, so very cold. I could feel my skin freezing as I swam toward her. I floundered about, trying to see the shadows cast by the sun through the wavering surface. I spotted a flash of yellow, tinted dark by the water. I reached for one of her thrashing arms, and she clutched at me, and then suddenly she was dragging me down.

I kicked upward, but now the woman's weight was on me. In her panic, she was using me like a ladder, allowing her own head to stay above the surface. I felt one of her heels dig into my shoulder, and I realized she was *standing* on me.

My lungs began to burn, and terror began to take me, too. I swatted at her legs and got a leather toe in the face in return. I saw her begin to rise. I kicked as hard as I could after her, chest threatening to breathe in the icy water that would kill me.

Then I felt something seize my cravat. It yanked me up, like a noose, and my head finally broke the water.

I gasped, inhaling the sweet, cold air. I had a moment of terror when I felt myself sinking again, but Tom had me. He released my cravat, grabbed me under my arms, and flung me like a doll to sprawl next to him on the dock.

The lady was already there. Sally, plus two more onlookers who'd come to help, had pulled her from the water, soaking dress and all. Amazingly, she hadn't even lost her mask. She stared through the dripping velvet in confusion. Then she kicked me in the head.

"You vagabond!" she screamed. "You blackguard! You tried to kill me!"

I couldn't believe this. *She'd* pushed *me* down to save herself. One of the men helping tried to reassure her. "Calm yourself, please, mademoiselle," he said. "It was an accident. It was the other man who caused all the trouble."

She wouldn't listen. She continued to hurl insults at me as she lashed out. She landed a couple more blows before Sally and the men managed to pull her away. "I want your name!" the lady shrieked. "Give me your name! I'll have you *flogged*!"

I'd had enough. "I'm Jacques de Molay," I said. "And I'm staying in the Great Tower."

I ignored the rest of her curses and looked out over the river, trembling as the air and the water chilled me to the bone. The assassin had finally righted himself in the boat. He rowed away with powerful arms, his face covered once more by the hood of his cloak.

"Are you all right?" Tom said.

Sally was holding a dagger, the one the assassin had thrown at me. She must have picked it up. My sopping clothes clung to my skin, and the only bit of warmth I felt was my anger. I grabbed the knife from her hands and, without thinking, hurled it after the assassin.

It arced over the water. We watched, he and I, as it flew,

then fell short, splashing into the Seine five feet from the boat.

The assassin's laughter carried him away.

Tom lent me his cloak to keep me warm. The men who'd come to assist us dragged the howling girl off, insisting she get inside before the chill killed her. That only seemed to add to her curses as we walked away. "Cretin! Peasant! I'll see you burn for this, Molay!"

Tom cocked his head. "That's actually rather funny, when you think about it."

I was too cold to see the humor. Tom and Sally wrapped their arms around me as they hurried me toward Maison Chastellain. At Marin's house, we shuffled past a surprised servant loading a horse with saddlebags, and Tom thumped on the door.

I was too close to freezing to be polite. "Just . . . get me . . . inside," I said, teeth chattering.

Sally opened the door and led us in. Colette, carrying a stack of linens, stopped in the entryway, a little startled by our intrusion. Simon, at the top of the stairs, paused in swinging a fur cloak over his shoulder. "Christopher? What happened?"

"The . . . Seine," I said.

"Why on earth . . . ? Get up here." He rushed me into Marin's study and placed me in front of the roaring fire as Colette hurried to bring me some blankets.

The heat felt like God's own love. I cast off Tom's cloak and began pulling away the rest of my clothes as well. Marin, sitting in his comfortable chair, swirled brandy in his glass and looked at me fondly. "Gone for a swim, eh?" he said. "Ah, the pleasures of youth."

Colette arrived with the blankets. I stripped naked under one made of bear fur and sat as close to the fire as I dared without actually burning my skin. Rémi, attending Marin as usual, stepped from his place against the wall and poured me brandy from his master's decanter. I almost drank it before I remembered.

"How long has this brandy been sitting there?" I said.

"As long as possible," Marin said cheerfully.

"I decanted it yesterday, monsieur," Rémi said.

"I meant today," I said. "How long has it been beside Marin?"

Marin laughed. "Also as long as possible."

"He's been here since lunch," Simon said. "Why? What is going on?"

"The assassin," I said. "We saw the assassin. Is everyone here all right?"

"Why wouldn't we be?"

"Because when Tom first spotted him," I said, "I think he might have come from your house."

CHAPTER 34

SIMON'S JAW DROPPED. "*HERE?*"

I nodded.

"But . . . no one's been inside. It's just me, my uncle, and the servants."

"It's a big place," I pointed out.

He blinked. Then he whirled on Rémi. "Gather everyone in the great hall immediately."

They left to collect the rest of the staff. As the brandy was safe—the assassin couldn't have poisoned it while Marin was there—I downed the glass Rémi had given me, letting the burn warm me from inside. Colette returned with a heavy woolen robe. I gathered it around me and, leaving the fire reluctantly, went down to join the rest in the great hall.

"They're all here," Simon said. He spoke to the staff. "Did any of you see anyone on the grounds?"

The servants looked at each other inquiringly. When no one spoke up, Rémi said, "No one, monsieur."

"Search the house, then."

After the slightest pause, Rémi said, "Of course, monsieur. But . . . what are we looking for?"

"Anything out of the ordinary. Go."

The servants did as commanded. Simon wandered the grounds, too. We'd have helped, but we didn't know the place well enough to be useful. I could only warn Simon to be on the lookout for subtle things: traps, poisons, and the like.

"*You* should look for poisons," Simon said. "You know more about them than I do."

He took us into the kitchen and ordered the servants to bring me all the food from the pantry and the wine from the cellar. I inspected everything, and it was when I was examining the bottles from the cellar that I stopped.

"Simon?" I called out. "Have any of these been opened before?"

He came in from the dining hall. "They shouldn't have. Why?"

"This cork isn't level."

I showed him the bottle I'd been inspecting. The cork was raised slightly from its mouth. Simon pulled it out with a pop and smelled the wine. He frowned, opened a second bottle, and sniffed at that one, too.

"Do these smell different?" he asked.

I tried them both. I wasn't sure if I smelled anything, or whether his question was making me imagine things, but I could swear I detected a slight difference in the fragrance.

He laid a finger on the bottle that had had the raised cork. "Did this one smell sweeter?"

That was it. I'd thought the same thing exactly.

"Could that just be a difference in the wine?" Sally said.

That was the problem; it could. And the cork could have been not level merely because that's how it was bottled.

"It's not worth the risk," Simon said. "We'll just throw it all away. Such a waste." He shook his head, exasperated. "But the wine's not important. I want to know more about this assassin."

He already knew about the snake. I told him the rest:

the attempted poisoning in England, this morning's wasp attack, and what had happened at the river.

"You saw him climbing over our garden wall?" Simon said.

"Not yours. This was on Rue Poulletier."

"Poulletier?" He frowned. "You can't sneak into here from there. Not without going into the street." He regarded me, arms folded, tapping his cheek. "I think you might have this all wrong."

"It was definitely the assassin," I insisted.

"That's not what I meant. I'm saying he might not have been *here*, at Maison Chastellain."

"Why else would he be on the Île Notre-Dame?"

"Because he was following *you*."

"*Me?*" That made me stop. "Why would he be following me?"

Simon looked at me incredulously. "Christopher . . . you've been a thorn in this man's side since the beginning. You've interfered with his plans three times—and now you've just chased him into the river. If I were him, I'd come for you before I even *thought* about striking again at the king."

I slumped in my chair. Why did these things always happen to me?

"Listen," Simon said. "I'm leaving for Normandy. Before I go, I'll have Rémi replace all the food and drink in this house. I'll also have him hire guards, and station them around my uncle's home. Except for you three, they'll have instructions to let no one in or out but my servants. Does that sound sufficient to ward off any possible assassins?"

I nodded glumly.

"Good," Simon said. "In that case: Would you like to stay here as well?"

That came as a surprise. "Stay?"

"You'll be much safer here than at the Palais. At least you'll know everyone around you. You can even have Master Benedict's old room."

I realized I'd rather like that. But I couldn't. My charge was at the Palais. I couldn't abandon it because I was now in danger.

"Then what if I hire guards to follow you?" Simon said.

That was another surprise. "The expense—"

"Is nothing. You're a blessing to my uncle, and I still owe you any number of apologies for yesterday. Troubled finances or not, Christopher, we can certainly afford a few more *sou*."

It was an equally tempting offer—and, sadly, equally

necessary to refuse. Our hunt for the Templars' treasure needed to be kept private. If our discovery at Notre-Dame had shown me anything, it was that we couldn't have prying eyes following us around, watching what we uncovered. Especially ones we didn't know we could trust.

"We'll be fine," I said.

Simon didn't think that was wise—I don't think Tom or Sally did, either—but he didn't argue. He called for Rémi and gave him his instructions. The only sign the servant gave of the unusual nature of Simon's commands was a slight raising of the eyebrows; otherwise, he bowed and said, "Right away, monsieur."

Rémi began to instruct his underlings, who scurried off to arrange what Simon had ordered. As for Simon, he stood and wrapped his fur cloak about him. "All right," he said. "I have to leave, before the entire day is through. Unless you need me to stay?"

"Really," I said, "I'm fine. We'll go spend some time with Marin."

He clasped my hand in farewell, then swung himself onto the horse outside and galloped off. As promised, we returned to the study to see his uncle—which was the reason we'd come here in the first place.

Rémi escorted us up the stairs. Feeling guilty, I turned to him—here, I didn't have to pretend I was a noble; I could actually apologize. "I'm sorry for making more work for all of you," I said.

"Ridiculous, monsieur." There was that trusty French-servant rudeness. "The safety of monsieur le Comte is paramount."

"Still. I don't think you'd planned on searching your master's house for assassins."

Rémi allowed himself a little smile. "Perhaps, at my age, I was hoping for a little more quiet. Then again, monsieur, I cannot complain that I am ever bored."

Thoughtfully, Colette had strung my clothes in front of the fire to dry them out. Remembering my lesson from Sir William, I pulled my blade from its scabbard to let it dry, too. Everything was still damp, so I kept myself wrapped in the robe as I checked on my apothecary sash. It was as wet as everything else, but the corks had kept the water out, and the ingredients inside seemed none the worse for wear. I'd managed to hold on to most of my tools, too—including, most thankfully, the Templar florin Marin had lent me—but the magnet Simon had played with as a child was gone, now resting at the bottom of the Seine.

Colette laid another blanket beside the fire, in case I needed it. I smiled in gratitude, and when I did, she reached out, cupped my chin, and turned my head gently to examine where the assassin's dagger had grazed my cheek.

She leaned in. I could smell the sweet scent of her dusting powder. "You've been wounded, monsieur."

Sally spoke sharply. "I'll handle that."

Colette stepped back, looking like she'd been caught reaching for the mistress's biscuits. She curtsied and left as Sally stood before me, hands on her hips.

"It's just a scratch," Sally said sourly, but she rooted around in my sash for the vial of honey and dabbed it over the cut. "What were you thinking, chasing that man?"

"I *wasn't* thinking," I admitted. "It's just . . . if we could have seen his face . . ."

"He nearly got you in the eye." She frowned at Tom. "Can't you talk some sense into him?"

"What difference would it make?" Tom said. "He never listens to me."

"I always listen to you," I protested.

"He does, it's true. He just doesn't do what I say."

"Will you please stop talking like I'm not here?"

Marin watched with amusement. I changed the subject

before Sally or Tom could chastise me further. "We've been following Voiture's poem," I said. "And I think we've found something."

Marin's eyes lit up. "Really? Then sit, boy, sit. Have a drink."

I didn't really want another one, but I let Rémi fill my glass to be polite.

"So?" Marin said. "What have you found?"

"There was a secret written on the statue of le Bel in Notre-Dame," I said.

Marin seemed astonished. "The statue?" Then he laughed. "How appropriate. What did it say?"

"Have you ever heard of Arcadia?"

The effect on Marin was startling. He stared at me, half rising from his chair. "I knew it," he whispered. "I *knew* it."

"Knew what?" Sally said.

"Poussin. I always knew it was Poussin."

Tom and Sally looked to me, but I didn't recognize the name. "Was he one of the knights who escaped with the treasure?"

"No," Marin said. "Nicolas Poussin is a painter."

And with that, the memory finally shook loose.

CHAPTER

I SMACKED MY FOREHEAD. "*THAT'S*
where I've seen it!"

"Seen what?" Tom said.

"The *painting*." I sprang from my chair and paced in
front of the fire. "That's where I saw the word 'Arcadia.' It
was on a painting in the Louvre. There were these shepherds, and they were reading an inscription on a tomb."

Marin nodded. "That's Nicolas Poussin. *Les bergers
d'Arcadie—the Arcadian Shepherds.* A stunning work."

"And it fits!" I said. "Look!" Colette had laid open the
paper with my master's handwriting in front of the fire to
dry with the rest of my clothes. The water had smudged

the ink, but it was still readable. "It fits the next verse of the poem!"

King is broken, man remains
Answer hidden in the stains.

"Hidden in the *stains*." I waved the paper at them. "It's talking about the *painting*. We have to go back to the Louvre."

"No need," Marin said. "I have the Poussin here."

"You do?" I said.

"Of course. I've had it for years."

"Uh . . ." Tom, Sally, and I exchanged a glance. I remembered what my master had said in his letter to Simon. *Do not try to correct him; it will not help.* "All right. Well . . . might we see it?"

He looked amused. "You are seeing it. It's right there."

He pointed to the painting that hung over the fireplace. It was a scene done in the Dutch style, with two men on horses standing by a riverbank and a third in the background, tending to cattle, in front of rolling wooded hills.

I glanced over at Rémi. I wasn't sure how to politely suggest we go prepare Marin's medicine.

Marin saw that. His eyes twinkled. "You think the old man's lost his mind."

That made me flush again. "No, I—"

"It's all right." Marin grinned. "Take it down," he said to Tom.

"Sir?" Tom said.

"Take the painting down. Go on."

Tom looked to me. I nodded, and he went over to the fire and lifted the painting from its hook.

"Remove it from its frame," Marin said.

Again Tom glanced at me, but he did as asked, popping the painting out of the wood. The canvas stretched around the inner frame, held to the wooden support with nails.

"Now take the painting off the mounting board."

I handed Tom a little pry bar from my sash to work the nails out. As he did so, I blinked.

There was a second canvas under the riverbank. When enough nails had been removed, Tom pulled it out and held it up, surprised.

"That's it," I said, amazed. "That's the painting from the Louvre."

It showed three shepherds, all carrying staves, and a maiden, inspecting a large stone tomb. The tomb stood alone in a pristine pastoral setting, under a blue but increasingly cloudy sky. Two of the shepherds pointed to the inscription carved into the stone.

ET IN ARCADIA EGO

"What does that mean?" Sally said.

"I am even in Arcadia," I translated.

"And what does *that* mean?" Tom said. "Whose tomb is it?"

"No one's," Marin said. "The 'I' refers to death itself. It is saying that, even in utopia, death is still there. The work is a memento mori: a painting intended to remind you that you, too, will die."

"As if I needed reminding," Tom muttered.

"But . . . how did you get this?" I said. "I could swear I saw this very same painting in the Louvre."

"You did," Marin said. "That's the original. This is a copy."

"It looks exactly the same."

"Because this is no ordinary copy. It is from the hand of Poussin himself. I commissioned it specifically. Paid quite a sum for it, too."

"Why?" I said.

"Because, like the Voiture poem, I was certain the painting was related to the Templars."

"You think a Templar paid him to paint this?"

"No," Marin said. "I think Poussin *is* a Templar."

CHAPTER
36

I STARED AT HIM. "WHY WOULD you think so?"

"It has to do with his time in Paris," Marin said. "Though French by birth, Nicolas Poussin lived in Rome for most of his youth. In 1640, however, Cardinal Richelieu called him back to be first painter to the king. Though he didn't want to come, he agreed.

"As much as he didn't want to be here, others were jealous of his talents and position. There were many petty slights against him by the king's courtiers, one of which involved a young boy. The boy was afflicted from birth: He had a rounded face and almond eyes, and his mind and speech were quite slow. These men at court thought it would be a great joke to give the boy to Poussin as a servant.

"To their surprise, Poussin didn't send him away. Instead, he took him into his household, where the boy served him faithfully and well. Nonetheless, Poussin grew disgusted with the scheming in Paris and, two years later, announced he was returning to Italy.

"The boy was devastated—other than his own mother, Poussin was the only person who'd ever treated him kindly. He wished to go with the painter, but the boy's mother was too ill to travel, and he couldn't leave her. Poussin praised the boy for standing by his mother, and, as a gift for exemplary service, gave him twenty *louis* before he left. An extraordinary sum—and yet Poussin also gave him something even *more* precious. Would you like to guess what it was?"

It came to me. "A florin," I said. "Stamped with a Templar cross."

Marin nodded in satisfaction. "Exactly."

My mind raced. "Is the boy still in Paris? Could we speak to him?"

"Sadly, no. Proud of his service, he told the wrong man of the gift he'd received. He was murdered for Poussin's gold."

Sally gasped. "That's horrible!"

"It seems the Templars thought so, too. The king's guard discovered the killer one morning, hanging dead outside the Bastille. The twenty *louis* were in a bag at his feet."

"What happened to the florin?" Tom said.

"It was never found. Taken back by the Templars, I presume. Anyway, that's why I believe Poussin is one of them. And this painting is particularly mysterious. When I saw it, I was so convinced it was a clue that I wrote to Poussin himself in Rome, begging him to paint it again. He agreed, as you see. Though I think he had the last laugh."

The old man rose and went over to his desk. The papers he'd pulled from the secret compartment in front of the fireplace were still there. He sifted through them and handed me a letter in French. I read it out, translating it into English for Tom.

Monsieur le Comte de Gravigny,

In receipt of your payment, I have produced another copy of my shepherds, in the exact style you have commissioned. I hope you enjoy it, but as you seem a man of decent character, I feel duty bound to tell you: Whatever it is you are looking for, you will not find it here.

Nicolas Poussin

I read the letter a second time. "The poem," I said to Marin, "led us to this painting."

"Yes."

"It also says the answer is 'hidden in the stains.'"

"Yes."

"But there's no clue in this version of it, is there?"

Marin sighed. "No. And that's what I can't figure out. Because, you see, these two paintings are absolutely identical. I have every brushstroke memorized. I've stood in front of the original for days, trying to see the difference. There isn't one."

"Do you think Poussin lied?" Sally said.

"No. Which means, whatever he hid, it's only in the original."

"So what do we do now?" Tom said.

"I think there's only one thing we can do," I said. "We'll have to take the painting from the Louvre."

THURSDAY, NOVEMBER 19, 1665

Sext

CHAPTER
37

THE MOON WAS STILL UP WHEN I
tried to pull Tom from his palliasse. "Come on," I said.
"We're going to be late."

He rolled away from me and placed his pillow over his
head. "You're really overplaying this joke," he said.

"It's not a joke. Come *on*."

"I'm not stealing a painting from the Louvre!"

"I told you, we're not going to steal it. We're going to
swap it." I yanked the pillow from Tom's hands. "We go
to the Louvre. We take the original. We replace it with
Marin's. No one will know the difference."

"That's stealing," Tom said.

"How is it stealing? We're leaving something behind."

"With Louis's permission?"

"Well . . . no. But, look." I unrolled the canvas. "It's the same painting. It's even by Nicolas Poussin himself."

"I don't think the king will see it that way."

"The king won't even know it's happened," I said. "I don't know what your problem is. Lord Ashcombe said we had Charles's permission to break any law we needed to in order to stop the assassins."

"He also said that if we get caught, we're on our own. Do you know what that means?"

I sighed. "A dungeon."

"Not *a* dungeon," Tom said. "*The* dungeon. The *Bastille*. Do you know what they do to you in the Bastille?"

I couldn't listen to the bread story again. "Just get moving, will you? I promise we won't get caught. I have a plan."

"That makes me feel *so* much better."

If you think that's bad, I thought, *just wait until I tell you what it is.*

Tom's voice rose about three octaves. "We're going to *what*?"

I tried to hush him. "It's fine, I promise."

"He promises." Tom turned to Sally and clutched his

cheeks. "How did I get here? What am I doing?"

I'd taken advantage of my place as Minette's guest to come watch Louis rise again, which gave us a reason to return to the palace. Then, when the others had gone for breakfast, I'd begged off and dragged Sally away from Minette's retinue. We'd need her to pull off this plan.

She didn't moan like Tom. She did, however, look at me like I'd lost my mind. "I really don't think we should set fire to the Louvre," she said.

"We're not setting fire to it," I said. "We're just making it *look* like we did. We're going to make a smoke bomb."

I pulled two vials from my sash. Both held fine white crystals: sugar in one, saltpeter in the other. "Can you keep watch while I make this?" I asked Sally. "It wouldn't do for anyone to see Baron Ashcombe cooking like a servant."

I made Tom borrow a pan from the kitchen. He looked even more put out when he returned. "The cooks yelled at me."

We searched for an empty room with a working fireplace. Then I set Sally at the door and prepared to make the bomb. I mixed both vials together, then dumped the crystals into the heated pan, stirring them with my silver spoon. Tom continued to pester me about my plan, which, in turn, made *me* annoyed. I was doing delicate work. If the recipe got too hot, I'd set it off right here.

Finally, I'd had enough. "Will you leave me alone?" I snapped. "Go stand with Sally. And stop being such a baby."

Tom's eyes narrowed. He looked like he was about to say something, but he just clenched his fists and walked away.

I regretted what I'd said instantly. I'd made Tom genuinely angry—and he never really got that angry. I tried to puzzle out why he was so worried about swapping the paintings—I'd got him into much worse schemes than this before—and I realized he'd already told me, without saying the words.

He was scared. Here he was, in a strange country, surrounded by strange people, where he couldn't even speak the language. If we got caught and ended up in some dungeon— the Bastille or otherwise—he'd be jailed far from home, and, without me, he'd be well and truly alone.

A thin smell of caramel smoke brought my attention back to what I was doing. My recipe had started to melt. I stirred it, and once the whole thing turned dark brown, I poured it onto a piece of paper to let it cool.

I inspected my work. It looked just like it should—a

shapeless brown lump. I took it over to the others. Tom wouldn't look at me.

I sighed. "All right, here's the plan. The Poussin is upstairs, in the second floor viewing hall. Tom and I will go up there and wait. Sally, give us a couple minutes to get in place. Then go to that curtain behind the couch and rub this into the bottom corner."

I handed her a vial of fine black powder. "What is it?" she said.

"Just charcoal," I said. "Once the smoke bomb's done its work, it'll look like the fabric started to smolder, and that's where the smoke came from. When you're ready, just place this lump"—I handed her the bomb—"underneath the curtain, and use a candle to set it off. Leave the candle on the ground next to it, so it'll look like that's what caused the problem. But make sure it doesn't touch the curtain. We don't want to start a real fire."

Sally nodded. Tom came upstairs with me, still refusing to look my way. I tried to tell him I was sorry, but he just turned his shoulder and wandered off to look at the paintings. I promised silently that I'd make everything up to him. Food usually did the trick. Maybe I'd ask the chef at the Palais if he could make chops in sauce.

But that would need to be later. For then we heard Sally scream.

"Fire! Fire!"

I could see smoke drifting up the stairs. From below came the sound of running feet and terrified cries. I joined my voice to theirs.

"Fire!" I shouted, and the few souls in the viewing hall ran down, calling out.

"Water! Bring water! Help!" And we were alone.

Now.

Poussin's shepherds hung in the center of the wall. Tom and I pulled it down. If we'd just planned to steal it, we could have cut it from the wood and run away. Instead, we'd need a little more time.

We popped the painting from its frame. Like Marin's copy, it was nailed to its mounting. I kept watch while Tom used my pry bar to work out the nails. Unfortunately, these were hammered more deeply into the backing board. I was horrified to see how much longer it was taking to get them out.

I listened at the doorway. The sounds of alarm had diminished; they'd already put a stop to the smoke. "Hurry up," I said.

I hadn't meant it unkindly; I was just getting worried. But it finally made Tom snap.

He slammed his hand down. "Don't rush me!" he said. "I'm a baker, not an art thief! If you wanted quick, you should have asked me for hot cross buns!"

I cringed. "Shhh!"

"Don't 'shhh' me! This is all *your* fault! And now look! I'm bleeding!" He thrust his wounded thumb at me. "I shouldn't be here! I should be in London, making breakfast rolls! Not in Paris, stealing puzzled Greek shepherds from a Frenchman!"

"All right," I said. "I'm sorry—"

"But nooooooo! Monsieur Christopher had to throw a bottle of poisoned wine at the king!"

"What are you two doing?" Sally, flushed from running, hissed at us from the top of the stairs. "The smoke's out, but now the queen's scared, so they're searching the palace to see if any other candles have fallen."

"Don't you talk to me, either!" Tom said. "You're as bad as he is!"

Sally looked confused. I waved my hands and said, "Find out where they're going first."

Finally, Tom worked out the last nail. He yanked the canvas from the frame and shoved it into my hands. Then he pulled the copy from beneath his cloak, and wrapped it around the frame as I rolled up the original.

Sally ran into the room. "They're coming!"

We had no time to nail the copy to the mounting board. We'd have to hope the frame itself would hold the canvas in place. We jammed it back in, hung the frame on the wall, then darted through the exit on the far side of the room. A voice came from behind us: Louis's herald, announcing his liege's entry. *"Le roi! Le roi!"* The king! The king!

I peeked back through the doorway. And my guts dropped.

"Oh no," I said.

Tom and Sally looked. They gasped.

The painting. The *painting*. We'd put it in upside down.

There were tears in Tom's eyes. "I'm going to the Bastille," he said.

"Just . . . let me think," I said.

It was too late to do anything about the painting. Louis, followed by his entourage, had already begun to enter the room we'd just left.

I ducked back. "What do we do?" Sally whispered.

And then it came to me.

I thrust the stolen painting at her. "Hide this under your dress. Then get out of here. Meet us downstairs, at the entrance."

She fled out the far exit. In the next room, the king's valet had spotted the Poussin. "What's happened here?"

Time for our way out. I ran to the paintings on the walls in this room and began flipping them upside down. "Tom! Help me!"

I was grateful he didn't ask any questions. He just began turning them over. When we were nearly finished, I laughed, as loud as I could.

Tom stared at me in horror. I motioned to him to laugh, too. He didn't do it very well.

But they heard us. *"Le roi!"* came the call. *"Le roi!"* And then Louis, with his entourage, entered our room.

Everyone stared at us. Tom and I stood frozen, holding the king's paintings, in the process of hanging them upside down. I tried to look guilty. Tom didn't have to try at all.

I couldn't read Louis's expression. "How very amusing," he said.

The king's valet didn't seem to think so. He stomped toward us, brandishing his cane. "Playing pranks, are you," he growled, "when the palace might be burning down around your ears?"

I'd rather hoped my status as a noble might, for once, spare us a beating. It didn't. The valet bent us over the table, and we took our lumps. The king's courtiers laughed, enjoying the show. *"Touché!"* they shouted, cheering with every blow.

When it was over, I could barely stand. I didn't dare look over at Tom. Not that I'd have seen him; my eyes were watering.

The valet, panting from the thrashing he'd administered, prodded us forward with his cane. "You idiots put every painting back the way it was. And if I catch you playing with His Majesty's property again, I'll feed you to the dogs."

We flipped all the paintings back over. The courtiers booed; the king's brother the loudest of all. "Oh, leave that one, Baron," Philippe said. "It's better upside down."

When we finished, we limped out of the room. Louis watched me. As I passed him, the tiniest smile danced over his lips. *"Very* amusing."

We made our way downstairs. I could feel Tom's heat coming off him in waves. As soon as we were out of earshot, I tried to make things right.

"Now, Tom," I began, "I think Louis actually found that funny, so that's a *good*—"

Slowly, Tom reached out and grabbed me by the cravat. He pulled me upward until my feet dangled, my nose almost touching his.

"When all this is done," he said calmly, "we're going back to London. And when we reach the channel, I'm going to tie you to the stern of the boat. And you can swim home."

I couldn't tell if he was joking.

CHAPTER

SALLY MET US JUST OUTSIDE THE
exit. Spying Tom's face, and how gingerly we were walking, she rather wisely decided not to comment. She slipped
the rolled-up painting from beneath her dress.

"Let's go to Maison Chastellain," I said. "We need to
examine this, and I'd rather not do it anywhere near the
royal family. Besides, Marin knows the work better than
anyone; maybe he can help." I looked at Tom tentatively. "Is
that all right?"

"Whatever Monsieur Christopher decides," Tom said
acidly.

"You go ahead," Sally said. "I need to stay."

It turned out that, last night, after we'd returned to the Palais, Sally had made some inroads toward befriending the comtesse de Colmar.

"The ladies weren't lying," Sally said. "She's so lonely. You should have seen her when we spoke, like a frightened rabbit. I think she thought the other girls had put me up to playing a joke on her. The day before, they'd put a spider in her hair." She shook her head at the cruelty.

"Did she say anything about her husband?" I said.

"Not yet. But I can tell she's bursting to talk to someone. She was clinging to me this morning, all the way to the Louvre. She made me promise I'd have lunch—"

"Mademoiselle!"

Speak of the devil. The comtesse herself was hurrying toward us, calling Sally. "Mademoiselle Grace. I—"

She stopped when she saw me. She looked embarrassed, and a little scared—like a rabbit, as Sally had said. She was probably thinking of my confrontation with her husband.

I needed to put her mind at ease. *Courtly grace,* I told myself, and I bowed with a flourish. "Comtesse. Please accept my apologies for yesterday. My words to the comte were hasty, and ill bred."

That relaxed her a bit. "Forgive me," she said. "I didn't

mean to intrude." Though she clearly *did* want to intrude, as she looked anxiously at Sally.

I nodded toward her. "The Lady Grace was just saying how nice it was to have come to Paris and already made a friend."

"I'm so glad to have met her," the comtesse said, and, from the relief in her voice, I could tell she meant it. "In fact, the duchess has decided we're going shopping. All the ladies are going. You'll come, too, won't you, mademoiselle?" Her eyes were practically begging. *Please, please don't let me go alone.*

"Of course I will," Sally said. "And I've so wanted to do some shopping. You're incredibly kind to invite me." She paused. "Though . . . I don't have any servants to carry things for me."

Tom cleared his throat. For a moment, I thought he was going to switch sides, and he very well might have if the grateful comtesse hadn't interjected. "Please use mine, Mademoiselle Grace. We'll weigh them down nicely."

The young woman actually managed a smile. Sally grinned back, then waved me away. "Thank you for the conversation, Baron."

A very noble dismissal. I bowed, and Tom and I left

them. I heard giggling, and when I turned back Sally was whispering in the comtesse's ear. The woman was blushing.

"Maybe she's getting *too* good at this," I muttered.

"Perhaps then Monsieur Christopher should find himself a wife," Tom said.

I sighed.

We headed for the Île Notre-Dame. I did take us on a slight detour to a pâtisserie I'd spotted yesterday at the Place Dauphine, just off the Pont Neuf. There I loaded Tom up with sweets until he stopped calling me Monsieur Christopher. It cost a lot.

Tom, now speaking to me once more, was still a little woozy from all that heavy cream by the time we got to Maison Chastellain. As promised, the guards Simon had hired let us into the house, and Marin, in his study with his brandy as usual, seemed to be in good spirits, though the way his eyes flicked from me to Tom made me wonder if he knew who we were.

The painting he recognized immediately. "Poussin." He nodded. "There's a secret in here."

Now that was the problem. Where was it? The poem was supposed to give us the answer.

King is broken, man remains
Answer hidden in the stains.

"Well," Tom said, pausing for a moment to stifle a belch, "where do you think it is?"

"What do you mean?"

"That's what that other clue asked, didn't it? On the statue?"

Right—I'd forgotten. *La soluzione è dove pensa.* The answer is where you think.

The problem was, I had no idea what I thought. The first thing that came to mind was a cipher. *"Et in Arcadia ego,"*

I said, reading the tomb along with the shepherds. "That's where I'd look first. Maybe there's a code hidden in here."

"What kind?" Tom said.

I didn't know. If there was a code, then there should also be some sort of clue, either in the poem, or the painting itself.

Arcadia, the clue on the statue had said. Was that merely to direct us to the right painting? Or was there a hidden meaning in the word as well?

Marin liked the idea of looking at the inscription. "I've always thought the shepherds pointing meant something, but I've never been able to figure it out."

I looked more closely at the painting. The shepherd on the left was pointing directly at "ARCADIA." More specifically, he was pointing at the letter *R* in the word. I wondered if that was a clue. As for the shepherd on the right . . .

"Wait a minute." I frowned. "This shepherd's *not* pointing at the inscription."

Tom peered at it. Sure enough, the shepherd's finger missed the engraving entirely. "What's he doing?"

We leaned in as I traced a line from the shepherd's fingertip across the painting. The path just missed the top of the first shepherd's shadow on the tomb. It continued across the stone, ending at his forehead.

"Masters of misdirection," I whispered. "That's it."

When Tom and Marin looked at me, I said, "The shepherd. The second shepherd. Look where he's pointing. He's pointing *exactly where you think*."

"Where am I supposed to think he's pointing?" Tom said.

"Not where *you* think. Where you *think*. Do you see?" I tapped the canvas. "He's pointing at the other shepherd's *head*."

CHAPTER

39

MARIN LOOKED STUNNED. "WHERE you *think*," he said. "*Mon Dieu*. I would never have . . . but . . . no. I've spent years studying this painting. There's nothing here."

"I think you saw nothing because you didn't look deep enough," I said. "The poem says the answer is hidden *in* the stains."

Marin blinked. "You mean . . . the paint itself?"

I nodded. "It explains why Poussin said the copy wouldn't help. Because I'm guessing the next clue isn't in the part of the painting you can see. It's *underneath* it."

"How would you see underneath the paint?" Tom asked.

"The obvious way," I said.

It took him a moment to grasp what I meant. Then his eyes bulged. "You want to scrape off the Sun King's painting?"

"Actually, I was thinking we'd dissolve it." I pulled a vial of turpentine from my sash.

Tom buried his head in his hands. Even Marin looked shocked. "This is a masterpiece," he protested.

"And the best part is, when I'm finished, it still will be. There's a literally perfect copy in the Louvre."

"I suppose that's true, but, Peter . . . this is taking it rather far, isn't it?"

Tom and I exchanged a glance. Who was Peter?

I didn't correct him. Instead, I said, "We exchanged the paintings, so this one is yours now. It's up to you. But I really think the answer is beneath the oil."

"Well . . . all right. If Benedict trusts you, I do, too. Go ahead."

It took me a moment to put it together. He still recognized I was Master Benedict's apprentice—just the wrong one. He thought I was Peter Hyde, the apprentice my master had had before me.

Marin asked Rémi to fetch us a rag. I pulled the cork from the vial of turpentine, filling the room with its acrid stink. As I made to pour it, I hesitated, realizing what I was about to do. I sent a quick prayer heavenward—*Please don't let this be a mistake*—and then I dripped the liquid onto the kneeling shepherd's head.

I stirred it, and the oil paint started to liquefy. I dabbed it away with the rag, bit by bit. And then my heart thumped even faster—mixed with a deep sense of relief.

"It's there," Marin whispered. "It's *there*."

Letters. There were letters behind the painting, written directly on the canvas. I went faster now, dissolving more and more, until I'd uncovered the full message.

Or, I should say, all *three* messages.

le roi meurt. sauvez-le

the square reveals the key

khmbegzsbyejceajivxavutpvccism

"Another code," Tom said.

But it was more than that. "It's not just a code," I said with glee. "It's one I already know how to solve."

CHAPTER
40

TOM STARED. "YOU CAN SOLVE *THAT* just by looking at it?"

"No," I said. "I mean I know *how* to solve it. I understand the clue."

I pointed to the second line.

the square reveals the key

"Do you remember," I said, "when we found that code in the assassin's cloak, I mentioned the Vigenère cipher? Well, that's what this clue is saying. It's Vigenère."

"How do you know that?"

"Because the Vigenère cipher has another name: Sometimes it's called Vigenère's *square*."

I showed them why. I took a blank piece of paper from Marin's desk and wrote out the tool needed to decipher Vigenère. True to its name, it looked like a square.

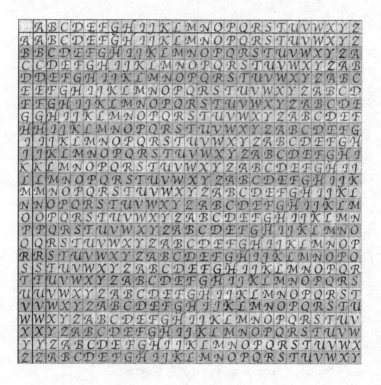

"That's . . . a mess," Tom said.

"It does look complicated," I said, remembering my own befuddlement when Master Benedict had first taught me how to use it. "But it's actually pretty easy. I'll show you."

I took another piece of paper and began to write. "You've seen a simple letter shift before. Suppose you have some words that you want to encipher." I wrote them down.

HELLO THERE

"To use a letter shift, all you do is decide how much you want to shift it by—say three, to the right—and then you shift each letter that much."

A B C D E F G H I J K L M N O P Q R S T U V W X Y Z
D E F G H I J K L M N O P Q R S T U V W X Y Z A B C

"Then you swap the letters according to the code, and 'hello there' becomes . . . "

H E L L O   T H E R E
K H O O R   W K H U H

"You can't read it anymore," Tom said.

"No. But this is really simple to break. All you have to do is try different shifts. Eventually, you'll find the right one."

"So then you need something more complicated," Tom said.

"Right. That's where Vigenère comes in. At its heart, Vigenère is a letter shift, like I showed you. What makes it unbreakable, however, is that the *amount* you shift each letter changes every time."

"If it changes, how do you know how much to shift it?"

"That's the most important part. Because what defines that shift is what we call a *key*. Watch."

I took a new piece of paper from Marin's desk. "Suppose again we want to encipher this message, 'hello there.' To use Vigenère, we choose a key. Let's keep it simple."

TOM

"What we do is take the original message, and above it, write out our key, repeating it as many times as we need to get to the end of the message."

T O M T O M T O M T
H E L L O T H E R E

"Now here's how we use the square. Take the first letter in the message—*H*—and find the row that starts with *H*. Then move along the columns to the first letter in our key: *T*. And then we swap the letter *H* with the letter that matches up with the *H* row and *T* column. In this case, that's the letter *A*."

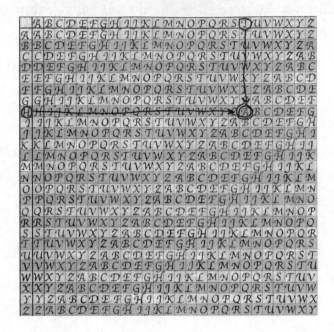

TOMTOMTOMT

HELLOTHERE

A

"Then we move on to the second letter. In our message, it's an *E*. In the key, it's an *O*. So according to our square, you replace it with . . . "

"An *S*," Tom finished.

"And so, like before," I said, "we write that down."

T O M T O M T O M T

H E L L O T H E R E

A S

"Now just keep going," I said, "and you get your new code. 'Hello there' becomes . . ."

T O M T O M T O M T

H E L L O T H E R E

A S X E C F A S D X

Tom mulled it over. "That's actually not that bad," he said. "See? I told you."

"But that's not what we're doing." He pointed to the code on the canvas. "We need to *de*cipher this."

"Yes."

"So . . . don't we need the key?"

"Absolutely. Otherwise, because the letters keep shifting, we'd never crack it. But do you see? The Templars already *gave* us the key."

I pointed to the inscription on the tomb. *"Et in Arcadia ego,"* I said. "I am even in . . ."

ARCADIA

CHAPTER
41

"THAT'S THE KEY," MARIN SAID,
surprised. "Arcadia *itself* is the key."

"It has to be," I said. "It's the same as the clue on the statue. So we can decipher the code right now."

"Do you do the same thing as before, then?" Tom said.

"Almost. It's just a small change to decipher something. First, write the code out. Then, as before, write the keyword above it."

A R C A D I A A R C A D I A A R C A D I A A R C A D I A A R
K H M B E G Z S B Y E J C E A J I V X A V U T P V C C I S M

"To decode it, then, here's what you do. Start on the row with the first letter of the *key*: A. Then move along the columns until you find the letter of the *code* that goes with it: K. From there, move up to see what the letter is at the top of the column. That's the first letter of the deciphered message: K."

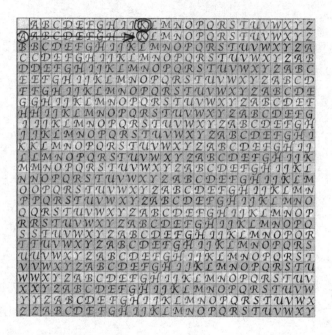

A R C A D I A A R C A D I A A R C A D I A A R C A D I A A R

K H M B E G Z S B Y E J C E A J I V X A V U T P V C C I S M

K

"Now move on to the next letter. It's R in the key . . . and H in the square . . . which goes up to Q."

ARCADIAARCADIAARCADIAARCADIAAR
KHMBEGZSBYEJCEAJIVXAVUTPVCCISM
KQ

"And just keep doing that until you're finished," I said.

Which is what I did. But the longer I wrote, the more my heart began to sink. Because when I was finished, what I had was . . . gibberish.

KQKBBYZSKWEGUEASGVUSVUCNVZUISV

"It doesn't work," Tom said.

I slumped in the chair, dejected.

Marin put a hand on my shoulder. "A moment, Peter, before you despair. We haven't yet addressed everything beneath the painting."

He pointed to the first line on the canvas.

le roi meurt. sauvez-le

"Is that French?" Tom said.

"Yes," I said. I hadn't missed it, exactly; I'd just thought the key to the code was "Arcadia." "It says: The king is dying. Save him."

Tom's eyes went wide. "Wait . . . are they talking about Louis?"

"They can't be. This painting is almost thirty years old. Louis wasn't even born when this message was written."

Marin agreed. "Other than Molay's curse, none of the riddles I've seen have ever included a threat."

The king is dying. Save him. Marin's comment made me wonder. "Might this be another reference to a prince of the blood?"

"Perhaps." Marin tapped his lip with his thumb. "Though 'save' is a curious instruction. I wonder if it's related to the next verse in the poem."

We did still have one more to decipher.

King is rotting, man upstart
Find the city's very heart.

"I don't suppose you know where the city's 'very heart' is," I asked Marin.

He sat, sipping pensively from his brandy. "It's a question I've pondered for ages. I'm not entirely certain how to view it. The *oldest* part of the city, from which the rest of Paris sprang, is the Île de la Cité. One might consider further that, spiritually, the Cathédrale Notre-Dame is the heart of the island."

That didn't sit quite right. "We've been to Notre-Dame," I said. "The first verse directed us there, and the second verse showed us where they'd hidden the next clue inside. I don't think the poem would then tell us to 'find' it, would it? Hasn't it already been found?"

"Possibly. Though remember: As always, the Templars are masters of misdirection. I suspect, if you keep that in your mind, that'll lead you to the key." He thought about it some more. "The Louvre might be another possibility. It's been, in a way, at the heart of Paris since it was built in the twelfth century. Since then, it's been a fortress, a treasury, a prison, and, for the last hundred and fifty years, the residence of the king. Politically, the Louvre is the heart of the city—and so the nation as well."

All these loops upon loops; they jumbled my brain. Suddenly I felt incredibly tired. It was deflating to come so close to an answer and end up with nothing. And the warmth of the study was lulling me to sleep. "We should get back to the Palais."

As Marin's mind hadn't been quite right—alongside

my own, it felt like—I took the time to make my master's recipe for his calmative and left it with Colette. Then Tom and I said our goodbyes.

We didn't talk much on our way back. Tom kept glancing behind him to see if we were being followed by any cloak-shrouded assassins, and I was mostly lost in thought.

As we passed the Louvre, Tom paused. "Why don't you think this might be the city's heart?" he asked.

I shrugged. "It just doesn't feel right. These riddles were set by the Templars, and if there's one thing we can be sure of, it's that the Templars don't like the kings of France. Would they really refer to their enemies' home as 'the city's very heart'?"

"I guess not." Tom thought about it. "What about the old Templar grounds, then? That would be *their* heart, wouldn't it? Would that fit the poem?"

"Maybe. Though there haven't been any Templars there for centuries. And no one even uses the Great Tower any-more. Would they call that the city's very heart? It's more or less been abandoned."

Unless, like Marin said, that was more misdirection. Rather petulantly, I kicked at the door to the Palais as we entered. Was it too much to ask to have *one* thing be simple?

"What do we do now?" Tom said.

All I really wanted to do was lie down. We returned to our quarters, but as soon as I'd flopped onto the bed, there was a scratch on the door from a fingernail, which was the style in royal Paris, instead of a knock.

Tom opened the door. One of the page boys pressed a letter into his hand. "Message for monsieur."

Tom handed me the letter as the boy hurried off. I looked at the name on the back.

Baron Christopher Ashcombe
Le Palais-Royal

I recognized the handwriting, with its loopy swirls. "It's from Sally," I said, surprised. I opened it and read the message inside.

My dear Lord Ashcombe,

Are you enjoying your time in Paris? Being out in the city has been a delight, but the unfamiliarity of everything has begun to wear, and now I feel so terribly homesick. Would you share a cup of chocolate with me when I return to the Palais? Oh, please do say yes. I so miss talk of England.

The Lady Grace

Tom was confused. "What's this about?" he said.

"The assassin," I said, voice rising. "It's about the assassin." I held the letter up. "I think Sally's figured out who he is."

CHAPTER
42

TOM BLINKED. "WHERE DOES IT say that?"

"It doesn't, exactly," I said. "It's the fact that she sent the letter at all. Sally was going to learn from the comtesse who her husband's business partners were." I stood, pacing. "She must have found something *big*, because the only reason to send this message is to make sure I know she's learned something, and it can't wait until tomorrow."

"But if she knows who the assassin is, why not just write that? 'It's Francois, *le butcherre. Arrestez* him.'"

"Because I think she's worried."

"About what?"

"About who'll read this message." I lowered my voice. "The fact she *doesn't* say it outright is a clue. I think the assassin is here *now*."

"In the Palais?" Tom said, startled.

I nodded. "I think that's what this reference to England means. Like at the party: The assassin's worked his way into the palace, posing as a servant."

"But . . . that could be anybody!"

I bit my lip. "None of us should go anywhere alone."

Tom looked scared. "We're not going to go looking for him, are we?"

I considered it. If we found him here, identified him, we could try to stop him right now. On the other hand, he'd thrown a dagger at me yesterday in the open street. What would he do if we cornered him inside the Palais?

And that was if I'd understood Sally's message correctly. The smart thing to do would be to see what she knew before we decided how to handle it. I think Tom was as surprised as he was relieved that, for once, we were going to do the smart thing and not hunt for the man while we were blind.

That didn't mean I wanted to wait until this evening, however. "Let's go see that page," I said.

We wandered the halls nervously until we found the

boy downstairs, carrying a message for another guest. "This letter," I said, showing him Sally's note. "Where's the courier who brought it?"

"He left, monsieur," the page said.

"Do you know where he went?"

"No, monsieur."

I tapped my lip. "The duchess went shopping today. I don't suppose you know where that is."

He shook his head. "Could be anywhere in the city, monsieur. Many merchants serve Madame."

"And she'll return . . . ?"

"Late, monsieur. Madame is something of a night bird."

No luck, then, after all. Frustrated, I let the page go. "We'll just have to wait," I grumbled to Tom. I arranged for an evening pot of chocolate from the kitchen, then wrote a carefully-worded letter to leave on Sally's bed.

My dear Lady Grace,
I would be delighted to see you this evening. Please
send someone to my quarters when you arrive. I'll
collect you from yours and escort you to the library for
our chocolate. It's lovely there at night, with the fire.
The Baron Ashcombe

"Hopefully she'll understand she should send someone first," I said. "I don't want her walking these halls alone."

"But what if the assassin reads this?" Tom said. "Won't he know where we're going to be? What if he lies in wait for us?"

"Let him. We're not going to the library. We'll find somewhere where there are plenty of palace guards instead."

Still, I realized all this dancing around could have been avoided if I'd set things up better beforehand. "Remind me when this is over," I said. "I'm going to think up a secret code just for the three of us. That way, the next time there's an assassin around, we can pass each other messages in safety."

Tom looked horrified. "What do you mean, the *next* time?"

We returned to our quarters. To be on the safe side, Tom and I shifted my bed to block the door. Then I lay back down, while Tom began to practice with his sword.

My mind raced, wondering what Sally had discovered. Eventually, I forced myself to shove those thoughts from my head. Sally was doing her job. I needed to do mine.

That verse. That last verse. *Find the city's very heart.*

I pulled out Lord Ashcombe's map and studied it. As Marin had said, Paris had begun as a settlement on the Île de la Cité. It had grown over the centuries, spreading outward beyond the river, roots digging in north and south of the Seine.

The city's very heart.

I sat against the wall and traced a circle around the map.

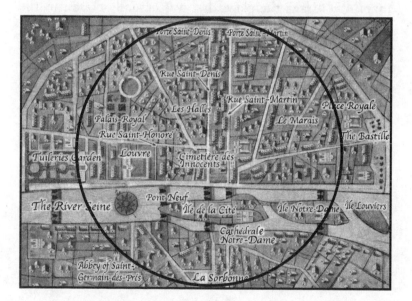

The center of the circle landed to the north of the Île de la Cité. I peered at what was closest.

Toward the south was the cathedral itself. I'd already discarded that idea.

The Louvre was there, too, to the west. Again, not likely.

Les Halles was nearby. Now that was interesting. Les Halles was the biggest market in Paris—in all of France, really. Everyone from peasants to kings bought something there: food, clothing, and every other human need. In a way, one could consider that the heart of the city.

I mulled it over. As I did, my gaze drifted across the map. And I saw: the place that was actually closest to the middle of Paris wasn't the market.

It was the cemetery.

Le Cimetière des Innocents was practically at the center of the circle I'd drawn. And, as I stared at the map, I heard Tom in my head, talking to Sir William, when we'd first entered Paris. The moat had stank; the streets had stank; the mud had stank. And the farther we came, the worse the stink got, because of the cemetery.

It's kept the bones of Parisians for five hundred years, Sir William had said.

And Tom had replied, *Who builds a city around a cemetery?*

The people of Paris did. Which meant that here, when you died . . . you'd be buried at your city's very heart.

CHAPTER
43

I LEAPED FROM MY BED.

Tom backed off, surprised. "In case you hadn't noticed, I'm swinging a sword here."

"Well, keep a grip on it," I said, drawing my own blade. "Because we're leaving."

"Where?"

I didn't quite want to tell him yet. We pulled the bed away from the door, then opened it with flat of my blade, as if it were trapped. When nothing happened, I poked my head into the hallway.

No assassins waiting—or at least none that I could see. "Come on."

We crept through the Palais, trying to avoid everyone. It wasn't until we approached the exit that we sheathed our swords; it wouldn't do to charge into Paris brandishing steel.

We hurried along the streets, then, watching once more to see we weren't followed. It wasn't until Tom was fairly certain there wasn't an assassin behind us that he finally remembered he didn't yet know where we were going.

When I told him, he stopped in horror. "The *cemetery? Why?*"

"Because it makes the most sense," I said. "It's at the center of the map. Plus, it fits the poem. It's confusing enough, yet straightforward enough, to be misdirection. And it focuses on the true heart of any city: the people. It's the people who make Paris what it is. And they've been buried there for five hundred years."

The Cimetière was only half a mile away from the Palais, directly east on Rue Saint-Honoré, but I decided we should take a more circuitous route, in case we'd missed someone shadowing us. If we'd been going anywhere else, we might have got lost, but all we needed to do was follow the stench.

Tom wrapped his cloak over his nose; I did the same. It didn't help much. The stink of rot got worse the closer we came. Even Bridget, flying overhead, kept swooping down and cooing, as if trying to warn us away from the smell.

The cemetery grounds covered as much area as the Louvre. They were surrounded by a stone wall, ten feet high, so we couldn't see inside from the road. And, as we soon learned, that was a good thing.

Inside those walls was a grim and terrible sight. The land was pitted with mass graves. Hundreds, *thousands* of bodies lay tangled in piles in the mud. The groundskeepers had covered them with quicklime, but the caustic powder seemed to have little effect. The rotting stench of decay didn't merely fill the air. It *was* the air.

My stomach roiled. "Christopher—" Tom said, gagging, and then he ran back outside. I joined him, retching, as we vomited what remained of this morning's pastries in the street.

All that cream wasted. Tom wiped his mouth. "I don't like the Templars anymore," he said.

I wasn't sure I did, either. But back in we had to go. Spitting out bile, I pulled the rosewater from my sash and poured it over his collar and my cravat. We held them to our faces as we made our way back inside.

The horror within didn't end in the ground. *Millions*

of Parisians had been buried here over the years, and of course there was no room for millions. To make space, the keepers had exhumed old graves, in which the bodies had already decayed. They'd moved the bones to the charnel houses instead, the depositories in the arched supports that ringed the interior of the cemetery's walls. Beneath cracked shingles, we could see the skulls. Hundreds of thousands of them surrounded us, staring down with hollow-socket eyes.

"This is a place of horror," Tom said. "Please, Christopher. I want to go."

"All right," I said, head bowed. "Go back to the Palais. I'll come get you when I'm done."

Tom looked like he was going to cry, but he didn't leave me. I was deeply grateful. I don't think I could have borne this place alone.

There were several men inside, working the graves. We turned away from them as they dumped a cart full of bodies into another pit. Then we hurried to the church in the northeast corner of the grounds.

The priest we found was a stolid sort, quiet and expressionless. He didn't introduce himself. He simply asked how he could be of service.

Now I had to figure out what to look for. I thought of

the clue under Poussin's painting. *The king is dying. Save him.* "Are there any kings buried here?" I asked, trying to breathe as little as possible.

"No, monsieur. The kings of France are buried in the royal necropolis, at the Basilica of Saint-Denis."

"Where's that?"

"In the town of Saint-Denis, north of the city. Around six miles away."

That clearly wouldn't be the right place. "Is there anything here about kings at all?"

"Only one king treads this ground, monsieur: the King of Kings, our Savior the Lord, who abandons no one, no matter how poor."

I desperately didn't want to spend any more time searching this place than I had to. I decided to be more direct. "What about the Templars? Is there anything related to them?"

And to my surprise, he said, "Yes, monsieur. There is a crypt underneath one of the charnel houses, the *charnier des Lingères*. The tombs are said to hold the remains of Knights Templar who were interred here before the construction of their headquarters." He pointed us to the south, to an entrance along the wall, and wished us the blessing of God.

We went where he directed. Painted on the stone, underneath the bones of the charnel, was a *danse macabre*. The mural showed Death in his skeletal form, leading away all manner of people: pope and emperor, doctor and peasant, lady and infant, cardinal and king. The ultimate memento mori: Everyone dies.

The entrance led to a narrow staircase. The darkness down here was profound, so I returned to the church and bought some candles to light our way.

We held the candles aloft, Tom and I, the flames flickering away the darkness. And we stared, surprised, as the walls flashed back.

They were gold.

CHAPTER
44

I FROZE. *THE TREASURE*.

But it wasn't, for no hoard could have remained here this long, even in a place so untraveled. What had made my heart skip a beat were golden plates, rectangular tomb markers, set into the walls in pairs. There were sixty of them, one above, one below, circling the chamber. Underneath each was a copper name plaque, all now unreadable, corroded over centuries by verdigris.

But the plates themselves were pristine. Not merely untarnished, but polished—and recently. To someone, somewhere—perhaps the Templars themselves—these tombs still mattered enough to be cared for.

"This must be it," I said.

Tom relaxed a little. Not only would we not have to stalk the cemetery anymore, the smell down here wasn't nearly as bad. It was musty but carried little stench of rot. "So what are we actually looking for?" he said.

The king is dying. Save him.

With the name plaques obscured, the only clues were the plates that covered the tombs. At the top of each, the same symbol was hammered into the gold: two circles with images we'd seen before.

The one on the left showed the two brothers on one horse, riding with lances at the ready. The other held the Dome of the Rock, their headquarters in Jerusalem. A Templar cross rested within the circles near the top, with words in Latin carved around them: SIGILLUM MILITUM DE TEMPLO CRISTI. The Seal of the Soldiers of Christ's Temple.

In the center, every plate depicted a different scene. Half of them were of warfare: knights riding into battle with lances held high, Templars and Saracens clashing blades, skirmishers volleying arrows at their foes. Other panels showed more mundane events: a farmer tending to his sheep, a man fishing from the prow of a boat, girls carting laundry down to the river. And then there were the fantastical. On one plate, a knight fought a dragon, swinging a wickedly spiked morning star into the monster's breath of fire. In another, a man in a hood spoke to a woman with the head of a lion.

One of these images had to hold the answer. Tom and I worked from opposite ends, studying the plates. They reminded me a little of the stone carvings we'd seen inside the Great Tower—though, spying a man riding a winged horse, I imagined these weren't meant to be taken so literally.

I felt certain the symbols would be the key. I noticed that some of those here were the same as we'd seen at the order's former grounds. Every plate had the Templar seal at the top, of course, but I also recognized the sun on two of the plates. In the middle of both suns was the equal-armed, flared-end Templar cross, like in the Great Tower, on the scene of the nine being blessed by King Baldwin, and on the panel Philippe le Bel had damaged in his rage.

Kings, I thought. Both of those men were kings. Le Bel hadn't been depicted in the Tower carvings, of course, but Baldwin had. We'd recognized him by . . .

"His crown," I said. "Look for a crown. Anywhere."

It was Tom who found it. "Christopher."

I went over to him, standing before a pair of panels. He pointed at the bottom one. "Look."

The plate depicted a battle scene—or, rather, the aftermath of one. On the right lay three men, heads wrapped in turbans. They were dead, each with a sword stuck through his chest. Behind them were overlapping sand dunes and five tall palm trees with long, droopy leaves. On the left, a knight lay on the ground, mouth open. A second knight knelt over him, tipping a goblet above the man's head. Behind them, strangely, was a fox eating a rooster.

"Why do you think—" I began.

Tom tapped the bottom left corner of the plate. That's when I saw what he'd spotted.

Hidden in the border was a crown. It looked like it had slipped from the head of the knight on the ground and rolled into the corner.

I grabbed Tom's arm. "You've found it."

"Wonderful," he said. "Now what?"

Good question. *The king is dying. Save him.* "How do we save the king?" I muttered.

"The goblet the knight above him is holding," Tom said. "Is that some kind of medicine?"

I didn't know. The king's mouth was open, as if ready to drink whatever the knight was giving him. But despite the goblet being upside down, nothing poured from it. If I was supposed to figure out what medicine he was getting, I'd need to know what was wrong with him.

I peered more closely at the engraving. And I frowned. "Do you see a wound here?"

Tom shook his head. I looked at the fallen Saracens.

There was no mistaking their problems: They'd been stuck with swords.

"If the king has no injury," I said, "then why is he dying?"

"A disease?" Tom said.

A disease would explain the goblet; the knight giving him medicine to cure it. But the king's skin wasn't marked, so if it was a disease, I had no way of knowing which one. Unless the fox eating the rooster was a clue.

"Does that mean anything to you?" Tom asked.

I wasn't sure. Though I got the strange feeling I'd seen these symbols before. Unlike "Arcadia," it *hadn't* been recently. I kept thinking of Master Benedict.

Some medicine he'd taught me? Or something else?

"What about the trees?" Tom said. "What are those?"

"Probably date palms," I said. "They're quite common in—"

That was it.

"The desert," I said. "They're in the *desert*."

"So?"

"Look," I said. "The king has no injuries, but he's dying. The man's trying to save him, but his cup is empty. So if there's no wound, and no disease, what else would kill the king?"

Tom's eyes went wide. "He's dying of *thirst*."

"Yes."

"So . . . we give him water? How do you give an engraving something to drink?"

"Remember my puzzle box?" I said. "Maybe there's a lever, like in that. Somewhere we could pour water in to open a lock."

We looked everywhere. On the plate, above it, below. We studied the cracks in the walls nearby, looking for a hole. We couldn't see anything.

"What now?" Tom said.

"Maybe there's a crack we've missed. Let's just try pouring water on the plate."

Tom looked dubious, but he didn't stop me. I pulled the vial of water from my apothecary sash and poured it onto the gold, letting it run from the knight's cup so it flowed down into the king's mouth. It trickled past, over his head, and welled in a small pool at the bottom of the plate, where it dripped over the edge and spattered on the stone.

And . . . nothing happened.

"That would have made so much sense, too," I said, disappointed.

"What about these?" Tom pointed at the fox eating the rooster. "We still don't know what they mean."

I studied the symbols again, and the more I did, the more something nagged at the back of my mind. What was I missing?

I closed my eyes. I saw my master, standing before me. *Think, Christopher*, he said. *What do those symbols signify?*

If I knew that, I said, *I wouldn't be standing in a crypt with my eyes shut.*

How very amusing. He sounded exactly like Louis XIV.

Sorry, Master.

Surely you haven't already begun to forget what I've taught you?

The thought horrified me. *Never, Master. I would never.*

Then think. For I've shown you these symbols before.

The rooster. Some time after I'd joined Master Benedict, he'd had me read a book about symbols. It said the rooster was one of the symbols for the Sun. I'd thought that was odd, until my master had pointed out what the rooster was most famous for: crowing in the morning, with the dawn.

So if the rooster was the Sun, then what was the fox? The Moon?

I frowned. I couldn't remember a fox.

Maybe I was going about this the wrong way. The rooster was the Sun. Another symbol for the Sun was—

"Gold," I said, surprised. "The metal on the plates is gold."

"All right," Tom said, puzzled. "And?"

And what is the fox doing? Master Benedict said.

He's eating it, I said.

And I had it.

"I know," I said, and my eyes opened wide. "I know how to save the king."

CHAPTER
45

"HOW?" TOM SAID.

I began rooting through my apothecary sash again. "He needs water."

"We just gave him water."

"Yes, but it wasn't good enough. He's a king, right? So he needs *royal* water."

Tom frowned. "There's royal water now?"

"Yes," I said. "Aqua regia. It's something my master taught me to make, long ago."

I found the two vials I was looking for and pulled them from the sash.

"I don't understand," Tom said.

"That's because the name's a little misleading. Aqua regia isn't actually water. You remember oil of vitriol? The stuff that eats through certain kinds of metal?"

"Of course."

"Aqua regia is like that. Except it dissolves something very special. In all the world, it's the only thing capable of dissolving gold."

I tapped the plate in front of us.

"You're saying . . . we have to dissolve this plate?" Tom said.

"That's what these symbols mean. The rooster is gold. The fox is eating the rooster—dissolving the gold. That's the key. The king's dying of thirst, so we need to give him water: aqua regia, the royal water. *That's* what we drip into his mouth. It'll dissolve the gold and reveal what's inside this crypt."

"Is aqua regia hard to make?"

"Not at all. It's easy, and it only takes two ingredients." I held up the vials. "Aqua fortis, and spirits of salt."

"Can I help?"

I hesitated. "Actually . . . it's probably better if you go stand in that corner. The far one. Over there."

Tom's eyes narrowed. "Wait. Is this going to explode?"

"No, no. It's just . . . aqua regia gives off a gas."

"Which smells bad?"

"Yes."

He waited. "And?"

"It's . . . a little poisonous," I said.

Tom buried his face in his hands and moaned.

"We'll be fine," I assured him. "Though . . . if I start vomiting, could you carry me out of here?"

He went into the corner, muttering things that weren't very nice.

All right, time to get to work. I thought back to what my master had showed me. *Pour the spirits of salt into the vial. Add, with great care, the aqua fortis. The final mixture should be one-quarter aqua fortis, three-quarters spirits of salt. Stir together gently with a silver spoon.*

And do NOT breathe the fumes.

I did as he instructed, using the empty vial of water and the silver spoon to mix them. As I stirred, the liquid changed color: It turned yellow, then orange, and finally, a clear and brilliant red.

That wasn't the only change. I turned my head away, blinking, as the vial began to fume, filling the air with a sour stink. It didn't smell as bad as the cemetery—but then the cemetery air wouldn't kill you.

My eyes began to tear, and I started sneezing. I needed to work quickly, but also carefully. I didn't know how thick the gold was, and I didn't have aqua regia to waste. So, instead of pouring it, I used the handle of the silver spoon to drip the liquid onto the plate. When I'd dripped enough to run from the cup to the king's mouth, I placed the vial on the ground and went to stand near Tom, hacking to clear my head of the poison.

Dissolving the gold would be slow. I waited a few minutes, then went back to wipe off what I'd already poured and drip some more on the plate. The drying liquid came away in reddish crystals—dragon's blood, my master had called it—packed inside with hidden gold.

The fumes took their toll. The longer I worked, the drier my throat became. Worse, as the time passed, I began to get restless and agitated, a definite symptom of fume poisoning. When it got so bad I felt like vomiting, I had to go upstairs—though breathing in the wretched cemetery air did nothing to quell my nausea.

Still, there wasn't much else I could do. It took over an

hour for a rut to form in the plate, and another two before the aqua regia finally opened a hole in the gold.

I nearly collapsed in relief. We scrambled over, holding a candle close to peer inside.

I couldn't see anything. I stuck my finger in and poked around. "There's a metal bar in here," I said.

"More gold?" Tom said.

"I'm not sure. It feels like some kind of lever—"

It shifted under pressure of my finger. There was a click and the brief sound of scraping stone, and then the plate fell forward.

Tom caught it before it crushed my toes. We laid the plate down. Then we looked into the tomb.

It was empty.

The space inside was narrow, just large enough to hold a single body. But there were no remains here, and no evidence of anything left behind, either.

My heart began to sink. This *had* to be the right crypt. The symbols, the lever—everything led us right here. A terrible thought occurred to me: Had whatever once rested here been removed? Had someone else already found this hiding spot and taken it?

Tom frowned. "Christopher."

He pointed at the plate at our feet. We'd laid it face-down, so now we could see its back.

It wasn't gold on this side. The mechanism of the lever and the lock was hidden behind an iron cover, which was dull, and marred by streaks of rust. But as I looked closer, I could see what Tom had spotted: There were markings engraved in the iron.

I pulled the vial of lemon juice from my sash. I tore a strip from the bottom of my shirt, soaked it with the juice—it would remove the rust—and used it to rub the back of the plate. The linen turned brown as the rust came away, and within a few minutes I could see the symbols hidden beneath.

CHAPTER
46

Wherever you think I am, you will find me at the opposite.

"WHAT IS THAT?" TOM SAID.

I shook my head. "I don't know."

A thin circle covered about half the plate. In the center was a fleur-de-lis. Around the outside of the circle were five different groups of letters: *E*, *N*, *SW*, *S*, and *NW*.

"It looks like a compass," I said.

"Are those directions, then?" Tom said.

I frowned. Directions had been my first thought: east, north, southwest, south, and northwest. But if they were directions, they didn't line up right. On the opposite side of north was south, as one would suspect. But the other points of the compass were all wrong. East was closer to where west should have been. And northwest was between east and south, exactly the opposite as well.

As I studied the back of the plate, I noticed something else below the circle, still covered somewhat by the rust. I used the rest of the lemon juice to rub it away and saw that they were words, in English.

> *Wherever you think I am, you will find me at*
> *the opposite.*

"This is it," I said. "This is what we've been looking to find all along. I think this is a treasure map."

"It's just a big circle," Tom said.

"There are directions on it," I pointed out. "And a fleur-de-lis."

Figuring out what the directions meant, however, was something else. "Any ideas?" Tom said.

I stared at it, confused. "No."

"In that case, do we have to work it out here?"

He had a point. This false tomb might have been empty, but the others probably weren't. There wasn't any reason to remain among the dead.

Using the quill and ink from my sash, I copied the map onto the back of Voiture's poem. Then Tom and I locked the panel back in place and headed toward the Palais.

Once again, we took a winding route to make sure we weren't followed. Now that we had the final treasure map— and I was certain that was what we carried—I felt more vulnerable than ever.

We entered the Palais cautiously. The first thing we did was check if Sally was back, but the servants told us Minette hadn't yet returned. That was frustrating—all this creeping about was fraying my nerves—but it also meant that, wherever the ladies were, at least they were still safe. If there had been an incident, someone would have informed the palace immediately.

Regardless, there was nothing Tom and I could do about it. So we went back to our quarters to think. I sat on the edge of the bed and studied the treasure map while Tom polished his sword.

My mind kept returning to the strangeness of the directions. Why were some of them opposite to where they should be? Was that more misdirection? Or was it a clue to the message written beneath?

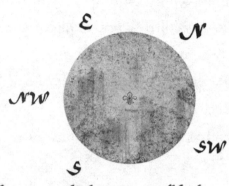

Wherever you think I am, you will find me at the opposite.

I tried to reorient the map in my head. The fleur-de-lis defined the center. There were five marked locations around the circle.

And the thought came, unbidden: Five.

I sat up, mind racing. Father Bernard's words burned in my memory. *If you think of the knights traveling away from Paris as a circle moving outward, then—*

"The knights," I said.

Tom looked up from his sword. "What knights?"

"The Templars. The ones who escaped le Bel. There

were *five* of them. And they went to—" I leaped from the bed. "That's it!"

"What is?" Tom said.

"This map. The compass directions don't make sense because they're *not* compass directions. Remember what Father Bernard told us? There were five knights who escaped. And where did they go?"

Tom thought about it. "One went to England. One went to Spain. One went . . ."

He trailed off as I tapped the letters on the map. I pointed to the *E*. "England." Then the *S*. "Spain." Then the rest of the letters. "*N* is Netherlands. *SW* is the Swiss cantons. And *NW* is—"

"Across the ocean," Tom said, surprised. "To the New World."

"They're not in the wrong place," I said. "They're exactly where they're supposed to be. This is a map of the world. The fleur-de-lis is Paris. The rest of the places are where the knights who escaped went. And one of those places holds the Templar treasure."

"So what does that warning mean?" He nodded toward the sentence at the bottom.

"More misdirection, I guess. If the clues we've found

tell us the treasure was sent to one of these places, then it was actually sent to the opposite side of the map."

Tom frowned. "That doesn't make sense."

"Why not?"

"Because . . . look. Suppose you think the knights took it to the Netherlands. Then that means they actually took it to Spain instead. But then you'd think they took it to Spain . . . so wouldn't that mean it was in the Netherlands?"

"I don't think that's how it works," I said dubiously.

"I don't think it works at all." He threw his sword on his palliasse. "We've spent all this time, worked out Voiture's whole poem, went digging in a bloody *cemetery*, just to find a map that tells us what we already knew when we started. That five knights went to five different places, and one of them had the treasure. Yet we haven't found a single clue as to which of those places he went."

That made me pause. Tom was right. We *hadn't* found anything to tell us the treasure's location. For all of our running around, we'd only gone in a circle, no closer to the treasure than when we'd left Father Bernard.

"No, wait," I said. "We *do* have one more clue. The code from behind the painting."

I took out the other piece of paper, the one on which I'd written Poussin's cipher.

KHMBEGZSBYEJCEAJIVXAVUTPVCCISM

The square reveals the key, it had said. "*This* must give us the location. We just have to work it out."

"But we had the code *already*," Tom said. "And we already knew where the five knights went. So what's the point of the map?"

Now I was confused, too. "I . . . I don't know. I guess . . . the code gives us the location, and the map . . . tells us to look in the opposite place?"

"You don't need a map for that." Tom flopped onto his palliasse, next to his sword. "You know what I think?" he said sourly. "I think someone's playing a joke. I don't think there's a treasure anymore at all."

The thought made my guts churn. Could he be right? Could this whole thing be nothing more than a prank?

A centuries-long prank. It seemed outlandish. Why would anyone do this? For what purpose? Was it like the florins, merely to taunt the kings of France?

It was nearly impossible to believe. But Tom's words

had planted doubt inside, and I couldn't seem to shake it. If this was all a joke, I'd wasted all this time, time I was supposed to spend protecting Minette. I'd been failing my mission right from the very start.

It couldn't be true. There *had* to be a treasure. There just *had* to be.

Oh, Master, I called up to him. *Please help.*

But this time, he didn't have any words for me. I crumpled onto my bed, deflated. What was I supposed to do now?

I had no ideas. Just the worthless treasure map, and the still-jumbled code from Poussin's shepherds. So I dragged myself over to the desk, pulled out the cipher, and stared at it for a very long while.

Gibberish.

The code was gibberish. It started as gibberish, Vigenère turned it into more gibberish, and gibberish was what I was left with.

"Arcadia" was the clue we'd found at Notre-Dame. *Et in Arcadia ego.* I am even in Arcadia. The square reveals the key.

Except the square revealed nothing. Arcadia revealed nothing. The code behind the painting revealed nothing.

I spent hours trying to figure it out. I studied the code and reworked it with Vigenère, in case I'd made a mistake. Played with it. Used a different language. *Et in Arcadia ego*: That was Latin; and I'd stumbled over the different Latin alphabet before. But redoing the cipher offered no solution.

"Arcadia" clearly wasn't the key. So I tried other keys. Et. In. Ego. The whole phrase. Poussin. Templars. Molay. Le Bel. Absolutely anything I could think of that might possibly work. I still ended up with nothing.

I was left staring, once more, between the undeciphered code and the map. And I wondered: What if we'd missed a clue along the way? It's not like we really knew what we were looking for.

My heart sank even further. If we'd really missed a clue, I had no idea where to find it. There were only two things left we didn't understand: what the purpose of the map was, and this stupid code. I kicked the crumpled papers toward the fireplace with the rest of my failed attempts and wished—as always—that Master Benedict was here.

Tom had dozed off, his absurdly polished sword across his lap. He woke as the paper I kicked bonked him on the head. "Hey," he said in protest.

"Sorry," I grumbled.

He rubbed his eyes and looked outside. It was dark. "What time is it?"

"I don't know. Late."

"Have you been at that all evening? Why don't you take a break?"

"I don't have time to take a break. Every day that passes is another day the assassins might kill Minette." Or us.

"Can I help, then?" Tom said.

I threw my quill down in disgust. "Only if you can solve this clue for me."

"Are you thinking about misdirection?"

"Always. And you know what the problem with that is? It just makes you doubt everything you're doing. Because whatever you're doing, it's probably wrong. By that measure, *anything* can be misdirection." I crumpled a blank piece of paper this time and booted the inoffensive wad into the flames.

"What about wordplay?" Tom said.

"What do you mean?"

"Well . . . like with the statue of le Bel. You thought 'underfoot' meant below the ground. But it was literal: It actually meant *under* his *foot*. The painting, too. There was a clue that said, 'The solution is where you think.' At first, you thought that meant the secret was where you'd think it would *be*. But the real answer, again, was literal: It was where you *think*, in your head."

I stared at him. "That is an *excellent* point."

He flushed with pride. "Well, I am a true son of England."

I laughed, my spirits brightened. "All right, you *goddon*. What should I be taking literally?"

"Well, what did the painting say? 'I am in Arcadia'? Maybe you should look *in* Arcadia, then. When Master Benedict taught you about it, did he ever say anything about what was inside Arcadia? Anything like a key?"

An interesting idea, though he'd got the translation slightly wrong. "It says, 'I am *even* in Arcadia.' Actually, it really says, 'And in Arcadia I am,' but it's a better translation to say 'even.'"

"So what about that, then? Could that mean something? And, or even?"

I thought about it. "And" had so many meanings: with, added to, also, repeated. "Even" meant lots of things, too. Level. Alike. Harmonious.

Harmonious?

I sat up. Arcadia was, by definition, a place of harmony. I pictured the painting in my mind, tried to see what was there. The sky, the trees, the tomb, the maiden. The shepherds, with their staves. There were three of them. One of them had been pointing at 'Arcadia'; specifically, at the *R*. And the code had been hidden behind—

Wait.

I'd missed it. I'd *missed* it.

I'd seen it before. But when I saw the second shepherd pointing and found the code behind the paint, I'd forgotten all about the *first* one.

He'd been pointing at the *R*. The *R* was the second letter in Arcadia. The second shepherd had been pointing at the second letter—

Even.

That was it.

That was *it*.

CHAPTER 47

I STARED AT TOM. "NUMBERS."

Tom looked puzzled. "Which numbers?"

"Even. Another meaning of 'even' is *numbers*. Two, four, six. They're called even."

"All right. I'm still confused."

"If you take *Et in Arcadia ego* to mean 'I am even in Arcadia,'" I said, "then maybe we *should* take it literally. Like you said. So then the key isn't 'Arcadia.' It's the even letters *in* 'Arcadia.'"

I grabbed another piece of paper. I wrote out the code again, this time using only the even letters in Arcadia: *RAI*.

RAIRAIRAIRAIRAIRAIRAIRAIRAIRAI
KHMBEGZSBYEJCEAJIVXAVUTPVCCISM

Then I used the square to decipher the code. It only took a few letters to make my heart thump even faster.

RAIRAIRAIRAIRAIRAIRAIRAIRAIRAI
KHMBEGZSBYEJCEAJIVXAVUTPVCCISM
THEKEYISTHEBLESSINGANDTHECURSE

It worked. The message revealed itself, plain as day.

The key is the blessing and the curse.

"What does that mean?" Tom said.

"I have no idea." I laid my head on the desk. "I swear, these Templars are trying to kill me."

"Maybe *they're* the assassins." Tom stretched. "Did Sally come back while I was asleep?"

"No." I frowned. "What time *is* it?"

I clearly needed to add a pocket watch to the collection of tools in my sash. In the meantime, hands on our blades, we left our quarters in search of a clock. We found one in the nearest study. I was startled to see it was almost midnight.

"Surely Minette should have come home by now," Tom said.

The halls were quiet. I moved cautiously, Tom following, until we came upon a servant putting out candles in the foyer.

"Has the duchess not returned?" I asked him.

"Of course she has, monsieur," he said. "After shopping, Madame had dinner at the Louvre, then went to watch a play. She retired around half an hour ago."

Half an hour ago? Then where was Sally?

I asked the man if he'd seen her, and he said, "Yes, monsieur. The Lady Grace returned with Madame."

My stomach began to twist. My note for Sally told her to call for us right away. So why hadn't anyone come?

Tom and I rushed to Sally's quarters and scratched at the door. A bleary-eyed chambermaid peeked her head out. "Monsieur?"

"I need to speak to Mademoiselle Grace," I said.

"She's not here, monsieur."

"What? Where is she?"

"I don't know. She left around twenty minutes ago—Monsieur!"

The girl stumbled back, shocked, as I pushed the door open.

Sally's quarters, unlike mine, weren't separate. There were five beds crammed in here, a young lady in each one, with a palliasse on the floor for her servant. The girls drew their blankets up to cover their bedclothes and shouted in protest.

I ignored their outrage and shoved the empty palliasse aside to get to Sally's bed. The letter I'd left for her had been opened. I picked it up.

"Did she read this before she left?" I said to the chambermaid.

"How dare you, Baron!" one of the ladies said.

Tom took the letter from me and looked it over. The servant girl backed away as I stepped closer. "I asked you a question," I said.

"Yes, monsieur," she said nervously. "Mademoiselle read it."

"Baron!" the lady said again.

I whirled on her. "Mademoiselle Grace is missing. Don't you care?"

Her expression told me that, in fact, she didn't. I remembered how Sally had said they despised her, and how they'd been tormenting the comtesse, and I was filled with a sudden, fervent desire to thrash every last one of them.

Tom stopped me. "Chr—" He caught himself. "Monsieur. Did you write the Lady Grace a new letter while I was asleep?"

"No," I said. "Why would I?"

He handed me the letter, confused. I read it.

My dear Lady Grace,

Of course I would be delighted to meet you.

However, I feel the deep need for prayer this evening, for when I last visited Notre-Dame, I felt as if I left something important behind. If you would join me, I have arranged for a carriage by the stables. The man inside will make sure you are escorted safely through the streets of Paris.

The Baron Ashcombe

I stared at it, not quite able to believe what I was seeing. Yet it wasn't the words themselves that shocked me the most.

"I . . . I didn't write this," I said.

Tom frowned. "But that's your handwriting."

It was. The message was a perfect copy of my own hand. In fact, it was so good, that for one dizzying moment, I wondered if I really *had* written this, and had just gone mad.

I couldn't hear the ladies' protests anymore. I couldn't hear anything but the rushing of blood in my ears. Sally had never come to get me because "I" hadn't told her to. Instead, she'd read between the lines of "my" message—*we missed something at Notre-Dame, come quickly*—and hurried there in "my" carriage, as she thought I'd asked.

The assassin had left her a trap, baited with my own forged handwriting. And now Sally was out in Paris, all alone.

We ran.

CHAPTER
48

MY SWORD WAS ALREADY IN MY
hand.

Tom carried his, too, anticipating not only what we'd
find at the cathedral, but the streets of Paris themselves. The
city was notorious for murders after dark.

But no one threatened us. Our way lit by moonlight,
we passed several men hidden behind cloaks—at this hour,
certainly *not* noblemen—but whether it was our naked
blades or Tom's size, everyone left us alone.

We were panting by the time we arrived; Notre Dame
was over a mile from the Palais. We skidded to a stop and
listened.

The church was quiet, shadowed in darkness. I heard cooing: Bridget, perched high up on one of the statues, calling to us from above. I heard something else, too, a soft nickering. Horses.

The carriage.

We followed the sound. We found the carriage tucked in the shadows behind the church. The horses stood quietly, breathing soft puffs into the chill. Swords on guard, Tom and I inched around to the carriage doors and tipped the curtains aside with our blades.

Empty.

There was no sign of Sally, nor the driver. We returned to the front of the cathedral, listening again. Hearing nothing further, we entered the church.

It was dark now, just a few dozen candles flickering against the night. The nave appeared to be empty. From the entrance, it was too dim to see much past the choir. I moved to the right side of the nave and motioned to Tom to take the left. I lost sight of him as he passed behind one of the great pillars.

Cautiously, I went forward, step by wary step. I passed the Portal of Saint Stephen at the southern end of the transept and approached the treasury to the right of the choir. I tried the door. It was locked.

I saw nothing, heard nothing. I returned to the transept, tested the Portal of Saint Stephen. That, too, was locked, so I went back to the entrance to the nave.

Tom hadn't yet returned. I saw a faint glimpse of his shape and candlelight reflecting from his sword at the other end of the church. Once more, I stopped to listen.

There.

I heard something. It was coming from the entrance. From outside.

I returned to the cold. The night carried the sound, crisp and clear. The flapping of wings.

Bridget landed at my feet. She ran over my boots, cooing insistently. When I stepped back, she took off again.

She flew around me in tight circles. Then she soared upward, disappearing into the darkness around the south bell tower.

And then I heard the cry.

"Tom!" I shouted into the church. "Tom! They're in the tower!"

I heard his heels echo from the far end of the cathedral. But I didn't have time to wait for him to come. The door to the bell tower was outside the church; I ran there and sprinted up the spiraling stairs.

"Sally!" I shouted.

"Christoph*mmmm*!"

Sally's voice faded, cut off like someone had clamped a hand over her mouth. I ran faster now, boots pounding on the stone as I climbed the hundreds of steps. They opened onto a wooden platform. A massive church bell, eight feet tall, hung suspended in the center of the tower. Thick beams jutted from every angle; past them, I saw shadows moving in torchlight.

Over there. A pair of low, narrow doors led outside to the walkway that joined the two towers. The shadows moved toward them, struggling.

"Sally!"

I heard rustling now, fighting. A blow, and the rush of air from lungs. "Christopher!" Sally screamed. "They're s—"

Her voice cut away with a horrifying *thunk*. My heart dropped as I squeezed through the door onto the walkway, and, in the moonlight, I saw her.

She was dangling in the grasp of the assassin; the same bull-man we'd seen outside Maison Chastellain, hidden as always beneath his cloak. He stood, his back to me, by the parapet at the front of the walkway. Sally, unconscious, hung in his left hand by the collar of her coat. In his right, he gripped an iron-shod club.

The wind blew cold. "Stop!" I shouted, and he turned. As before, his face was covered, but, this time, not with his cloak. Instead he wore a scarf, wrapped around his nose, so only his eyes were visible under his hood.

He stared at me, eyes narrowed. He dropped his club and grabbed Sally under both arms.

"No," I said. "No!"

Then he threw her over the side, to the stone, one hundred and fifty feet below.

CHAPTER
49

HE'D KILLED HER.

He'd *killed* her.

My guts went hollow. Then they filled with despair, a sinking, crushing anguish I hadn't felt since I'd found my master's broken body in our shop.

I stood there, unable to move. I felt the sword in my hand, the hilt rough against my skin. My heart pounded, echoing thundering crashes in my skull.

Then the world went red. The sky turned red; the stars turned red; the stone turned red. The wind howled in my ears like a demon's shriek. It was cold, but I wasn't cold. I burst with a fire so hot it burned my brain.

And I felt the sword in my hand.

I ran at the man, hacked at him. I used no skill, no finesse; I had none, and even if I had, in my rage, I'd have thrown it away. With both hands, I chopped at him like my blade was an ax, trying to fell a tree so thick one could swing a million times and never reach the other side.

The assassin had drawn his own sword as I advanced. He used it to ward off my blows. Sparks brightened the night as my blade clashed upon his, ringing like a hammer on an anvil. I swung, over and over again, no thought to defense, no thought to anything but one: I would kill him. I would hack him until there was nothing left. I would send him from this world into the arms of the Devil, where he could burn in anguish for all eternity.

He staggered under my blows. Surprised, he backed away; I followed him, chopping madly. He took the strikes, pressed against the parapet, seemingly about to falter. Then he stepped to the side, and I missed.

The force of my swing threw me off balance. The assassin kicked out, and his boot landed in my gut. I swung my sword back toward him, but his kick had winded me, and now his blade turned mine away easily.

Steel rang against steel, echoing into the black. His parries were clean and perfect. My edge never came close to touching him, and in the back of my mind, I understood: This was a swordsman. He didn't have the exquisite perfection of Sir William Leech, or the efficient brutality of Lord Ashcombe, or the hot-tempered brilliance of Simon Chastellain. But he knew how to handle his blade, and he did, with a mocking, almost contemptuous style, like a man swatting at a gnat.

And swat me he did. When he tired of batting away my sword, he spun on his heel, out of its path. With me off balance again, he stepped in close and punched me in the back, low and hard.

The shock was enough to pierce my rage. Pain burst in my side as my whole body seized. He punched me again, twice more, each blow like a giant's fist. I sprawled against the parapet and tried to twist my blade toward him. I barely had the chance to turn before he cracked me across the jaw with his hilt.

The blow rocked my head into the stone. I tried to step away, but the world was spinning. My feet found no purchase on the walkway; I slipped; I stumbled; I fell.

On my knees, I tried to raise my blade in defense.

He slapped the sword from my hand with his own. My weapon bounced off the parapet and fell, ringing against the stone far below.

I looked up at him, barely able to focus. I saw only his eyes. They sneered at me, and then his boot landed in my gut, right below my ribs. I collapsed, retching, paralyzed.

He placed his sword against the back of my neck. Its point pricked blood from my skin.

Get up, my mind screamed.

Get up, my body howled.

Get up, my master said. *I need you to get up.*

But I couldn't.

I'm sorry, Master. I failed.

The sword began to drive its way in.

Then I heard a voice. It came in a half whisper, high, melodic. A girl's. The whisper masked it; I couldn't tell if I'd ever heard it before. But it was cold, colder than the wind that burned my face.

"No," she said.

The blade hesitated, a fraction of an inch below my skin. Then I felt it press forward again.

"I said *no*."

The assassin stopped, this time for good. He pulled his steel from my neck.

I tried to push myself to my feet. Something hard struck the back of my head, and I collapsed. I heard footsteps getting fainter, and then I was alone, all alone, on the stone.

CHAPTER
50

I HEARD COOING.

Christopher, a voice said.

Christopher.

Large, gentle hands lifted me. They held me as my head fell back, my eyes blinded by the moon.

"Christopher," Tom said. "Are you all right?"

As sense returned, so did my despair. "She's dead," I said.

Tom steadied me, his voice rising. "Who's dead? What happened? Where's Sally?"

"He killed her," I said, though my mind screamed: *You killed her, Christopher. When you failed.*

Tom stared in horror as I pushed away. He shook his head. "No."

That's what the girl had said. No. "He threw her over the wall."

Tom ran to the edge. Bridget was there, cooing. Had she been there the whole time? Had she watched the assassin beat me down? Had she seen Sally die?

"No," Tom said again.

Even in the moonlight, it was too dark to see the ground below. I was grateful. It spared us the sight of her broken body. Though that respite wouldn't last long.

Bridget cooed at me and flapped her wings.

"She . . . ," Tom said. "She could have . . ."

I shook my head. We were a hundred and fifty feet up, a hundred and fifty feet down to paved stone. Nothing could survive that fall.

Tom covered his mouth with his hands. I sank and placed my head against the parapet, as if its cold could draw out the sickness in my chest.

Bridget cooed. She came over, still flapping her wings, so the breeze from her feathers brushed my face. I pushed her away.

"We can't leave Sally down there," I said to Tom. "We have to take her home."

Tom nodded. I had trouble standing; he had to help me. We limped away.

Bridget cooed at me. She flew up, circling, spinning closer and closer.

Then she landed on my head. Her wings beat against my ears, startling me. I waved my hands at her, and she flapped away, coming to land on the wall.

"What are you . . . ?" I said.

She cooed, insistent. Then she dove down into the dark, swooped back up to the wall, and cooed at me once again.

I stared at her, then I looked over at Tom.

"It's not possible," I said. "It's not *possible*."

Together, we rushed to the edge. I couldn't see anything but stone. "Get a light," I said.

Tom ran to the bell tower and returned with a torch. He held it over the side.

And we saw a gleam.

Four feet below, something winked at us from the head of a gargoyle jutting from the church facade. A flash of silver.

Tom stretched the torch out and leaned over.

And we saw the soft tumble of auburn hair.

It was Sally. The girl dangled in the breeze, head bowed. For a moment, I couldn't make sense of it. Then I understood.

Just below the parapet, the stone was sloped. When the assassin had thrown her over, she'd slid down it before falling from the side. She would have plummeted to her death then, but for the tracery of the stonework—and her chain.

Her silver chain. Her medallion of Saint Christopher, the one her grandmother had given her. It had caught on the gargoyle. Now it held her, hooked under her jaw, suspended a hundred and fifty feet above the stone.

Bridget cooed.

"Get her!" I shouted, but Tom was already ahead of me. He leaned as far over as he dared, stretching his giant arms.

He couldn't reach her. The chain was still a few inches away.

We didn't have time to wait. If we took too long, the necklace would choke her, like a noose. If it didn't break first.

"Move," I said, and I swung a leg over the edge.

Tom yanked me back. "Are you mad?" he said. "I'll get her. Hold me down."

He leaned over again. I wrapped my arms around his

legs, a counterweight, as he tipped forward over empty space.

He looked afraid. But he stretched, ever closer. He leaned farther, and I pressed back, until he teetered, almost upside down. Then his finger slipped under her necklace.

He began to lift. Steady, steady.

She rose. The chain bit into Tom's finger. It swelled, glowing red with blood in the light. Still his strength raised her up.

Suddenly he gasped. "The chain!" he shouted.

The silver chain, strained to the breaking point, stretched. Then it snapped.

Time stopped. For a moment, Sally seemed to remain there, hovering, as if held by the hand of Saint Christopher. The silver medallion fell into the darkness.

Then Sally began to drop.

Tom caught her by her collar. The weight of the falling girl dragged him down. I slid forward, and I knew, unless I let them go, that we'd all tumble over the side.

I didn't let go. I'd never let go. I dug my heels into the parapet and prayed. I felt my boots scratching, scraping against the stone, and I don't know how we didn't fall. The hand of my namesake again, maybe.

And then Tom was pushing himself up. From one hand, Sally dangled. He dragged her over to our side of the wall, then toppled backward with me.

We hit the stone. Sally fell on top of us, her face against mine. Her lips pressed softly against my chin.

We lay there, together, Tom and me gasping for air. He sat up and stared, mouth open, as if he could see the saint that had blessed us.

"A miracle," he croaked. "We just witnessed a miracle."

Bridget cooed.

CHAPTER

THE JOY OF FINDING SALLY QUICKLY

turned cold. I cradled her, and her head lolled back, mouth open. I felt a warm wetness on my hands.

It was blood. I remembered the blow I'd heard in the bell tower, the club the assassin had dropped. It had disappeared from the walkway, taken when he and his companion had fled.

I pressed my hand against her skull to stop the bleeding. "Sally. Sally!"

She wouldn't wake.

"We have to get her to the surgeon," I said.

Tom reached out to take her. I held her close. "I'm carrying her."

Tom hesitated, but he didn't argue. We ran down the steps of the tower and into the square. My sword lay on the flagstones. The carriage beside the cathedral was gone.

Tom picked up my blade and carried it with his own, wards against further blackguards on the street. We rushed back to the Palais, my chest huffing, lungs burning. Sally wasn't heavy—maybe eighty pounds, with the dress—but as the near-mile dragged on, so did her weight.

Still, I wouldn't let her go. She woke as I ran. She looked around, one eye cockeyed, both of them glazed.

"It's me," I said. "It's Christopher. You're going to be all right."

"It hurts," she said.

"I know. I have you. No one's going to hurt you anymore."

"That's the river," she said, as we sprinted over the Pont-Neuf. "Are you going to throw me in?"

"Not today."

"I smell apples."

I couldn't smell anything but blood.

"No one ever pays attention," she said. "Did you see?" Her eyes unfocused.

My feet thumped against the stones as we sprinted toward the palace.

"I smell apples," she said again. Then she cursed. "Traitors."

"Shh," I said. "Don't talk. Just rest."

"Will you read me a story?" she said, and she rested her head on my shoulder. "It's the only time I ever feel safe."

Then she didn't speak anymore.

We battered our way through the door of the Palais.

"Help!" I shouted. "Somebody help!"

A dozen guards came running. So did a dozen servants, dressed in nightclothes. They stared at us: me on my knees, gasping for breath; Tom standing over us, a sword in each hand; Sally lying on the parquet, blood smeared from her hair against the wood.

"She's been attacked," I said. "Find the surgeon."

One of the guards ran from the palace to get him. I moved to pick Sally up, but Tom was already there. He scooped her in his arms before I could find the breath to protest and carried her into the nearest study.

I didn't know what to do. I remembered Sally said she'd been in pain, so I ordered a pot of boiling water for the poppy from my apothecary sash. I never got to make it.

The surgeon, Palissy, came in, took one look, and said,

"Get her to the kitchen." I carried her this time. We went, and I laid her on that long wooden table where Lisette, the chambermaid, had lost her leg.

Palissy pushed me aside firmly. He leaned over Sally and ran his fingers along her skull, pressing. Then he rolled up his sleeves.

"Everybody out," he said.

The servants and guards shuffled off as Palissy's apprentices came forward. They opened their leather satchels and began drawing out the surgeon's tools, laying them on the table. Knives, saws, picks, prods.

I stayed. "You, too," Palissy said. Still I remained, until he turned to me and said, less gruffly, "Go on, son. I need to work."

Tom took my arm and led me out. He walked me along in a daze until I found myself in the chapel of the Palais. Tom knelt before the golden cross. I knelt beside him.

And we prayed.

FRIDAY, NOVEMBER 20, 1665

Nones

CHAPTER
52

THE SURGEON SHOOK ME AWAKE.

I sat up. I'd dozed off in the chapel, sleeping on the stone next to Tom, who was still on his knees, praying. The morning's sunlight streamed through the stained glass windows, painting our skin with color.

"She's alive," Palissy said, and I felt the hollow inside get less empty.

Tom and I stood. "Can we see her?" I asked.

Palissy nodded. "I've moved her back to the study." I made to leave, but he put a hand on my shoulder. The look he gave me made my heart sink.

"Her skull wasn't fractured," he said, "but there was

bleeding in the brain. I've drained it, and wrapped the wound, but the likelihood of her recovery is not good. And even if she does survive . . ."

He didn't have to finish. I'd seen similar injuries while working with my master. If she woke, she might not even be Sally anymore. I felt like throwing up.

We went to the study. Sally lay on the couch, her head wrapped in linen. At the back, the cloth was stained crimson.

Look, Christopher, I thought. *Look at what you've done.*

"Stop it," Tom said.

"I didn't say anything," I said.

"I know what you're thinking. This is not your fault."

"She's here because of *me*. You both are."

"She chose to be here," Tom said. "And so did I. There *are* people who are responsible, but they are not you, nor me, nor Lord Ashcombe, nor the king. So stop blaming yourself and do something useful. Pray."

He knelt in front of the couch, pulling me down with him. I remained beside him, praying, as the hours passed. Most of the nobles staying at the Palais joined us for a time.

Minette was the first. She spoke kindly about Sally, then said she was going to mass to entreat the Lord for her recovery.

She invited us to join her, but I didn't want to leave Sally's side.

Not long after Minette came the comtesse de Colmar. Her eyes were red from crying.

"Will Mademoiselle Grace be all right?" she asked.

No thanks to your wretched husband, I thought.

"Was it one of the ladies?" she said.

"What ladies?" I said.

"The ones who've been tormenting me. Did they do this?"

I was about to tell her no. Then I remembered the voice I'd heard at Notre-Dame. *It came in a half whisper, high, melodic. A girl's.*

I looked up at the comtesse. "Why do you think one of the ladies did this?"

"Because, when we were with the duchess, something they said frightened her."

I stood. "Tell me."

She stepped back a little, startled by my anger. "It was yesterday, when we were out. We'd been talking about my h—" She cut herself off, embarrassed. "We'd been talking. Then we got separated, in the tailor's shop, and when I saw her next, she looked scared."

"What scared her?"

"She wouldn't say. I saw she'd been speaking with the

other girls, and she told me they'd said something unkind. But she wasn't sad. She was afraid. She excused herself, wrote a letter with the tailor's quill, then sent one of the servants off with it."

That would have been the message I'd received yesterday. She'd sent it, not after talking to the comtesse, but to one of the ladies?

I had no idea what it meant. But from what the comtesse had said, I'd just got further from understanding who the assassins really were. And whatever Sally had learned, it had all but gotten her killed.

I asked a few more questions of the comtesse, but she had nothing else to tell me. She left, following Minette to mass. Once again, guilt churned in my gut, and though I tried to calm myself with prayer, anger began to smolder alongside it.

Palissy returned in the afternoon to change the dressing, reporting no change in her condition. I didn't think there would be, so soon, but by the time the sun was low in the sky, my despair had faded, swallowed completely by rage.

I'll find them, I swore. *I'll find these assassins, and I'll kill them. I'll watch them burn.*

And in my fury, my master came to me. *Calm, Christopher. You must remain calm.*

I'll kill them! I shouted. *I will! Leave me alone!*

But he wouldn't go. *Calm, my child. Be calm.*

Still I raged. *Why should I?*

Because the angry make mistakes, he said. *And you need to not make mistakes. You need to put an end to this.*

I will put an end to this!

Not that way. You cannot beat them like this. You fell to the assassin's sword. You saw his skill. Even you and Tom together couldn't stand against him.

Don't say that!

Would you run from the truth? he said. *Is that what I taught you to do?*

And I cried, my heart breaking. *Why are you saying this to me?*

Because if you face them with anger, Christopher, you will die.

I don't care. Do you understand? I don't care.

I do understand, he said gently. *But I care. You must master your anger, not let it be your master. In this way only might you defeat them.*

But I don't know what to do. Oh, Master, please. I don't know what to do.

Yes, you do. You already have the answers. You just have to understand.

Understand what? I said. *I don't know anything. I don't know where the treasure went. I don't know what that code means. I don't know why all this happened. Why did they have to hurt Sally? I was the threat. Why didn't they kill me instead?*

I'd meant it only as a cry of despair. But Master Benedict nodded.

Ah, he said. *Finally, you ask the right question.*

And the vision shattered. His words burned inside me. *The right question.*

Why *didn't* they kill me?

They could have, and easily. Last night, I'd been at the assassin's mercy. All he had to do was push his sword in.

But the girl had told the man no. She'd insisted. She hadn't wanted me dead.

I was the thorn in their side, not Sally. *I* was the one following the path laid out by the Templars. *I* was the assassins' true rival. Whatever Sally had discovered, she'd never even have been here if it wasn't for me.

And yet they didn't want me gone?

What did the assassins gain from keeping me alive?

I looked over at Sally, still sleeping. *She knew something. And they knew she knew it.* I thought back to the tower, past the fear, past the rage, past the despair. Sally had called to me.

Christopher! They're s—

They'd silenced her. But she'd spoken to me again, when I'd carried her back, after they'd thought they'd killed her. She'd been confused. The smell of apples. Back in the orphanage, me reading her stories.

Traitors, she'd said. *No one ever pays attention,* she'd said.

Her words echoed in my mind. She'd said the same thing to me somewhere else.

I remembered. It was back in England, in Oxford. We were in the library, after I'd stopped the poisoned wine from being drunk.

No one ever pays attention to—

That was it.

I understood.

I *understood.*

The scales fell from my eyes. I knew why they'd tried to kill Sally. Why they hadn't wanted to kill me.

And with that, more pieces fell into place. My mind raced, and from the tempest came clarity. The same clarity that revealed the villains shook the Templars' final riddle free as well. I stood, trembling.

"Pick Sally up," I said to a surprised Tom. "And take her to our room. Put her on my bed. Don't leave her side."

I ran from the study before he could ask what I was up to. I hurried through the halls, looking for palace guards. I found two of them, wandering toward their quarters, having just been relieved of their duties.

I paused. Could I trust them? I'd figured out who some of the players behind the assassination attempts were, but I had no way of knowing how many other people were involved. Yet even as I worried, I realized I didn't have a choice: I'd have to take a gamble and hope these men weren't part of the plot.

I stopped them. "What are your names?"

They looked a little surprised at the question. "I'm Adelard, monsieur," the taller one said. He pointed to his companion, a squat man with a single eyebrow. "And this is Sanguin."

"Come with me," I said. "I have a job for you."

They hesitated. They'd already been on their feet for twelve hours. They were tired, and they wanted to go to sleep, I knew. Still I ignored their weary looks and marched them up to my quarters. Tom was already there, Sally lying unconscious on my bed.

"We have to leave for a time," I said to the guards. "I want you to watch over this girl while we're gone."

"Our day's duty is finished, monsieur," Adelard said bluntly. "We're—"

"When we leave," I said, "I want you to lock the door behind us. You are not to let anyone in—*anyone*—except Tom, me, or Palissy, the surgeon."

"Monsieur, I told you—"

"We'll return in a few hours. When we do, I'll examine the Lady Grace. If she's harmed in any way further, you two will get nothing. If she's untouched, I'll give you this."

I opened my hand. In the center of my palm were two gold *louis* that I'd pulled from my purse. Their jaws dropped as they stared at the coins.

"Or should I get someone else?" I said.

"No!" Adelard said. "I mean . . ." He snapped to attention. "It is our honor to serve, monsieur. She'll be as safe as the king; I promise."

I instructed them to call for the surgeon immediately if she woke. Then I motioned to Tom, and we left.

"What's going on?" he said, puzzled.

"I know who the assassins are," I said quietly. "Or, at least, I know who's working with them. And I'm also pretty sure I've figured out where the Templars sent their treasure."

Tom stared at me as we made our way to the exit. "Well? Are you going to tell me, or what?"

"I will. Just not here."

He glanced around. "It's not safe here?"

"It *is* safe here. That's the problem. I have to tell you somewhere that it *isn't*."

CHAPTER

RÉMI LET US INSIDE MAISON

Chastellain. He looked haggard.

"Monsieur is not well this evening," he said, though he needn't have. I could hear Marin ranting from here.

"Traitors!" his voice echoed from the study. "Get out!"

"I'll make his medicine," I said. Rémi bowed with gratitude and called Colette to escort me to the kitchen. She collected the ingredients I needed while Tom went upstairs to see if he could calm Simon's uncle.

When I joined them, Master Benedict's calmative steaming in my hand, Tom was holding Marin's cane high so the old man couldn't reach it. From the welt on

Tom's neck, he'd confiscated it for good reason.

Marin stretched for it. "Give that back, you great brute." He spotted me. "Benedict! Tell this monster to give me back my cane."

"I think he doesn't want to be hit anymore, Marin," I said.

"He's a big boy; he can take it."

Tom gave me a look that said, *Please don't give him back the cane.* I didn't intend to. Instead, I made the grumbling Marin drink his medicine, then asked Rémi to keep him warm in the study.

"We're going to step out back," I said.

Rémi seemed a little surprised. "Will you not remain with the comte this evening?"

"I'd hoped to," I said, "but I've uncovered some important information, and now that I see him, I'm afraid what I've discovered might agitate him further. It's better Tom and I discuss it in private. Could you remove the guard from the garden?"

That surprised him even more. But he opened one of the windows in the study and called the guard inside. "Colette can help you if you require anything further," he said to me.

The girl led us out to the garden, waiting by the French

doors at the back entrance. "Could you leave us, please?" I said.

She hesitated before curtsying and going back inside. Tom wrapped his arms around himself. "Will you please tell me what's going on now? Why are we out here in the cold?"

"I just wanted to make sure we had some privacy." I peered into the garden, as if looking to see if anyone was there. I glanced upward; the window right above us was still open, just a crack. "I know where the Templars hid their treasure."

"Was it in the code in the painting?" he said. "The thing about the key being—"

"No, no," I said. "That tells you how to remove the traps."

"What traps?"

"The traps that guard the treasure."

Tom looked confused. "There are traps now?"

"Of course. Don't you remember the clue?" When he started to speak, I cut him off. "Never mind, they're not important. I already know how to get past them. The important thing is where the treasure is."

I pulled out the map I'd sketched of the plate at the Cimetière des Innocents. "It's right here. It finally makes sense. You gave me the answer."

"I did?"

I nodded. "It's what you said, about taking things literally. I realized that that's been true about every one of the Templar clues we've found. Underfoot. Where you think. Arcadia." I shook my head. "Riddles, by nature, are cryptic. So when you give someone a puzzle, their mind immediately starts to think about what it means—the *hidden* meaning. And so you miss what's right in front of you. That's what the Templars have been taking advantage of all these years. They've been hiding the truth in plain sight."

I held the map out. "Look at this again. What does it show?"

Wherever you think I am, you will find me at the opposite.

"The places to where the knights escaped," Tom said. "Where one of them must have taken the treasure."

"Right. And what does it say underneath?"

"'Wherever you think I am, you will find me at the opposite.'"

"So that means?"

"If I think it's at one place on the circle, then it's on the other side of the circle. So, if you think it's in the Netherlands, it's actually in Spain."

"No."

"No?" Tom threw his hands up. "Then I have no idea what you're talking about."

"Except *you* were the one who said it, don't you remember? If I think it's in the Netherlands, then it's in Spain. But if I think it's in Spain, then shouldn't it be in the Netherlands instead? Follow that logic, and you'll just keep going around in a circle."

"You said that wasn't what they meant."

"I know. But then you pointed something else out. We've gone through all this trouble, solved all these clues, to end up learning nothing more than we started with."

I paced along the hedgerow, my voice rising. "That, right there, is the key. After all this time, *we haven't seen a single clue that even hints at where the Templars sent the treasure. And *that's* the actual clue."

"That's . . ." Tom shook his head. "You're not making any sense. The clue that tells us where the treasure went . . . is that there's no clue that tells us where it went?"

"Exactly."

"My head hurts."

"I think that's what the Templars were aiming for," I said. "But here, I'll make it simple. The map says wherever you think the treasure went, you're wrong. But it also offers no clue as to where the treasure went. So if I have no clue, then don't I just have to guess?"

Tom thought about it. "I suppose you would."

"All right. But if I guess, there has to be a chance that I'm correct, right? If it went to one of five places, then pure guessing means I'd be right one in five times. So how can they *know* I'll be wrong?"

He scratched his head. "Because . . . it's not there after all?"

"Precisely. Whatever you think, it's the opposite. But what have they made you think? That it's on the circle. So that means it's *not* on the circle. Do you see? *They didn't send the treasure to anywhere on the circle at all.*"

"But . . . if they didn't send it to one of these places, where did it go?"

"To the only other place marked on the map," I said.

Tom studied the map. "There *is* no other place here."

"Sure there is. It's so obvious, you're not even seeing it."

"The only thing . . . Wait." He frowned. "Do you mean the fleur-de-lis?"

"Yes," I said.

"Isn't the fleur-de-lis supposed to be Paris?"

"Yes."

"But . . . then that would mean . . ."

"Yes," I said. "The masters of misdirection pulled the ultimate trick of misdirection—on Philippe le Bel himself, three hundred and fifty years ago. All those knights that escaped . . . they were carrying nothing but straw.

"The Templars never actually moved the treasure," I said. "It's still here, in Paris. And I'm pretty sure I know exactly where."

CHAPTER

TOM STARED AT ME. "WHERE IS IT?"

I pursed my lips, let him hang for a moment. Then I said, "I just have to work one thing out before I'm certain. As soon as I am, we'll go get it."

"Tonight?"

"Absolutely not," I said, trying to sound shocked. "Do you want to cart the Templars' treasure through the streets of Paris after dark? I'll go early in the morning, before anyone else is awake. In the meantime, we should get back to the Palais."

"What about Sally? You said the as—"

I raised a hand. "Let's say goodbye to Marin."

We went back upstairs to say our farewells, then Colette escorted us out. As we began to walk down the lane, I whispered to Tom, "You were excellent."

"I don't have the faintest idea what you're talking about," he said.

"I know," I said. "That's why you were excellent. Your reactions were very authentic." We turned the corner on Rue Poulletier, walking behind a high brick wall opposite the house where we'd spotted the assassin two days ago. As soon as we were out of sight, I said, "Come on!"

Tom, startled, followed me as I scrambled up and over the wall. Crouching, we crept through the bushes until we got to the gate. I poked an eye around it; from here, we could just see Marin's front door.

Tom, hiding next to me, huffed. "You're driving me mad," he said. "Are you going to tell me what's going on or not?"

"We're waiting for one of the assassins," I said.

"We're *what*?"

"Look."

We remained hidden in shadow as the door to Maison Chastellain opened. Colette stepped outside, wrapped in a warm woolen cloak. "I have to go to les Halles for Monsieur's medicine," we heard her say to the guards. Then she hurried down the street, out of view.

"We need to follow her," I said, clambering over the gate back into the street. "Make sure you keep out of sight."

In Tom's case, that meant ducking to conceal his height every time Colette looked around nervously—which she did quite a bit. It made her rather hard to follow. She slipped through the heavy Paris traffic down the bridge to the north side of the river, then turned west. We had to hide behind carriages and stalls often enough that we lost sight of her in the crowd several times. Each time, she reappeared farther away, until we finally lost her for good.

I cursed, kicking a nearby stone into the mud.

"Where did she go?" Tom said.

"Do you recognize where we are?" I said.

He looked around. "Close to the Palais?" When I nodded, he said, "She went inside?"

"The garden behind it, I'm guessing. She's probably contacting her accomplices right now." I sighed. "I suppose we'd never have got close enough to see who it was without getting spotted, anyway."

"Then . . . Colette is one of the assassins?"

"Yes," I said. "Maybe not a killer herself—that girl I

heard last night wasn't Colette—but she's definitely working with them. Or at least she's working for Rémi."

"*Rémi?*" Tom looked flabbergasted. "*Rémi's* one of the assassins? How on earth do you know?"

I drew a breath. "Ever since last night, I've been asking myself one question. When Sally learned something that might expose them, they tried to kill her. But *I've* been doing more than anyone to stop them. So why didn't they try to kill *me*? They had me at their mercy. Why leave me be?

"I couldn't make any sense of it. And then I finally understood. The only reason to keep me alive was that *I was more valuable to them alive than dead*. And the only way that can be true is simple: I'm solving the problem they couldn't. While they've been trying to murder the royal family, I've been solving the Templars' actual clues."

Tom frowned. "But how would they know you were succeeding? Have they been following us the whole time?"

"They didn't have to. Because *I* kept bringing the answer to *them*. Think about it: Who knows everything I've discovered? You. Me. Sally. Marin. And . . . ?"

"Rémi!" Tom gasped. "He was there, in the study, the whole time!"

I nodded. "We made it easy for him. He was there

when Marin told us about Voiture's poem. He was there after Notre-Dame, when we told Marin about the Arcadia clue. He was there when we revealed the code in Poussin's painting. Almost everything we discovered, we talked about at Maison Chastellain. Except for Marin, only Rémi heard everything we said."

Tom looked troubled. "Then couldn't Marin be working with them, too?"

"He could," I said, "except he's so sick. No one in his state could manage any kind of plot, especially one this complicated."

"What if he's faking it?"

I'd worried about that, too. It *was* possible that Marin was involved. Yet . . . I just couldn't bring myself to believe it. He'd been too good a friend to Master Benedict.

Did that make me blind to possible treachery? I had to admit, it did. Nonetheless, I couldn't believe someone my master had cared for his whole life could be so wicked. Besides, he'd been pursuing the Templar treasure for decades. After all this time, would he really change his mind and decide to kill the king?

"How did you know Colette was part of it, too?" Tom asked.

"I didn't," I said. "I was certain about Rémi, but I didn't know if he had any allies in Marin's home. That's why I dragged you there to talk about the map, then acted so secretive. Did you notice Rémi left the study window open to listen? After what I'd said, I knew he'd have to alert the killers. I didn't know Colette was with him until I saw her leave."

Tom shook his head, amazed. "Rémi. I never even paid attention to—" He stopped, realizing what he'd been just about to say.

I nodded grimly. "No one ever pays attention to servants. That's what Sally was trying to remind me of last night. They're always around, so, soon enough, they disappear into the furniture. And you don't even remember they're there."

"There might be more of them at Maison Chastellain, then, mightn't there?"

"It's possible."

"But if Marin's not part of the plot," Tom said, "then he's in danger!"

"No. He knows too much about the Templar treasure. Like me, he's more precious to them alive." I sighed. "Poor Marin. Without even knowing it, he's been the cause of all this."

"He has?"

"Remember what Simon said about chasing the thieving servants from the house? I suspect they weren't just stealing Marin's money. They'd been with the man for years; they knew how much he knew about the Templars. They probably got the idea to go after the treasure from him. But when Simon chased them away, they lost access to what his uncle knew. I'd bet anything that when Simon began to hire new servants, Rémi went deliberately to take their place."

"I wouldn't like to be him when Simon finds out," Tom said.

Nor would I. Blood would be spilled at Maison Chastellain. I wondered if I should tell the king's guard first, so Rémi and Colette would be properly tried and executed instead.

Meanwhile, Tom was pondering something. "So one of Marin's old servants . . ."

"Is likely one of the assassins," I said. "And I bet they've found work in there." I pointed to the Palais-Royal. "I think *that's* what Sally discovered yesterday: that one of the ladies at the Palais had hired one of the old servants from Maison Chastellain. She probably realized exactly what that meant."

"So what you said, about the map, and the treasure

never leaving town: That was a lie? A ploy to reveal Rémi as a traitor?"

"No, I'm certain the treasure's still in Paris. And I'm equally certain I know where it is."

"Well," Tom said, his patience fading, "since we're no longer being spied upon, are you finally going to tell me?"

"Sure," I said. "It's in the Great Tower."

CHAPTER

TOM BLINKED. "THE GREAT TOWER? You mean . . . the old Templar dungeon?"

"The ultimate misdirection," I said. "Le Bel went there to get it, and went away empty-handed. But the Templars had it in there the whole time."

"How is that possible? We've been in the tower; it's empty."

"I think there's a secret vault somewhere—probably hidden behind one of those stone panels in the basement. And I think that's what this riddle means."

I pulled the deciphered code from beneath my sash.

The key is the blessing and the curse

"That's certainly clear," Tom grumbled.

"Actually," I said, "I bet it is—and as literal as all the other clues. I just don't know what it means yet. I'll have to see the panels again to figure it out."

"Then . . . you were serious about going back there?"

"Absolutely. And I'm returning early tomorrow, as promised."

"Won't the assassins follow you?"

"I certainly hope so," I said. "My whole plan depends on it."

"What plan?" Then Tom's eyes went wide. "Oh no."

I frowned. "You haven't even heard it yet."

"Does it involve surrounding yourself with a hundred armed guards?"

"No."

"Then, as I said . . ."

"There's no other way to play this out."

"Why?" Tom said. "Why can't we get all Minette's guards, lure the assassins to the tower, and arrest them?"

"On what charge? With what evidence?" I shook my head. "We don't have any proof that what I've said is true. And even though they think I'm a baron, remember: I'm a foreigner. No one will take my word over their own countrymen's.

"There's another reason, too. We still don't know who we can trust. Suppose I'm right, and we find a secret vault. Would you really like to be surrounded by armed men who suddenly find themselves knee deep in treasure?"

Tom looked troubled. "I hadn't thought of that." Then he brightened. "What about Simon? He can fight. Why not wait for him to return?"

I bit my lip. "I'm not sure if Simon can be trusted." When Tom looked shocked, I said, "He did hire Rémi, remember? And we never *saw* him chase the old servants off. Maybe he hadn't been fooled, after all. Maybe *he's* the one who's been lying to us the whole time."

It was a terrible thing, not knowing whom you could trust. At least I always had Tom. I threw my arms around him and gave him a hug.

He looked down at me, wary. "You're not leaving me behind again, are you?"

"Not a chance," I said, letting him go. "You're the most important person here." And I told him what I had planned.

He stared at me in horror. "And I thought it would just be *moderately* bad."

"It'll be fine," I assured him. "All you have to do is wait for me to whistle for you."

"Why can't I stand with you?" he asked. "We could capture them together as soon as they show up."

"Because we need them to talk," I said. "That's the only way we'll find everyone that's involved in this. If we fight them right away, if they get killed . . . we might not learn anything at all. And then we'll *really* set ourselves up as a target. You have to promise, Tom. And I mean *promise*. No matter what you hear, no matter how horrible it sounds, you can't come until I whistle. If they don't talk, we'll fail. And we'll die. So promise. Not to me. Promise before *God*."

Tom still looked dubious, but he didn't really have an argument against what I'd said. "I promise," he said grudgingly.

I was glad he let it go, because, in reality, there was a different reason I didn't want him with me when I first confronted the assassins—and if I told him, he'd be so scared it would cripple him.

The fight at Notre-Dame had made it clear: If it came to swords, it was Tom, not me, who'd have to face the assassin. And that man was far too skilled for Tom to beat him. He'd carve my friend to pieces—unless I evened the field first.

So that's exactly what I planned to do. "I need to get a

few things ready," I said quickly, before Tom could think of some other protest. "But let's go inside. I want to make sure Sally's safe."

She was. When we got to our room, the guards I'd hired wouldn't even open the door until we convinced them we were who we claimed. When they did finally unlock it, they had their swords ready to skewer us in case they'd been fooled.

They sheathed their blades. "See, monsieur?" Adelard said proudly, motioning to Sally on the bed. Bridget lay nestled in the crook of her arm. "Safe as can be."

I sat next to her and brushed the curls from her face with my fingers. "Did anyone try to come for her?"

"Yes, monsieur," Adelard said. "A girl scratched at the door an hour ago, saying she'd come to change the lady's dressing."

A girl? I stood. "Who was it?"

"We don't know, monsieur. We didn't open the door. We didn't even say a word. After her first call, she scratched at the door again, said, 'Is anyone in there?' and then left. Did we do right?"

Inwardly, I cursed. They'd missed a chance to identify a suspect. Still, what they'd done was best to keep Sally safe.

"Indeed you did," I said. I doled the two *louis* I'd promised into their eager hands. "Listen, I know you must be tired, but will you remain and stand watch over us tonight? There's another *louis* in it for you, if you do."

They looked like they couldn't believe their luck. "Absolutely, monsieur," Adelard said. "You and your man can sleep soundly. We'll keep you safe."

"All right. Then one of you stay here with Tom and the Lady Grace, the other one come with me."

"Where are you going?" Tom said.

"I'll be back soon," I told him. "I just need a couple of things for our plan. A strap of leather, and some ribbons." I scratched my head. "And I'll need to see if anyone here has a goose."

SATURDAY, NOVEMBER 21, 1665

Vespers

CHAPTER
56

WITH THE MORNING CAME A BITING, bitter cold. An hour before sunrise, I crept from my room in the Palais and made my way down Rue Saint-Denis, my breath turning to fog in the moonlight. The streets were mostly empty—too early for honest folk, too late for brigands and thieves. Nonetheless, I walked the mile to the Great Tower like a thousand arrows were trained on my back. Though I saw nothing, I could *feel* them following me. My skin itched.

When I arrived at the old Templar grounds, I snuck first into Saint Mary's. The keys Father Bernard had used when we'd come to visit still hung on the hook behind the stairwell next to the transept. I lifted them slowly, so they wouldn't jingle, then unlocked the Great Tower and went inside.

It was cold in here, too. I used flint and tinder from my sash to light one of the torches that hung in the brackets near the door. It flared up, casting shifting shadows over the panels on the walls. I warmed my hands over it for a moment, then took it through the corner turret to the dungeon below.

The darkness made me shiver, piercing deeper than the cold ever could. Alone, waiting, I felt the soul of every Templar who'd been held here, 350 years ago. And then, within my frozen breath, I swear I saw an image come to life: an old and bearded knight, mail coif covering his head, blood-red cross on his tunic of white. Jacques de Molay, twenty-third grand master, still standing duty over his charge.

I wondered what they thought of me, these spirits of Templars long dead. I prayed they wished me well. Because from the sound of the creaking door above, I didn't have long to find out.

There was nowhere to hide. Hiding wasn't the point, anyway. I simply stood in the center of the tower, the carving of le Bel's florin between my feet, and listened as they came down the stairs.

They carried their own torch. The man in front, clomp-
ing on the stone like a bull, wore his cloak; like at Notre-
Dame, a separate cloth hid his face. Behind him came a
girl, and though her face was covered, too, I was startled to
realize I recognized her.

She wore the same yellow dress she'd worn on the Île
Notre-Dame. The same velvet mask hid her features. It was
the noble girl the assassin had thrown at me on the quay, the
girl I'd knocked into the Seine.

"You were together," I said, understanding. "He used
you to help him escape."

She ignored me. She looked steadily around the room,
behind every wooden box, every iron bar. Then, when she
was finally satisfied we were alone, she nodded to her companion, and both of them took off their masks.

The girl was a few years older than me—seventeen at
most—and, other than that day at the quay, I knew I'd
never seen her anywhere else. I'd have remembered her
without question.

She wasn't merely beautiful. She was *stunning*. She was
a statue of Aphrodite come to life, with soft blond curls
and smooth alabaster skin and doe eyes so big as to melt
the heart. And yet her beauty was marred by a coldness, a

cruelty in her expression, that chilled deeper than the late November frost.

The man who accompanied her was the exact opposite. Not in cruelty; there was plenty of that in his gaze. But he was ugly, profoundly ugly, with a squashed nose and crooked teeth and a mouth twisted in a permanent scowl. His wide face fit well his bullish body: a Minotaur to serve his Aphrodite.

My guts quavered. They'd let me see their faces. I knew very well what that meant. I needed to get them talking, and quickly.

"Who are you?" I said.

Aphrodite didn't answer. "Take his weapon," she told the Minotaur.

He stepped forward, drawing his sword. I reached my hand across my body, let it hover over the hilt at my side, as if to draw my own blade in return.

"Do you think that's a good idea?" Aphrodite said curiously.

I didn't. Slowly, I moved my hands away from my belt, held them out.

"You don't have to hurt me," I said.

"That's a very good attitude, Baron." Aphrodite smiled. "Throw your sword over here."

I stepped back, trembling. "I told you, you don't have to hurt me. I won't fight."

"Take it," she ordered her companion.

The Minotaur raised his blade until its point poked into my chin. He held my eyes with his, and the tightness of his jaw told me he wanted nothing more than to drive the steel in. He reached down to pull out my weapon.

Then he yelped.

Aphrodite flinched as her partner leaped back. Then the Minotaur raised his sword and bashed me across the jaw with its hilt.

It felt like he'd struck me with a hammer. My brain rattled in my skull; my legs went weak. I fell to my knees. My torch rolled away, sending sparks fluttering like fireflies into the air.

"What did he do?" Aphrodite said. "What did he do?"

"He stabbed me!" the Minotaur said, cradling his hand against his chest.

"Stabbed you with what? His hands were in the air."

"Look!" He held his hand out so she could see. On his palm were two swelling dots of blood. Puzzled, Aphrodite stepped forward, bringing her torch low.

Then she threw her head back and laughed.

The flames illuminated my sword, still in its scabbard. Wrapped with a leather strap and ribbons, goose feathers adorned the hilt, two of them broken down to the quills.

"The feathers!" She lost her breath with laughter. "You stuck yourself with the decorations on his sword!"

He flushed. "It's not funny."

That made her laugh harder. "What a baby!"

The girl's mockery infuriated him. He took it out on me. He stepped forward and kicked me right in the stomach.

It drove every ounce of breath from my lungs. I crumpled, forehead against the stone, unable to see. I gasped for air, great heaving sobs, as my whole body clenched from the pain. If I'd eaten anything this morning, I would have thrown it up.

The Minotaur pulled my sword from my scabbard, making sure this time to touch it only by the crosspiece. He hurled the weapon against the wall in disgust.

Aphrodite dabbed tears of laughter from her eyes. "Stand him up."

The man grabbed my hair and pulled. I wobbled on my feet, stomach still roiling from his kick. He'd sprung the trap I'd left for him on my sword hilt, but I knew it would need time to take effect—if it worked at all. And this conversation wasn't going as I'd planned.

Who *was* this girl? Despite the finery she wore, from her rough manner and country accent, she clearly wasn't a noble. I thought again about Sally's discovery.

No one pays attention to servants.

Was she one of the ladies' servants? Was that what Sally had seen, that had made her a target? And if Aphrodite was just a servant, who gave her those clothes?

I needed to get her talking *now*. "Who *are* you?" I said again.

"I'm asking the questions, *chéri*," Aphrodite said. "Where's the treasure?"

"What treasure?"

The Minotaur punched me, going once more for my gut. His iron fist made me double over, and the only thing that held me up was his grip on my hair.

Aphrodite watched me, eyes flashing with pleasure as I retched. She stepped forward as I righted myself, and pushed the Minotaur's hand from my head with the tip of her finger. Then she cupped my chin, stroking my cheek with her thumb.

"That's it," she said. "Breathe. Just breathe. There we are. All better now."

"Listen," I gasped. "We can make a deal."

"Oh?" She stared at my cheek, as if fascinated by the way my skin felt under her thumb. "A deal? You think you're going to fool me with a deal?"

"No, I—"

She slipped her thumb between my lips. Then she dug her nail down, stabbing into the flesh below my gums. I howled, and my mouth stung with the coppery taste of blood.

"You have *vexed* me," she hissed. "Ruined carefully crafted plans at every turn. You and that scrawny little mouse of a girl. I was *punished* because of you. I took *beatings* for you."

She drove her nail in deeper. She leaned in, so close I could feel her breath.

"You think you're so *clever*," she said. "Do you know what I'd like to do to you? I think I'd like to cut out your tongue."

Deeper still went the nail. The pain was so sharp, so shocking: a knife carving its way into my flesh. She twisted her hand, and the agony drove me to my knees. It hurt so much I couldn't even beg her to stop.

Then she let go. Blood dripped from my mouth, spattered on the stone, sending little crimson beads into the grooves of the florin carved into it centuries ago.

Aphrodite stood over me. "Yes," she said. "My little English baron. What a prize it would make, your tongue nailed to my wall. How clever do you think you'd be then?"

She motioned to the Minotaur. He hauled me to my feet.

She cupped my chin again, her touch gentle once more. "Don't worry, *chéri*," she said. "I'm not going to cut out your tongue. You need it. You need it to tell me everything you know. But do you know what you don't need to talk?"

She reached down and clasped my hand in hers. She brought my hand up, until it hovered in front of my eyes.

"Your fingers," she said.

And then she drew out her knife.

CHAPTER

I PANICKED.

I'd got this wrong, so wrong. Every other villain I'd faced couldn't *wait* to tell me what they'd done. They'd practically glowed with pride in the wickedness of their plans, wanted me to be proud of them as well. Not this girl. I was nothing to her. She wasn't being cruel because she thought she had to be. She *liked* it.

And I still had no idea who she was. I'd never get her to talk, not on purpose. My brain screamed at me. *You've made a mistake. Call Tom. Call him call him call him NOW or you'll die.*

A lone voice answered. My master. *It's still too early, Christopher. If you call him now, you'll* both *die.*

Aphrodite brought the knife up.

"Wait," I said. *"Wait."*

She placed its edge against my index finger. The blade bit into my skin.

"WAIT!"

She stopped. A drop of blood ran down the edge of the knife, dripped to stain my boots.

"Do you have something to say?" she said. "Is it clever? I can't tell you how much I hope it's *clever.*"

"There's a code," I gasped.

"I already know that. You found it under the painting."

"But I worked it out. I know what it says."

"Show me."

"My hand. I need my hand."

For a moment, she held on to it, as if deciding whether or not to keep cutting. Then, with a peal of silvery laughter, she let me go.

I reached toward my belt. The Minotaur grabbed my wrist.

"Careful, now," Aphrodite said.

The Minotaur pulled my shirt up to see what was underneath. It was my sash, tied tightly around my waist. Some of the vials had broken, a gift from the Minotaur's iron fists.

"The code's beneath it," I said.

"Take it off," Aphrodite said. "Slowly."

The Minotaur laid his blade across my throat. I reached back and undid the buckles that held the sash in place. The paper fell from behind it, fluttering onto my boots.

"Throw the sash away," she said.

I tossed it aside, the Minotaur's blade still at my neck. When she was satisfied I had nothing more hidden under my shirt, she picked up the paper and read it.

"'The key is the blessing and the curse.'" She frowned. "What does it mean?"

"I'm not sure," I said.

Her eyes hardened.

"I swear," I said quickly. "I haven't had the chance to work it out. I think it's referring to the carvings."

I motioned to the Templar stories that ringed the dungeon. She looked around, suddenly interested, as if seeing them for the first time.

"Well, then, you clever thing," she said. "Get to work."

I moved to go to the nearest panel. Aphrodite stopped me.

"And just so you don't try to play a trick on us," she said, "I'm going to give you two minutes to figure it out. If you don't, one of your fingers will go." She smiled. "That gives you twenty minutes before I start in on the rest of you."

I stared at her in horror.

"Well, don't just stand there, Baron," she said. "Tick tock, tick tock."

Panic rose in my chest. This was madness. Two minutes. I'd made such a terrible mistake. I needed a way out. But there was no way out.

Then I heard my master's voice once more. *There is a way out, Christopher. You just have to find it. Literally.*

It took me a moment to process what he'd meant.

Literally.

Yes. That was it. All the Templars' clues were literal. So this one would be, too.

The panels. I picked up the torch and ran to them, began to scan.

The first panel showed a battle. A group of knights— nine of them, I counted—rode their horses into a band of Saracens, lances down. The Saracens, in return, waved heavy, wickedly-curved swords. Their faces were covered by cloth, so only their eyes could be seen. My stomach tumbled as I thought of the Minotaur behind me, his own sword dragging on the stone.

"Ninety seconds," Aphrodite said.

Above the panel were words, carved in Latin. *Hostiles repulsantur,* it said. The enemy repelled.

This was not it. It held neither blessing nor curse. I moved on.

The next panel showed the same nine knights sitting around an oasis. Broad-bladed trees stood tall in the background, in front of sandy, windswept dunes. The knights were eating; dates, it looked like. Again there was a phrase in Latin. *Dominus providet.* The Lord provides.

I stopped.

The Lord provides. *That* was a blessing.

"Sixty seconds."

My blood pounded in my ears. I couldn't *think.*

My master returned to me. I felt the warmth of his hand around my heart. *Focus on the problem, Christopher.*

I can't! I cried.

You can, he whispered. *I believe in you.*

The blessing. Here was a blessing. Where was the curse?

I scanned the stone, the trees, the men. I saw nothing. It wasn't here.

"Thirty seconds."

It wasn't here. Move on.

The next panel was the damaged one, the one that

showed the treasure, the one the Templars had used to taunt le Bel. I could see only three knights on this panel, though there might have been more, hacked off by the Iron King's rage. As before, it was impossible to tell what the treasure had been: some kind of box, with an angel statue remaining at one end.

Treasure, I thought. That would certainly be literal. Treasure here, behind the treasure?

I peered closer. Something stirred in me, as if the angel statue should matter, like the treasure should be something I knew. But without the full stone, I simply couldn't tell what it was. I scanned the parts I could see, but there was no phrase in Latin here. All that remained was the golden yellow sun above, emblazoned with the Templar cross.

I was looking for something literal. This panel was nothing if not literal. But it couldn't be right. *The key is the blessing and the curse,* they'd said. I saw neither blessing nor curse.

"Fifteen seconds," Aphrodite said.

Now I couldn't quell my panic. I moved on to the next panel, mind screaming in terror. Here a single knight stood upon a platform.

"Ten seconds."

The knight wore a simple coif of mail, the links intricately carved. His sword hung in a belt by his side. His mouth was open

"Five."

and his arms were upraised. The

"Four."

crowd in front of him was

"Three."

multitudinous, a sea

"Two."

of faces in rapture

"One."

at his words

"Time's up," Aphrodite said.

"No," I begged. "It's not enough. It's not *enough*—"

A rough hand grabbed my collar. I tried to twist away, to run. I managed a couple of steps toward the stairs before the Minotaur flipped me off my feet. I landed heavily on the stone.

"No!" I shouted.

The Minotaur pressed his blade to my throat. I scanned every inch of him, trying to see if there was anything different in his motion: some tremor, some fault, some way in which he'd been weakened. I saw nothing. My trap on my sword hilt had failed.

"Hold him," Aphrodite said.

She straddled me. She grabbed my hand.

I thrashed. I screamed. I pleaded. All I could see was the ice in the Minotaur's eyes, the cruel pleasure in hers.

Call Tom, my mind shrieked. *Call Tom.*

No, Christopher, Master Benedict said. *Call him now, spare yourself, and he dies.*

I couldn't. I couldn't. Aphrodite placed the blade against my finger, the same place she'd cut it before.

"I'm afraid this is going to hurt," she said.

I couldn't sacrifice Tom. And I knew, because I couldn't, they would take me here, and carve me like a hog, under the cold light above us of

the faded

Templar

sun

I remembered.

I *remembered.*

CHAPTER

"IT'S THERE!"

My scream echoed in the cells. Unlike my begging, this made Aphrodite stop.

"You're lying," she said.

"No," I said. "It's there. It's there. It's right on the wall behind you."

Dubiously, she swiveled her head to look across the dungeon.

"No. Him. Behind him." I motioned to the Minotaur with my head. "The sun. On the panel. It's the sun."

She stood. She peered at it. "I see nothing."

"The blessing. The sun. The blessing *is* the sun."

She looked doubtful. "That's hardly—"

"Upstairs," I said, "in the central tower, there's a panel." I closed my eyes, remembering, my chest heaving with my breaths. "It shows the Templars, their order being created by King Baldwin. There are words above it, in Latin. *Deo et hominibus benedicti.* 'Blessed by God and man.'"

"What does that have to do with this one?"

"The sun," I said. "The *sun.* It's the only other panel with the sun."

She looked around, eyes narrowed. "Keep him there," she said.

She went back upstairs. I waited, the Minotaur's sword at my throat, almost too scared to breathe.

Aphrodite returned, her face flushed. "He's right," she said. "It's the only other panel with a sun." She returned to the damaged panel. "I see how that's the blessing. But I don't see a curse."

"That's because it's not there anymore." I wriggled my arm out from underneath the Minotaur's knee and pointed to the broken stone. "The Iron King took it away."

"The missing stone?"

"Not the stone itself," I said. "What was on it. The priest in the church next door told me. The Templars carved a taunt for le Bel: *This shall never be yours.* That's it. That's the curse."

She looked from the sun to the broken stone. "Blessing," she whispered, "and curse."

Her eyes lit up. She slipped her dagger back into her belt and peered more closely at the panel. "How do I open it?"

"I don't know," I said. "There must be a mechanism of some kind. Try pressing it."

She poked at the carving. She traced her fingers along its edge. She pried at it, trying to pull it loose. The more she tried, the more frustrated she got.

"Get over here," she snapped.

The Minotaur hauled me up and pushed me toward the panel. I stepped forward, scanned it, trying to stall for time.

"Do you need another two minutes?" Aphrodite said.

I swallowed and took her place prodding the stone. I pressed harder than she did, pulled harder. Twisted. Wrenched. Nothing seemed to work.

Feeling both of them looming closer, I began to hammer on it. All over the panel. It was when I got to the sun that I felt something shift.

"Did you hear that?" I said.

They looked at me, puzzled. I pressed on the sun. It resisted for a moment, and then I felt something snap. Stone dust trickled down as the circle of the sun slipped into the rock.

Aphrodite gasped. She waited, breathless, for something to happen.

So did I. But nothing moved.

"Wait," Aphrodite said. She ran upstairs. When she came back down, she shook her head. "The sun up there doesn't move."

Meanwhile, I found myself remembering another secret door in a wall, not so long ago. Then, we'd needed to pour things into the holes to open it; the keys were various—

Keys, I thought. *The key is the blessing and the curse.*

It came to me in a flash.

Aphrodite had been watching me. "You know what to do," she said.

"I don't—" I began.

The Minotaur slammed me against the wall.

"After all this time," Aphrodite said, "you're still not taking me seriously."

I didn't wait for the knife. "The florin," I croaked.

She stopped. "The what?"

"The florin. The coin with the Templar cross on it. I think that's the key—literally. The Templars have used them to taunt the kings of France on their coronation. But they also give them to people who've done them a kindness."

Realization dawned on her. "The blessing . . . and the *curse*. Then we need a florin to open the door?"

I didn't try to hide anything this time. Rémi would already have told her, through Colette. If I lied again, I would face Aphrodite's knife for sure. Besides, there was something else much more valuable that the truth—the partial truth—would give me: a second chance to properly spring my trap.

"I have Marin Chastellain's florin," I said, trying to sound defeated. "It's in my sash."

"Get it," she told the Minotaur.

He shoved me against the wall again, this time just because he could. He went over to where I'd thrown my sash, picked it up, looked at the dozens of pockets. "Which one?"

Now.

"It's next to the vial with the wax top," I said.

Please work, I prayed, and he reached his fingers in.

Then he howled.

Aphrodite had the knife on me right away. "What did you do?"

The Minotaur drew back his hand. A sharpened goose quill was stuck in his middle finger, deep below the skin. He pulled it out, cursing as he came toward me. "You did that on purpose!"

Aphrodite saved me from the beating. "Stop whining," she said. "It's just a feather. Find the coin."

With a murderous look, he turned back, but this time, he didn't bother to search the sash. He simply tipped it upside down and shook it. Half my things fell, vials shattering out their ingredients, tools ringing on the stone.

The florin fell, too. It bounced and rolled away. The Minotaur chased it clumsily, finally stepping on it to make it stop. He held it up, triumphant.

"Put it in," Aphrodite said.

He pressed the florin into the sun. Both slid into the rock. Still nothing happened. They looked at me.

"I think you have to drop it," I said.

He let it go. I heard the coin scraping through the

stone. Then there was a dull *ping*, metal hitting metal.

Click.

The panel came unsealed. Aphrodite stared at it, her doe eyes glinting with greed. Then she pulled the panel open and stared into the dark.

CHAPTER
59

STAIRS.

A steep, narrow set of stairs led down. Grinning, Aphrodite took a step forward. Then she stopped.

"I almost forgot about the traps," she said. "You go first."

The Minotaur smacked me on the back of my head, revenge for sticking him with the quill—or, more likely, just the beginning of revenge. Reluctantly, I led the way down.

It was forty steps to the bottom. The stairs ended on rough and bumpy rock, a jagged-edged tunnel leading away to the north. The Minotaur slapped me forward again, and I went, holding the torch in front to light the way.

We walked. The tunnel seemed to go on forever. Deep underground, I lost all sense of place, but it felt like we traveled half a mile, at least. I kept looking back at the Minotaur, trying to make it seem as if I was questioning whether we should continue.

"Move," he growled, "until I tell you not to move."

I nodded. In reality, I was trying to find a sign that the trap in the sash hadn't failed like the one on my sword hilt. If Master Benedict's notes were right, the paste I'd filled the goose quills with should have affected him already.

When it's fresh, my master had warned. And what I'd used was anything but fresh. It was at least several months old, possibly even years. If it didn't work, I was finished. I couldn't think of any other way out.

"What's wrong with you?" Aphrodite said.

For a moment, I thought she was talking to me. Then the Minotaur answered. "It's warm."

"Are you mad? It's freezing."

I turned, watching him intently. The man rocked his head back and forth, as if trying to stretch his neck.

"I don't like it down here," he said.

"You'll like it fine when we have the treasure," Aphrodite said.

The tunnel widened and began to slope upward. My eyes followed the path up, and it nearly got me killed.

I put my foot down—and found no ground. I teetered, arms flailing, and saw the giant pit opening before me. I knew I was about to fall.

A long-nailed hand grabbed me, pulled me back. Aphrodite let go of my collar and smoothed it out. "Careful, Baron. You can't die on me yet. There might be more of those along the way."

I sidestepped the pit, trying not to look down. It didn't seem as if it had been carved deliberately. It looked like a natural opening.

"I know where we are," Aphrodite said suddenly. "This is one of the old gypsum mines." The passage branched for a short distance to the left, where falling rocks had sealed up the tunnel. "Must have been closed off by a cave-in."

The Minotaur grunted. He was working his jaw from side to side, as if his ears had become blocked by water.

My heart leaped. This was what my master had said would happen. My plan *was* working. I just needed a little more time.

Except it didn't look like I was going to get it. The tunnel we followed opened abruptly into a giant, naturally formed cavern.

It was extraordinary. The ceiling of the cave rose fifty feet above us, the rock curved and smooth. Giant stalactites hung over our heads like monstrous teeth, dripping water into pools turned milky white. Equally large stalagmites pierced upward from the floor, and in the center, a single column tapered from floor to ceiling, thicker than an oak tree at the ends, thinner in the middle than a baby's finger. One of the milky pools spilled over, its cloudy liquid trickling across the rock to drip down another one of those pits into which I'd nearly fallen. Several of them ringed the open space.

I could have stared at this cave for hours. But something even more extraordinary caught my eye.

Gold.

Aphrodite pressed me forward, and suddenly we were surrounded by treasure. What seemed like a million golden coins lay scattered on the cavern floor, like dunes of glittering sand. Among them were piled thick bars of silver, tarnished nearly black from centuries in the cave, stacked thirty high, side by side. And everywhere, everywhere, *everywhere* were spectacular works of art: golden chalices, silver bowls, crosses and candlesticks, endless priceless artifacts that outshone even the Louvre.

My head spun. The Templars' treasure wasn't a treasure. It was a dragon's hoard.

Aphrodite shrieked, bounding forward like a little girl. She skidded to a stop in front of the sea of coins and stood there for a moment. Then she dived in.

Her laughter echoed through the cave. She splashed her arms like she was in the Seine, sending Templar florins flying like golden drops.

The Minotaur seemed just as awed, but he didn't follow her. He still held his sword in one hand; with the other, he rubbed at his arm and shoulders. He saw me watching him and snarled.

Aphrodite played some more, grinning as she crawled her way out of the pile. She squealed with delight as she shook her shoe, flinging away more coins that had slipped inside. Then she turned back to me.

I saw the gleam in her eye. The gold was found; the traps were bypassed. There was nothing left that I could do for her.

I backed away.

She gave me a look that seemed almost kind. "Don't be afraid," she said. "I'm grateful to you for working this out. I promise, I won't hurt you anymore. It'll be over quickly."

There was no more time, there were no more riddles; I had only one trick left to play. I stuck two fingers between my lips and whistled as loud as I could.

Aphrodite looked amused. "What do you think that'll do? Raise an army of Templars?"

I whistled again. The sound pierced the cavern, loud enough to shake the walls.

She stepped closer. "Or are you thinking of your overgrown friend? I'm afraid he won't be coming. We locked the door to the tower behind us when we entered."

"Where did you get the keys?" I said.

"Who needs keys when you can pick a lock?" She waved at the Minotaur, who was flexing his fingers as if he wasn't quite sure they were working. "No, *chéri*, that door is secure. And the tower was built to withstand a siege. Unless your man has a battering ram, there's no way he could get in."

"Not *after* the door was locked," I said. "But how about before?"

She scoffed. "You didn't bring him with you. We saw. We were following you, remember?"

"I said *before*."

Suddenly it dawned on her what I meant. The smile slipped from her lips.

"That's impossible," she said. "He couldn't have got here before you. We were watching your room all night. You both went in. Only you came out."

"Only I went out the *door*," I said. "You're forgetting about the window."

"The window . . ." She trailed off, stunned. "He couldn't have! Your room is two floors up!"

"Yes. Tom was very cross with me. But bedsheets tied together make a perfectly decent rope. He's been in the tower for hours, hiding in the upper floors. He doesn't like waiting, by the way. And he especially hates waiting in the cold. So if I had to guess . . ." I nodded toward the entrance to the cave. "I'd say he's about to take it out on you."

CHAPTER
60

SHE TURNED IN HORROR.

Tom stood in the entrance. He held my apothecary sash in one hand, his polished sword gleaming in the other. And he really didn't look very pleased.

Aphrodite whipped her dagger from her belt. "You think this matters? We'll kill two of you just as easily as one. If anything, you've made it simpler to finish off your sweetheart at the Palais." She turned to the Minotaur. "Get him!"

The brute was already on his way. Tom dropped my sash and stepped forward. He raised his sword high in defense.

I held my breath. The Minotaur looked sluggish, but not

paralytic. I had to hope my trap had worked well enough.

The Minotaur lunged first. The man held his blade low, then swung wide on his right. Tom brought his sword across to meet it. Their steel clanged loudly in the cavern.

The man lunged again, once more toward the right. Tom moved his blade to parry as before, but this attack was just a feint. The Minotaur switched his line to the left, and Tom, taken by surprise, couldn't get his weapon over in time. The man's blade cut into Tom's upper arm, and he staggered back, blood staining his shirt.

My guts twisted, even as the Minotaur's blade flashed in the torchlight. Tom hurried backward, trying desperately to get out of the way. The Minotaur pressed the attack, and, after a flurry of heart-stopping parries, Tom tried a riposte. The Minotaur slapped it aside contemptuously, then swung his own counter-riposte at Tom's neck.

A bright red line appeared on Tom's skin. For one sickening moment, I thought the Minotaur had cut his throat. But the wound was shallow. Still, Tom staggered back, terrified.

My heart sank. What had I done? It wasn't enough. It hadn't been enough.

As much as I despaired, Aphrodite was infuriated.

"What are you doing?" she shrieked at the Minotaur. "Stop playing and finish him!"

And suddenly I saw an opening: telling her the truth.

"He's not playing," I said. "He's poisoned."

She looked at me sharply. "How could you have . . . ?" Then her eyes went wide. "The quills!"

I put on a smile. "The quills. The goose-feather quills, filled with a poison called urare. Do you know what it does? It paralyzes you. First you get warm and dizzy. Then your neck feels like it's getting stiff. Then your arms and legs go numb, and, finally, you collapse."

She looked back at the Minotaur. And fear crept across her face.

"You should run," I said. "Run before the poison brings him down. Run before Tom comes to kill you, too."

She thrust her knife out, point toward me. She eyed the treasure to her side.

"No," she said. "No! Kill him! Kill him *now!*"

I didn't know how much the Minotaur had heard of our conversation. But he heard the panic in her voice, and it seemed to fuel his own. He could see how basic Tom's skill with the sword was; he should have been able to chop him down within seconds. But I saw the way the Minotaur shook his arms, and I knew he felt it. His body slipping, his limbs beginning to fail. The poisoner, laid low by poison.

Desperation drove him forward. He needed to end the fight before it was too late. He advanced upon Tom and let loose a frenzy of blows at his head. Tom, back almost against the cave wall, held his blade high to block the man's strikes. Sparks flew. One, two, three, four, five—then, suddenly, the man's blade dropped low.

It was a brutally effective line of attack, as Sir William himself had taught us. Make an inexperienced opponent defend one area, then shift and strike at what's left exposed. And if the Minotaur hadn't been poisoned, he would have moved too fast for Tom to react.

But he *had* been poisoned. And—just as important—Sir William had been an excellent master. The Minotaur's blade thrust upward, inches away from Tom's gut. Yet this was an attack Tom had seen two times too many.

Tom swept his blade down in an arc, slapping away the Minotaur's sword. And then, in one smooth stroke, he thrust his own weapon out in riposte.

It pierced the Minotaur's chest. Tom drove forward, and his steel plunged through the man's back.

They both stood there, staring at each other in shock.

Then the Minotaur's sword fell from useless fingers and clattered on the floor of the cavern. Tom pulled out his blade, and the Minotaur fell to his knees. The man reached toward Aphrodite, pleading. Then he toppled to the stone.

Fire ran through my veins. Every ounce of my body screamed. He'd done it. He'd really *done* it.

Tom swayed. I thought he might faint. He looked like he couldn't believe he'd won. Aphrodite looked even more disbelieving—and then she began to panic.

She backed away, dagger held out. She aimed her knife at Tom, then at me, as if uncertain whom she should threaten.

Tom, finally recovered, saw what she was doing. He advanced, blade high.

Aphrodite stepped toward me. "Back. Back!" she commanded him.

Tom hesitated. I could see the clockwork turning in his mind. Could he get to me before she could?

She decided not to give him time to figure it out. Aphrodite snatched a platinum goblet from the hoard. She plunged it into the pile of florins, scooping up gold. She clutched her prize to her chest like a swaddled child as she moved away, knife out. "Don't come any closer!"

Tom stepped in front of me protectively as she backed toward the exit. *No,* I thought. Knife or not, we couldn't let her get away. She'd told us nothing of who else was working with her. We needed to capture her; if she escaped, none of us would ever be safe.

I hefted a bar of silver from the pile of treasure beside me. It wasn't much of a weapon, but the Minotaur's sword was on the other side of the cave.

Aphrodite flinched, took another step away. She could see I wasn't going to let her go without a fight. I stepped forward, and she stepped back again, and that ended the final battle before it began.

She hadn't been watching where she was going. Her eyes widened in shock as her final step found no ground. Off balance, she whirled her arms, sending the goblet of florins flying. Then she fell backward into the pit.

Her scream cut off quickly. We ran to the edge, skidded to a stop. Then we leaned over to see.

The fall wasn't that far: fifteen, twenty feet. If the pit had been smooth, she might not even have been that badly hurt. But this was a natural cave. Aphrodite looked up at us, face drained of color, as her hands went to her stomach and found, instead, the rock.

A stalagmite pierced upward through her abdomen. I had to look away.

"Help," she cried softly. "Please. I'm sorry. I'm sorry I hurt you. Help."

The platinum goblet lay beside her, dented from the fall. Gold coins surrounded her like stars.

"Please," Aphrodite said. "It wasn't me. I'm not to blame. It's my mistress, the comtesse de Colmar. I just work for her. Please help."

I stared down at her. "The *comtesse*? Amyot's *wife*? *She's* behind all this?"

"And some man. I don't know who he is. He's somewhere in the city. He sends a girl with instructions when we need them. Please."

My mind raced as the pieces fell into place. We *did* know the man, and the girl he sent: Rémi and Colette. But . . . the *comtesse*? "It's not Amyot himself?"

Aphrodite's breath heaved in her chest. "No. Madame hates him; she tells him nothing. Please. I don't know anything more. Please help me."

Tom looked to me for what to do. I shook my head.

There was nothing we *could* do. Even if we helped her from the pit, the injury she'd sustained was too great. In truth, the stalagmite was probably the only thing still keeping her alive. As soon as we pulled her off it, she'd bleed to death.

I turned away. Tom didn't look happy, but he turned with me.

"No!" she cried. "Please! Don't leave me all alone in the dark! I beg you, Master! Have mercy!"

My blood boiled. Mercy? She'd nearly murdered Sally, to say nothing of the scores of others she'd have been happy to kill. That the comtesse was the source of her orders changed nothing. She *deserved* the fate she'd earned.

Yet still I stopped. With the rock sealing the wound, she could live like that for hours. Maybe even days.

I hated her. I hated her for what she'd done to Sally, what she was ready to do to me. I *burned* with hatred. Yet I wondered: If I walked away now, what would happen to those flames? Would they dwindle to coals, and then cool? Or would that burning never cease?

I called up to heaven. *What should I do, Master?*

I didn't hear an answer. But I did see his face.

I sighed. Then I picked up my apothecary sash. Most of the vials had spilled out when the Minotaur had shaken it back in the tower. I looked through what remained, then chose one. It was filled with tiny black, kidney-shaped seeds.

I returned to the pit, where Tom still waited. I held out the vial so Aphrodite could see it. Then I dropped it so it landed on her chest.

She clawed at it with trembling hands. She looked up at me, hopeful.

"That's madapple," I said. "It's poison—just like the two of you fed to others. Chew the seeds, and your pain will end."

And so, deserving or not, we didn't leave her all alone in the dark.

It didn't take long to finish. When it was over, Tom and I went back to the center of the chamber, where the Templar's treasure waited. I spied the Minotaur's body and realized just how close we'd both come to the end.

I threw my arms around Tom. "You were *brilliant*," I said. "Sir William—and Lord Ashcombe—and the *king*—they'll be so proud of you."

"And you," he said, "were utterly mad."

I laughed, then let go and stared at the treasure.

"What do we do now?" Tom said.

"I—" I stopped. I'd heard something.

I glanced quickly to the side of the cavern, to the pit where Aphrodite had fallen. But the sound hadn't come from there. They were footsteps.

And they echoed from the tunnel back to the tower.

CHAPTER

TOM RAISED HIS SWORD. I PRESSED
against him, clutching the silver bar as a weapon once
more. The figure that entered stopped when he saw us and
raised his hands in return.

"I am unarmed," Father Bernard said.

Tom looked to me before lowering his blade. Father
Bernard let his hands fall, too. "May I sit?" he said. "It's a
long walk here from the tower."

I nodded. He wandered over to where the Templar
treasure lay piled. He brushed some florins off the stack of
silver bars that had furnished my weapon, then sat on it,
joints cracking.

"Congratulations," he said. "In three hundred and fifty years, you're the first to succeed."

He looked around the cavern. There was interest in his gaze, and curiosity, but no greed, nor even surprise, at the sight of the treasure, or the Minotaur's body beside it. And I understood.

"You're a Templar," I said.

He nodded. "Since I was barely older than you."

"So you knew this was here the whole time."

"Not exactly. The grand master never told me what I was guarding. My task was only to keep what remains of our old headquarters in good repair. But, for decades, I've believed the treasure was here."

He rubbed his leg, working out the soreness from his walk. "Our order has always valued secrecy, so we're never told more than we need to know. Yet being priest at Saint Mary's has given me an opportunity available to none of my brothers. Over the years, every rumor, fable, and clue about the treasure made its way to me. I've read the poems, the puzzles, the riddles, the codes. I've even tried to work out a few myself, just for amusement's sake. Together, they pointed me here. But it wasn't the riddles that convinced me. Do you know what it was?"

Tom and I shook our heads.

"Molay's story," he said.

I thought about it. "Because he was *caught*," I said. "He supposedly sent the treasure away, but he remained even though there was danger."

Father Bernard nodded. "Molay clearly saw what the Iron King was going to do; why else bother with the ruse of the knights and their wagons? Yet, if he knew, why not leave with the treasure himself? There's another reason, too, though only our order would know it: We *always* leave ourselves an escape route. It was impossible that there would be no such route at our own headquarters. And that passage would have been a perfect place to hide a treasure."

"But Molay never used it," Tom said. "Even after he knew the treasure would be safe, he stayed in the dungeon. Why didn't he ever try to escape?"

"Ah. Now that, I *was* told." Father Bernard stared thoughtfully at the exit. "You have to understand what was happening at the time. The Knights Templar was an order in decline. Its original purpose was to protect the Holy Land, but enthusiasm for the Crusades had begun to wane. The kings of Europe had their own agendas, and none of those involved defending a place half a world away.

We'd become, after all that time, an inconvenience.

"Le Bel may have brought us down, but he wasn't the only one who wanted us eliminated. We had power, wealth, prestige—and if there's one thing kings can't stand, it's those things in the hands of anyone else. If the Iron King hadn't struck at us, eventually, some other man would have. Molay saw *that* coming, too. And so he made a sacrifice.

"The Knights Templar needed to change. We could no longer be a military order. Instead, it was decided our real power would be held in shadow: We would work *behind* the scenes, using knowledge and influence to keep our civilization safe. But you can't work in the shadows when all upon you is shining light. So Jacques de Molay—twenty-third grand master, but *not* the last—came up with a plan.

"Our order would be destroyed. The whole world would watch us fall, so completely, so shamefully, that only those given to conspiracy theories would believe we still existed. *Humiliation* would be our cloak, and under that, we'd find our shadow. Jacques de Molay, greatest of our grand masters, gave his own life, along with his bravest men, so the Knights Templar might live on. And we remain to help to this day."

"Doing what?" I asked.

"If you want to know that, you'll have to join our order."

It took a moment for us to realize what he'd said.

"Us?" Tom gasped. "Become *Knights Templar*?"

Father Bernard looked amused. "We need to find new brothers somewhere. You don't think I'm three hundred and fifty years old, do you?"

Tom's mouth worked, unable to speak. I didn't do much better. "I . . . I . . ."

The priest laughed. "I'm not asking you to give me an answer now. You're still a bit young to undergo the initiation, anyway. It's just something to keep in mind; perhaps we'll revisit it another time. At the moment, you have a different decision to make."

He scooped up a handful of florins and let them run through his fingers, waiting.

That also came as a surprise. "Wait," I said. "You're not taking back the treasure? You're letting us keep it?"

"You earned it," he said. "You solved the riddles fairly, and harmed no innocents along the way. The conditions are met; the treasure is yours. Though I dare say you'll need to find a few people to help you carry it." He looked at me carefully. "But if you do choose to keep it, I must warn you: You'll be putting yourself in quite a bit of danger."

"From other Templars?"

"No, no. From France."

I frowned. "I don't understand."

"Remember how this all started," Father Bernard said. "The whole reason Philippe le Bel arrested us was to get his hands on this treasure. He never did, but the laws he signed declared all Templar properties part of the crown. Those laws were never erased. Which means—technically—this belongs to Louis the Fourteenth.

"If you keep it, you'll have to sneak it out of France. And even if you succeed, you'll find you still have a problem. Many of these objects"—he waved at the assorted artifacts—"are quite famous. If you display them, or sell them, well, you might get away with one or two. But eventually, someone will realize where they came from. And the florins, of course, will give the game away immediately. You could melt them down—it would be a shame to see that happen, but you could—but your instant wealth will still raise quite a few eyebrows. And Louis will be very, very angry."

I hadn't even thought of that. Lord Ashcombe had ordered me not to inflame tensions between England and France; our nations were already on the brink of war. If I made Louis angry, King Charles would be, too.

I didn't much like the idea of making an enemy of kings. "What if we just told Louis we found it?"

Father Bernard nodded. "That would be the better choice. Louis is a decent man, and a generous one, as well. If you brought him the treasure, he'd grant you a great deal of land, and a title—plus a portion of this wealth itself. Not a king's portion, mind you, but still enough to make you, Tom, and Sally three of the richest people in Europe."

All the color drained from Tom's face. My own legs had gone a bit wobbly, too. Though there was a catch in the priest's voice that made me pause.

"You don't want us to do that," I said.

"No," he said.

"Why not?"

He studied me for a moment. "You have to understand our perspective. When the Iron King laid claim to this treasure, the way he did it was unholy. He didn't trade, or negotiate, or ask us for assistance. He didn't even fight us, defeat us in honest combat—we were a military order; we understood the way of things. Any of those we could accept.

"Instead, he attacked us in a manner most wicked. He

struck at the very heart of who we are. We dedicated our life in service to the Lord. But he called us heretics, blasphemers, enemies of God. To this day, holy men still spit upon our name. Of all the things he could have done, that's the most unforgivable."

"Is that why you leave a florin on every new king's pillow?" Tom said.

"That," Father Bernard said, "and also because it doesn't hurt to remind a king there remains something greater than him."

"But Louis isn't responsible for what le Bel did," I said.

"No, he isn't. Which is why—except for le Bel and his sons—we've never harmed a single king of France. In fact, quite the opposite: Several of our order have worked secretly for the fleur-de-lis, to support it—including men currently in Louis's service. But there remains a difference between blaming them, and not wishing them to profit from our demise."

I bit my lip. "So what is it you want us to do?"

"Nothing," he said. "I would like you to do nothing. Tell no one—absolutely no one—what you've found. Just go back to your room at the Palais and wait. If you do this, then later today, a letter will be delivered to you. You'll know what to do when you get it."

"We *can't* do nothing," I said. "Exposing the treasure was the whole reason we began searching for it in the first place. Those two"—I waved toward the pit and the Minotaur's body—"were only part of the conspiracy. If it remains hidden, Minette and the rest of the royal family will still be in danger."

"The letter you receive will take care of that."

I stared at him. "You know the comtesse de Colmar is behind this? You can stop her?"

All he said was "If you return the treasure to us, then I promise you, the danger to the royal family will end."

A million thoughts ran through my brain. If we took the treasure, we'd be rich beyond imagining. But we'd make powerful enemies of both England and France, and betray the orders of our king. I'm not going to say I didn't *want* the money, but the truth was, we didn't *need* it: Master Benedict's legacy had left me with more than enough to keep me, Tom, and Sally safe from poverty for our entire lives.

If I gave the treasure to Louis, we'd still be rich, and we'd make a valuable friend of him as well. Both of those sounded just fine to me. On the other hand, if we returned the treasure to the Templars, then *they'd* be our friends—and from what Father Bernard had told us, they seemed even more powerful than kings.

As I struggled with the answer, a different question arose in my mind. "There's still one thing I don't understand," I said. "If you don't want anyone revealing the treasure, why all the riddles telling people how to find it? Why not just keep it for yourselves?"

"For two reasons," Father Bernard said. "The first is as I told you: The Knights Templar are always in need of new recruits. The puzzles act as a kind of test: We watch, and whenever someone shows enough skill to get close to the treasure, we invite them to join our brotherhood. So far, it's been extremely effective in finding talent. We would have already approached you three, in fact, but you discovered everything so quickly, and there were too many players on the board to remove a piece. Which brings me to the second reason.

"The Templars could never disappear completely. The influence we wield, however subtle, could always reveal our existence to an astute observer. So, to protect ourselves, we direct that curiosity. As the most visible sign of our existence, the treasure hunt is always the first place people begin to look for us. And as they follow our clues, we watch *how* they search. Are they kind, or cruel?" He nodded toward the body of the Minotaur, still lying on the floor of the cavern. "In this way, we reveal their intentions. Will they be our enemy, or—"

"Your servant," I said, understanding.

He smiled. "Sometimes, prophecies do come true."

I turned to Tom. "What should we do?"

He folded his arms. "Don't even *think* of asking me. This is all *your* fault."

I couldn't decide what was best. I couldn't ask Sally, either. So I sent the question to my master. *What do I do?*

Whatever you decide, he said, *I stand with you.*

And that would always be enough for me.

I gave one final look of longing at the treasure before I sighed. "All right," I said. "We'll do as you ask."

"Thank you, Baron," Father Bernard said simply, and pushed himself to his feet. "I have little time to work, so you'd better go. The letter will arrive by tonight."

As Tom and I made to leave, the priest stopped us. "I

almost forgot. There *is* one thing you should do. I understand you brought some items with you from England." He looked at me meaningfully. "If I were you, I'd ensure none of those are in your room by this evening."

A fair warning. I thanked him, and we went. At the exit, I stopped.

"Father Bernard?" I said. "I'm not really a baron, you know."

He laughed pleasantly. "You don't say. Well, you're still young. Give it time."

CHAPTER

WE HURRIED BACK TO THE PALAIS, stopping only to collect my sword and the tools the assassin had shaken from my apothecary sash onto the dungeon floor. Adelard and Sanguin, weary but eager to serve, were still watching over Sally when we returned.

Thinking of Father Bernard's warning, Tom and I collected my box of poisons and Master Benedict's notes along with my sash and carried them from our room. Tom groaned when I told him where I planned to hide them.

"The *cemetery*?" he said. *"Again?"*

"I can't think of anywhere else that's safe," I said. "We can't trust Maison Chastellain, and I'm not going to throw my master's things in the Seine. The false tomb in the Templar crypt is the only place."

He grumbled, but he came. To make it up to him, I stopped at a pâtisserie on the way home. It cost a *lot*.

We were praying over Sally when the scratch came at the door. After a glance to see if it was safe, Adelard opened it.

It was one of the palace pages, the same boy who'd brought me Sally's message. "A letter arrived for you, monsieur."

It was addressed to "Ashcombe" and sealed with unmarked red wax. I opened it and was surprised to see that what it contained was another sealed letter. This one, however, was intended for someone else: Louis's most trusted advisor, the man I'd met after watching the king wake.

Jean-Baptiste Colbert
The Louvre

Leaving the guards behind to keep watch, Tom and I hurried to the palace. Though the sun had already set, Colbert was still working in his office. When his assistant ushered me in, I found him sitting behind his desk, writing in a ledger.

"Ah," he said, without pausing in his writing. "Baron. Welcome. How may I help you?"

I handed him the letter. Still writing, he broke the seal with his free hand. It wasn't until he began to read that the quill stopped scratching.

He stood. "Where did you get this?"

"Some boy I've never seen before, monsieur," I lied. "He handed it to my guard at the Palais and bade him deliver it to you."

Colbert read through the letter again. "Do you know what this says?" he asked.

"No, monsieur."

He regarded both of us for a moment. "Come with me," he said.

We followed him to the outer office, where he spoke quietly to his assistant. The man looked rather shocked at what his master said, but he nodded and hurried out. Colbert then walked us outside, where a score of the king's guards had begun to assemble.

Colbert called two of them over. "Return to the Palais," he said to us. "These men will accompany you. Please, Baron, remain in your quarters until told otherwise."

We did as we were commanded—not that the king's

guards gave us a choice. We stayed in our room until Colbert, now accompanied by even more guards, came to collect me. He ordered Tom to remain.

I followed him nervously through the corridors of the Palais. Beyond the tromping of the soldiers' boots, I could hear the sound of an argument. The guards pushed the assembled crowd of nobles from the door of the study and ushered us in.

A dozen more of the king's guards were already there, squared off against two of the duchess's guests: a red-faced Amyot and his frightened wife, the comtesse.

"Colbert?" Amyot said. "How dare you hold us like this! Let us go!"

Colbert didn't answer. He waited until four more guards pushed through the crowd, carrying two bodies covered with shrouds. They laid them in front of the couple.

"What is this?" Amyot said.

Colbert drew back one of the shrouds. It was the Minotaur, the sword wound in his chest. "Do you recognize this man?" Colbert said.

The comtesse went pale. Amyot just looked confused. "No," he said.

Colbert threw back the other shroud. "And what about her?"

It was Aphrodite, in her yellow gown. The crowd gasped at the terrible wound in her stomach.

"Yes," Amyot said, even more confused. "That's my wife's chambermaid. What happened to her?"

Everyone stared at the comtesse. She looked like she was ready to faint.

"Wait . . . isn't that your dress?" Amyot asked her. "Why on earth is *she* wearing it?"

"These two," Colbert said, "were found in an alleyway in the Cour des Miracles near Porte Saint-Denis. A report I received indicated they were murdered after discovering an ancient cache of Templar treasure and delivering it to their mistress."

"After *what*? Are you suggesting—"

Colbert held up a finger. "I am suggesting, monsieur, that you remain silent." When Amyot shut his mouth, Colbert said, "Well, Comtesse?"

She could barely speak, just a whisper. "I . . . I don't . . . I had nothing to do with this."

Two more soldiers tromped into the room, carrying an ornately carved chest. They laid it at Colbert's feet.

"This is yours, is it not, Madame?" Colbert said.

Now the comtesse looked confused. "Yes."

"The key, please."

She drew the key from a chain on her neck and handed it over. The soldiers opened the chest. At the top was a folded satin gown. When the soldiers removed it, the crowd gasped again.

The chest was filled with treasure. There were several jeweled artifacts: goblets, crosses, and a silver frame, all nestled in a heap of golden florins.

She looked shocked. "How . . . how did those . . . Those aren't mine!"

"You just handed me the key," Colbert said.

"But I didn't . . . I couldn't . . . I never even saw . . . *him*!" She pointed at me.

"It was *him*!" she shrieked. "*He* did this! He's *framing* me! He's not even a baron, he's an *apprentice*! The other one is a *baker*!"

Colbert remained stone-faced as she ranted. The rest of the crowd stared in shock—and a fair amount of gossipy delight. Her husband seemed stunned. "Darling," he began.

She recoiled from his touch and backed away until she was pressed against the wall. "All I wanted to do was go *home!*" she cried. "Why wouldn't you let me go *home?*"

Colbert drew a paper from his waistcoat. "This is a writ from the king," he said. "The Templar treasure is confiscated, and you are hereby invited to be his guest at the Bastille."

"No," she pleaded as the guards grabbed her arms. "Please. I'll tell you everything. Please don't take me to the Bastille!"

The crowd scrambled aside as the guards hauled her off, avoiding her like she carried the plague. Her cries echoed all the way down the hall.

The guards marched me back to my quarters. When we arrived, I saw they'd ransacked my room. Everything inside was on the floor. Even my mattress and Tom's palliasse had been cut open, feathers and straw scattered across the parquet. Tom stood against the fireplace, holding the unconscious Sally, a flustered Bridget on his shoulder, as he waited nervously beside Adelard and Sanguin.

"Anything?" Colbert said.

The soldiers shook their heads. Colbert looked the guards I'd hired up and down. "Who are you?"

"I'm Adelard, monsieur," Adelard said, "and this is Sanguin. We work for the duke."

"What are you doing here, then?"

"The young monsieur asked for us. To keep watch over the lady when he went out."

"Have you been here long?"

"Since yesterday."

"And in all that time," Colbert said, "have you seen these boys do anything strange?"

"Strange, monsieur?" Adelard looked over at me.

As casually as I could, I laid a hand on my coin purse. Adelard looked at Sanguin, who shrugged.

"No, monsieur," Adelard said. "We've seen nothing strange at all."

NOVEMBER 22–30, 1665

Compline

CHAPTER
63

WITH THE ARREST OF THE COMTESSE
de Colmar, all attempts on the lives of the royal family
ceased. As for the comtesse herself, gossip trickled out
of the Bastille. At first, she tried to recant her words to
Colbert, laying all the blame on Aphrodite, her way-
ward chambermaid, whose real name turned out to be
Marie-Louise. Finally, under pressure, she admitted the
truth.

According to the comtesse, she'd been recruited to
the plot by someone else, whom she refused to name. The
unnamed man had placed Aphrodite in her service, promising the comtesse enough wealth to ensure that her fool of

a husband couldn't ever render her family penniless again. The comtesse claimed she didn't know who the Minotaur was—he had been Aphrodite's pet—but, after considerable pressure, she promised to speak more of her co-conspirator in exchange for a sentence of exile instead of death.

Louis himself took a keen interest in the case, and the entire aristocracy of Paris jockeyed for a place in the gallery in the court where her trial would be. But their entertainment was spoiled. The morning it was supposed to begin, the comtesse was found dead in her cell, an apparent victim of suicide. She'd swallowed poison, came the report—though no one could quite determine how she'd acquired it.

I already knew who the co-conspirator was: Rémi, at Maison Chastellain. Still, the question nagged at my mind. Why hadn't the comtesse named him? The gossip was that she'd been terrified the unnamed man would wreak some dreadful revenge on her if she had. But what could be worse than being executed outside the Bastille? And, since Rémi had placed Aphrodite in the comtesse's service, why had Aphrodite told us in the cave that she didn't know who he was? What horror could Rémi promise that would make her deny him, even when she was already nearly dead?

I itched to go to Colbert and tell him what I knew. Except that would put me squarely back in the plot. And a much worse possibility than Rémi remained.

"You don't really think Simon was working with them, do you?" Tom said.

I didn't want that to be true. But I didn't know.

Tom shook his head. "It doesn't make sense. If Simon was in charge, then Rémi would have told him we knew where the treasure was. So why wouldn't he show up with Aphrodite and the Minotaur? It's not like they were going to let us live, right? In fact, why would he even leave the city?"

That was the best argument for Simon *not* being involved. If he had been, he never would have left the city when he knew we were so close to discovering the prize. Except . . . "What if he didn't leave the city after all?" I said. "What if he was here the whole time, hiding, and he just pretended to leave so we wouldn't suspect him?"

"Now *you're* running your mind in circles," Tom said.

Maybe. There was only one way to find out. Still not sure whom I could trust at the Palais, I went first to Saint Mary's to see Father Bernard. There I discovered that a brand new priest, Father Jerome, had taken over the church.

"I'm afraid Father Bernard has left, monsieur," he said.

"The Vatican has transferred him to a parish in Arles, in Provence."

I didn't believe that for a second. The question was: Did Father Jerome?

"Are you . . . ?" I said.

He looked at me oddly. "Am I what, monsieur?"

I sighed. "Never mind."

I suppose I should have expected it: Templars, and their secrets. Unfortunately, it still left me looking to find someone I could be certain wasn't working for Rémi. I figured the most likely candidate would be Colbert. When I returned to his office and asked him if he knew of a reliable courier, he found me a boy of sixteen, whom I presented with a letter.

"Take this to Normandy," I said, "to the appanage of the comte de Gravigny. You must hand it directly to his nephew, Simon Chastellain—no one else. If he's not there, find out the last time he was. Then return immediately to me. Go quickly."

It took more than a day for the courier to ride there and back. My heart sank as the boy handed me the letter.

"Simon wasn't there?" I said.

"I'm sorry, monsieur," he said. "I just missed him."

I looked up sharply. "Wait. So . . . he *was* there?"

"He had been. The *maître* of the estate said Monsieur Chastellain arrived on Thursday, and spent the next few days around the appanage, setting his uncle's business in order. When I got there, he'd just left for Paris. I must have passed him on the road."

I slumped in my chair, relieved. The courier's report meant Simon couldn't have known. So it was only Rémi, Colette, and whoever else was with them on Marin's staff that we had left to worry about. I asked Adelard and Sanguin to accompany us—for far less than a *louis*, this time—and hurried over to Maison Chastellain.

When we got there, we discovered that Simon, traveling more slowly than my courier, had just arrived home. Still covered with dirt and dust from the road, he looked bewildered.

"Christopher?" he said. "What's going on? What happened to Rémi? The staff tell me he's disappeared."

I'd promised Father Bernard I wouldn't tell anyone about finding the treasure. So I told Simon only what the rest of Paris had seen: the comtesse arrested, her trunk filled with Templar gold, and her servants found murdered.

I did say, however, that I believed Rémi had been

working with them. "I think that's how they found the treasure. One of the riddles we discovered pointed to the Cour des Miracles, where the bodies were. The only person who heard me say that was Rémi."

Simon stared at me, flabbergasted. Then he shouted for one of the footmen. "Gaspard! When did you last see Rémi?"

"Saturday night," Gaspard said. "His bed was empty in the morning. Colette is gone as well, along with Claude and Jacqueline. They gave no notice."

Simon seemed horrified that, this time, *he* was the one who'd allowed so many blackguards into his uncle's home. He ran upstairs, and we followed him.

We found Marin in his chair in his study, reading and sipping his brandy. He looked up and raised an eyebrow. "What's got into you?"

Simon sighed, relieved. "Just glad to see you're well, Uncle."

"Why wouldn't I be?" He cast a critical eye at the nearby decanter. "Though I'm dangerously low on drink."

As the days passed, things only got better. With the end of the intrigue, I returned to the Cimetière des Innocents to collect my sash and my master's things. I spared Tom the trip this time, going back and forth twice myself instead. The second time I returned to the Palais, I heard a shout from the upper floor.

"Christopher!" Tom, leaning out of the window, waved his arms at me. "Christopher! Come quickly!"

I ran upstairs and skidded into our room. Tom stood there, beaming—next to Palissy, the surgeon, who was examining his newly awakened patient.

"Sally!" I dropped my master's notes and ran to her side. She gave me a weak smile.

Palissy elbowed me away. "Get back, boy, get back. Give me space." He probed gently at the bandage around Sally's head. "How are you feeling?"

"Thirsty," she croaked.

I called for drink as Palissy continued his examination. When he was finished, he sat back and said, "Well, we'll keep that bandage on for a few days more, and I wouldn't go bumping your head into anything. Otherwise, I'd say you're out of danger."

"It hurts."

"And it's going to for quite some time. But you'll be fine." He patted her leg. "You're an incredibly strong girl, do you know that? I've seen men twice your size finished by blows half as bad."

"I had someone looking out for me," she said, and it was after the surgeon left that she explained that she'd meant Saint Christopher. "Tom told me what happened." She stroked Bridget's feathers as my pigeon sat contentedly on her lap. "Did I really go back to Notre-Dame?"

"You don't remember?" I said. When she shook her head, I asked, "What's the last thing you *do* remember?"

She thought about it. "My grandmother gave me her medallion. Then the three of us went to . . . a church?"

"Saint Mary's," Tom prompted.

Sally seemed to be struggling. "I remember a bridge. But . . . that can't be right. It was so big. And there weren't any houses on it."

"That's the Pont Neuf," I said. "We were there."

"That's . . . I . . . I can't . . ."

"It's fine." I took her hand, and she intertwined her fingers in mine, holding them tightly. "Not remembering is normal. Master Benedict said that's common with a head injury. As long as you remember us."

"Thank you, Tom," she said.

"Wh . . . ," I began. Then she grinned. "That's not funny," I said sourly.

"It's a little funny. So . . . what else happened?"

Tom had already filled her in on the miracle that had saved her at Notre-Dame, so I told her everything else, from our trip to the Pont Neuf to the flight of Marin's servants. She listened, wide-eyed, and shuddered. "So it was Rémi behind everything all along," she said.

I had to suppress a shudder, too. It was chilling to know we'd been in the company of someone so cruel without even the slightest inkling of what was hidden under the mask. I thought of the comtesse, and Aphrodite, so afraid of him they wouldn't even say his name. The fact that he'd disappeared without a trace made me scared.

Simon had told us he'd hired investigators to search for him, but so far, no one had any idea where he'd gone. He did say he'd checked Rémi's letters of reference with his previous master and had discovered the man had never actually worked there. The seals he'd provided had been forged.

Simon had buried his head in his hands. "How could I have let this happen?"

But we'd seen it happen before, how forged letters could take advantage of the desperate. And Rémi was about as good a forger as can be. Sitting with Sally on my bed, I showed her the letter that had drawn her to Notre-Dame.

"It's perfect," I said. "Even *I* would think I wrote it."

She read it over and over, struggling to remember. "But why did they go after *me*?"

In the aftermath of the comtesse's capture, I'd spent some time thinking about that. And I believed I'd figured out the answer. "Do you remember the wasp attack in the Tuileries? You told us one of the chambermaids ran from the bushes, the first to be attacked."

"I remember."

"That chambermaid," I said. "Was she really pretty?"

"She was stunning," Sally said.

I *had* been right. "That was Aphrodite," I said. "Marie-Louise. She was the comtesse's chambermaid. I think what happened was, the day you were out shopping, the comtesse brought her servants. And when you saw Marie-Louise, you realized not only was she one of the assassins, but the comtesse herself was part of the conspiracy."

Sally frowned. "I don't understand why seeing one of her servants would have—" She gasped. "The garden!"

I nodded. The day of the wasp attack, Philippe had

made the comtesse and her husband stay at the Palais. So there was no cause for Marie-Louise to be at the Tuileries. The only reason, in fact, would be because she *had* to be: to dart into the bushes and kick over the wasp's nest, which the Minotaur had left that morning for her to find.

"And she *couldn't* have been at the Tuileries," Sally said, "without having permission to go from her mistress." She looked amazed. "So the comtesse had to know all along."

"And you figured it out. They must have seen your reaction when you spotted Marie-Louise. Then, when they intercepted your letter . . ." I took her hand. Once again, she linked her fingers in mine. "As it was, you still helped. I only realized what was going on because of you."

She was quiet for a while. Finally, she said, "I'm glad you stopped them."

"Thank Tom," I said. "He's the master swordsman." Tom, practicing with his blade, flushed, pleased. "And now you're going to be all right, too. So all's well."

Despite what I'd said, I was worried about her. It was true that Master Benedict had said memory loss was normal with a head injury, but he'd also said it might not be the only effect. I noticed something odd whenever Sally stroked Bridget's feathers. I confirmed it when we brought her food, and I watched her eat. She'd stopped trying to use her left hand.

I waited until she was finished, then sat close beside her on the bed.

She looked at me with an expression I couldn't read. "What are you doing?"

"Mind if I check something?" I said.

"What?"

"Just humor me." I took her right hand in mine. "Squeeze my hand as hard as you can."

"Why?"

"It's an exercise," I lied. "Master Benedict told me it helped with recovery."

She kept her eyes on mine as she squeezed my fingers. When I was satisfied, I took her left hand. "Now squeeze again."

She pulled her hand away. "Can we do this later? I'm too tired for exercises."

"It won't take long."

"I said later. Tom, can't you take him somewhere he can set things on fire?"

"I only brought one pair of breeches," he complained.

Sally laughed and lay down. She looked up at me from my pillow with a sidelong glance. "If you really want to do something nice," she said, "you could read to me."

"All right," I said. "We'll get something from the library."

Tom and I left. Halfway down the hall, I paused.

"Wait here a minute," I said, and I went back to our room.

I made to open the door, but the sound from inside stopped me. I leaned against the wood, eyes closed, and listened as Sally cried, all alone.

Though our mission had ended, I delayed our trip back to England for a few days, giving Sally a little more time to recover. It was during one of those lazy days, as Tom, Sally, and I played with Bridget by the warmth of the fire, that the young page boy who'd brought me the letter for Colbert stopped by, struggling under an unwieldy package.

"Just arrived for you, monsieur," the boy said.

It came wrapped in sackcloth. When I pulled the cloth away, I found an elm box inside, carved with beautifully detailed leaf designs. The box was nearly five feet long, and one foot wide, locked with three brass latches.

And it wasn't for me. After the page had gone, I looked at the note attached.

Thomas Bailey

"For *me*?" Tom said. "What is it?"

"I don't know," I said. "I can't see through wood."

Tom made a face and popped the latches. Then he gasped.

The box contained a sword, nestled in deep red velvet. The hilt, large enough to fit two hands, was leather, wrapped intricately with fine gold wire. The pommel was a single polished moonstone, the size of a plum, that seemed to shine with an inner bluish-white light. Above the crosspiece was a broad blade of tempered steel three feet long, the metal itself inlaid with gold, an inscription on both sides, between two Templar crosses.

Tom's jaw hung open as he lifted the sword. He weighed it in his hands, then swung it around. The blade rang softly as it sliced through the air, and the sound made my heart thump: the sword was *singing* to him.

"It's magnificent," Tom said, awestruck.

More than that, I thought. It was magical. A weapon fit for a king.

"Who would give this to me?" Tom said.

I looked at him strangely.

"The *Templars*?" he said.

"Who else?"

"But . . . why?"

"A thank you, I'd guess. You beat a far more practiced swordsman—who would never have returned the treasure to them. And you saved my life *again*. I'd say you earned it."

He held it up. "This inscription. Is it Latin?"

It was. I read it out, one side of the blade, then the other. "'*Ego autem non exspecto aeternitatem,*'" I said. "'*Sempiternus sum.*'"

"What does it mean?"

"It means: I do not await eternity. I *am* eternity."

"Eternity," he whispered, staring into the moonstone. Then he looked back in the box, puzzled. There was a cracked leather scabbard to go with the sword, and nothing else. "Where's yours?"

I sighed. "I'm pretty sure the Templars have discovered I'm more a danger to my friends *with* a sword."

"That's not right," he said, indignant. "You should get a gift, too. You both should."

"It's fine," I said.

"I don't need anything," Sally said. "I'm just grateful you got my medallion back."

"What medallion?" Tom said.

"My Saint Christopher medallion. I'd have been heart-broken without it."

Tom and I looked at each other, puzzled. "We didn't get your medallion back," I said. "We lost it at Notre-Dame."

Now she looked puzzled. "But . . ." She pulled the silver chain from under her dress. "Look."

Tom and I couldn't believe it. For there, between her fingers, hung her grandmother's silver medallion.

She stared down at it in awe. "Are you saying . . . ?"

"I guess you got a gift after all," I said, shaken. How had the Templars found it? And how on earth had they placed it back around her neck?

"Then . . . wait," Tom said to me. "You're the only one who didn't get something? That's outrageous."

"Don't worry about it," I said, though, in truth, I was pretty disappointed.

Except, as it turned out, I did receive a gift. The next morning, as we set off to visit Marin and Simon, that famil-iar page boy ran up behind me.

"Monsieur! Monsieur!"

I turned.

"You dropped this, monsieur," he said, and placed a small leather pouch in my hand.

"This isn't mine," I said.

"Of course it is, monsieur. I saw you drop it."

"But—"

He ran back around the corner before I could stop him. Puzzled, I undid the knots and opened it.

I stared. Inside, I saw gold.

I pulled it out. It was a coin, a single florin, stamped with a Templar cross.

When we arrived at Maison Chastellain, Simon answered the door himself. His eyes were red and puffy: He'd been crying.

"What's wrong?" I said, heart already sinking.

"It's Uncle Marin," Simon said. "He's . . . he's gone."

For a moment, I hoped he'd meant Marin had just wandered off, as those with demency sometimes did. But, of course, he hadn't.

"It happened during the night," Simon said as he led

us up to his uncle's room. "He'd had a terrible day. Angry, confused. He wouldn't even drink his brandy. All he did was stare into the fireplace in his study. I tried to give him Master Benedict's medicine, but he just threw it at me.

"He refused to talk, so I spoke instead. I told him about what you'd done, about discovering that the treasure was hidden in the Cour des Miracles—though I didn't say the comtesse's servants had got there before you.

"That seemed to rouse him. He looked up at me and said, 'Benedict found the Templar treasure?' I said yes, he'd found it, but he'd lost it all again. And Uncle Marin just smiled and said, 'Tell Benedict we'll search for the new puzzle in the morning.'"

Simon drew a breath. "I suppose I should be pleased he died happy. It's just . . ."

He let the thought trail away as we entered Marin's bedchamber. A priest was already there, attended by four servants. We watched somberly as the priest anointed Marin's head with oil, offering the last rites to the departed. Then the servants wrapped his body in a shroud and carried him out.

"I have to arrange with Father Martin for a mass," Simon said. "Why don't you wait in the study? I'll join you soon."

"We should go," I said. "I'm sorry; we didn't mean to intrude."

"No, please stay. You were his friends. And . . . I'd rather not be alone."

We made our own way to Marin's study. The fireplace was cold, his brandy glass empty beside his chair.

Tom began to stack wood for a fire, then stopped. "It feels wrong without him here," he said softly, and I agreed. A sadness gripped me, not just for the loss of Marin, but that another one of Master Benedict's friends had gone. I sent a thought into the empty hearth.

Please, Marin. When you get to heaven, tell Master Benedict how much I miss him.

We waited until we heard a knock at the front door. A minute later, Simon joined us, holding a letter. He looked puzzled. "Did you tell anyone you were coming here?" he said.

"No," I said.

He frowned and handed me the letter. "It's for you."

He was right. The letter was addressed to me—not Baron Ashcombe, *me*. But what really made my blood freeze was the handwriting.

It was mine.

Christopher Rowe
Maison Chastellain
Île Notre-Dame, Paris

With trembling hands, I turned the letter over. The seal was stamped with a finely drawn, sharp-beaked bird. I cracked it and saw the message within, again a perfect copy of my own hand. And as I read it, the ice in my blood burrowed so deep it chilled my soul.

My dear Christopher,
I congratulate you on your victory. You have done the impossible: You found the Templar treasure, where others—including me—could not. Don't worry, I'll tell no one the truth of what happened; I like that you and I now share a secret. And, as vexed as I am, I must admit: It was fascinating to watch your mind at work. I see now why Master Benedict chose you as an apprentice.

Does the mention of your master surprise you? No doubt Benedict never told you about me, so I will: He was a thorn in my side for many years. Now,

though he has departed, you come to take his place.
And while I try not to begrudge you your success, your
discovery has cost me dearly. You owe me, Christopher.
And I always collect what I am owed.

 Your first payment is the life of Marin
Chastellain. No, he did not die from his illness.
I poisoned him—and in doing so, I left you a
clue. Before you go searching for it, I want you
to know that I did not kill him because he was
any threat to me. I did it because I knew it would
hurt Blackthorn, and, in turn, hurt you. It is, after
all, much more sporting to face an opponent who
understands the stakes of the game.

 I am going to do to you what I should have
done to your master years ago: I am going to make
you suffer. I will do this by taking away the things
you love, one by one, until there is only you and me.
And then, once I have stripped your life bare, you
will understand.

 Find the clue I've left for you. Ponder it. Then
reflect on what it might mean. There's no need to
rush; I have several plans in motion that must be

completed before our game can begin. So, until then, be well, Christopher. Savor your life, while you still have some of it left. For when I am ready, I will come for you.

The Raven

A FEW MATTERS OF HISTORICAL NOTE

They called it the City of Light.

By the time Christopher arrived at the Porte Saint-Denis, Paris was in the middle of one of the most incredible transformations any city had ever experienced. It was starting to leave behind its medieval roots and modernize—not by accident, but by design.

In 1601, the government of Paris was informed by Henri IV, Louis XIV's grandfather, that "His Majesty has declared his intention of making the city in which he plans to spend the rest of his life beautiful and splendid, of making [Paris] into a world unto itself and a miracle of the world."[1] And so

---

1. As quoted by J. DeJean in *How Paris Became Paris*, Bloomsbury, 2014.

he did, because, for the first time in history, a ruler rebuilt a city not by whim, but on the advice of professionals: architects, artists, and engineers.

This urban planning made Paris a city of firsts: the first bridge uncluttered by homes and shops at its sides, the first streetlights, the first sidewalks, the first public transit, the first postal service, the first numbered houses, the first police force. The changes were so remarkable that they turned Paris into the world's first tourist destination. And when those tourists—including Charles II of England—returned home, they brought Paris with them: design, architecture, fashion, music. Seventeenth-century Paris would come to influence, shape, and rebuild the entire Western world.

Much of Paris's ancient beauty remains, and you can visit it today: the stunning Cathédrale Notre-Dame; the endless rooms of the Louvre, now the world's most famous art museum; the Palais-Royal; the Île Notre-Dame, now known as the Île Saint-Louis; even the Pont Neuf (which is still so grand that it makes an appearance in pretty much every Hollywood movie shot in that city).

Sadly, however, many of the treasures of that time are now gone. In the French Revolution of 1789, in trying to eliminate all reminders of royalty, the rebels destroyed many artifacts. The giant sculpture of Saint Christopher at Notre-Dame, for example, was lost in that purge. And the Great Tower, that final remnant of the Knights Templar in Paris, was torn down, too.

As for the Templars themselves . . . well, who knows? But if you're looking for the key, I already gave it to you. Ivnvnyvi gsv kfaaov xfyv?

ACKNOWLEDGMENTS

It's my privilege to have so many talented folks helping put these books together. I'd like to say thank you to the following:

To Liesa Abrams, Ben Horslen, Tricia Lin, Dan Lazar, and Suri Rosen, all of whom offered insights that made this story immeasurably better.

To Mara Anastas, Mary Marotta, Jon Anderson, Katherine Devendorf, Karin Paprocki, Julie Doebler, Jodie Hockensmith, Christina Pecorale, Lauren Hoffman, Michelle Leo, Greg Stadnyk, Hilary Zarycky, Laura Lyn DiSiena, Victor Iannone, Gary Urda, Michael Selleck, and Stephanie Voros at Aladdin, and to copy editor Brian Luster and fact-checker Daphne Tagg.

To Kevin Hanson, Nancy Purcell, Felicia Quon, Sheila Haidon, Andrea Seto, Jacquelynne Lennard, and Rita Silva at Simon & Schuster Canada.

To Cecilia de la Campa, Angharad Kowal, Torie Doherty-Munro, and James Munro at Writers House.

To the publishers around the world who have embraced the Blackthorn Key series.

To Terry Bailey, and to Alma, for their assistance with Latin translation, and to Colin Grey for his assistance with French. Any errors remaining are my own.

And, as always, to you, dear reader: Thank you for joining Christopher on this adventure. There are plenty of places yet to go.